TO NEVER HEAR THE SONG

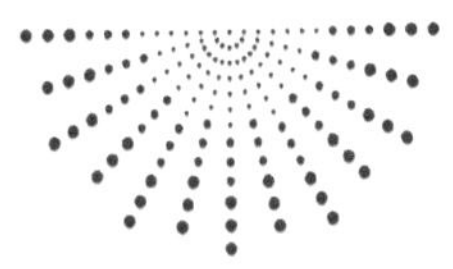

E.G. STONE

For all the warrior women

CONTENTS

Hullgard
Iron Mountains
Red Desert
Red Palace
Salusian Empire
No Man's Land
Shinalea
Aerial City
The Pits
Stone Tower
Mardego
Southron

PROLOGUE

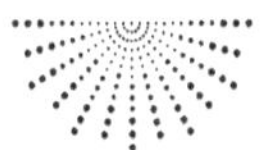

The battlefield before his claws was bloody. The ground, three days since the end of this mighty war, still sank and swelled with the remains of the dead. His own scales, usually white as dawn, now matched the redness of his eyes. The dragon surveyed all that had happened, all that had come from this war. And he wished that he could weep.

"You have no need to remain behind." A voice, deep, ancient, sounded in his ear. The dragon lifted his head and looked at the one walking slowly up the hill to rest beside him. The newcomer's wings were limp, hanging at his sides as if he could not be bothered to furl them. His scales, a myriad of greens that shifted to blues, were rough and dull. The tip of one of his great horns that curled over his head like antlers was broken.

"We have wrought death," the white dragon said, feeling small in the shadow of his elder. "Should not some of us remain behind to see the results, Qiaseri?"

Qiaseri let out a great sigh. His claws curled into the dirt. "This battle—this war—was not our fault, young one. This war was always inevitable. It is not our fault that we fought and that others died."

"Then why do I wear blood like humans wear clothes?"

Qiaseri lowered his head and touched the white dragon with his snout. A flash, and then the white scales were now clean. The young dragon recoiled. "You should not have done that!"

"My magic is strong enough for that, though it be that I require an extra day. With the great sleep upon us, what is one more day?" Qiaseri let out a chuckle, though there was not enough heart in it. He looked out at the field, at the humans and elves lingering there, seeing to the dead. He looked and saw the corpses of races that would likely not be seen again for a hundred generations. Dragons were not the least among them.

"Do you think that things will improve in the time that you are to sleep?" the white dragon asked. Qiaseri shuffled his wings until they lay flat on his back.

"I think that the world will be a vastly different place. We dragons may require the great sleep to replenish our magic and our souls from what was achieved in this war, but the rest of the world will continue. Yes, I have great hopes for the future of this world." Qiaseri looked out towards the horizon, towards some future that the young white dragon could not see.

"I fear the future," he said.

"We all fear the future. But you must not let that fear overwhelm you. I would not be what I am had I remained swallowed by fear."

"Would this war have even happened had we not been afraid?"

Qiaseri fixed a sharp eye on the young dragon. "You think that this was wrought because people were afraid?"

"I know it," was the response.

"Then it is good that you are remaining behind while we sleep. Maybe then you will learn the truth of things."

Qiaseri turned and started the slow, stately walk back down the hill. The white dragon remained behind, words dying on his tongue. Though a thousand cycles would pass, he knew that the answer would not change. Fear had wrought this death, this horrid thing. And he would never allow it to do so again.

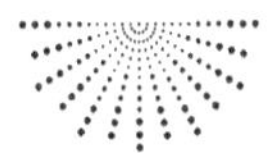

CHAPTER ONE

*M*iska remembered every heartbeat of the attack that had ruined his hearing. He had been nine cycles, a child desperate to fit in with the others of his village. The closest in age was a boy of ten who had the rest of the village children wrapped around his fingers: Qilas. He was the very image of the perfect desert boy, with his light brown skin and cunning dark eyes. He preferred fighting and hunting to any other activity and was one of the youngest who managed to bring back food every time. He was well-liked and destined to be a great leader, maybe even a soldier in the royal army.

Miska wanted to be just like him.

It had been one of the rare sunny days at the beginning of the monsoon season that hit the Red Desert every cycle. The rains only came for a few weeks, but they were powerful, dangerous, and not much could stand in their path. Qilas and the other village children had been running around just on the outskirts of the settlement, enjoying the slight crispness in the air.

Miska had been doing chores for his mother.

"Bring back enough oil this time or I'll have you whipped,"

she hissed. Miska wondered, on occasion, what it was like to love your mother. Even as a child, he had understood that there was something missing in their relationship. She was a tall, thin woman who blamed Miska for her low status. Perhaps it was because he hadn't looked like her. His skin was a rare reddish brown colour that had people whispering of the legendary red devils, the demons who haunted the night. Or perhaps it was that she had a decent life and was to be married to the settlement's advocate before falling pregnant with Miska. He never knew why she did not love him and he did not love her. But he still tried to do his best by her anyways.

"Yes, Mother." Miska bowed at the waist before running off to do as he was told. He blocked his ears off so he wouldn't hear the sneered words thrown in his direction as he left. They always came. And he always heard.

"Maybe this time don't come back at all!"

Miska had run through the settlement to the oil woman's house, hoping to beg or barter some of the precious liquid from her. It was one of the few commodities his settlement had in the desert and they treasured it highly. Other places, like the almost-mystical Red Palace, sported oases; some had vast deposits of minerals. Most, though, were like his settlement. Barren but for a few sun-dried mud-and-straw houses, and the few precious things they managed to cultivate.

A foot flashed out and tangled between Miska's churning legs, catching him off guard. With a yelp, he fell to the ground. His palms scraped open on the packed dirt and blood trickled down his eyebrow. He looked up and saw Qilas sneering down at him, four other children beside him.

"Look what I caught!" Qilas crowed to a pretty girl with dark brown hair. The girl was older than Miska by two cycles, but it had not stopped his heart from beating rapidly each time she passed. Now, she looked down at him with malice and contempt in her gaze. Miska closed his eyes so he would not see any more. The words though, kept coming.

"Pitiful excuse for a red devil," the girl said. Miska squeezed his eyes harder. "He did not even put up a fight!"

"I thought they were supposed to be ferocious," another boy sneered. Qilas' unmistakeable laugh rang out in the narrow alley. For a beat, Miska hoped that a grown-up would come and hear the commotion, perhaps rescue him from this torment. No one came.

"Maybe it's just when they're full-blooded, and not mongrels," Qilas said. Miska cracked his eyes open to see the utter triumph on the boy's face. All admiration he had held for the other boy slipped away. All his hopes of ever being like him, of ever being accepted in this settlement, they slipped away as well. What was left was staring him in the face, his laughter ringing in Miska's ears.

"Get up and fight," the girl demanded, aiming a kick at Miska's side. He shuffled away from the blow, puffs of dust flying as he moved. Qilas frowned.

"The mongrel does not want to play," Qilas said. The others snickered. "Well, why should he? He doesn't belong here, does he?"

"No!" the others agreed, their shouts edging towards gleeful.

"Then let's show him what we do to people who don't belong!" Qilas surged forwards, faster than Miska could counter. This time, the blow struck home. Miska let out a strangled cry as his ribs smarted. He scrambled to his feet as fast as he could, holding up his hands.

"Leave me alone," Miska snapped, trying to look braver than he felt. Qilas exchanged another glance with the girl. They both burst out laughing before advancing on Miska.

"Now, mongrel," Qilas said, advancing like a jackal before its dying prey. "Why would we do that?"

Miska was found some hours later, after the rains had

already begun. Maybe his mother had raised a cry when he didn't return home with the oil. He doubted it, though. More likely, one of the residents of the settlement had stumbled on his prone form, the rain washing away the blood to reveal the full extent of what had been done to him. Ribs broken, left ankle shattered, skull fractured. But the worst of it was, no matter what Miska tried to do, he kept hearing the taunting voices of Qilas and the others. Over and over, it was almost louder than the echoes of his own screams. It took Miska two days to realise that it was all he could hear. All he would ever hear again.

* * *

WITH A SHARP INHALATION OF BREATH, Miska sat upwards, his heart pounding. He winced and pressed his hands to his head; it was throbbing something fierce. He needed to find Warra, the healing woman, and get it seen to, otherwise he would not be able to function at all, let alone put on a smiling face for Ravenna.

Ravenna!

The memories of the last few days surged into Miska's mind. Suddenly, the headache was not the most of his problems. He remembered that Ravenna, the most giving creature he had ever met and his deepest love, had fled the Red Desert to warn her people—the winged sylphs—about Lord Davorin. Davorin was the Firstborn Son of the Salusian Empire. A man set on conquering the known world to prove his worth, he had settled on the Red Desert as his first conquest. The isolated island of sylphs would be next, giving him a chance to have the almost mythical beings as his personal slaves. Many people would think the sylphs to be angels, messengers of the divine, and would never dare challenge Davorin with them at his side.

Miska had heartily wished Ravenna well. He hoped she found her people and warned them in time. He hoped that she was safe and that nothing would happen to hurt her again. She deserved so much better than life had given her. He also wished that he hadn't been left behind.

Of course, if Miska *hadn't* been left behind to stand with Queen Lenore of the Red Desert against the tyrant conqueror, then he would not have witnessed her fall. He would not have seen his home turn into nothing more than another conquered people, bowed to the cruelty that was Davorin. Lenore had told him with a desperate twist of her mouth to run and save the Red Desert.

Miska had obeyed without question.

He went to look for Ravenna. Instead, he had found himself in the foothills of the Iron Mountains, terrified, dehydrated, cold and alone. And there was something else…

Miska pressed the heels of his hands against his temple, hoping that the pressure of his headache would lessen even a little. There was something else that he needed to remember. Something had happened to him to bring him here, wherever here was.

Miska lifted his head and brushed his brown hair out of his eyes. He looked around and frowned. This was unlike any dwelling he had known. He was used to the mud-stone of the small desert dwellings, or the massive Red Palace, carved from the desert rock itself. This was a rounded room that rose to a point in the ceiling. The floor was draped with furs and thickly woven rugs. A fire crackled merrily in the centre of the room, the smoke drifting upwards and out through a slight opening at the top. Miska wracked his brain and finally came up with the word that explained his surroundings. A tent.

Who would have a tent in the desert?

And, for that matter, who would bother with dressing Miska's few scratches with a salve and then putting him to bed in a cot wrapped in furs?

A flap in the tent wall opened, catching Miska's attention. A man with a small leather-bound book in his hands walked in, looking like nothing Miska had ever seen. For one, he had hair that was as sand under the moon. His skin was pale and marbled with purple where his veins showed faintly through, highlighting sharp features and bright eyes of a strange crimson hue. He wore dark robes that almost brushed the floor and went all the way down his arms. Under the robes, he wore clothes equally strange: tightly fitted pants that looked to be made of leather, a long tunic that looked thicker than any clothes Miska had ever owned, and a leather thong around his neck with a long, curved claw hanging from it. But strangest of all, two horns of darkest obsidian black rose from the man's head. They started just below his hairline on his forehead, curving up and back like crescent moons in ridges that looked sharp enough to cut.

Miska was so absorbed in staring at this man—he had seen and known Ravenna with her night-black wings of legend, but this was something entirely different—that he missed seeing the words on the man's lips. When the man tilted his head in question, Miska blushed. He hated not seeing what people were saying. It made them act like something was wrong with him.

The man repeated the words and Miska focused intently to make up for his earlier blunder. But the movement of the man's lips and tongue and jaw was completely unfamiliar to Miska. He only caught something that could have been, "Ngao, talu… miisa?"

Miska shook his head. The man frowned, the movement somehow more curious than disapproving. It was as though he was something of interest, a curiosity in this strange world of tents and furs and fires. Well, Miska definitely agreed with that.

The horned man spoke again, this time moving his mouth differently. A different set of possibilities filtered through Miska's mind, but none of them made sense, either. After a moment, he realised that the man was trying to speak to him in different languages.

Mouth suddenly dry, Miska wanted nothing more than to look away. He was much, much farther from home than he had thought if he couldn't even speak the language. Even Ravenna spoke Ionan, though the way she formed her words had Miska imagining the most beautiful accent. She had told him that the language the sylphs spoke was very similar, probably because their two languages had only diverged a short time before. But now, Miska was on completely unfamiliar ground.

Being deaf was hard enough. He had to pay constant attention to people, searching them for the tiniest of clues as to what they were trying to say. He had to watch the way their tongue touched their teeth, or their lips curved on a vowel. He had to watch the muscles in their face for emotional cues. He had to watch their eyes. Their brows. And that was when he *understood* the language and could interpret the movements of their mouths. This? This was an impossible situation. Miska would not last long.

Finally, the horned man stopped trying out languages on Miska. His frown deepened. The sharp grace of his features made the movement somehow more profound. Miska considered saying something, considered at least trying to communicate.

Then, a *sound* burst into his head, louder than anything Miska remembered hearing. He screamed and pressed his hands to his ears. The sound withdrew, almost shocked, then softened and soothed.

Be calm, human, it seemed to say. *I will not harm you.*

Miska whimpered, scrabbling uselessly at his ears. He had not heard anything for twenty cycles. For so long that it was more normal for him to hear nothing than to remember those moments of hearing anything.

"I cannot hear," he said, saying the words both inside his

head and out loud. It had taken cycles of training to be able to speak properly and now he felt as though all of that was slipping away because of this *sound.* "I cannot hear," Miska said again, reassuring himself.

Is that why you did not answer my questions?

Miska blinked back the tears that sprang to his eyes. He wanted the sound to stop!

The horned man approached Miska and knelt down before his cot. Miska flinched; he hadn't noticed the man moving in his distress. The man made no move to speak, just gave a gentle smile. There was something calming in the motion, something ageless and powerful and wise. It was like Warra's smiles, but less loving. The man reached up and pulled Miska's hands away from his ears, shaking his head.

My voice is in your thoughts, not your ears. It will not hurt you.

Miska flinched slightly, but this time the sound was not so harsh. It was almost like bells, ringing gently through his mind. Their tones were deep and resonant. Powerful. He blinked. The sound... it was coming from the man kneeling before him. But... they did not speak the same language.

"My language," Miska said out loud.

I am speaking to your thoughts. Language is irrelevant here. The man smiled, blinking his crimson eyes. Miska found himself staring again when he saw that the man's pupils were slitted vertically, like a desert snake coiled in the sun.

"I don't understand," Miska breathed. The man nodded and pressed his hand against Miska's forehead. There was a burst of music inside his head. Miska screamed again and tried to pull away. When the man's hand broke contact with his skin, the memories returned.

He had been running from Davorin. Climbing up into the hills of the Iron Mountains, hoping desperately that this was the way that Ravenna had gone. Something had caused Miska's instincts to sharpen. The hair on the back of his neck stood up and he had run. He tripped over an unseen dip in the ground. Then, there was a monster's head hanging over him. Sharp, angled, with horns as long as his arm, scales that shone white, and eyes of deep crimson.

A dragon.

I feared you were injured, the horned man explained. *So I brought you over the mountains to the Peoples of the Stone. You are safe here.*

"You're a dragon!" Miska exclaimed. He backed away from the horned man—the dragon taken human form—and took him in, completely astonished.

Indeed, young human. I am a dragon.

"But... but that's impossible! Even Ravenna thought that dragons were long dead, and she had access to the tomes!" Miska's words flowed out in a desperate rush. He was not even certain he had properly articulated some of the words. If the dragon were speaking to him through his thoughts, then it wouldn't matter, though.

Tomes? Ravenna? Both ancient words. Where did you learn them, young human?

"R-Ravenna is a sylph," he said. Even before the words were spoken, he wished he could take them back. Ravenna being a sylph was already causing a great deal of trouble for her; it was the reason Davorin now sought out her people instead of keeping her alone as a divine symbol. It could be very dangerous for more people to know of her existence. The dragon, though, just widened his eyes in astonishment and his jaw dropped open to reveal slightly pointed teeth.

I think you have rather a story to tell, young human. I am Cavaris. What is your name?

"Miska," he said quietly. "My name is Miska."

Well, Miska, I have a feeling that what you have to say may turn this world on its head.

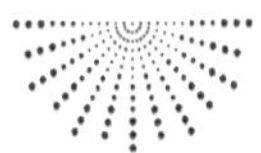

CHAPTER TWO

Queen Lenore of the Red Desert stood before the hammered silver mirror in her room, staring blankly at her reflection. She tried to find a spark of joy for the beautiful job that the royal dressmaker had done on her wedding gown. It was done in the fashion of the desert, with layers of sheer fabric in a burnished red wrapped tightly across her bodice and flowing gently to the floor in waves. With the gold and copper beading sewn into the skirts and across the neckline, she looked like she was wearing a living flame. Her auburn hair, normally tied tightly in a multitude of tiny braids, hung loose around her shoulders and waist, a few strands pinned up for the benefit of showing off the earrings that her intended had given her for the occasion.

Lenore reached up and touched the dangling red gems. They matched the tiered necklace tied tightly around her throat. She shuddered; it was more a collar than a gift. And those who could not see that were fools.

"My queen," a voice whispered, causing Lenore to stiffen and turn. She wanted to rub at her eyes to blot out any tears that might have shone in their depths, but that would ruin the dark eye powders her attendants had spent hours on. The person standing in the door was female, but she had no wings. Why, Lenore wondered, had she hoped that Ravenna would be there? That Ravenna would save her?

"Come, Blodwen," Lenore murmured. The woman slipped into her chambers as easily as if she were floating. She was the serving woman provided to her from the retinue that had arrived during the wedding preparations. Davorin had spared no expense and had sent for a whole new set of servants to work in the Red Palace from the Salusian Empire. Lenore knew it was to spy on her, to make certain that her people were kept well and truly under control. She hated the way that the servants deferred to her, as if they actually believed she held power. Blodwen in particular.

She was a trim girl, perhaps taller and broader than others but very neat. Her hair was the dark brown that seemed common in the Empire, and she still had yet to replace her clothes from the heavier fabrics of the cooler land to the lighter fabrics of the desert. Lenore thought it strange the way that Blodwen's long kirtle and over gown remained, despite the heat. Just another sign that this woman did not belong here.

None of these new people belonged here. But Lenore had no choice.

She was to marry Lord Davorin the Firstborn Son of the Salusian Empire. And his horrible servant, the dragon-spirit that he called Dagan, after his long-dead brother, that inhabited the body of his former Captain, Nadezhda, would be watching gleefully nearby. Whether the being was Davorin's dead brother or not mattered little; both were monsters. She shuddered.

"There's naught to be worried about my queen," Blodwen said cheerfully, taking her shiver for nervousness. No, Lenore was not nervous. She had thus far upheld her end of the bargain. She would marry Davorin and allow him to take the name of King-Consort to the Queen of the Red Desert. He, in turn, would keep from razing her kingdom to the ground and killing her people in the process.

"I am not nervous," Lenore said in a flat voice. It was meant to intimidate, meant to cow this servant into some semblance of obedience, but Blodwen just softened her expression and brushed her rough hand over Lenore's arm.

"It is a great honour to be wed to one such as Lord Davorin. He will be a good husband, and he will protect you and this land," Blodwen said. Lenore lifted her chin. She wanted to have fire flash in her eyes, wanted some reminder of the power and might she had once wielded without question or thought to be in her movements. Instead, all she could muster was a sense of dread and misery.

"Protect this land," Lenore breathed, closing her eyes. It would take a miracle if her people were not conscripted into Davorin's army and made to march on their neighbours. Her own soldiers, the ones she had called friends, had already been ordered by Davorin—through her—to join with the mercenaries they had so bravely fought. They were to become the first in the private army of the Firstborn Son.

Lenore had not seen Vareis, the training mistress for the army, or General Garreth Murdoch during her pronouncement. She wondered if they were dead. So many had been killed before the slaughter by Nadezhda and Davorin had ceased. Lenore had been confined to her room, unable to attend the burials. But she had watched from her room overlooking the gardens as the smoke rose to the skies. Her eyes, though, had been dry and her heart shattered.

"M'lady?" Blodwen's voice drew Lenore back to the present. The girl had the audacity to look concerned. "Is it... is it the bedding that has you worried?"

Lenore scoffed, tossing her head with what little spirit she had left. Bedding Davorin would be the least of her worries. Though, he was likely as cruel a lover as he was a warrior. But she imagined he would want to keep her in one piece in order to produce an heir. No, that was not her worry. Blodwen did not need to know that, though.

Lenore strode over to the windows that overlooked her gardens. They were still lush and green, full of the plants that could only grow in the unusual environment of a desert oasis. The birds still sang and the flowers still bloomed, though summer was drawing to an end. It was just as beautiful as it had ever been. "What do you know of Lord Davorin?" Lenore asked Blodwen, her voice cold.

Blodwen skittered around behind Lenore; she could hear the girl's ridiculous skirts moving around as she walked. Then, Blodwen moved to Lenore's side so that the Red Queen could see her out of the corner of her eye. She wanted to look away, but she forced herself to watch Blodwen. To look her enemy in the eye.

"Well, as you know, Lord Davorin was not the original First-born Son," Blodwen started. Lenore inclined her head. "Lord Dagan was always a favourite with the Royal Court, but he was not around that much. He was usually away with the army, expanding the Empire and bringing those poor people into civilisation. Lord *Davorin* was around much, much more but I cannot say that he was every terrible noticed by the Court. He was not known for any great skill. I mean, that is, of course he was—*is*—very capable! He's very smart. Read so much from the Royal Library. And everyone in the Court knew he had a silver tongue. But he wasn't, well, he wasn't Lord Dagan."

"Dagan is dead," Lenore stated. No matter what Davorin said about the being inhabiting Nadezhda's body, the real Dagan was dead. Blodwen winced.

"Yes," she murmured, almost as if it were a personal loss. "I don't think the Emperor ever really recovered from Lord Dagan's death. He was so distraught, claiming outright that he did not think Lord Davorin would serve the Empire in the way that Lord Dagan had. The Emperor even went so far as to see if the Code of Kings could be modified so that the Lady Seraphina could inherit. But she is already married, so that is impossible."

"His father hates him?" Lenore asked, slightly surprised. She had known that Davorin came to the Red Desert with fewer resources than one would expect of a Salusian Royal, but had always assumed that it was simply because he was prudent. But if the Emperor refused to support him…

"Oh, no!" Blodwen shook her head vehemently. "No, the Emperor loves his son! He just did not want Lord Davorin commanding the army in Lord Dagan's place. It… it wouldn't be right, see?"

Lenore saw. Saw beyond the words that Blodwen was saying. Perhaps if she could appeal to the Emperor, things would be different. Perhaps the Red Desert could be saved, after all. Even as she thought it, though, she knew it would be impossible. Her marriage to Davorin was in a few short hours. And with the demon at his side and whatever foul magic he now possessed, not even the Emperor of the Salusian Empire would be able to stand up to Davorin.

Ravenna was Lenore's only hope. Ravenna and Miska. Both gone. Perhaps dead.

"After news came that Lord Davorin was marrying you and allying your countries—bringing the Red Desert into the Empire—well, the Emperor threw his full support behind Lord Davorin. Oh, the Court was so relieved. They had been worried that the Emperor would leave no clear line of succession to the throne and that the Empire would fall into chaos. But, well, the Emperor is getting old and I suppose it just took him some time to come to terms with Lord Dagan's death," Blodwen said.

Lenore sighed softly. Would this woman ever stop talking? She had already kindled Lenore's hopes, only to dash them again in the next breath. With her marriage in such a short time, and the end of her reign—perhaps the end of her people—to come soon after, she was not certain she could handle such hope.

"M'lady," Blodwen said. Her voice changed, slightly, drawing Lenore's attentions. The Salusian woman looked at her with a serious expression, her eyes worried, brow furrowed. Blodwen lay a hand on her shoulder and dropped the cheerful act altogether. "I only ever met Lord Davorin once, when I came here. But I believe him to be a good man. I believe that he will do what he can to make the Red Desert all it can be, now that it is to be part of the Empire. I believe he will make a good husband and a good king."

Lenore shuddered and drew away from Blodwen. She turned her gaze firmly to the gardens. Then, her voice as cold as the ice in Ravenna's eyes, she said, "Then you believe wrongly."

Blodwen recoiled as though Lenore had struck her. She frowned, eyes wide with horror and confusion. "How could you say such a thing?"

Lenore scoffed. "Have you seen the demon that he keeps at his side? The scaled woman with red skin and the cruel smile?"

Blodwen nodded. "That's his captain… he said she was imbued with an ancient magic. And after he has *seen* the angel, and plans on calling on her and her kind, how could you doubt?"

"Captain Nadezhda is dead," Lenore spat. "She was a dangerous, horrible woman, but even she would not have been able to slaughter my best soldiers without being scratched once. Even she could not be so heartless as to *laugh* at the burning of *my people* while I was locked up here, unable to fight back!"

Lenore regretted the words immediately after she spoke them. The servant from the Salusian Empire grew stiff, her expression hardening. She went so far as to curl her lip and sneer at Lenore. "What would *you* know? Some savage playing at queen out here on the outskirts of the Empire? Lord Davorin only wanted to marry you to avoid bloodshed. Your pathetic country isn't worth wasting Salusian blood."

As foolish as they were, the words stung. Lenore had once cared what people thought of her, whether or not she was a good ruler. She recalled the wary glances of her councillors and allies from the city-states to the south. She had tried so hard to please them and their endless demands couched as suggestions. It had nearly ruined her country and helped no one but outsiders. She had thought she had grown a spine. Ravenna had commented on the fact, even, and had made Lenore's heart soar even as it now ached.

But to have people believe that her country, her people, were backwards, uncivilised, savage, simply because they lived amongst the sand and stone, well that was almost too much to bear. Lenore was a queen, though. She was the famed Red Queen of the Red Desert. She might have to bow to Davorin for the sake of her people, but she would not bend before this woman. She would not break.

"And what would you know?" Lenore returned, putting all her fire into the words. "You, nothing but a servant brought from the Salusian Empire to the outskirts where you have not the luxury you demand, nor the recognition you crave? Why were you brought here, Blodwen? Was it by choice, or a punishment? Servant to the conquered queen of the second son?"

Blodwen blushed, eyes flashing. She blinked rapidly, her dark eyes filling with tears. Lenore had struck a nerve and she did not regret it in the slightest. She shook her head, flinching slightly at the unfamiliar feel of her loose hair over her shoulders. She might not regret the words, but she was not foolish enough to make a true enemy of Blodwen. This intruder into her life might be the only ally she would have in the future. Miska was gone. Ravenna was gone. Her hope was gone with them.

Lenore sighed and reached out to touch Blodwen's arm. It

felt strange to have such thick fabric as a barrier between touch, even with someone she disliked. "Look, Blodwen, I'm sorry. I... I would think much the same if I were ever in the Empire."

"No," Blodwen sniffed, though she did not pull back, "you wouldn't. The Empire is wonderful!"

"We have our merits here, too," Lenore murmured. She gestured to the gardens. "Have you ever seen anything so beautiful?"

"It's... fine," Blodwen said. Lenore nodded; it would have to be good enough. In the background, she could hear a commotion and knew that her time was up. Any moment now, someone would fetch her to the Great Hall. A cleric would stand before Davorin and herself. And she would be wed.

Even as she thought the words, the doors to her chambers swung open as if by an invisible wind. She flinched, tightening her grip on Blodwen's arm in fear. The servant winced accordingly, searching Lenore's face. Lenore, though, was staring in horror at the creature that had come to fetch her to her wedding.

Surely, even Davorin could not be that cruel?

The dragon-spirit creature that had taken over Nadezhda's body stood before Lenore. Its skin shone blood red, the largest veins throbbing black against its skin. Around its vertically slit eyes lay scales in a lighter shade of red, some peeling up and some looking as though they were just smudged with dirt. The former Captain of Davorin's armies had once had cropped hair that brushed her skull. This creature had let the hair grow out until it was long enough to touch its chin. The strands were greasy and dull. It wore black trousers and a grey tunic belted at the waist with a single blade at its left hip. Lenore recognised the signature curved blade of the Salusian Empire and shuddered.

The beast that had slaughtered twenty of her people in less

time than it took to suck in a breath to scream, had come for her wearing a delighted and cruel smile.

Your groom awaits you, it said. Lenore closed her eyes and swallowed down a plea for help. This was the beast that Davorin so blatantly claimed was the spirit of his brother, Dagan, come to inhabit the body of his former lover. She knew better. This was a magic that should have remained dead. This was torture incarnate.

"I come," Lenore said, her words wooden. She loosed her hand from Blodwen's arm.

"M'lady!" Blodwen said, looking between Lenore and Dagan.

"I come," Lenore repeated. Dagan nodded its head and held out an arm. She blinked back a single tear and strode forwards to place her hand on its arm.

Wherever you are, Miska, Ravenna, please... save me. Save us all! Lenore thought. She spared a single backwards glance for Blodwen and saw confusion there, mixed with a tinge of fear. Then, Lenore was swept from her chambers towards the Great Hall, where her fate awaited her.

* * *

The closer they drew to the Great Hall, the faster Lenore's heart pounded. Soon, it drowned out every sound but her thoughts. She did not want to go through with this. She did not want to be wife to Davorin. She wanted to continue on as before! If she did not do this, though, her people would suffer. Davorin had promised that he would treat her people as any other citizens of the Empire if she cooperated with him. She had no reason to doubt his word, as dangerous as he was.

She still wanted to turn and run.

Lenore tried to take steadying breaths to calm her heart. She tried to quell the fear that rose like bile in her throat. No one was coming to save her, she realised.

So Lenore did something she had not done since she was a young girl. She prayed.

To The One Who Watches, she thought, her steps seeming to slow as the words formed in her mind. *Please, keep my people safe. Let this not be for nothing. And let Miska be well. Let him find Ravenna so that she can come and... I don't know why I'm placing all my faith in her. But please. Let this not be for naught.*

The One Who Watches was the deity most worshipped by the desert folk, though they assimilated many different religions into their practise. But The Watcher was meant to be above the other gods, was meant to be powerful where the others were weak, was meant to have armies and accolades and the ability to change the world with a whisper. Only, The Watcher was most often silent.

Lenore heard nothing, not even a whisper.

Her breath faltered for a moment as she and the beast Dagan reached the heavy wooden doors of the Great Hall. As with the doors in her chamber, they opened with some invisible power, revealing the place that had not two moons before, been the sight of death unchallenged. Now, not even Lenore could recognise it.

The walls had been draped with fabric of many different colours. There were shields and sigils embroidered into the fabric in threads of bright metallic colours. Some symbol of the conquered people of the Empire? Some sign of marriage? She did not know, only that the banners and tapestries looked garish against the red desert stone. A bright red cloth stretched along the floor from the entrance of the hall to the throne. On either side of the cloth stood people wearing finery the likes of which Lenore had never seen.

One woman, dark haired and clad in a dress that looked to be made from liquid copper with gold embroidery and an elaborate headdress of shining metal, inclined her head to Lenore. Even without the opulent dress, she would have recognised the family resemblance anywhere. Her stomach dropped. Davorin's sister had come to see her be wed? Was the massive man with his hand on her shoulder a lover or a husband? Or would he be the one to execute Lenore if she did not perform?

No, Lenore shook herself. The creature on her own arm, smiling falsely, would be her executioner.

Trumpets sounded, the tinny noise echoing harshly against the stone. Dagan moved forwards, dragging Lenore with it. She forced herself to walk forwards. She tried to ignore the people smiling at her on either side of the cloth. Their leers told her just how much of a prize she was. Lenore focused her attention on the people waiting at the end of the Hall.

She nearly froze. There, standing next to Davorin in all his finery, was a priest. Not a cleric for The One Who Watches. But a priest, wrapped in heavy embroidered robes of a deep blue, a hood on his head, beard neat and trimmed and a shining white. On his hand were several rings and in the crook of his arm was a leather bound book. The defining mark, though, was the knife at the priest's belt. This was a priest from the Salusian Empire, for the warrior god Materior. She would not even be married under the rites of her own people.

"Welcome, Lenore," Davorin said as she drew close enough. He stood there, deceptively pleasant in demeanour. His dark hair was still cropped close to his head and he still wore the twin blades at his hip. In truth, except for the fact that his clothes and leather work were gilded with fantastical designs of dragons and sylphs—angels, Lenore reminded herself bitterly—Davorin looked exactly as he always did.

Cunning. Dangerous. Deadly.

"Lord Davorin," Lenore said, her voice barely more than a whisper. Dagan released Lenore's hand and she took the final few steps to stand beside Davorin. The demon creature stood off to the side, opposite Seraphina. Lenore did not miss the leer that Dagan threw to Seraphina. She, to her credit, ignored it except for a slight flaring of her nostrils.

Davorin held out his right hand, expectant. Lenore rested her left on top of his, a shiver forcing its way to the surface. Her normally golden skin looked pale and wan against his dark tan hand, so much larger and scarred than hers. He inclined his head to the priest.

"We are gathered today under the warrior sun of Materior, to call upon the forces that make up this world to join these two in union binding," the priest said. His tones rang out over the Hall, silencing anyone who was whispering or muttering behind raised hands. Lenore's heart sank further.

"By the will of Materior, do you swear that there is nothing standing between your union?" The priest eyed Lenore warily. Davorin spoke first.

"There lies no impediment," Davorin said, voice strong.

Yes! There does! Lenore cried out in her thoughts. Her mouth, though, repeated Davorin's words. "There lies no impediment," she breathed, barely loud enough for the priest to hear. He nodded, ignoring her completely.

"Then let the ceremony begin!"

Lenore closed her eyes for a heartbeat. She reminded herself that she had chosen this fate and that the alternative was much, much worse. She opened her eyes and focused her attention back on the priest. She let her spine straighten. Her chin lifted. And somewhere deep inside, she started building a core of iron so that she could continue to do her best by her people.

The priest droned on about how Materior knew that conflict between people was as natural as the sun conflicting with the moon. That despite the conflict, people would still be joined together into something better and stronger. It was nonsense to Lenore's ears, but she knew nothing about the Salusian god.

After a goodly amount of time musing on the nature of

Materior and matrimony, the priest reached for the knife at his belt. He gestured for her hand; she hesitated, confused.

"Give him your hand," Davorin hissed through a pleasant smile. Lenore hid a wince, but did as Davorin asked. This was something that had never been in any of the wedding ceremonies she had seen. The priest snatched her hand and flipped it so that the palm was upright. Then, he drew the point of the knife across her hand in a swift stroke.

Lenore sucked in a breath and blood welled in her palm. She hardly noticed when Davorin's hand was also cut open, only thought it ironic that her married life would begin with blood. Davorin's bleeding palm was joined with hers so that their blood could mingle. The priest tied a thick embroidered ribbon across both of their hands and made a sigil over it.

"By the might of Materior, by the blood spilled in witness, I bind you together in matrimony. Two, separate, may break. One, together, will stand."

Davorin repeated the words, and Lenore belatedly did the same. Then, she was grasped by her shoulders and spun around, her hand still tied to Davorin's and starting to throb. The faces of the people watching the ceremony became too-bright figures, enemies, leering at Lenore. They erupted in cheers, their shouts filling the Great Hall and echoing off the richly carved stone.

Davorin lifted their joined hands, a triumphant grin on his face. The cheers grew louder. She tried to smile, but that was gone. So she stood there, trying to look regal and proud and not in the least diminished by her new union with Davorin. She was not certain she succeeded.

The time after the ceremony passed in a whirl. Lenore was dragged to the library where she signed official documents declaring her marriage to Davorin, the joining of the Red Desert to the Salusian Empire, and the instatement of Davorin as King Consort to her throne. She was then pulled by their joined hands to a celebratory wedding breakfast, followed by dancing and music and Davorin gloating over the gifts that had been given to them.

Lenore did not remember much after the first document had been signed. She did not see much point.

Somehow, though, the day managed to slip past until it was evening and the married couple was being ushered back to their chamber. Blodwen and the other servants had set up a separate chamber for the purpose. Neither Davorin nor Lenore wished to share their usual rooms with the other. At least there was that.

Once they were safely ensconced inside the room, Davorin tore the bloody ribbon from their hands. Then, ignoring her completely, he ripped his palm from hers and stalked to the window overlooking the gardens. Lenore let out a quiet sound as her wound was torn open again. She cradled the appendage against her chest, ignoring the fact that her dress was likely to be spotted with blood.

"Well, husband," Lenore said, doing her best to keep the mockery out of her voice, "you have gotten your prize. What now?"

Davorin took a deep breath, his broad shoulders rising and falling easily. "You know perfectly well what I intend to do next."

Lenore bit back a fiery retort, pacing her anger off. "You will not find the sylphs quite so easy to subdue."

"You doubt me, wife," Davorin said, his own mockery much greater than Lenore would have expected. Did he not want this marriage to her, as she did not want it? Why, then, had he bothered to go through with it? "I have a new army at my disposal. I have *magic* flowing through my veins. And you think I cannot conquer an island of peaceful birds?"

"Ravenna was not peaceful," Lenore spat. Davorin turned from the window and was before Lenore in an instant. His hand wrapped around her jaw, forcing her head up and her mouth closed.

"Do *not* speak to me of Ravenna," Davorin snarled. He took in a deep breath, running his nose up Lenore's neck. "You know nothing about it."

"I know that you killed the only other person who could have told you where to find the sylphs," Lenore taunted, though it was difficult to speak. She knew that her words would simply provoke Davorin, but she could not help herself. The fire burned brightly in her belly, now that the marriage was official. Her self-pity had vanished. There was no changing her fate now, so she might as well embrace it. "Or does the being you call Dagan still have access to Nadezhda's memories?"

Davorin tightened his grip on Lenore's jaw until she was scrabbling at him with her bloody hands. Davorin saw the liquid on his arm and pulled away, a disgusted sneer on his face. "I do not enjoy forcing a woman into bed, wife, so take comfort of that where you will. But I *will* have you, one way or another."

Lenore barked out a laugh. "You may have won my hand in marriage, drawn a new border for your precious Empire, but you have not broken me."

Davorin set his own bleeding hand on the hilt of one of his twin swords. A single drop trickled down the carved handle. "Do not try my patience. You are my wife."

Lenore held out her arms. "I know my *duty*, husband. And I will do it. But you cannot break me."

Davorin spoke three words. "We shall see."

Lenore smiled.

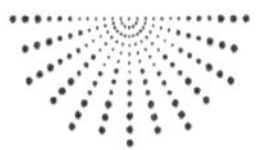

Ravenna was intently focused on the words forming beneath her quill. She had plucked a fresh quill from her own wings just that morning and was busy writing out an account of her foray into the human world. At the moment, she was describing Miska, the human who had stolen her heart and whom she had left behind. Everything else fell away as she recalled the touch of his hands on her shoulders, her wings. The distinct cadence of his voice that produced such precise words all because he could not hear. The way his eyes—green, and so unlike anything Ravenna had ever seen before on Shinalea— shone with mischief or joy at the slightest provocation.

Ravenna threw down her quill and whirled from her chair, drawing one of the two blades that were sheathed against her back. She pointed the tip beneath the chin of the sylph who had interrupted her. Kratos swallowed, holding up his hands in desperation. His golden wings fluttered nervously behind him.

Ravenna sighed and lowered her blade, replacing it in its sheath. "What can I do for you, Kratos?" she asked blandly.

The other sylph wavered. He was shorter than Ravenna and much, much wider, but his wings stretched almost twice the distance that her own black wings did. Kratos, head healer of the Intellecti and, at the moment one of the few sylphs who treated her with anything close to friendship, could fly. Ravenna could not.

"The Council asks for you," Kratos said. He mopped the nervous sheen of sweat from his brow with a scrap of silk. Ravenna sighed, sinking back into the chair. She closed the tome she had been writing in and secured its lock. It wouldn't do to have a curious sylph reading her private thoughts. Not while she was alive, at least.

"I'm busy," Ravenna said after a moment. She toyed with the quill she had been writing with, the night-black sheen of her feather catching in the light of her personal quarters in the Stone Tower. It was separate from the Aerial City where most of the sylphs lived and suited her perfectly well. The other Intellecti, though, seemed to be nervous about Ravenna's inhabiting their home. Six moons ago, they would not have given it a second thought. Then, she had been nothing more than Tacitus' heart-daughter, his flightless ward who was learning the ways of the Intellecti as best she could. Since then, Ravenna had been captured by humans, learned to fight, and experienced enough pain for a lifetime. She had returned to Shinalea barely two moons before to warn her people of the threat against them.

Like it or not, the sylphs would shortly be at war.

The Council had begged her to take the Winged Crown and be the Chosen Queen to lead them through the war. She had refused. Instead, she was now their Warlord, preparing their army and training their people as best she could. The Council wanted to control her, know everything she was doing. Ravenna was not so easily controlled.

"They say it is urgent," Kratos replied, wringing his hands. Ravenna sighed again. Kratos had been one of the few sylphs to support her without question, though it was obvious to her that he had more than a few.

Ravenna stretched her arms above her head. The four parallel scars that ran from her left shoulder across her chest to end above her right breast pulled uncomfortably with the movement. She had earned the scars in a desperate fight with a mad desert lion. It had left her with the wounds, nearly killing her. She had left it lifeless. She had saved Miska, and that was all that mattered.

Ravenna wondered if he were still alive.

"They always say it is urgent," Ravenna snapped. She forced herself to pay attention to the business at hand. Thoughts of Miska were for her tome. She could ill afford to be distracted otherwise. Not when none of the other sylphs knew she had given her heart to a human, the very threat they were fighting against. Well, attempting to fight. "I have to train their army this afternoon. The Sharpwing Company is scheduled with me today. The others are off running the courses."

Kratos let out a little puff of air that might, in anyone else, be considered a sigh. He folded his wings a bit more and stepped farther into Ravenna's room. She tried not to bristle, instead letting the older sylph sit on a spare stool. "We all know that what you're doing is important. More than important; it could be our saving grace. But disregarding the Council will not serve you well."

"They want to control me like some trained falcon," Ravenna said. "I have already been invited to seven dinners with various Council members and their families, so that they might 'thank' me for my work. They want me to be beholden."

"Yes," Kratos agreed readily. "That is how they have worked for generations uncounted. The Chosen Monarch may have ruled our people, but the Council moved around support for laws and social approval. Your grandmother was unusual, in that she could do almost whatever she pleased without worrying about Council approval. Because she was a good ruler.

But the Council controls the will of Shinalea. Fly carefully around this issue, Ravenna."

"The Council may do what it pleases. I will do exactly everything to prepare our people for the war that is coming."

Kratos shook his head. He may have been a healer, but he was trained in all the ways of the Intellecti, including the deep rational paths that served to undergird the factual analysis the Intellecti pursued. He was, now that Tacitus was gone, the closest thing that Ravenna had to a mentor.

Oh, Tacitus—

Ravenna slammed an iron wall down on that line of thought. She shoved the desperate plea for her dead heart-father into the recesses of her mind, instead letting the sharp rationalism that she had so carefully cultivated take its place. Since fleeing the Red Desert, it was all she had to keep from spiralling back into the wing weariness. She had lost so much; it would help no one to think of such things. So she didn't.

"If you had taken the Winged Crown, perhaps that would be possible," Kratos said. Ravenna blinked, raising her brow in surprise. Kratos allowed himself a small smile. "Yes, I know that the Council offered you the crown. Not many do, since your refusal was seen as a failure."

"How?" Ravenna asked. She had imagined the Council would want to keep that very quiet. Her relationship with them and the rest of the sylphs was tenuous enough now that she was their Warlord.

"Tacitus told me," Kratos said. "He said that the Council would offer you the crown. And that he would be dead before he knew what decision you made."

"He already knew my decision," Ravenna said.

"Perhaps before you left," Kratos replied evenly. "But after you returned? You came back different, Ravenna."

She said nothing. She simply placed her quill crossways on her tome and rose, wings stretching out behind her. Kratos rose as well, following her to the door. To see if she went to heed the Council, or to see if she would go train? Ravenna did not know the old healer as well as she had once done.

"I am not Tacitus," Kratos said softly. Ravenna kept walking, her steps even. "But I think I can speak for him when I say it was a good thing you did to not take the crown. But do beware. The Council will be giving you orders, and you must follow them."

Ravenna paused, her wings brushing against the cold stone of the Tower. She was not foolish. She had known exactly what she was doing when she refused to take up the mantle of Chosen Queen. Still, something nagged in the back of her mind. She was uneasy about being given orders by the Council. By anyone.

"I know," she said. "It seems as though the humans are not the only ones to practise slavery after all."

Ravenna did not wait for an answer. She knew that she was not the same sylph that had left Shinalea all those moons ago. She had returned hard and cold and scarred. She no longer cared about what others thought, only what was necessary. She had left everything behind when she returned to her people. And every night, she prayed to the human gods—she did not care which ones—that Miska and Lenore be safe.

Ravenna emerged onto the mossy courtyard, the bright sun hitting her like a shot to the chest. If she let her eyes blur, then the greenery looked almost like the gardens of the Red Desert. But they weren't. They were the hardwood and pine forests of her home. The undergrowth was sparse ferns and dead leaves, not the thick exotic plants of a desert oasis. Ravenna rubbed the knot from her chest, keeping her expression forcibly calm so she wouldn't burst out into an angry snarl.

A shadow passed overhead.

With instincts built up over a lifetime, plus battle skills acquired when survival was everything, she drew both her blades from the sheaths on her back. She raised the left one over her head and held the right one at her side in a Dalketh position known as Blocks the Sun. The descending shadow paused an inch from her blade.

A voice let out a choice curse and the shadow quickly moved off, flapping clumsily as it moved. A moment later and Crispinus settled onto the ground, his golden wings flared wide with alarm. His charcoal-ash skin was flushed slightly with alarm and anger as he spluttered. "What was that, Ravenna?"

"Instinct." She shrugged, sheathing her swords. "Why were you diving at me like prey?"

"Prey? I wasn't!" Crispin said. "I was coming to fetch you for training!"

"That usually requires settling down and *asking* if I wish to be flown to the plateau. Not plucking me up from the ground like one of your rabbits," Ravenna snapped. She shook her head. "I am not Desarra. It would be well that you learned that."

Crispin stiffened at the mention of his mate and Ravenna's sister. Desarra, needless to say, was not pleased about the fact that Ravenna had returned to Shinalea with enough power to be one of the most sought after sylphs on the island. Ravenna hadn't cared at all. They'd never had a close relationship, and since returning she had not bothered to try and mend things between them. Desarra had made things abundantly clear long before Ravenna left.

"I… sorry," Crispin said. She blinked. This sylph, along with her sister, had bullied her for most of her life. The two of them had been the reason she initially discovered that she was flightless. And they had taunted her for it for cycles, never wasting an opportunity to make their dislike of her known. Now, for Crispin to apologise after a minor disagreement? It was unexpected, to say the least.

"Very well," Ravenna said, ignoring the apology. "You may fly me to the plateau, if you wish."

Crispin bowed slightly at the waist before surging forwards and scooping Ravenna up in his arms. He used his forwards momentum in tandem with the beating of his massive wings to take to the skies with as little effort as it took Ravenna to draw her swords. She felt that familiar longing for her own wings to be able to do as Crispin's did. She wanted to feel sky beneath her feathers, wanted to feel the air currents and the joy that would come from flight. She wanted to feel Dalketh in the air, to revel in the strength of her wings. Instead, they hung limp so as not to interfere with Crispin's flight.

The island of Shinalea sped beneath them. Crispin rose higher than Ravenna would have imagined necessary and the trees became one massive green blur. From that height, it was possible to see the mainland. Her heart ached for a moment, but she quickly looked away, instead focusing on the feeling of flying. Crispin turned in mid-air, his wings spiralling them upwards, sun glinting off the feathers.

Then, with a snap so strong that it rang through Ravenna's bones, Crispin's wings flared open as far as they would stretch. The world stood still before them. Clouds hovered at eye level. The ground below disappeared if one did not look down. The winds seemed to hold their breath. Then, reality started to return. Gravity took effect. Crispin started to fall towards the ground, his wings flexing to turn the fall into a manageable dive. Air rushed past her ears, the sound filling her with something stronger than she had known before. Her black hair, wrapped in a neat braid down her back, whipped around her face.

Ravenna glanced at Crispin, expecting to see nothing more than a sylph carrying out his duty in flying her to the plateau above the cliffs where the Aerial City was carved. Instead, she saw pure, unadulterated joy.

This flying, these aerial acrobatics, were what Crispin loved.

Perhaps even above Desarra. But there was no doubt that he was an artist. A master at his craft.

Crispin pulled out of the dive sooner than Ravenna would have liked. She wanted to feel the pounding of earth beneath her feet when they landed, but Crispin was gentle as he set down. He released her from his arms without a word and continued to say nothing as she took a few steps away.

She took a deep breath, looking about the grassy plateau. It was one of the few places on Shinalea where trees did not grow. Instead, it was full of long grasses and wildflowers. It was a popular place for Kratos and other healers in the Aerial City to gather herbs. Ravenna had only stepped foot here a few times in her life. It was something she always associated with the Aerial City. A place of flying. A place where she did not belong.

Now, it was a place almost exclusively reserved for her purposes. It was the only place large enough to gather the fighters of Shinalea. Barely two thousand, but the males and females who chose to rally behind her were strong willed and capable. She hoped.

"I want you to be general of my army," Ravenna said. For a moment, she thought the wind had snatched away her words.

Then, "What?!"

Ravenna turned to face Crispin. "I need a second in command. I need you to be a general. Direct command over half the army. The Sharpwings. The Harrowers. Others. You would pick your own people to lead under you."

"I don't understand," Crispin said. His wings were folded tight against his body. She quirked an eyebrow at the obvious sign of agitation. "I… I thought you didn't like me!"

"I don't," Ravenna said easily. Crispin flinched, but did not draw away. A good sign. "You were the bane of my life here. I looked for you around every corner, behind every tree, hoping that you and Desarra wouldn't be there waiting to trip me as I came up the Stone Stair, or to tug on my wings and scorn me for being flightless. You were cruel and a bully. I still do not like you. I may never like you. But things are different now."

Crispin swallowed, flashing his teeth like a scared cougar. "I still don't understand. If I was all of those things to you—and I suppose I was—then why offer me such a position now? Surely things have not changed that much?"

Ravenna scoffed. She pulled aside the collar of the loose tunic she wore, revealing the long lines of her scars to Crispin. He recoiled. Then, she lifted her tunic and pulled down the edge of her tight breeches, revealing the brand burned into the skin on her hip. She would have showed him the long line that ran down her spine, another scar courtesy of her experiences on the mainland, but that would mean unstrapping her swords, and Ravenna was loath to do so.

"Things have changed more than you know," she said. Crispin's wings still fluttered nervously, but he started to stand up straight again. Ravenna pointed to the sky. "I saw your face just now, as we were flying. You were happy. Even carrying me, you were happier than I have ever seen you. You fly better than anyone I have ever seen. And I would be willing to stake my swords that you would be willing to fight for that. So, no, I don't like you. But I trust you to fight. Right now, that is all that matters."

Crispinus was silent. He lifted his head to study the clouds painted against the impossible blue of the sky. "You're right," he said after a few heartbeats. "I will fight for that. I will be your general."

Ravenna inclined her head. "Good."

Another shadow crossed the plateau, moving swiftly. Ravenna had the foresight not to draw her blade, even as the sylph staggered to the ground only a few feet in front of her. It was Kratos, heaving for breath. He pressed his hands to his knees and sucked in great breaths. Between them, she could make out words. "Desarra… Council… Chosen Queen."

CHAPTER FOUR

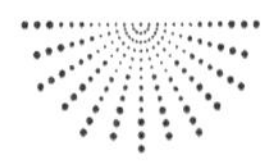

Ravenna burst into the Council chambers without ceremony or pretence. Her wings were flared wide behind her and with her eyes spitting ice, the most powerful sylphs on Shinalea all flinched. The Council was only half assembled, with most of them looking as though they were leaving for the day, but it would be enough to express her anger.

"You bastards," Ravenna spat. Strygis, the unspoken leader of the Council, smiled widely. The loose, flowing tunic and trousers of the sylphs barely covered his enormous girth. His wings brushed the ground when he walked. And yet, somehow, this sylph managed to hold untold influence over others.

Ravenna hated politics. That was part of the reason why she had turned down the crown. Part of her longed to just draw her swords and remove all facade of obedience. But she was one against a society. If she wanted to protect the other sylphs on Shinalea, then she would need to be sanctioned by the Council and by the Chosen Monarch.

Who was, now, her sister.

"My sister?" Ravenna asked, clenching her hands into fists to keep from hitting Strygis. Her expression cracked a little, revealing the fury beneath. A moment later and the fury was gone, replaced by her cool ice. "You could not convince me to take the Winged Crown, so you offered it to my sister?!"

"Desarra is a good candidate. She is also the granddaughter of the last Chosen Queen. Add to the fact that she *is* your family and you gain a good deal of credibility amongst our people," Strygis said.

A taller, worn sylph woman stood beside Strygis. Her charcoal-ash skin was heavily wrinkled and her amber-fire eyes seemed weary. But at Strygis' words, she lifted her chin high and spoke. "You did not want the crown, Warlord. Since we have not the time nor the resources to hold a Choosing while we are at war, someone had to fill the position. Desarra was the granddaughter of Mariala, as well as your sister. She was the best candidate for the position."

"Of course she was, Tytira," Ravenna said. "She was the best way for you to control *me*."

Strygis brushed a golden hand down the front of his robes. "I never took you to be arrogant, Ravenna Wingsword."

Ravenna laughed, the sound sharp and disbelieving. "Is that what they're calling me, now? Or is that your pet name to make me feel important?"

"Your insolence will not long be tolerated by this Council," Tytira spoke again. She was taller than Ravenna and her wings were larger, but the sylph failed to intimidate. None of these sylphs posed any threat to her. They all knew they needed her to train them in the ways of fighting that had been forgotten generations ago. They needed her to help to win the war.

Ravenna shook her head slowly. "You think Desarra is capable of holding the Winged Crown? She is a vain female, who thinks more about appearances than strategy or politics. She will be a pretty figurehead, but she will not be a good Chosen Queen."

"You are rather harsh on your own sister," Strygis said

mildly. Ravenna clenched her fist tighter, nails digging into her palm. "She is your only family, since your grandmother died. Not to mention she will soon be your monarch."

"She will be *your* figurehead," Ravenna said again, this time baring her teeth sharply. "Look how well I obey *you*."

Strygis and Tytira looked at each other in alarm. Strygis' golden skin grew an unhealthy shade of orange and Tytira seemed to become more grey than charcoal. Strygis took a step closer to Ravenna, taking in a deep breath. He paused just before her, close enough to lay a hand on her arm and smart enough not to. "Fly carefully, Ravenna," Strygis murmured. "You have only the authority we grant you. You could be denounced in an instant if we so chose."

Ravenna leaned in, her ice-blue eyes mere inches from Strygis' amber-brown ones. "And who, then, would fight your war?"

Strygis stumbled back a few steps, his wings clumsily stretching to help him regain his balance. Tytira spread her wings wide to support him. She looked down her hooked nose at Ravenna. "You are nothing more than a flightless, arrogant ingrate who expects too much! Who's to say that this war of yours is nothing more than fabrication?!"

"Tytira!" Strygis drew back in shock.

Ravenna just laughed drily, sketching a bow with her wings. "Perhaps I am all of those things, Councillor, but if I were lying, why would I have bothered to come back?" She did not say that Shinalea had nearly destroyed her before she had a chance to stretch her wings. Had Tacitus not been so good a sylph, she likely would have been.

Strygis shook his head, his frown deepening as Tytira simply sniffed and said nothing, arms folded. "You know as well as I what the scouts reported after Ravenna's return," Strygis said.

Ravenna straightened. "Scouts? You sent scouts?"

"It was necessary, to see if you were telling the truth," Strygis muttered through gritted teeth. "And you were."

"She still defies our authority at every turn!" Tytira snapped.

Ravenna sighed. This was why she disliked dealing with the Council. She hated getting drawn into their political games. Either she was their duly appointed Warlord, or she was some spiteful land-walker, determined to cause chaos. If she bowed and scraped to their every whim, they would lose this war. And yet, if she stepped too far outside their authority, then the other sylphs would not do as she was demanding of them. Ravenna had never wanted to lead anything. Yet here she was, leading an army.

"She is doing the best she can!" Strygis returned, clenching his fists. Ironic, given that a few minutes before he had been demanding that she do exactly as Tytira asked. Some rifts ran deep, evidently. "We are not a people prepared for war. There are many things that may have to change in the future if we want to come out of this alive. We cannot expect that our society will come out of this unscathed!"

"If we let her have her way, then our society will be nothing more than the tatters of the grand thing that it is," Tytira hissed. "All our efforts at enlightenment, at philosophy and art and music and science and improvement—lost!"

Ravenna spoke, thinking of a night long ago when she learned to dance in a society ready for war. "None of these things will be lost. Only adapted to a wider understanding of the world. One which we have lost. I have *seen* the tomes that talk of the Stormbringers. I *know* that we were once a people ready to defend ourselves. We were legion and we were powerful, yet we did not give up our pursuit of knowledge or art or philosophy. Generations of peace have brought us to lose our knowledge of war, but that does not mean it is wrong."

Strygis raised his eyebrows in surprise. "You speak well, Ravenna. And it has, indeed, been long since the Stormbringers were talked about as more than myth."

Ravenna shook her head. "I was raised as an Intellecti. Yet you see me as nothing more than a weapon."

"You are *dangerous*," Tytira said flatly, slicing her wings through the air to accentuate the point. Ravenna could feel the Councillor's stare focused on the blades at her back. There would be no convincing Tytira. Capitulate and obey, but she would still be treated with fear. Unfortunately, there were many who probably considered her that way.

Her wings sagged a little, suddenly heavy. She brushed a strand of hair out of her eyes and looked between Strygis and Tytira. She would not hurt them. She had never displayed violence in all her life except when she was on the mainland. Yet suddenly, her knowledge and her plan and the skills she possessed made her dangerous.

"Desarra is your choice, then," Ravenna said quietly. Strygis nodded. "And you think that having my sister, who loathes me, giving me orders is the best plan for us all?"

Strygis blinked. "She does not like you? But you are family!"

"In blood only," Ravenna said. "She hates me. She has always hated me."

"And what of you?" Tytira asked gravely, snidely. Ravenna knew precisely what the older sylph meant. She would have happily sworn off all connections with Shinalea if it meant she could return to Miska and live in peace. On this island, though, Miska did not exist and peace was a dream lost in fog. The truth of the matter was that she did have connections here. Tacitus was dead, but his spirit remained. Kratos was a friend, if perhaps not a great one. Crispinus was her general. And Desarra? Well, before she had left, Ravenna had hoped desperately for some sign of affection from her sister. Now? She wasn't certain it mattered.

"Desarra is my blood, whether or not I hold her in affection," Ravenna said. "My mother and grandmother are dead. She is all the blood family I have left."

"You believe that Desarra does not think the same way? That she will not accord you some respect?" Tytira tilted her head, looking like some curious eagles that occasionally roosted in the Aerial City.

"I think that Desarra does not know anything about fighting a war."

"We will guide her," Strygis interrupted. Firmly. "After all, she does not have the previous Chosen Queen to guide her. She will be relying on the Council heavily to perform her duties."

"You want to clip her wings?" Ravenna asked, narrowing her eyes. She might not love Desarra, but to be given an empty throne seemed worse than being ruled by her sister. It would crush Desarra. And Ravenna would feel the weight of the Council even more.

"Of course not," Tytira snapped before Strygis could make a political response. "She will be our Chosen Queen!"

"Very well," Ravenna murmured. "I think you are making a mistake, but it matters little. If Desarra is your Chosen Queen, then I will pledge to serve her, as I serve Shinalea."

There was immediate relief on Tytira and Strygis' faces. Their wings lifted slightly and their shoulders no longer looked so burdened. Even some of the fear that they held in their eyes dissipated. Ravenna looked away.

She did not wait for a dismissal, just spun on her heel, wings flaring behind her, and left the Council chambers.

Strygis' voice followed in her wake. "We will notify you regarding the ceremony!"

* * *

BY THE TIME Ravenna returned to the plateau above the city, the Sharpwings and Cloudbreakers were already gathered. Allowing Crispinus to fly her to the plateau had given Ravenna extra time to challenge the Council, but now she was late. She would have liked to observe her two companies for a moment, to see how they interact. But with her moon-pale skin and her night-black wings, she stood out like a bent feather and her presence was spotted immediately.

Brianna, one of the more vocal sylphs, strode forwards. She reminded Ravenna of her grandmother, Mariala, both in the proud way she walked and the way her golden skin was spotted at the fingertips with charcoal-ash. Her wingspan was one of the widest amongst the sylphs, reaching almost twenty-one feet, and she was one of the best fliers next to Crispin.

"Where have you been?" Brianna demanded. Ravenna was not intimidated by the way Brianna's wings stretched in supposed dominance. She just stood there, her own ten foot span pathetic compared to Brianna's. But it was the other sylph who backed down, folding her wings behind her so they rose up over her head. "Crispinus was saying something about being made a 'general', whatever that is. And you weren't here and we need to start training—"

"Yes," Ravenna said. She had to remember that only a small fraction of the sylphs who had volunteered to fight—only two, in fact—had been trained as Intellecti. The terminology surrounding war and fighting would be new to most all of them. Though, she admitted to herself, she had picked up the word "general" from her times with the humans. "I will explain everything after training. When all of the companies are assembled."

"All of them?" Brianna asked, feathers bristling. Ravenna inclined her head. She only wanted to explain this once. The other eighteen companies of a hundred sylphs were meant to be flying around the island or gathering supplies. It would take time for them to gather. But her words were important. She needed to organise them, to establish a hierarchy. In a battle, orders would need to be followed without question.

But that could wait until after she had gone through the training for the day.

Ravenna followed Brianna back to the gathered sylphs. Crispin was waiting, looking a little nervous. As Ravenna drew closer, the gathered sylphs fell silent. No matter that it had happened every day for nearly two moons, the sensation still sent an unpleasant tingle up Ravenna's spine. She disliked being at the centre of so much attention. Coming from sylphs who had ignored her and pretended she did not exist for most of her life, it was definitely unusual.

"Wingsword," one of the males said, ducking his head. So, the Council hadn't been making the moniker up.

"Alright," Ravenna said, her voice snapping out in the thin air on the plateau. She could not bellow as well as Vareis, the human female who had trained her in the Red Desert, but she could make herself heard. "First things first! Don't call me Wingsword. I am Ravenna, nothing more."

"You are our Warlord," Brianna pointed out. Ravenna's feathers bristled.

"I am," Ravenna agreed. "But I have done nothing to earn a title, especially not Wingsword."

"Are the rumours true?" the dark sylph who had called her the name spoke again. "Is there to be a new Chosen Monarch?"

"There is," Ravenna said, offering no more information. They would find out in due course. She would not let the announcement be tainted by her own feelings regarding the situation. "The Council will make a formal announcement within the week. The crowning will take place sometime shortly after."

Murmuring broke out amongst the gathered sylphs. Ravenna let them speculate for a few moments; a new Chosen Queen would affect all of them. Once the murmuring turned into whispered conversation, though, she snapped her wings wide and let out a bellow Vareis would be proud of. "Enough!"

They fell silent.

"We are here to train. As far as you are concerned, politics does not exist on this field unless I say it does. You will have time to speculate later. Now, run through Dalketh," Ravenna said. She saw more than a few wings rippling in shock or fear or some other strong emotion. If she had not been so used to hiding everything behind her calm expression, she would perhaps have felt something. As it was, she preferred they feared her rather than loved her.

Ravenna watched as the sylphs shuffled into a series of ten lines, twenty sylphs per line. They spread out far enough that their wings would not touch each other as they went through the motions of the ancient art of Dalketh.

Dalketh was a series of movements that were often used to teach the young how to fly. It involved flowing slowly from one position to another, all limbs and wings shifting slightly. The art was an ancient one, and she had discovered that it was meant for more than flying. It was meant for fighting.

Of course, most of the sylphs now barely remembered movements that they had learned as children. Often, once a sylph learned how to fly, they no longer bothered with the movements of Dalketh. Ravenna had been unusual; being flight-less, she had incorporated the movements into her every day life so she could run through the forest indiscriminately, jumping over logs and boulders, leaping into the branches of trees and jumping through the air like a squirrel. Then, after she was taken by the humans, Dalketh became her means of survival. She winced at the jerky motions of the sylphs before her.

Crispinus was in the front lines, his expression set into one of concentration. He was one of the best at Dalketh, and even that was pitiful. Ravenna sighed as his wings slid out of position. Many of the others, watching Crispin for cues, copied him.

"Stop, stop," Ravenna said, shaking her head. The assembled slid out of position and watched her expectantly. "Did none of you practise Dalketh since last we met? You call yourself Sharp-wings? Cloudbreakers? The Harrowers managed to make it through a whole set! And the Wind Through Feathers did it double time."

"This is child's play," a male complained. Ravenna narrowed her eyes on him. He was tall and broad, with wings that were bunched with muscle. The green tunic he wore was stretched tight across muscles, even when the fashion was for loose clothing. His golden skin was ruddy in comparison to some others and the typical burnished gold hair of the sylphs was nearly shaved off his head, leaving only a single braid falling off his left temple. She was shorter than him by a hand, at least, even though she was slightly above average height. So when she walked over to him, she lifted her chin to stare him down.

"I beg your pardon…?" Ravenna trailed off, seeking a name.

"Itonus," the male growled. "Why are we doing this? Dalketh is a pitiful way to exercise. Why do we not actually learn to *fight*?"

Ravenna smiled up at Itonus, the gesture restricted to her mouth. Her eyes remained as cold as ever. "Ah, yes. As an army, you should be learning to fight. Did I not explain why Dalketh was necessary?"

Itonus frowned. "Something about the ancient arts having been forgotten. Something about what the Stormbringers used to do."

Ravenna nodded. She took a step back so the others could see her better. She spread her arms out wide and her wings lifted over her head. "Did I not *demonstrate* why I am your Warlord? Were my scars not enough?!"

No one said anything. Ravenna shook her head. "Very well," she said, voice echoing the ice in her eyes. She reached over her head with both arms and drew her twin blades. They were thin, triangular blades made by the best smith in the Red Palace. Another reminder of the world she had left behind.

A few of the sylphs near her flinched at the sight of the blades. Ravenna would have to remedy that as well. The art of weaponry had long been forgotten on Shinalea. Excepting for a few hunting knives, most sylphs only used blades for preparing meals. What use could a peaceful society have for weapons?

Ravenna took her own swords and thrust the tips into the ground so they swayed there, standing upright. She walked a few steps away from her blades, then pointed to Itonus. "Attack me."

Itonus' heavy wings folded close to his back and he shook his head, braid swinging. "With respect, Warlord—"

"That was not a request, warrior," Ravenna said, curling her lip. "You wanted to know why we were practising Dalketh? Then attack me! And you," she said, pointing to all the others, "had better watch closely."

There was a flurry of wings as most of the sylphs rose into the air to get a better vantage point on their Warlord. Crispinus took a step towards her, then hesitated. He retreated to stand by her swords. After a moment, Ravenna and Itonus stood facing one another in a circle of sylphs. They were watched from all sides and from above. Ravenna blinked and was immediately transported back to an arena carved from a sinkhole in the desert. The sun beat down on her without mercy. The crowd called out vulgar insults and cheers for blood. In a box situated above the rest, a vulgar woman lounged, leering down at her with greedy gaze.

Ravenna blinked again and she was out of the Slave Pits, Itonus bearing down on her. His wings were spread open halfway to give him balance as he rushed forwards. She slid into her Dalketh stance and easily sidestepped the massive sylph. He staggered beyond Ravenna for a few steps before turning back to face her. He charged again, this time tilting his wings into the wind for speed.

Ravenna let him get close enough to strike. Itonus swung

with his left hand, reaching for her head to cuff her ears. She had time enough to bob her head under his swing. Then, she used his own momentum against him. One hand grabbed his outstretched arm and pulled him forwards, her knee connecting with his stomach. Ravenna hopped backwards, wings folded in front of her. Itonus growled, clutching his stomach.

Then, the fight began in earnest. Itonus had size and strength on his side. Ravenna was the faster. And she knew what she was doing. Every time Itonus got close enough to strike, he would swing at her vulnerable spots. She was never there, though, darting away with a slice of her wings. She buffeted at his head with her wings. She hit him in the soft centre with palm-strikes. Her legs blurred into aerial kicks augmented by her wings. Never once did Itonus manage to hit back.

Eventually, he grew so angry that he took to the sky, letting out a roar of fury as he gained altitude and did the one thing that Ravenna could not: fly. He rose far enough into the air to give him decent momentum when he dove. With a snap, his wings folded to his back and Itonus surged towards Ravenna.

She had never fought against an aerial enemy before, but figuring out what to do was nothing more than applying the instinct from nearly twenty cycles of practising Dalketh daily and the fighting spirit instilled by the humans. She had learned from nightmares come to life. The angry sylph flying towards her was nothing more than an annoyance.

Ravenna brought her right wing over her head, as if shielding herself from Itonus' attack. When she could feel his hands reaching for her feathers, Ravenna whipped her wing wide. The force of her blow knocked Itonus from the sky. One of his wings caught on the ground and he tumbled head over feathers to lie on his back, gasping for breath. She strode over, looming over him. She looked over his wings, noting that neither seemed injured. None of his golden-brown feathers were even out of place.

"You will be fine," Ravenna said flatly. Then, she looked up at the sylphs still flying overhead, their eyes wide as they watched. "Now do you understand?!"

Crispinus stepped forwards, holding out her swords. Ravenna took them and slid the blades back into their sheaths. "We understand," Crispin said in a soft voice.

"Good," she said. "Back into formation. It's time we start from the very beginning."

CHAPTER FIVE

*C*avaris was perhaps the most frustrating being that Miska had ever met. That first morning, the dragon had coaxed the barest of facts from him while saying nothing about himself. Then, he had vanished, leaving Miska to fend for himself until dark. This absurd routine continued for nearly a moon. Cavaris had learned his life story, including all his recent experiences with Ravenna, the supposedly mythological being, and Davorin the monster. Miska had still learned almost nothing about his new companion, nor had he learned any news of the people he had left behind.

Every day, Cavaris would bring food for Miska to cook over the fire in the centre of the tent. They would share the breakfast and a strong cup of tea. They would sit outside the tent, looking at the forest. Miska usually shivered through the entire ordeal, despite the fact that Cavaris let him use some of the furs as blankets. The dragon, in his human guise, would ask him questions. In turn, he would be instructed on the language of the Iron Mountains.

It was a bit frustrating exchanging valuable information for the word "tree" repeated several times over, with a corresponding hand motion thrown in. Miska had heard of a signed language meant for people like him who could not hear, but no one at the Red Palace had known of such things. Consequently, he was not only struggling to read this new language on Cavaris' lips, but he was trying to mimic the hand motions, also.

His patience often ran thin.

After Miska's language lessons, the dragon would vanish for most of the day, off doing whatever it was that he did. Miska would tend the fire, clean the tent, and wander around the forest. He never strayed far enough to get lost. But eventually, the trees felt more like comfortable protection than ominous threats. He entertained thoughts of trying to find Ravenna, but he never ventured far enough to consider seeking her out. Nor did he venture in the direction of home. So he recovered and told Cavaris everything and tried not to tremble when he thought of what he had left behind.

This day, though, was different.

Miska had been doing his best to gather firewood. He never saw Cavaris gather the wood; it was always just there. The fire seemed to just keep burning, no matter how long had passed since he tended it. But gathering wood was better than sitting around doing nothing, so he bent and picked up sticks.

Something tapped Miska on the shoulder and he spun, dropping all the sticks but the one he held in his right hand. Some long-quiet instinct had him raising the stick as if to strike. Cavaris stopped it with ease, his pale hand flashing out and grabbing the stick from the air. He ripped it from Miska's grasp as though he were plucking a blade of grass. Then, the dragon raised a single brow.

Were you expecting to be attacked?

Miska muttered something, scuffing his now-worn leather slippers on the dirt. His toe poked through the left one and made it painfully obvious when he stepped on a pinecone. "I thought you were away."

Cavaris gestured to a hulking figure behind him. *I have brought someone. I think it time your internment here ended.* The figure stepped forwards. Miska took a mirroring step backwards, a flash of fear rising in him.

The figure was a man, though larger than any Miska had ever seen. He towered head and shoulders above both Miska and Cavaris. His skin was light, marked with many scars that looked to be from both blades and claws. He had hair that was the colour of fresh dirt and sported a beard that covered most of his jaw. His eyes burned bright blue. He wore clothes of thickly woven fabric and had a few dark furs slung over his shoulder as some sort of patchy cloak. But what had Miska retreating was the giant battle axe wrapped in his right fist. His left hand was nothing more than a stump covered with a piece of steel and held in place with rivets.

"Miska," Cavaris said out loud, his voice as calm and soothing as ever. "This is Sisu. He will help you."

"Help me what?" Miska asked, the unfamiliar words feeling strange on his tongue. He tried to make his mouth do as it was told, but the slight furrowing of Sisu's massive brow had him frowning. He wanted to be home, where people understood him and he understood them. Not here, in this unfamiliar place with people who were more likely to scorn him or laugh at him. He had to *help* Lenore. Not waste away.

Cavaris turned to say something to the massive Sisu, then turned back to Miska. *Sisu will take over your training.*

"My training?" Miska blurted in Ionan. Sisu frowned at the language, but Miska focused his attention on Cavaris. "What training? I have to help Queen Lenore!"

Indeed. I have confirmed your story. It took many days of flight and watching from above, but what you say is true. Even the part about the island with a sylph civilisation flourishing there. Cavaris' eyes gleamed. He inclined his head, horns brushing a low hanging branch. *You have my apologies for doubting you.*

Miska curled his lip. "You were there?" he asked. Cavaris nodded. "And you did not take me with you? You could have returned me to Queen Lenore! You could have taken me to Ravenna! She would have helped!"

Sisu said something, his mouth moving too swiftly for Miska to pick apart. He caught two words, "what" and "saying" as well as a flurry of others. The man wanted to know what Miska was saying, probably. He wanted to throw something at the massive man, just standing there and letting Cavaris mock him. For his part, the dragon just blinked languidly and shook his head, fine white hair moving gently as he did so.

And what of your sylph's efforts for her people? She could not have sent them after your Queen Lenore in their current state. You wish to help; I understand. But you can do nothing as you are.

Miska blinked back furious tears. "And what am I?"

At the moment? Alone. Cavaris stepped forwards and lay a gentle hand on his shoulder, the claws brushing his skin. Miska wanted to throw the dragon off, but he just stood there, fists clenched at his side. Cavaris paused a moment, then drew his hand back. *I have brought Sisu to help you. He will teach you the ways of the Iron Mountains. And, once you are ready, he will bring you before the Elders of Hullgard to speak your case. If you are successful, then they will march with you to the Red Desert.*

Hope flared through Miska. "You can promise this?" he breathed. Cavaris smiled, an ancient giant looking down on a minuscule ant.

I can only present the opportunity. Sisu is the one who has offered to teach you.

"And what about you?" Miska asked, pointing at Cavaris. "Will you help?"

Miska could only imagine what a dragon—a *real dragon*—could do against Davorin and that monster that slew the soldiers in Lenore's throne room. It was like walking amongst all the stories told to him as a child. Magic, sylphs, dragons. He had spent a moon conversing with Cavaris, learning a language, but the awe of him being draconic had not diminished. If he brought Cavaris to the battle, then the war could already be won!

Cavaris shook his head. *I will not fly again into the affairs of humans until magic reappears. True magic, the song of the earth, not the corrupted thing that human who claimed your lands has brought into existence.*

Miska's shoulders slumped. "You will not fight?" he asked. Cavaris shook his head, no. Miska swallowed back a plea and once again examined Sisu. Training with him could take moons. He had no idea how long it would be before Sisu determined him "ready". And what of Lenore in the mean time? What of Ravenna? Still, Cavaris was right. Miska could do nothing as he was. He couldn't fight. He couldn't even communicate. He was…alone.

"Please," Miska begged Cavaris. "Don't let them die while I do this."

I will watch. Cavaris turned to the tent and walked away, leaving Miska standing before Sisu, feeling tiny by comparison. The big man lumbered forwards, surprisingly graceful for someone who looked as though he could bend trees. He looked down at Miska, his long dark hair swinging forwards and revealing a multitude of braids woven with feathers and black stones inscribed with runes.

Miska took a breath, his heart pounding in his chest. With all its might, it told him to run away. Run back to the Red Desert and do what he could from there. Maybe he could start a people's uprising. Maybe he could sneak into the Red Palace and subvert Davorin from there. Maybe he could make his way to Shinalea and learn under Ravenna's tutelage, ready to fight at her side. At the thought of her, his heart ached. He had barely told her how he felt before she had fled the desert to save her people. She had told him she loved him, but she did not *need* him with her. Maybe he did not need her either. Maybe he could help in his own way.

"Sisu," Miska said the man's name, carefully tracing his tongue over the path that Cavaris had followed. The man nodded. "I… go with you?"

"Yes," Sisu said.

* * *

MISKA WAS WOEFULLY unprepared for what came next. Sisu had gestured for Miska to follow him, then started on a brisk march through the woods and the mountains. He tried to keep up as best he could, but the big man walked faster than he could have imagined. He was practically running to keep up. And there were unfamiliar things that got in his way. Tree branches fallen to the ground, rocks that seemed perfectly hidden under masses of undergrowth, pine needles that kept wheedling their way into his soft leather shoes. Miska tripped and stumbled and scraped his hands more times than he cared to count. All the while, Sisu just kept walking along, strolling as though he had not a care in the world.

Eventually, Sisu turned and watched Miska's progress. He paused, the enormous battle axe glinting in the sunlight. Miska tried not to stare at it or the lack of left hand. He staggered to a halt. He leaned against a wide tree, the scrapes on his hands tingling. He stared at the red lines that had appeared after an unfortunate encounter with a ditch.

Sisu's singular hand reached out and looked at Miska's hands. He bit back a flinch and looked up at the man. Sisu was frowning. His mouth moved and Miska tried to understand the words. "How… live… desert?"

Miska shook his head. "What?"

Sisu growled, shaking Miska's hands. "How… you… live… desert?"

"How did I *live* in the desert?" Miska asked, his tongue stumbling over the pronunciation. Sisu nodded, then repeated his words back, his own mouth moving slowly, his single hand moving in the twists and turns that Cavaris had taught him. Miska only caught three of the movements, but he parroted back the corrected pronunciation well enough to make Sisu smile. The man nodded, the beads flashing in his hair.

To further explain, Sisu gestured to Miska's bedraggled clothing, torn and dirty, and the scrapes on his hands. Miska understood. Sisu wanted to know just how he managed to survive in the desert without seriously injuring himself. He must seem so weak to this man. Was that why Ravenna had left him behind? Because he was weak?

Miska tucked his hands into his abdomen, hiding the injuries from his travelling companion. He straightened and, letting his brown hair fall into his eyes to hide their anguish, started off in the direction that Sisu had been taking them. Sisu put his hand on his shoulder, turned him, and pointed in an entirely different direction.

Miska flushed. There was an obvious path—perhaps a game trail?—moving through the woods. Sisu started down it and, with a single look back at him, led the way once again. He did notice, though, that Sisu made an effort to walk slower.

Some several hours later, Miska had stopped wondering when they were going to stop. He put one foot before the other as a matter of pure routine. His arms hung limply as he walked. He did pay attention to where he was stepping, though that was only a precaution to keep from falling. His thoughts had long since stopped revolving around the lost Ravenna and the people Miska himself had left behind. He stopped wondering why Cavaris had shunted him off onto this human instead of teaching him. After all, Cavaris could communicate with him. Sisu had to make do with repetition of the simplest phrases and wild hand gestures that hardly made sense at all.

Miska ran into a solid wall. He stumbled backwards, landing flat on his back. He shook his head and looked up at Sisu. The man looked a little bemused by Miska lying on the ground. He gestured to the area they were in and said something.

Miska furrowed his brows, repeating the movements of Sisu's mouth. "Sleep?" he thought he said. Sisu nodded, grinning eagerly.

"Sleep!" he said, gesturing again to the trees around them. Miska glanced around. There was nothing remarkable about this spot as opposed to others. The trees seemed just as thick. The ground might have been a little flatter, but it was difficult to tell. Though, the sun was beginning to set and this seemed as good a place as any to make camp. Wistfully, he longed for the pleasant warmth of Cavaris' tent. He hoped he would not freeze to death in this mountain air.

Miska rose to his feet and immediately felt his muscles waver beneath him. Sisu steadied him. He nodded his thanks and looked around. Okay, now what?

Thankfully, Sisu seemed to know exactly what to do. Miska had only ever slept rough on the journey from the Red Desert to the Iron Mountains. He had huddled against whatever natural shelter he could find and hoped that animals did not eat him. Now, he watched as Sisu swept a broad space clear of undergrowth, picking up and placing stones in a circle. That much, Miska recognised. He quickly went to gather sticks and larger logs so that they could have a fire. He tried not to show how much his muscles were trembling as he carried an armful of wood to Sisu.

Sisu grinned, saying something that made him laugh and nod approvingly. Or at least, he hoped it was approving. He had rarely tried to read the facial expressions and movements of someone with so much hair. It covered many of the finer muscles around the mouth and made Sisu's emotions appear either nonexistent or powerful to the point of overwhelming, depending. Miska dropped the wood beside the man and fairly collapsed himself.

Sisu fumbled at his belt and handed him a sack of some sort filled with a liquid. He unstoppered it and sniffed it to find water. He drank eagerly. Sisu snatched it back after a few precious mouthfuls and stoppered it. He gestured to the water sack with his stump hand and said something. Miska frowned, shaking his head. Sisu mimed something, about pouring something into something else...

"Ah!" Miska said, sitting straight. Sisu wanted him to find more water and fill the sack. Miska nodded and took the sack back from Sisu, as well as an empty one that had been folded into a tiny square. He stood, his legs screaming protest as he did so. He wanted to sleep so badly. He was so tired. Tired of trying to communicate in an impossible language so far from home. And, now that he was doing more than walking numbly, the thoughts that had fallen from his head flowed back with desperation.

Most of them focused on Ravenna.

The sylph was unlike anyone that he had ever met. She was stubborn and seemed to care little for herself. But she could fight with an ease that even Vareis, the training master, had said she could not match. Ravenna was beautiful and strong. She was cold, with a mind that was quick and sharp. Yet, she cared. She was not cruel or mean, like some others. She never seemed to care that Miska couldn't hear her. She just loved him for him.

Why, then, did she leave him behind?

Miska fell into the stream before him. The water was like ice, jolting him awake far better than hours of walking had. He hadn't even realised it was there; who knew where water lay in these unfamiliar places? He had just been going slightly downhill, hoping that something would turn up. And there it was! Sisu must have known it was nearby when he decided to stop to camp.

The water was cold enough to set Miska's heart racing. He scrambled out of the water, his worn trousers dripping and falling to pieces even more. Cavaris had never mentioned anything about his clothes. He had tried to keep them clean, washing them as best he could. But it seemed that the last remnants of his desert life were falling to pieces before his very eyes. He sighed, shaking some droplets of water off his hands.

There was nothing he could do about it, now. Nothing he could do about Ravenna, either. She was gone. He understood why, but it still hurt. At least he knew she loved him, as he loved her.

Miska filled the two water sacks. The material stretched under his hands, holding much more than he had ever thought they could carry. He held up one and examined it. The material was like a supple leather, but it did not soak through and there were no seams. In the desert, they used waxed fabric soaked in animal fat. These, though, looked oddly like some of the more exotic delicacies that had graced Lenore's table during events with foreign dignitaries.

Miska dropped the sack he was holding, only to snatch it up again as it fell into the stream and nearly floated downstream. They were not sacks at all. They were animal stomachs, treated and fitted with stoppers.

What sort of horrible place had he come to be in?

What had Cavaris meant when he told Miska that he was to be *trained* by Sisu? He closed his eyes and swallowed. He had a feeling this was not going to be the training he would have expected in the desert, working with Vareis. That would have been working with weapons, learning basic fighting and then increasing that ability carefully. This... this was going to be something different.

Miska swallowed his disgust before refilling the spilled water and heaving both stomachs into his arms. They weighed a considerable amount, considering there was nothing but water.

Miska staggered up the hill with them, trying to remember which way the camp was. He wandered for a good five minutes, his already weary muscles growing more tired with each shuffled step. Finally, he spotted a light through the trees.

Sisu grinned broadly at him as he walked back into the camp. He dropped the stomachs unceremoniously on the ground. Miska pointed at his abdomen, then to the stomachs. Sisu watched the motion a couple of times before he tilted his head back and howled laughter into the darkening sky, shoulders shaking with the mirth. The man's face lit up with humour, to the point where even Miska couldn't help the slight smile that touched his mouth.

Sisu pointed at him and shook his head, tears falling from the corner of his eyes. Eventually, even Sisu had to stop laughing. He took big, heaving breaths. Then, pointing to his abdomen and the stomachs holding water, he gave the word for stomach in his language. Miska's tongue twisted as he tried to replicate the movements. Sisu said the word slower; this time Miska could replicate it. Then, Sisu pointed again to the water stomachs and said, "Skin. Water skin."

Miska knew the word for water. He repeated the other. Sisu nodded, blue eyes glinting.

Thus began Miska's language lessons with Sisu. While the man hung one of the water skins over the fire and threw in ingredients that had been wrapped in a ball of fabric into the water, he also said the word for each and every thing that he could point to with his metal-covered stump. Some of them, Miska knew, others he repeated faithfully until Sisu nodded. Sometimes, Sisu threw in a hand motion that Miska tried to replicate. Those were much more difficult for him to remember, but he tried.

The soup was cooking gently over the fire and Miska's head was starting to hurt. He was so tired that he almost felt beyond hunger, but the scents that drifted from the cooking food woke something in him. And there was Sisu through all of this. He seemed perfectly at ease, throwing bits of dried meat into the soup as it simmered. And he just kept talking. The situation, if it hadn't been so odd, would almost have been relaxing.

After what felt like hours, Sisu declared the soup done. He handed a crudely carved wooden spoon to Miska. Given that they had no bowls, they took turns scooping out soup from the skin until his hunger was gone and Sisu was scraping the inside of the water skin for more. Somewhere during the meal, the language lesson had stopped, leaving his thoughts to calm and his body to fall into complete weariness.

He did not even notice when he closed his eyes. He only felt a large cloak of furs being placed on him as the songs of nights long past played quietly inside Miska's head where he was the only one to ever hear. He wondered if this forest sounded the same as the oasis back home.

Then, nothing but darkness.

CHAPTER SIX

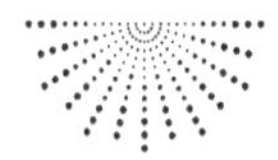

The next day, Miska followed Sisu with an almost blind faith. His fingers were so cold and his nose was dripping from the harsh mountain air that flowed through it. He wore Sisu's cloak even as they walked. He did not know what was in the multitude of pockets that lined the inside, only that he was glad of the weight and did not care that his stiff muscles were protesting loudly. It was warm.

They did not walk nearly as far, nor as fast. Sisu walked beside Miska, helping him when he stumbled or pointing at something and having him say what it was. That was one thing that Miska seemed to be managing, at least. His language skills were definitely improving.

Sometime after midday, while he was chewing fervently on some of the dried meat that Sisu produced, the forest seemed to just fall away and a whole new world opened up before him. He nearly dropped the food as he stared in awe.

Miska had grown up in a small village in the Red Desert. It was hardly more than a tiny dot on any map. And moving to the Red Palace had been like stepping into a dream, but it was an isolated building in the middle of an oasis. He had heard of what a city would be like. Sometimes Ravenna had described the Aerial City that the sylphs inhabited, but even she admitted that it was fairly small since the population was no more than three or four thousand.

What faced Miska as he looked into the valley was something entirely different. It was vast, with buildings rising from the ground like impossibly tall boulders. Some were made from wood, some were carved from the remains of a mountain. They were as varied as they were many. Some stood impossibly close together and some stood alone in a vast space. Still other empty spaces were filled by some of the heavy tents like the one Cavaris had lived in.

He looked up at Sisu. The man nodded, his expression solemn for once. He gestured with his left arm, the metal cap on it gleaming in the weak mountain sun. "Hullgard," he said. Miska did not even have to ask him to repeat the word. It sent shivers down his spine. This was where the Elders were. They were the ones who would determine his fate, and the fate of his people.

The city, as large as it was, still sat a good distance away. Perhaps another half-day's walk. He expected Sisu to start for the city immediately. Instead, he turned and walked along the rim of the valley. Miska frowned, but followed.

They walked for another hour at least. As they did, the trees seemed to close in on them once again and Hullgard fell out of view. If this was the way to the city, then Miska could understand why no one from his part of the world had made it that far. Sisu did not seem concerned, though. He just kept walking, his shoulders straightening and his chin lifting. A few moments later, Miska understood why.

The land opened up again to reveal a slight valley, nowhere near as vast as the one containing Hullgard. Tents and small structures made of wood filled the valley with spaces between large enough for the people, horses, and few wagons that moved about. This must be the encampment that Cavaris had mentioned. It was smaller than Hullgard, but Miska still felt his heart beating faster. This was bigger than the Red Palace. There were more people here than he had ever seen in his life. He was expected to live here?

Sisu clapped Miska on the shoulder and gestured to the town. "Rygirfel."

Miska's tongue slipped around the unfamiliar word. It was similar enough to whatever language Sisu was teaching him that it seemed somewhat natural. But it was still a mouthful and he was slightly disappointed when Sisu made the movements for "close enough."

Maybe Miska was meant to feel a sense of awe as Sisu led him into the mountain town, but all he could feel was bile rising in his stomach. He closed his eyes and reminded himself that he was doing this for his queen and for his love. They needed him to succeed here. Anything else would be unacceptable. And, Miska thought, it could be worse. He could still be the injured boy he had been, newly deaf and unable to move for nearly a moon.

Instead, he was just hungry, cold, dirty, and in desperate need of sleep.

Sisu greeted almost everyone they passed with a smile and a few words. Miska tried to pay attention to everything, but he could not take in the structures around him, the horses larger than anything he'd ever seen, furs laid out to dry, people wearing the strangest clothes, weapons being made and handled freely, and the eyes of the overwhelmingly curious. Sisu was, by far, the largest of the people that he had seen. But many of them looked just as scarred or capable, especially the men. Though, it seemed that each woman carried either an axe or a hefty sword on her back.

Miska suddenly felt very underarmed.

Sisu led Miska to a large tent that rivalled Cavaris'. It was decorated similarly with furs on the ground and a large fire in the centre. There was a raised platform that was obviously where Sisu slept, and a smaller one, presumably for Miska. The big man threw down his axe with relative carelessness, then turned to Miska with a wicked gleam in his eyes.

Miska swallowed nervously.

Over the next few hours, he was led to a small, freezing stream where he bathed faster than he ever had in his life. His hair was combed roughly by a couple of well-meaning grandmothers, then beads were braided into the relatively short strands. Miska suspected that the grandmothers were exclaiming over the colour of his brown hair and reddish skin the entire time. From what he saw, Ravenna was more like to find people of her sort there. Well, without the wings, of course. He was dressed in trousers lined with a light fleece and given a second pair lined with rabbit fur—presumably for the colder moons—then given a tunic of the same thickly woven fabric that Sisu wore, as well as an over shirt and a mantle of dark fur from some beast he could not name. Miska was fed with roasted chunks of meat and a large portion of root vegetables, so different from the food he was used to and so much heavier.

By the time he staggered after Sisu into the tent for the evening, he felt simultaneously like he was going to collapse into sleep and burst from food and questions. The former won out and he barely wasted any effort for a good-night to Sisu before darkness was upon him again. For better or worse, this was his life now.

* * *

THIS WHOLE TRAINING situation that Cavaris had told Miska to do was a complete waste of time. He was not learning anything that could help him. Lenore had asked him, in her moment of complete desperation in the face of a monster too horrible to consider, to save them. He had sought out Ravenna, the only person who could possibly put together a force and come to the rescue of everyone in the Red Desert. Instead of being with her, though, Miska was here. Gutting fish. With a trio of women older than the grandmothers who had made him appear as though he somewhat belonged in this mountainous society. And they would not stop talking!

Miska was, for once, glad that he was deaf. He tried to keep up with their words, trying to piece together what they said with the phrases that he could understand. But he still only caught one full sentence in ten. Watching their movements, for as much and as fast as they spoke, was extremely trying. Not to mention that he also had a knife in his hand and was meant to be gutting fish.

Fish was not a desert meal. Miska had never eaten fish in his life, let alone gutted it. Ravenna had described what fish was like, even drawn pictures of the animals. He did not recall any of her pictures or descriptions telling him what it was like to cut the creature's head off and then filet it, scooping out innards and washing it in a bucket of increasingly-red water. So far, he'd only thrown up once.

The great-grandmothers, as Miska thought of them, were constantly pointing out his errors. He learned very quickly the words for "wrong" and "knife" and, unfortunately, "egg sack". Apparently, the eggs were a delicacy here. The mere thought made Miska gag again.

Frankly, he thought this was a complete waste of time. Sisu had dropped him here early in the morning and then promptly left. Miska was annoyed to see a band of men, Sisu in the lead, going past a few minutes later, smiling and carrying weapons meant for a hunt. Three of the men carried bows—another unfamiliar desert weapon, though he had seen one once—that were nearly as tall as them. The others carried knives, swords, and of course Sisu's axe. Miska had risen to follow them, but was pulled down by the closest great-grandmother, a woman with one blind eye and a permanently grinning expression.

She shook her head. "No, you stay here," she had said, articulating the words slowly so that Miska could read them. He was a little surprised he had understood, but that shock was quickly devoured by the disappointment. Sisu, it seemed, was merely an escort. Miska was instead going to be "training" with women who needed his help to stand.

He swung his knife in an angry arc and the fish's head came off almost easily. The great-grandmothers drew his attention with their applause. They did not seem to be mocking him; they genuinely seemed pleased by his effort. Miska then noticed the fact that they, too, managed to get their fish heads off in one go. He flushed, half in embarrassment, half in anger, at this fact.

No wonder Sisu had shunted him off onto these women. Miska was weak enough that he could barely gut fish properly. Had he always been this weak or was it just his time travelling from the Red Desert and doing very little with Cavaris? Miska tried to remember things he did in the Red Palace. Cleaning? Hardly much work. Running messages for Lenore? Well, that depended on how fast he ran. Playing nursemaid to foreign dignitaries? His head usually hurt after that, but little else.

It was a bit disconcerting to realise how soft his life had been. Once upon a time, Miska had wanted to be the greatest hunter ever. He had wanted to be a warrior in the army. He had wanted to run and fight and hunt and be nothing less than the strongest and the best. And while he still had the strength of youth, he was soft. Weak.

Cavaris had been right. Again. He was no use to Ravenna in this state.

With another angry swing, Miska cut the tail off his fish. The effort did not seem nearly as difficult, this time. And he had earned another appreciative bout of applause from the great-grandmothers. Fine, Miska thought, doing his best to gut the fish efficiently and without taking his fingers off. He would work with these women. He would train. He would grow stronger and hopefully convince Sisu and the people of Hullgard to help him.

Miska just hoped that no one died in the mean time.

So, for the next week, he worked with the great-grandmothers. He watched them talk for hours of the day, gutting and cleaning the fishermen's catch from the lake not half-an-hour's walk from Rygirfel. He salted the fish and stowed large barrels of the food in an underground cache for the winter. Those that weren't salted, Miska ate with the evening meal. He ate with those same great-grandmothers, ignored by everyone else and never invited by Sisu to join in, if Sisu was around, that is. The nights he spent sleeping in Sisu's tent, trying to make sense of the "training" he had received that day.

The two days following that, Miska tried to be positive. He tried to tell himself that things were just going to take a while for him to assimilate. He was definitely getting stronger and surer with a blade. Gutting fish was now no longer something he had to concentrate on. He could actively pay attention to the great-grandmothers' conversation and pick up a whole lot more of the language. He even found himself talking with them a little bit, pleased with the smiles of encouragement they gave.

But the problem was, he was not learning anything else. Sisu just delivered him to the great-grandmothers every day. Then, without fail, he would wander past with a band of others, ready to go off and hunt or train or something. Frankly, Miska was growing angry.

On the ninth day, Miska decided enough was enough. He hated losing his temper. It rarely did anyone any good. But he had been told to come here by Cavaris, with the promise that Sisu would train him and that he might be able to convince Hullgard that he needed their help. This was supposed to let him save his queen. And he was doing nothing.

Sisu wandered past the area where the old women were sitting, their knives and quick hands already slick with fish blood, talking about someone's upcoming nuptials and the food being prepared for it. Miska threw his fish into the salting barrel by his seat and jumped up. The great-grandmothers' mouths stopped moving, but he was too busy placing himself before Sisu to notice.

"I've had enough," Miska growled. He would have supposed Sisu hadn't understood by the way the man raised his eyebrows and smiled, but Miska knew better. His language skills were becoming more than conversational. Once he got the trick of things, it was not hard. He did not know what his accent sounded like, but he knew that he was understood by the hard-of-hearing women he had been working with. Miska raised his knife covered with watery blood and fish scales. "You were meant to be training me!"

"And you think you are ready for this?" Sisu asked, putting the metal cap on his stump against the blade of his axe. Judging by the wince a few of the other men gave, the sound wasn't pleasant. Miska just bared his teeth like Ravenna did when she scared the living daylights out of him.

"Cavaris sent me here to be trained, not to waste my time," Miska snapped.

"Cavaris sent you to be trained by *me*," Sisu said. Behind his great beard, the man's mouth twitched, making him all the angrier. "I say you are not ready."

"I say I am," Miska said. He wanted to tear the beads out of Sisu's hair. He settled for tightening his grip on the handle of his knife. He could feel the leather rasping in his grip. Sisu's eyes widened as he took in the blade in Miska's hands. The man raised his hands in surrender, a grin on his face.

"A weak thing like you? You barely made it back to Rygirfel. Let alone know how to hunt!" Sisu said. He looked over his shoulders and the three others flanking him flashed mocking grins. They turned to one another and said something which Miska did not catch, being unable to read their mouths properly.

What he did catch was the way Sisu's hand flicked inside his cloak and drew something out. It was long, shining, and Miska's instincts screamed at him to do something. He did, left hand reaching out to control Sisu's wrist, the right hand pausing a hair's breadth from Sisu's neck, knife edge shining. "Teach. Me. As you promised," Miska said through gritted teeth.

Sisu smiled, genuinely this time. "There you are. I was wondering when you would come out."

Miska stepped back, frowning. He held the knife out, just to be sure, though. But he had the unsettling feeling that this whole situation had been a test. To see how long he would wait before demanding to be taken off fish-gutting duty? To see how long it would take for him to lose his temper? Or to see what would happen when Miska was threatened with a weapon?

Sisu stepped forwards and closed the distance between them, wrapping Miska in a massive hug. Miska snarled. He was set down and Sisu clapped him on his shoulders, the metal plate striking his bones and sending a ringing through his shoulder. "Welcome to the Claws of Bears!"

"Bear?" Miska said, habit having him mull over the unfamiliar word. A man with shockingly blonde hair that brushed his shoulders and a neatly trimmed beard stepped forwards, holding his hand out for him to shake.

"You shall see," he said, grinning. "I am Asgeir."

"Miska," he introduced himself. Asgeir clapped his hand to Miska's and, like Sisu, pulled him into a hug. Asgeir released him and gave him a look up and down, then turned to Sisu and said something Miska' did not catch. Sisu nodded, laughing.

Sisu gestured to the others and all started walking again, this time with Sisu at the back, his arm slung around Miska's shoulder. Miska pointedly did not look at the man next to him, not wanting to see anything that was said. He wanted to be trained, yes, but not like this. Not with subtlety and trickery.

"I think I hate you," Miska said after a few minutes, voice barely loud enough to hear. He looked at Sisu at last.

The man was nodding, his dark brown hair turning to black in the shadows of the trees. He blinked, took in a breath, nodded again. Then, "I understand. I think I would hate me, too."

CHAPTER SEVEN

*L*enore was furious with herself. She was sitting alone in the breakfast room, a small room set between some of the suites in her wing for eating breakfast without having to deal with others. The low stone table was laden with food, from the choicest fruits from the coast lands to the meats and cheeses favoured by those from the Salusian capital. She was eating a piece of bread spread with honey from the royal gardens. Only, her hand was shaking, making the bread wobble before her very eyes.

Lenore set the bread back on her plate, no longer hungry. "Pull yourself together," she murmured.

"I beg your pardon?"

Lenore jerked and looked up, eyes wide. Seraphina was gliding into the breakfast room, dressed in a ridiculous robe that looked as though it had been woven from pure silver. It had tiny crystals on the hem to weigh it down, and she wore a tiered necklace of silver with green gems to hide the indecency of the neckline. She had several rings on her fingers and tiny silver beads woven into her hair. Surprisingly, though, Seraphina wore no face paints, leaving her skin clear and unadorned. It made her eyes, the twin brown orbs to Davorin's, all that more striking.

"Good morning, Lady Seraphina," Lenore said, rising from the stone bench. Seraphina flapped her hand dismissively and sank onto the bench opposite Lenore. With that expression, she looked like nothing more than a woman fond of jewels who had come looking for a meal. Lenore knew better.

"Please, call me Seraphina, or Sera," she said with a smile. She reached out and snatched up some of the fruit and meats and cheeses, piling her plate high. "After all, we are family now."

Lenore managed a weak smile. "Would you like some tea?"

"Oh, yes, please! I haven't had a good strong cup of tea in ages," Seraphina said. She held out her cup for Lenore, who took it. "My husband, Baldur, is much more fond of a drink brewed from the roasted fruit of a plant grown far to the south of our lands. Thank goodness for me, it doesn't seem to grow anywhere up here."

Lenore wondered absently what it was like to live in Southron. What was beyond the borders of that country. Perhaps there would be something there for her, as opposed to here. Her hand still shook as she poured the tea. A few drops spilled over, enough to cause her to flush with shame. She put the pot down and handed the cup back to Seraphina, careful not to spill more. She did not meet Seraphina's gaze.

"Is my brother such a cruel husband?" Seraphina asked, the question bland and unassuming. She seemed more interested in sipping at her tea than whether or not Lenore was able to control her limbs. Lenore picked up her bread again, simply to have something to do other than answer.

"He is not all that inventive a lover," Lenore said at last. She was not lying, either. After that first, horrible, coupling, Davorin had been rather tame. He just demanded that she did her duty, took his pleasure, then was gone. So far, he had only come to her twice. As their marriage was three days prior, she considered herself fortunate.

Seraphina giggled into her tea. "Oh, my dear, that is no secret! My brother Dagan, may Materior keep him, was always known as the wild one. I'm actually quite surprised by the fact that Davorin managed to pull off his little coup in annexing the Red Desert. I suppose it makes him cleverer than I thought, but I never expected him to be interesting!"

Lenore managed a weak smile and took another bite of bread. Seraphina shrugged one shoulder and stabbed a piece of meat with her knife. Lenore found herself staring at the knife, wondering how hard it would be to kill Davorin. Would his terrible magic stop her if she killed him while he slept? Or would that murderous creature inhabiting Nadezhda do the deed for him? She knew that her people would suffer greatly if she did manage to kill him. If not from the Emperor himself, then from Seraphina. Who, despite her smiling and simpering, was another dangerous enemy.

"Is it really true that my brother wields magic?" Seraphina asked after a moment's pause.

Lenore jerked, spilling some of her tea. She had to set down the cup to keep from crushing it in her fist as anger roared through her. If Davorin did not have that magic, then none of this would have happened. "Yes," she said simply. "I don't know how well he controls it. He is linked by it in some way to that..."

Seraphina snorted. "The thing he calls Dagan? Oh, yes, I'm well aware of it. Davorin has tried to keep it quiet while my retinue and I are here, but it's rather difficult to hide something so... vile. I wonder how he managed to do it. Bring magic here after all the time it's ben gone. Enough to summon whatever it is into the body of that woman. Who was she? She looks familiar, I think."

Lenore frowned at the thought. She may have hated

Davorin's former Captain, but she would never wish such a fate on anyone. "Captain Nadezhda. She commanded his army."

Seraphina's brows rose, eyes widening. "Oh, really. How very interesting."

"Why? She was a brute of a woman, but she didn't deserve to be turned into whatever that thing is."

Seraphina did not answer for a moment. She took her time cutting a slice out of her fruit and then placing it delicately on her tongue. She washed it down with a swallow of tea, then dabbed her hands on the fine silk napkins that adorned the breakfast table. Seraphina lifted her eyes, flashing with some unnameable emotion. Pleasure, perhaps. Or cunning. "Captain Nadezhda was formerly in Dagan's service. She commanded *his* armies. A position that suited her quite well, given that she had trained under my brute of a brother—oh, don't look so surprised. Dagan's death was well-deserved, despite what my father says. He might have made the Empire look strong and powerful, but he would have overextended its resources within another five cycles."

"Then why did Davorin bring her in?" Lenore asked before she could stop herself. She clamped her mouth shut. It was far too easy to talk to Seraphina. She *knew* the other woman was dangerous, but that didn't seem to stop her from wanting to talk. Not to mention she was giving Lenore such interesting pieces of information about her new husband. Information that could well be to her advantage.

Seraphina flapped her hand dismissively. "Likely something about wanting to upstage Dagan or some such nonsense. Davorin always did have such a flair for dramatic indignation. Always growling quietly about what Dagan was doing to ruin the Empire. Always claiming he could do things better. Well, he's had his chance and now look at where we are. Him married to the most beautiful woman in the desert with a new country brought within the borders of the Empire."

Lenore frowned, flicking her eyes down to her plate. She clenched her fists in her lap, doing her best to keep a straight expression. Ravenna had been a master of the neutral expression. No matter how difficult things got, the sylph was always calm. Lenore feared she had too much fire in herself to be quite so calm; at least she could try not to give anything away to this woman. Seraphina must have seen something on her face, though, because she let out a tinkling laugh.

"There is no need to look so distraught!" Seraphina said, smiling. She reached out and lay a hand on Lenore's arm, her rings cold to the touch. "Now that the Red Desert is part of the Salusian Empire, you have little to worry about. Davorin is very careful about maintaining the power of the Empire. He wouldn't be so foolish as to waste the resources you've brought him."

Lenore inclined her head. She reached for the teapot and poured herself another cup. This time, the trembling in her hands was from anger. "I am simply glad that it was Davorin and not Dagan who brought the Red Desert into the Empire."

"Oh, well, perhaps. I think you might have held out longer against a military incursion, even with all the resources of the Empire," Seraphina said. She put a hand to her mouth and let out another laugh. "I've said too much. No, I should be celebrating with you on your marriage."

Lenore said nothing. She fixed her eyes on the cup with its steaming liquid, watching the vapour swirl into the air and disappear. Even when she heard the clatter of Seraphina's knife against her plate, she kept looking at the tea.

"When I first married my husband, I did not love him." Lenore looked up at Seraphina in shock, but for once, the other woman seemed to be wearing no pretence. "Baldur was a good match. He came from a strong tribe and was powerful enough to prove promising in the future. He was—is—not wildly intelligent, but that can be worked around. And, best of all, it got me out of the way of scheming courtiers in the Empire. If I had married within the Empire, then my husband would have been in line for the throne and Dagan and Davorin would hardly have stood for that. I would likely have been a widow within the cycle. But marrying *outside* the Empire… not only did it grant a measure of safety to Southron, but I earned my freedom."

"I don't see what this has to do with me," Lenore said flatly. She did not need some sob story about poor Seraphina, who had not been in love with her husband but over time had learned to be content. She had seen the way Baldur followed his wife around like a lost dog. Seraphina hadn't married into a situation anything remotely like hers.

Seraphina gave Lenore a dry smile. "I am just saying that I made the most of my marriage and you can, too. I married strategically. Perhaps not for the, ah, noble reasons that you did, but it is not dissimilar. You are intelligent, Lenore. You are not weak. You need only be subtler than my brother and you can make the best of your situation, as I have."

Lenore lifted her chin, though she was careful enough not to sneer down at Seraphina. "And what would you suggest I do to gain the upper hand?"

Seraphina skewered another slice of meat, bringing the morsel to her lips. Her tongue darted out to taste it before she smiled at Lenore. "Knowledge, my dear, is everything. You need only ask yourself one question: what would Davorin do to save the Empire from incompetents who would tear it down, knowingly or not. Even if those incompetents are—or were—close to him. Very close."

Lenore kept her mouth shut, let the question percolate through her mind. She knew the implications that Seraphina was presenting. She knew that there had been bad blood between the brothers, that Davorin had been convinced Dagan would bring the Empire to ruin. But then, why name that monster after his brother? Why pledge to lead the armies—or to go conquering—in Dagan's place?

Seraphina finished the last of her breakfast then rose, robes swishing quietly with her movements. She stepped behind Lenore and put a hand on her shoulder, the pressure both a comfort and a threat. Lenore looked up at Seraphina, who was smiling down at her. "I am glad that he married you, and not that serving wench I employed in my camp the last time he was at the borderlands. You are a woman deserving of this role."

Cool understanding flooded Lenore. She found herself smiling, revealing her teeth in what must have been a feral grin. "Thank you, Seraphina," Lenore said, inclining her head. "It was lovely talking with you."

Seraphina grinned, then turned and walked out of the room. Her task was done. Lenore knew that the cat had been set amongst the birds, that Seraphina meant to cause chaos and strife in her brother's household. And she did not care one iota.

* * *

LENORE KNEW PRECISELY where she would find her husband. In the Red Palace, there were many places a person could hide if they wished to be alone. But when it came to understanding the running of the kingdom, one inevitably ended up in the library. Over the two moons prior to their marriage, Davorin had made the library his home. He spent hours in there, combing over records and documents regarding the mineral outputs of various places around the Red Desert, what the smaller, outlying settlements had to offer, even what the cost of updating the army's weaponry was.

The fact that the library had been so completely brought under Davorin's control rankled Lenore to no end. Not only was it *her* library, but it had also been the place where Ravenna spent most of her time, when not training with Vareis. The sylph had made the library seem almost a sacred space. She had reminded Lenore the pleasure to be had in the pages of a book, or the power that knowledge could bring. It was one of the few places that still stirred up such vibrant memories of the sylph upon whom she placed almost all of her hopes.

Now, it was another conquest by the Empire.

Well, no more.

Lenore threw open the doors to the library, silently smirking when they banged loudly against the stone walls. Davorin, sitting at his table with pages and letters and ink before him, jumped. The glass pen he had been holding clattered to the stone floor, splattering ink onto the hem of his breeches. Unlike her servant, Davorin had adopted the clothes of the desert and was currently wearing a pair of almost-white trousers that were loose and comfortable, with a blue tunic-vest that left his shoulders bare. He still wore the twin blades at his hip, though. A constant reminder of his power. Or perhaps his fear.

"Hello, husband," Lenore purred.

"Lenore," Davorin replied warily. He picked up his pen, not taking his eyes off of Lenore as he did so. She did not miss the way his left hand strayed to one of the swords. "It is early. What do you want?"

"I've already enjoyed breakfast with your sister. She was polite enough not to ask where you were, but your presence was missed," she said. It was not even close to the truth. She knew full well that Seraphina had been more than happy to have Lenore to herself. She walked forwards and ran her fingers along some of the papers. Why would Davorin be interested in goat leather production along the southern border?

Lenore made a show of looking around. "Where is your pet? I would have thought 'Dagan' never left your side."

Davorin cleaned the ink of the nib off the pen with a spare rubbing cloth. He remained seated, instead looking up at her. Though caution was written plainly on his face, he obviously did not think her enough of a threat to directly confront. "The details of running a country hold little interest for it."

Lenore pressed his lips together in a thin smile. "I do not know why you concern yourself with such details in the running of my country. After all, while the Red Desert is now a protectorate of the Empire, you are technically only a King Consort."

Davorin curled his lip, though his words remained as pleasant and calm as always. Ever the polite snake. "It is merely a matter of perspective. As a protectorate of the Empire, the authority of the Emperor and his heir supersedes that of its ruling body. The monarchy may not have been dissolved, as is done so often when we bring some place into the Empire, but do not mistake your position for power."

Taking a deep breath, Lenore forced herself to count to three thrice over before she replied. The fire in her belly demanded that Davorin pay for his words. She wanted to fight back. She wanted to rally and scream, but none of that would help her. Lenore picked up a book of records. It detailed the price of mint exported over the cycles. One of the few crops that grew almost exclusively around the Red Palace, it was actually highly desirable for many of the surrounding nations. There, she was calm again.

"I have successfully managed the Red Desert for cycles... I could help you properly integrate it into the Empire. I know you are already busy with managing the economies within the Empire and trade without. I... please do not shut me out of my country. These are my people." Lenore was a little shocked by how desperate she sounded. She had hoped that Davorin would simply see her ability as something useful, but it was really so much more than that. In agreeing to marry him, she knew that everything she had come to love would be destroyed. The Red Desert may have been an annexed protectorate, but that would change. The only reason she still remained Queen was because

Davorin had not yet found the law to declare himself King, not Consort. He was right, though. Her power was in name only, and it remained simply because he coveted her title.

"A week ago, you would do nothing to help me. You *dared* me to break your spirit on our wedding night, all but openly declaring that you would do your best to rebel against me at every turn," Davorin said. His words were even and measured, but there was a touch of fury on the edges that had Lenore's shoulders tensing. "Why should I believe that this request is anything but a means to subvert my efforts from within?"

Ah, yes. There had been that. Lenore winced.

"I was… perhaps over hasty," she said. The words burned on her tongue. She would happily rebel against Davorin, but not at the expense of her people. "The fact is that my people will always come first. And now, there is no changing the fact that the Red Desert…belongs to the Salusian Empire. The best way to help my people is to make the transition smooth. To ensure that our country does not fall apart during this change. Your sister mentioned that you would do anything to protect the interests of the Empire. The Red Desert is now the Empire, so—"

"And what else did Seraphina have to say about me?" Davorin interrupted, ire dripping off his tongue. He slowly capped the inkwell, as if controlling that movement was all he could manage. Lenore bit back a shudder as best she could, instead clenching her fists behind her back.

"She talked about how things have changed, now that you are Firstborn Son instead of Dagan," Lenore said carefully. She had not been careful enough in choosing her words, though. Davorin's expression darkened and something like lightning crackled across the desk, scattering papers and books to the walls and floor. Lenore could not hide her flinch, now.

"Seraphina is nothing more than a manipulative power-seeker, scheming to have that which does not belong to her. She will twist every inch of the truth in order to achieve her ends. And sowing the seeds of discord between myself and my new wife would be exactly what she wants," Davorin said. He lay his hands flat on the table, his bare shoulders hunching with the effort of containing his anger. He was not succeeding.

"Your sister merely described your dedication," Lenore said. She lifted her chin and felt once again the unfamiliar feeling of her loose auburn hair on her back. She wished Davorin would let her have it in braids. "Though perhaps she did not explain its overwhelming intensity as being quite so paranoid and absurd."

"Curb your tongue," Davorin snapped. His fingers pressed into the wood.

Lenore slammed her own hand onto the table, ignoring the way the inkwell jumped. "You *promised* that my people would be taken care of if I agreed to wed you. Well, we are wed, Davorin. Uphold your promise!"

"I am doing just that. I simply do not see why you think *you* are the best means of fulfilling that promise." Davorin took a breath and shook his head, chuckling. "You are more capable than most, as your records show. But despite our titles, I am the one who controls things, now. You have given me no reason to trust you and have been antagonistic from the beginning. So, *wife*, you will do as I tell you. Now go away."

That furious fire roared inside Lenore. The edges of her vision turned blurry, though that could have been from the angry tears that filled her eyes. Her heart beat loud enough for her to hear it in her ears. She wanted to strangle Davorin. She wanted to kill him here and now without a care for the consequences. That would be beyond stupid, though. Instead, Lenore bared her teeth and leaned over the table, drawing close to Davorin.

"Wife, is it? I do not know why you even bothered, when you take your pleasure elsewhere," Lenore seethed. Davorin raised his brows, bemused. After a pause, he chuckled, the sound grating on Lenore's ears.

"Is that what Seraphina tells you? Oh, my sister is quite talented in spreading her particular brand of chaos. But what does it matter to you? You are still my wife. By the laws of the Empire, and the rites of Materior, I may take my pleasure with you when I please. What I do otherwise is none of your business." Davorin picked up his pen again, as if to return to work and send Lenore scurrying away like the dutiful wife she was meant to be.

"In my religion, The Watcher calls for fidelity. Or does keeping your promises matter less to your warrior god?" Lenore spat. She straightened and brushed her tunic shirt so it lay flat. "By your reasoning, then, I may take my pleasure as I choose."

Davorin's eyes became a storm. Tiny arcs of lighting—this time sharper and definitely coming from Davorin—flashed from his fingers, reaching for Lenore. They fell short, though, instead burning into the table. She took a step back. This was that same horrid magic that the false Dagan seemed to exude. Only this time, Davorin was the instigator. What was he? Ravenna had mentioned nothing about magic.

For the first time since Davorin had won Lenore's consent to marry him, she felt fear tighten its grip on her heart. Her anger snuffed out, fleeing back inside that tiny core of iron deep within her. Davorin's dark eyes gleamed, as though he could sense her fear.

"If my heir is not like me in looks, then you will know far more than a lack of control over your people," Davorin said. "I can promise you that."

Lenore turned and strode from the room without a backwards glance or a word to mark her exit. She walked slowly enough to not be seen as running from her husband; the truth was there all the same. If she wanted to do *anything* to save her people from Davorin's clutches, then her hopes would have to lie somewhere other than with herself. A true rebellion, rather than a quiet and insidious one.

She barely noticed as she brushed past Blodwen on her way out of the library. Lenore's only thought was to get as far from Davorin as possible. She fled through the halls of the once-familiar Red Palace. Her feet knew the way, her thin leather slippers marking a familiar path through the stone halls. But the servants were wrong. The guards were dangerous rather than friendly. Even the light seemed harsher.

Lenore pressed her hands to her ears, hoping to drive out the cruel laughter that seemed to follow her. She reached her chambers and barely had enough presence of mind to close the doors behind her. She slid down the wall, staring at her hands. They were shaking again. And this time, she doubted that it would ever stop.

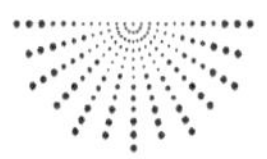

CHAPTER EIGHT

Ravenna supposed that a confrontation between herself and her sister was inevitable. Since her return to Shinalea, Desarra had been surprisingly absent. She had not openly refused to see her, but each time Ravenna met with Crispinus about training or marched her way up to the Aerial City to deal with the High Council, Desarra was nowhere to be seen. She had received a single note on the death of her heart-father, Tacitus, expressing condolences. Ravenna had not expected anything more.

So, to now be practically summoned to Desarra, three days before the Crowning and the fete celebrating the new Chosen Queen, was a bit out of character. Though, it was not unexpected.

Ravenna had never been to her sister's apartments in the Aerial City. Being the granddaughter of the former chosen queen, and mate to a Lord of the Wind, she supposed that Desarra and Crispin would live in relatively nice quarters. She did not expect that Desarra would have already moved into the chambers reserved for the Chosen Queen.

The last person to hold those chambers had been Mariala,

Ravenna and Desarra's grandmother, a female of incredible strength, intelligence and colour. Her quarters had displayed the wild colours and personality of its owner, with tapestries and rugs, throw cushions and interesting art from artists throughout the population. It had been one of the few places on Shinalea where Ravenna felt happy. Now…

"Ravenna!" Desarra cried, surging forwards over the now-bare floors, her wings spread to balance her. Desarra threw her wings around Ravenna, their feathers brushing. Ravenna stiffened. Desarra pulled back, confusion written on her beautiful features, though it was soon brushed away with a smile. "Come and see what I've done."

Desarra linked her arm through Ravenna's and pulled her sister along. She noted, not for the first time, that Desarra was one of the true beauties on Shinalea. She had the aristocratic features that marked their bloodline. Her golden skin seemed to be tinged with health and her wings were mottled with various shades of brown, making them almost shimmer. Her hair was a shade of copper-tinged gold that gleamed almost red in the sun. For an instant, another queen stood before Ravenna, her own red hair tied up in a multitude of braids, her form graceful and strong. She, though, was human, and nothing alike in personality to the sylph tucked at Ravenna's side.

"Look at these chambers," Desarra said, waving her hand expressively. Ravenna obliged. The once-colourful rooms now boasted very simple designs. A single massive woven rug in a muted ivory covered most of the floor. The wide windows where sylphs could come and go at ease with their wings were framed in sheer curtains of the same ivory. The furniture was all wood with simple lines. There was no colour, no personality. It was, in a word, cold.

"The style suits you," Ravenna said. She forced herself to smile for her sister, to feel pleased at Desarra's accomplishment, even if her elevation to Chosen Queen was only to control Ravenna. "I'm surprised you moved in so early."

"Oh, it just makes everything easier," Desarra said, her wings shifting dismissively. "After the Crowning, I will be so busy that I would have hardly had time to do anything about this place. And of course, no one had done *anything* since Grandmother died. It was like a shrine."

"I... wish I had been here," Ravenna murmured, a tinge of true regret fluttering in her chest. She had returned to the island scarred and battered, only to learn that her grandmother had died and that Tacitus would soon follow. She did not even know how Mariala had died; though it was not a great surprise, given that her grandmother had been quite old.

"Well, you weren't," Desarra said, her voice taking on the edge of criticism. Immediately, she seemed contrite, offering a placating smile. "I mean, there was nothing that you could do. Nothing that anyone could do. And I'm sure she understood."

Ravenna gave a wing-shrug. "Still, I would have liked to say goodbye."

"Yes..." Desarra looked around the sparse room, perhaps seeking a new topic for them to discuss. Ravenna watched, her expression as guarded and cool as ever. Desarra had never been able to hold a conversation with her; their interests and lives varied too much. "How is training going? Crispin has been telling me so much, about the Dalketh and being a general. Oh, there is so much to do, I'm sure!"

Ravenna inclined her head. "Indeed. Running an army—let alone training one—is something that has not been done since the earliest days of our civilisation. Since the Stormbringers. There is much to learn."

Desarra gave a nervous laugh. She skip-stepped to a low sill with cushions in the same ivory and tossed her head. "Surely the Stormbringers are nothing more than a myth!"

Ravenna bit back a frustrated sigh. Instead, she ran her

fingers over the wooden table in the corner of the room before walking towards the windows. Outside, the Aerial City was as grand as ever. The whole city had been carved from the cliffs and it suited a race of flying beings perfectly well. Even as she stood there, three different sylphs flew past the windows with an effortless grace that came from a lifetime of touching the sky. Ravenna wondered idly if there was a place where she would ever feel effortless.

Being with Miska, perhaps. But no, that had been far from effortless. It was wonderful and the place she went in her dreams, but never effortless. Not yet.

A slight cough returned Ravenna to the present. She turned to her sister, ready to educate and to try not to lecture. "If Stormbringers were a myth, then why did the humans know of them? Why is it our Dalketh, which comes from the same time in our history as the Stormbringers, is perfectly suited to fighting—both on the ground and in the air?"

Desarra's great wings showed her discomfort with the situation. Still, she smiled prettily and fixed her with a benevolent look. "Then it's a good thing that you're leading the armies. You're so much better suited to learning these things than most."

"Is that because I was slave to the humans or because I am an Intellecti?" Ravenna asked, giving up with this ridiculous pretence that the two of them actually liked and respected each other. She knew they had to get along for the sake of the sylphs. Surely, though, that could be as little more than Chosen Queen and Warlord. As far as she was concerned, the earlier she established that she would do precisely what she wished as regards the safety and care of her people, the better. Desarra could have her throne. Let Ravenna have her independence.

Desarra, to her credit, did not flinch. She merely straightened and displayed some of the social grace that had made her a master at manipulating her way through society. "It was not my fault, nor Queen Mariala's, that Tacitus chose to raise you as an Intellecti. It was such an irregular situation, after all!"

Ravenna snorted. "You mean because our mother gave me into their care before she died, instead of entrusting me to Grandmother or another female relative. The fact that she was dead moments later meant nothing to anyone?"

"Well, I mean… Tacitus made it perfectly clear that he would raise you as his heart-daughter. What could anyone do after a declaration like that?" Desarra asked, spreading her hands in question. Ravenna shook her head at the familiar argument.

"Raised as an Intellecti, under *male* care, no less. In a society that follows the female line, it was unusual, but not unheard of," Ravenna said. She flicked her icy eyes to Desarra's and saw her sister flinch. "Had our mother been mated, I would have been cared for by a male in any case. No, it was the fact that it was the Intellecti who chose to raise me, wasn't it? Or shall we stop playing these ridiculous political games and just state the obvious. It is because I am flightless and of a colouring never before seen that my entrance into the same house as you was refused."

"How dare you!" Desarra rose, lifting her chin and displaying all of the regal stature that one would expect of a queen. Except, Ravenna had been in the presence of monarchs, true monarchs. Lenore was more a queen than ever Desarra would be. Davorin, for all the darkness within him, too held true power. Desarra's posturing meant nothing to her.

Ravenna took in a deep breath and spread her wings a touch, stretching muscles that were sore and tired with training. She worked with all of the companies, which meant that she often worked harder than any sylph under her command. Not to mention the paperwork that was starting to build up. Supplies. Food. Strategies. Even keeping the names and capabilities straight. Ravenna managed it all.

"Why have you called me here, Desarra?" Ravenna asked, her weariness betraying itself in her voice. "You have never liked me. We have never been friends. And even if we decided that we wanted to try and communicate like sisters who do not have twenty-five cycles of distance between them, what then? My background as an Intellecti and as a flightless wretch are insurmountable to you."

Desarra huffed, indignant. "The Intellecti choose to live separately from other sylphs. They do not understand how our society works, buried in their books like they are. Why should they have any say in the lives of the rest of us?"

"Because we study history and science and the facts afforded us to improve our society," Ravenna said, spouting off a familiar argument. She pressed her palm to her forehead, staving off a headache. "It does not matter," she murmured. "No matter what we say, people will always be as wary of us as they are influenced by us. Them, really."

"Oh, are you no longer part of the Intellecti?" Desarra's words were scathing.

"No," Ravenna said. "I am your Warlord. I am no longer an instrument of learning. I am an instrument of death."

Silence descended on the chambers of the Chosen Queen. Only Desarra's feathers, twitching and rustling as their owner wrestled with her thoughts, made any noise. Ravenna turned her attention back to the window, her wings folded calmly at her side. "No matter how we feel about each other, we must work together, or this will all be lost."

Desarra walked forwards to the window to stand beside Ravenna. "Are we…are things as bad as that?"

"Those carvings outside these rooms? The ones depicting sylphs fighting at the side of dragons, against elves and some other creature? What do you think of those?" Ravenna asked.

Desarra shivered, from the tips of her fingers to the ends of her primary feathers. "They're horrible! I wanted to have them removed, but they're history, so the Council overruled me. Such violence has no place here."

Ravenna smiled sadly and shook her head. "The reality, dear sister, is much, much worse."

"Oh," Desarra breathed, understanding dawning on her. She wrapped her wings about herself, staving off a chill that had nothing to do with the warm day. "I... I don't know anything about leading a people through war."

"It is new to me as well," Ravenna assured her sister. "We will learn together."

Desarra nodded. This time, the silence that fell was comfortable, if not companionable. The two sisters stood at the window for another minute, watching the sylphs flying by. The ones flying in formation were invariably soldiers training, using techniques that Ravenna pulled from tomes nearly falling to pieces. The other sylphs stayed out of the soldiers' way.

"Des?"

The voice had Ravenna whirling around, drawing the blades that were ever present at her back. She knew, even as she moved, that the voice belonged to Crispin, that he was here to see Desarra and that he posed no threat. But instinct drilled into her throughout her life, and especially in her time with the humans, said differently. She forced herself to relax, though her wings still bristled.

"Crispin!" Desarra said, flying to her mate's arms. She did not notice Ravenna's movements, thank goodness. Ravenna was as composed as ever by the time Crispin addressed her, though the look in his eyes said that her general had noticed her reaction to his entrance.

"Ravenna," he said, inclining his head politely.

"General," Ravenna replied. She started towards the door. "If you'll excuse me, I have a few things to see to."

"Oh, nonsense," Desarra said. Her body was folded neatly beneath Crispin's wings, her hand pressed against his chest. It was the most relaxed Ravenna had ever seen either of them. She had known they loved each other—that was why they had taken the mating bond, even though it was more common to fly from lover to lover—but seeing the reality was something different. Their closeness sparked something deep in Ravenna. Something that she shoved deeper until it could only come out at night. Longing.

She had that closeness, once. Now it was gone, perhaps forever.

"You'll stay and have supper with us," Desarra declared. "After all, we still have to discuss the Crowning ceremony. There are so many formalities that I must uphold. And the Council is weaving new ones to include you and I really must go over it beforehand."

Crispin spoke before Ravenna could drop the excuse that she had ready on her tongue. "You need to eat just as much as the rest of us, Warlord," Crispin said. The use of her title was not lost on Ravenna. It was a definitive statement of her position, a reminder that she had a duty to keep herself strong for the sake of others. She wanted to retort that she had not dropped into the wing-weary lack of caring for herself since she had first arrived at the Red Palace those many moons ago. She was fully aware of her responsibilities. More than either Desarra or Crispin knew.

"Very well," Ravenna said. Her wings fought to droop in defeat; she resolutely kept them still, though her muscles trembled a little. To hide the discomfort, she strode to the low table and sat on one of the cushions surrounding it. Desarra and Crispin were quick to join her. "How were the flight exercises?"

"Most of them have barely sorted out Dalketh on the ground, let alone in the air, but we're learning," Crispin reported. Desarra rang a silver bell, calling forth a servant. A young female appeared in the window, her wings spread for balance.

"A meal for the three of us, if you please," Desarra said, her voice pleasant and gentle. Ravenna raised a brow at the tone, having heard nothing like it from her sister before.

"Tomorrow, I want to start doing forest-running," Ravenna said almost absently, wondering what her sister's attitude could mean. Crispin brought her back to the present with the confusion in his eyes.

"Forest… running?" he asked.

Ravenna shrugged. "Manoeuvrability in all sorts of terrain will be essential when the battle formations fall to pieces. All the records of ancient battles I have read indicate that it is inevitable."

"I thought that there was little but desert between the coast and the mountains. Surely we won't be going that far?" Crispin asked. He drew a basic map on the table with his fingers, one Ravenna had made him and Brianna—her other general—learn.

"You two!" Desarra laughed, the sound a little too sharp to be pleasant. "How about we save the battle talk for another time, hmm? You must be so tired of it by now!"

"Of course, Des," Crispin said, reaching out to pull Desarra close. He kissed the top of her head, burying his nose into her hair and breathing deeply. "How goes planning for the fete?"

Ravenna kept silent, looking at the grain in the wooden table rather than watch her sister and her mate. For a brief instant, she felt phantom hands brushing over her feathers, tucking a strand of her hair behind her ears. Then, just as her heart sang out, the feeling vanished and Ravenna was left alone again.

* * *

SYLPH SOCIETY WAS NOT BUILT on religious wonderings, or superstition. The sylphs firmly believed in the facts that they had experienced or knew, through viewing the reactions to situations, to be true. Ravenna had, perhaps, become the most unusual in that regard, simply because she no longer believed that what they knew to be true, was true. Who was to say that magic was nothing more than a figment of historical imagination? Who was to say that the humans were wrong to worship their pantheon, or their Watcher, or the whims of fate? This was one area where her research did very little good; it was one area where she had to trust her instincts and her heart.

All the belief systems aside, the sylphs were very, very good at throwing fetes at regular intervals, despite the fact that they had no religious ceremonies to follow. A solstice required a fete. A harvest of the few crops they bothered to grow required a fete. A birth required a fete. A death required a fete. And the crowning of the Chosen Queen? Well, that would be a fete for the ages.

Hours before the fete was set to begin, Ravenna was standing in Desarra's chambers, looking outside the wide windows to where a host of sylphs were hanging wrought metal baskets with candles, or wicker baskets, or anything that would hold a light. The Aerial City looked as though it was showered in stars. She knew that the plateau where training was normally held had been converted into a banquet area for the sylphs of all ages to come and eat or drink with their friends. Dancing would start there and then take to the skies, with the sylphs flying amongst the candles and revelling in the celebration of their new queen.

Ravenna looked over her shoulder to where Desarra paced, unable to keep still. She wore the golden crown of metal feathers on her brow, having been crowned only a few hours before. Ravenna had stood through the ceremony at her sister's side, unable to suppress a slight feeling of pride at the way Desarra swore to protect and serve her people as best she could. The High Council had fairly crowed with delight when Ravenna had knelt, her wings spread submissively, and sworn to lead the armies at Desarra's command.

Now, her sister no longer looked so queenly. She just looked nervous.

"The hard part is done," Ravenna said, turning her back on the window. She caught Desarra's arm and forced her to stand still. "Why are you nervous?"

"It will be my first appearance as Chosen Queen," Desarra said. "What if I do something wrong? What if I don't know the right things to say? What if someone asks me for advice and I steer them wrong?"

"Then keep your head up and apologise," Ravenna said with a wing-shrug. "People do not expect perfection from you, Desarra."

"Don't they?" Desarra twined her fingers together, twisting them until the skin turned almost as white as Ravenna's. "This won't be discussing policy with the Council. Everyone will be looking at me! They'll expect me to do things and I won't know what to do to make them happy!"

Ravenna took a deep breath. She moved Desarra to sit on the low cushion before the windows. A slight breeze ruffled their feathers. Desarra moved her wings closer to her body. Ravenna revelled in the slight bite in the air.

"When I was in the human lands, I met a human queen," Ravenna said. Desarra recoiled; whether from shock at her revealing anything about her time away or from the fact that humans, too, had queens, she did not know. Ravenna just nodded and continued, as outwardly calm as ever. "She was as beautiful as a sylph and walked with strength and pride. Her people loved her unreservedly and her lands flourished in trade and power, though she ruled a desert. She told me, once, that when she first took the crown, she did everything she could to try and appease those who would criticise her or sneer down at her for making the wrong decision. She became so caught up in trying to do best by these people, about caring what they thought, that she neglected her lands to the point where slavers came and went as they pleased. Only when this queen stopped trying to please everybody and did what she *knew* was best for her people did her lands flourish and become the power I saw."

Desarra was silent for a moment. She pulled her wings closer, her feathers pressing together to the point that Desarra seemed smaller than she was. "A pretty story," she murmured.

"You don't believe me?" Ravenna asked, slightly surprised.

"You've told everyone how cruel and terrible the humans are. Why would one queen refuse to allow slavers in her country? No, I appreciate the sentiment—and the advice—but... things are not as easy as that," Desarra said. She stood again and started pacing once more, her wings still pressed flat against her sides.

Ravenna blinked. She had never been doubted in regards to her stories of the humans. Actually, she had never been doubted before when it came to knowledge or facts. Part if it was that she was Intellecti, respected for her knowledge. They were feared, but when the Intellecti spoke, one disregarded their words with caution. She had done her task too thoroughly. She had painted her picture too well if even Desarra did not believe her when she described the smallest of good in the humans. Another reason why she could never tell them about Miska and Lenore in truth.

"Desarra, you are far more capable than you believe," Ravenna said. She rose and went to her sister once more, unsure where the need to comfort her came from. Perhaps it was that Desarra was her queen, now. "You have never doubted yourself before."

"Haven't I?" Desarra snapped. She spun to face Ravenna, wings flaring wide. Finally, something other than worry. "For *cycles*, I have done nothing but doubt myself. What do I have to recommend myself, hmm? Beauty inherited from a dead mother. That is all. I was Mariala's granddaughter, but that does not mean much when it comes to judging capability! If you..."

Desarra paused and snarled, turning so quickly that her loose trousers flared like human skirts. "If you could fly, do you think that I would be here? That I would be Chosen Queen? They didn't even hold a Choosing! They just offered it to me, out of desperation. Because we are at war."

"They would not have offered it to you if you were not capable," Ravenna said. She was not certain her words were true, only that they were necessary. She believed that the High Council offered the crown to Desarra to control herself. Because she was dangerous and too independent. But surely they would not have gone through with it if they did not believe that Desarra was in some regards capable of ruling their people. After all, the war with the humans would not last forever.

Desarra said nothing. She just paced more, her wings moving as though she wanted to launch into flight at a moment's notice. She clenched her hands into fists and finally looked at Ravenna with tears blurring her amber-fire eyes. "Why didn't they give *you* the crown?" Desarra whispered.

Ravenna laughed darkly. "The other sylphs may follow me in war, because I know what it is that we face and I have the ability to fight and to cause bloodshed. They follow me in war because I carry two blades on my back and because I will not hesitate to use them. But do you think for a moment that once the war is done they will follow me any longer? I cannot fly. I am not trained in diplomacy the way you are. I was raised by a male and an Intellecti. I have been sneered at and taunted and abused my whole life. If it were not for this war, they would not want me at all."

Desarra recoiled. The tears in her eyes fell down her face, though she was hasty in wiping them away. "You can't really think that... can you?"

Ravenna shrugged, feeling the familiar weight of her swords between her shoulder blades. "You and Crispinus and everyone else thought it for my entire life, until I came back. Desarra, look. I'm not trying to create more distance between us. I just want you to understand; if I can train an army that did not exist three moons ago, if I can lead them into battle, if I can be entrusted with the protection of our people, then you can, too. You know them better than I. These are your people. You've lived among them. You've talked with them. You know their hopes and dreams and fears and passions. The only thing that has changed is now you wear a piece of metal on your head. That is all."

Desarra looked as though she were about to respond. She lifted her chin a touch and seemed on the verge of saying something when four female sylphs flew through the windows. They landed in a flurry of wings and fabrics, all carrying something that would make Desarra even more beautiful than before. At the sight of Ravenna, though, with her icy expression and her twin blades, they faltered, wings pulling in close.

The leader, a small, plump female with charcoal-dark skin and a kind smile, looked at Desarra. "Ah, apologies for the intrusion, my queen. Tytira, of the High Council, sent us to you to help you prepare for the fete. We… did not mean to interrupt your deliberations."

Desarra frowned. "Deliberations?"

"With Warlord Wingsword," the woman said, inclining her head slightly to Ravenna. Ravenna nodded sharply.

"Oh, but—" Desarra started. Ravenna shook her head.

"It is time I left. You have much to do before the fete and I have some papers to attend to," she said. Not a lie. She bowed to Desarra, wings sweeping wide, then left the room by the door, making her way to the stairs.

"Ravenna, wait!" Desarra called after her. She turned, quirking an eyebrow at her sister. "I'll see you later?"

"You enjoy yourself," Ravenna said. "We can talk tomorrow."

"You're not coming to the fete?" Desarra asked, a slight line appearing between her eyebrows. "But everyone is going. The chefs have outdone themselves. And the candles. And dancing!"

Ravenna shook her head, a cynical smile touching her mouth. She spread her wings, the black feathers glinting in the dying light of day. "If you haven't noticed, I cannot participate in the dancing. And I'm not really one for crowds."

She turned to leave again. Desarra's voice called again, halting Ravenna in her tracks. "Please?"

Ravenna turned to look at her sister and saw fear and pain in her eyes, something that had never been there before.

"Please?" Desarra repeated, the word almost impossible to hear. Ravenna closed her eyes, forcing down the bile that rose in her throat at the thought of going to a party. The last time she had been to a celebration had been at the human ball. That had been the first time Ravenna had felt beautiful. She had danced with Miska and known what it was, for a glorious moment, to be happy with no burdens.

"Very well." Ravenna inclined her head.

* * *

RAVENNA DID NOT KNOW what time it was. The sun had long set and the only light came from the glow of the moon and the star-candles set around the city. Musicians played from alcoves in the cliffs that allowed their music to echo throughout the whole city. Sylphs of all ages flew about in twining, graceful motions, their wings folding and spreading in time with the music, their arms weaving and their feet never once touching the ground.

Ravenna sat against a rock on the plateau, her wings laying limp at her sides. She supposed that she should care that they were getting dirty or that it was unnatural to have her wings so relaxed that she could not leap into a fighting stance. But, given that the drink in her hand was her third—fourth?—of the evening, she did not really care. The drink was keeping her company when she was feeling lonely and that was all that mattered.

"Oh, Miska," Ravenna murmured, closing her eyes and leaning her head against the rock. She tried not to think about him, about dancing in his arms, about his expression as she had turned away from him for the last time. It was difficult, though. All the other sylphs were off dancing excepting her and the children who were not yet old enough to fly. And they were still running about, chasing fireflies and shrieking with delight.

"What is a Miska?"

Ravenna's eyes snapped open. She discovered that even with four drinks in her she could still leap to her feet and reach for her blades faster than her opponent could react. Ravenna bared her teeth at Crispin, blinking furiously to keep her vision from blurring. "Damn it," she grumbled in the human version of their tongue. She stumbled a bit as the world spun, then took a deep breath.

"Are you… drunk?" Crispin asked, reaching out with his wings to steady her. Ravenna sheathed her sword, the movement practised and graceful. The rest of her, not so much.

"No," Ravenna snapped. "I'm just not used to sylph wine."

"You've been back for three moons," Crispin pointed out. He carefully pulled his wings back. Ravenna remained standing, without swaying involved, and frowned when Crispin nodded in satisfaction. "Surely you've gotten used to the wine since then."

Ravenna poured the last of her drink onto the flattened grass. "I don't normally drink. It lets the demons out without restraints."

Crispin nodded, as if that explained everything. Ravenna wanted to hate him for that. "What are you doing here on your own? The party is, well, everywhere else."

Ravenna snorted. She spread her wings and waggled them so that Crispin could see them even against the darkness. "In case you hadn't noticed, I cannot very well participate in the festivities. Desarra insisted that I come, so here I am. Where is Desarra?"

"Des is off dancing with anyone who will ask her," Crispin chuckled. Ravenna frowned, brows furrowing.

"Doesn't that bother you? She is your mate."

Crispin shrugged, feathers rustling. "We chose to be mates despite the tradition being a bit old fashioned. I know that most people don't care about long-term fidelity, or knowing that you are the father of a child, but it's different for Des and me. She can dance with whomever she likes. I know our bond will win out."

Ravenna shook her head. It was so strange seeing this sylph whom she had hated—or at least actively disliked—her entire life trust her sister so much that he did not care who she danced with. It was another facet, another aspect that made him more… real. For a flash, Ravenna longed for the time when she could just hate him in peace. He was her enemy, nothing more. Now, everything had changed.

If things had not changed, though, she would have never met Miska.

"Come on, Ravenna, dance with me," Crispin grinned, holding out his hand. "We wouldn't want our Warlord to miss out on all the fun."

Ravenna waggled her wings again. "Missing the obvious, aren't you?"

Crispin did not wait for a response. He just lunged forwards, his wings parting the air as though it was not even there. He wrapped her in his arms and, with two mighty downstrokes, had them in the air amongst the other sylphs. Instead of letting her fall, he kept his arms around her, wings moving in time to the music. Ravenna's feet rested on Crispin's and she found her wings picking up the almost-natural movements of the dance. It was easy for them to respond to Crispin's movements. It was easy for her to bend and sway as he did, so that they would stay aloft. She could provide no lift, but she was still participating.

The music swelled and Ravenna realised that she was dancing.

The hardness that she cultivated and sought out to protect her from the world melted a touch. Miska was not there. She was not dancing in his arms. She was not stumbling over his feet as he tried to teach her movements to a dance made for humans. She was with Crispin, her sister's mate and one of the generals of her army. But she still felt…happy?

Crispin tossed his head back and laughed, the sound shocking and feather-rustling and *right*. Ravenna allowed herself to smile.

Then, Crispin's arms vanished from around her. Ravenna angled her wings, but there was nothing she could do. She was falling again. Breath caught in her throat, barely holding back a scream of horror. Someone's arms wrapped around her, smaller than Crispin's. Ravenna snapped her eyes open and saw Brianna smiling widely at her, wings moving steadily to the music. Ravenna's other general spun closer to the musicians, her massive wings more capable than Ravenna could have known.

She understood. Crispin had not dropped her. He had passed her on to another partner. Brianna had caught her. These sylphs, her soldiers, were not going to let her fall. They were going to dance with her.

Ravenna forced herself to return Brianna's smile, then she let herself get lost in the music.

It seemed like hours passed, Ravenna doing the closest thing to flying that she had ever done. Her body knew exactly what to do. The movements took no effort at all and all she had to do was listen to the music. It swelled up and over her, her heart beating in time with the drums, her feathers waving in time to the strings and the flutes. Ravenna was passed from partner to partner, never without someone's arms around her for more than a second. She never fell, she never even came close.

She let herself trust.

"Wingsword!" Itonus cried with joy as Ravenna was passed to him. He pulled her closer than was perhaps strictly necessary, but then this was new for everyone. Bringing the flightless to a flying dance. They were all so strong to carry themselves and her extra weight. Ravenna found herself grinning widely at Itonus.

"This is marvellous!" Ravenna threw back her head, black hair long since escaped from its constraining braid.

Itonus laughed, the sound deep and booming over the music. "Never danced before?"

"Not like this," Ravenna replied. Her arms wound their way around Itonus' neck. She looked around at the other sylphs, all moving in time. The city seemed to surround her, the carvings looking more stunning and less imposing and out of reach than ever before. Everyone, finally, looked happy. "I've never seen the city like this."

"Fetes are great," Itonus agreed. "I'm surprised you've never done this before."

Ravenna tossed her head, "Who would have wanted to fly with me before?" She laughed and shook off her own cloud of misery that threatened to return. There was so much to do for her army. They needed more training, desperately. Davorin would find his way to them sooner than anyone would like. Ravenna needed scouts. She needed weapons. She needed Miska. But for now, none of that mattered. The war was a lifetime away. Miska would have smiled and laughed right along with her, but he was not there. Right now, she was dancing and flying and smiling, weightless.

Itonus' smile softened slightly. The music drew to a close and some sylphs touched air for a while, waiting for the next song. Others flew down to the plateau to get more drinks and food. The musicians retuned their instruments. No one seemed to think beyond the moment. That was perfectly alright with Ravenna.

Itonus led them to the plateau, letting Ravenna hop down and catch her breath while he settled into the grass beside her. "Do you want something to drink?" Itonus asked, reaching out his hand.

Ravenna nodded, breathless. "Absolutely," she said. Her body ached, but in a pleasant way. She knew that she would need almost a whole day to recover from the unusual exertion, but she did not care one feather just then. She grabbed Itonus' hand and was glad to be pulled off to where drinks were being served.

Ravenna downed the drink in one go. Itonus' grin turned to challenge and he matched her. Ravenna laughed, tossing her head again. "No need," she said, half-skipping away from the table. "You could outdrink me in a heartbeat."

"That's because you're so slight," Itonus said, catching up with her. He wrapped his wings around hers and smiled. Ravenna reached up and tucked the braided lock of his hair behind his ear.

"Does it ever get in the way?" she asked. Okay, she was probably wine-drunk. There was no way she would ever have asked such a thing before. But all that mattered just then was that Itonus tossed his head back and laughed, the sound echoing across the plateau.

"I'm used to it by now," he said, chuckling. "It's exactly what you would say with your braid, though I like your hair better down." Before Ravenna could ask something else, he threw his arms around her and returned them to the air. "Come on, a new song is starting!"

Ravenna closed her eyes and let the music and the night air flow over her again. She had never felt so much like she belonged here. It was heady and marvellous and it made her wonder why she had ever wanted to leave in the first place.

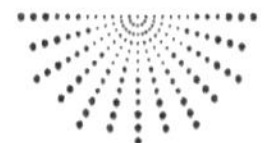

CHAPTER NINE

"**W**hat do you mean you cannot get the weapons?" Ravenna asked. She was in one of the lower rooms of the Stone Tower, having been given permission to use it from the Intellecti for purposes of planning for the war. Only Kratos ever offered her a smile upon her entering or exiting the room. Actually, only Kratos ever seemed to talk with her at all; the other Intellecti merely pretended she did not exist. She was too busy to be amused by the irony in her reversal of status.

Brianna shuffled her thin leather slippers on the stone floor. Ravenna noted another thing that would have to be gotten from a quartermaster; her army would need to be properly shod. Brianna rubbed her dark fingers over one of her covert feathers, smoothing the barbs. She seemed unconcerned by Ravenna's dismay.

"I mean that the metal smiths cannot accommodate such an order. We have limited metal supplies as it is, let alone ordering weapons and armour for an army of two thousand," Brianna said simply. Ravenna wished for a brief moment she had not given a general's status to the female. She was far too cavalier and seemed to ignore the import of most of Ravenna's words. But she was a magnificent flier, a promising fighter and she had the obvious admiration of the army. What else could Ravenna ask for?

"This was always going to be an issue," Crispin said. He sat in a chair at the small table in the room. It was strewn with papers detailing what Ravenna thought were reasonable requests to furnish the army properly. After all, if they could not match the humans in weaponry, what would be the point? They would be skewered and sliced to pieces before they could touch the ground.

"I was guaranteed that the necessary resources would be diverted," Ravenna said. Crispin shrugged, wings flaring slightly.

"The High Council was in no position to do such things," he said. "Desarra has been going over the supplies and we just cannot accommodate your request."

Ravenna wanted to snarl and hiss. She wanted to demonstrate just how poorly they would fare against an army of armed humans. Her two swords were the only swords on Shinalea and her people could never train properly if they did not have the appropriate tools. "I realise that Shinalea is an island and that our resources are limited, but surely the situation is not that grave?"

Crispin said nothing. Brianna said nothing. They just looked to Ravenna for answers, as always.

"How much can they manage?" Ravenna turned to Brianna. She folded her arms and pulled her massive wings in closer. The news would not be good, then.

"Perhaps enough metal plating in leather armour and daggers for... two companies," Brianna said. "No more than that."

"Two companies? That's a tenth of our force!" Ravenna snapped. She pressed her fingers against her temple, massaging the headache that was coming as best she could. Unfortunately, it seemed the headache was winning. "What other options do we have?"

"Can we manage without?" Crispin asked. Ravenna turned to stare at him, her normal composure slipping in complete shock. "We have enough lumber to make spears and perhaps some of those bows and arrows from the drawings that you found in those tomes. If we do it right, we wouldn't even have to get close to the humans."

"Archery is a dead art," Ravenna said. "We can revive it somewhat, but we will never be skilled enough for fighting a war that way."

"Fighting with Dalketh was a dead art," Brianna pointed out. Ravenna sighed and sank into her own chair, wings hanging limply at her side. She picked up a diagram of the bow and wished, desperately, that she had learned of such things during her time with the humans. But it was not something the people of the Red Desert used.

"Fighting was something I learned with the humans. I was able to apply something that already existed that every sylph was taught. Dalketh was always meant to be a fighting art, only its purpose had been changed over the cycles," Ravenna explained. She gave the paper with the drawing on it to Brianna, who frowned over it. "Archery survives in no form here. It was killed off completely some many ages ago, when sylphs decided that it ruined the sport of hunting. *That* is what our society has been reduced to. Discarding viable means of defence simply because it wasn't sporting for the prey!"

"Relax," Crispin said. He sat up straighter, wings bristling. Ravenna frowned; Crispin had been part of the Lords of the Wind, a group renowned for their hunting. Shouldn't he be defending her position? "We can learn archery, just like we learned this new way of Dalketh. I'll talk to the wood shapers and we can see if they can make us something to use."

"It won't be enough," Ravenna said, though something was surely better than nothing. "I have been studying war tactics in the tomes. The Stormbringers used archery, yes, but they also had to fight in close proximity to their enemies because of metal-plated armour, shields, even magic. Some of these things have been lost to the ages, even amongst the humans, but they are far from helpless. We will need a good deal of equipment to battle our enemies."

"And where would you suggest we get the supplies to make them, let alone the people to actually craft the weapons and armour?" Brianna asked. She tossed the paper onto the table. Ravenna watched it fall, her mind whirling. They had limited time, and it would take a good deal of it to determine where to acquire materials, let alone have the metal workers craft it. They had not done anything remotely like what Ravenna needed for countless generations. But there were some who had...

"We will purchase what we need," Ravenna said. Brianna and Crispin exchanged a look with each other.

"Purchase? As in...money? From whom?" Crispin asked. Ravenna sighed. If her own reaction was any indication, she doubted very much that her generals would like what she had to say.

"Who else?" Ravenna asked. "The humans."

All was quiet for a moment. Then, "*What?!*" It was not certain whether Brianna or Crispinus was the one to exclaim. Both seemed completely taken aback. Crispin surged out of his chair, wings spreading as wide as they would go. Brianna similarly bristled, her feathers spread in their most threatening stance. Ravenna merely raised an eyebrow and shook her head.

"Are you insane?" Brianna demanded. "Do you have any idea what you're suggesting? These are our *enemies!*"

"Some, yes," Ravenna agreed. "But not all."

"You've told us yourself that they're cruel, heartless

monsters, out only for blood," Crispin said. He licked his lips, desperation shining in his eyes. "We... we *can't*."

"As always, you look at the world in terms of yes or no. Right or wrong. Human or sylph. Things are far more complex, *General*, than you imagine. The humans are cruel beings, yes. They are the ones with whom we are at war, yes. But not all of them are seeking our destruction."

"Then why...?" Brianna faltered, unable to put all her questions into words. Ravenna understood. She was bringing into question everything that she had told her people thus far. She had painted her picture of the humans in broad terms. She had made certain that the sylphs understood that they needed to either fight or die. The alternative was not to be thought of. Yet here she was, suggesting that they go to the humans to fix their problems.

Ravenna pulled out a clean sheet of paper and picked up a feather quill. She drew a map of the human lands, one that she had memorised when in Lenore's country. It was crude and hardly explained the distances necessary to travel in the lands properly, but it would serve to explain. "This," Ravenna said pointing to a massive tract of land in the west, "is the Salusian Empire. They are led by Davorin, who is the one who seeks us out. This is Southron, an ally of the Empire. The Red Desert would once have stood against the Empire, but no longer. These countries, though, are still free and this one in particular will do exactly as we wish, as long as we can pay."

Ravenna pointed to a small triangle of land between the borders of Southron, the Empire, and the Red Desert. She did not know if it even truly existed as a country now, or remained a place where those desperate human souls would go. It was a place she had hoped never to see again. But her circumstances had changed. She knew full well that they could find what they needed there. If they could not, then there were other places. Places where sylphs were worshipped and admired.

"What is this place?" Crispin asked warily. Ravenna lifted her eyes from the crude map and met his gaze. He flinched and quickly lowered his eyes. Ravenna turned to Brianna, who also looked away.

"This is the place where I was made a slave," Ravenna murmured quietly. Crispin sucked in a sharp breath, but he did not say anything. Brianna, though, was far more vocal.

She slammed her hands onto the table, making the wood jump. "You're mad!" Brianna roared, the Tower echoing with her cry. Footsteps halted outside the door and then hurriedly scurried away. The Intellecti were too afraid to interrupt, even when their precious peace was in jeopardy. "You want to go *back* there?!"

"Do we have a choice?" Ravenna asked, her posture as calm as ever. She did not wish to return there, but she would do anything if it meant helping her people. Had she not already proven as much?

"There has to be another way," Crispin said after a moment. Brianna turned, fixing him with a furious stare, her eyes radiating more fire than was normal. "Why need we rely on the humans at all? Surely they are all as you describe. Especially these."

Ravenna took a deep breath through her nose. She straightened some papers, looking at the calculations for the army's needs. She let the breath out. "A crow is a carrion-eater," she said. "They are often mean, attacking other birds and animals who get in the way of their next meal, sometimes just for sport. They have been known to mob larger birds and can cause a good deal of damage. They can be a scourge."

"I don't—" Brianna started. Ravenna cut her off with a sharp look, her ice countering the general's fire. Ravenna rose to her feet and braced her hands on the table, her wings flaring wide and blocking out the small window in the stone behind her. The room darkened a few shades.

"When the bodies lie dead on the fields, and we are wading our way through sand mixed with blood, wings too weary to do more than drag behind us, the crows will be there to clean up the dead." Ravenna looked between Crispin and Brianna. For the first time, she saw true fear in their eyes. Not the wariness that came from dealing with a potentially dangerous predator. Not the awkwardness or discomfort that came from giving fealty to someone they had previously hated. This was true, heart-stopping, feather-wilting, back-breaking fear. Good. "Should the crows be reviled and scattered because of their nature? Perhaps. But they will perform a function that few others would ever willingly do. The humans are cruel, yes. They often seek blood before peace. They think first of themselves and their place in the world. But they will perform a function for us that few others can do."

"It is hardly the same," Crispin rasped, voice quiet.

"Isn't it?" Ravenna raised an eyebrow and sank back into her chair. "If you have a better idea, then please, do let me know. I would welcome any suggestions that keep me from that place."

No one had an answer. Brianna fidgeted, her wings twitching. Crispinus kept silent, his eyes fixed on the papers on the table. Ravenna let the silence linger. It would be pointless to say anything more. They knew her argument. She had perhaps impressed upon them too strongly the consequences. But she would rather that than the alternative. Anything but the alternative.

"H-how will we pay them?" Brianna asked with a flutter of her wings. "I doubt they'd agree to trade in the manner of the sylphs."

"You mean with services and kind gestures?" Ravenna asked. "It would be a bad thing to offer these humans. They would take advantage very easily."

"We have nothing they covet," Crispin pushed. "Nothing but ourselves."

"We have moulted feathers," Ravenna said. "That will be a start. The rest will require Desarra's approval."

"Approval for what?" Brianna asked. She shifted again, her agitation clearly showing. Perhaps it would be better concealed once their troops knew the plan. But that would not happen until after the first shipment of weapons and armour was made.

"The only other thing of value that we have that the humans would want are the jewels stored in the vaults beneath the cliffs. The Chosen Queen's permission is required to do anything with them," Ravenna said. She looked at Crispin, who let out a harsh sigh. He ran his dark fingers through his burnished-gold hair.

"You've got to be kidding me," Crispin snapped. "Des will never agree to such a thing. The Council will never agree to such a thing."

"The High Council need not get involved," Ravenna replied cooly. "The jewels are in the wings of the Chosen Queen alone. Can you persuade her to part with some?"

Crispin shook his head. He hunched his shoulders, wings pressing closer to his body. "I can try. I can promise you that Desarra will not like it. She's going to want a very, very good reason for doing this. They're our history!"

"Persuade her, Crispin," Ravenna said. An order to her general. She gathered the papers together in a single pile, signifying that their meeting was over. She froze Crispin with a look just as he was standing. "If you do not, then I will. And I will not be as gentle."

Crispin flinched. Brianna said nothing, only leaving the room as quickly as she could, her anxiety still lingering. Crispin paused at the door, revealing Kratos standing there nervously, his wings flaring and folding subtly. Crispin turned back to Ravenna, his expression a mixture of regret and pain. "I knew you came back differently, Ravenna, but I never would have thought you this... cold."

Ravenna scoffed, the sound a mockery of the laughter that

she had given freely at the fete only the week before. She shook her head. "Then you never knew me at all."

Crispin's spine straightened, but he said nothing. He just left. Ravenna expected nothing else.

She sank back into the chair, her wings fitting perfectly in the divots designed for that very purpose. She had done nothing but talk, yet everything ached. Her muscles were tired. Her mind was spinning quickly towards exhaustion, trying to run over every possibility, and she no longer trusted that she felt much of anything at all. It was much like the wing-weariness she had experienced in the Pits, the very place she was proposing to return to buy weapons and armour. This was a little different, though, because she was the one at fault for this wing-weariness. And there was little she could do to get out of it.

"You may as well come in, Kratos," Ravenna said. "I am too tired to move just now."

Kratos shuffled into the room, wings held tensely at his sides. Other than that, he looked more at ease with Ravenna than her own generals had. Perhaps if he had heard the conversation that had just transpired, things would be different. Somehow, Ravenna doubted it.

"You do not look well," Kratos said. He sat in the chair opposite Ravenna and frowned. She chuckled drily.

"Are you saying that as my healer, or as my friend?"

"Both," Kratos said. He rubbed his fingers against the grains in the wood, weighing his words. Ravenna's interest piqued, though she did not move from her weary slump. "You should take better care of yourself."

"I should," Ravenna agreed. This was an ongoing conversation between the two. Ravenna was like as not to neglect her own needs in favour of figuring out how to solve a problem or, in this case, train and prepare an army for war. She spent much of her time training, and when she did not train, she had these discussions with her generals or spent hours researching ancient war tactics and records and requirements so that she might better understand what it took to raise an army. The result was that her sleep was slim and her eating habits were irregular. She knew that she needed to be at full strength and mental ability for the sake of her people, but there was little desire to do so.

"Have you eaten today?" Kratos pressed. Ravenna smiled, amused.

"I have," she said. "And more than one meal, too. Breakfast, as you know since you were there with the other Intellecti. I took the midday meal in the hall with the soldiers of the Skydancers, Wingkeepers and Wind Through Feathers companies."

Kratos nodded, his plump face showing worry and his mouth drawn in a thin line. "Good."

Ravenna tilted her head. "Why don't you tell me precisely what it is that you wish to talk to me about?"

"It has been three moons since Tacitus died," Kratos blurted, almost before Ravenna finished speaking. She stiffened, her weariness vanishing as her posture straightened and her eyes sharpened, flashing shards of ice.

"Ah," she said. "Has it… has it really been that long?"

Kratos nodded. His feathers rose in agitation and he wrung his hands together. "It has."

Ravenna looked at the ceiling. She did not want to do this. Not now. Perhaps not ever. But it was necessary and it was unfair to Tacitus to deny him this rite. She just had so much else on her shoulders already. She blinked, surprised to feel her eyes filling with moisture. She took a breath, the air cutting through her.

"You do not have to do this," Kratos said, words rushing out. Ravenna looked at him, frowning. "I mean, the other Intellecti would be glad to take your place if you do not feel up to it. After all, Tacitus was a revered member of our order and—"

"No," Ravenna murmured. Kratos fell silent, worrying his lip between his teeth. "No, it is my right and it is my duty as his heart-daughter and the benefactor of his legacy. I am trained in the rite. What else is there to do?"

"I… checked this morning. His bones have been picked clean."

Ravenna closed her eyes. She swallowed, her grief catching in her throat. For three moons, she had pushed aside her grief and her need to mourn, not only for Tacitus but for the sylph she had been in the Red Desert. Her people here on Shinalea needed her more. They did not need a weeping, grief-stricken sylph who was more caught up with the desperation in her soul than preparing them to face a nightmare come to life. Ravenna was never one to be very open, in any case. But this… this hurt. And yet she could not deny Tacitus this final right.

"Very well," she said at last. "Tonight, we go to the Place of the Dead and we will gather his bones. Tacitus' last rite."

Kratos rewarded Ravenna with a smile. "He would be proud of you, you know."

"Would he? Sometimes I'm not certain."

"Tacitus loved you, sometimes more than I think he loved the Intellecti. We… we were a calling, a vocation. You were everything. How could he not be proud of you?" Kratos said. Ravenna's wings folded close to her.

"You were there at the end," she replied. "You knew things had changed."

"Everything changes, Ravenna," Kratos said, a hint of bite in his voice. "Surely you know this, after all your studies."

"I know that everything changes in the short term, but that the rest of the world seems to be stuck in the mire. War. Slaughter. Violence. Death. It's all inevitable. We've but escaped it for a short while." Ravenna rose from her chair; she did not wish to talk of this any longer. She did not wish to reveal just how much her beliefs had changed since being taken by the humans.

"Perhaps Life is the inevitable," Kratos said, rising with her. He bowed his head. "I will see you at the Place of the Dead as the sun sets."

Ravenna nodded, throat tight. Then she fled the room, recognising the irony just as sharply as she recognised the pain.

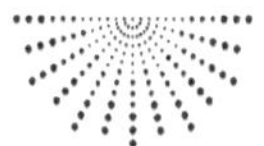

CHAPTER TEN

The mysterious task that Sisu, Asgeir and the others—twins named Cai and Ib—had done every day while Miska was shunted on the great-grandmothers, was to go hunting. Or, that was what Sisu said. So far, Miska hadn't seen much hunting being done.

He had been handed a bow almost as tall as himself, a set of arrows, a set of snares, and a hunting knife that now sat strapped to his thigh in the most unfamiliar manner. He wanted to grumble and complain, but he knew better. Instead, he followed Sisu through the forest as the big man laughed and joked with Asgeir. Miska focused on not dropping his bow.

After about an hour of walking, the five of them found themselves at the edge of a clearing wide enough to make seeing the trees on the other side difficult. The ground rose and fell in small hills, each covered with long grasses and fall wildflowers. Bees moved happily through the plants, and birds flitted from small bush to boulder to tree branch with a careless ease.

Sisu held up his right hand, the fingers curled in a fist. Immediately, Asgeir and Cai stopped. Ib walked around the edge of the clearing a little ways. Miska remained where he was just inside the tree line. Sisu turned and looked right at him. His mouth moved, but given the stiff and silent way the others seemed to be holding themselves, Miska doubted any sound was actually being made. He tried to follow the hand motions as well as the movement of Sisu's mouth.

"There's a herd of elk that like to wander this meadow," Sisu said. Miska wondered what an elk was and whether it was dangerous. "Be careful, though, and stick to hiding behind hills and trees. The elk will see you and flee before you can set up the shot if you're not careful. Patience is the key. If you get a shot, take it. They won't present another."

"Why are you waiting?" Asgeir said, turning to look between Miska and Sisu with a frown. "We need to get into position."

Sisu nodded and made some hand signals that Miska did not understand, but the others did. They started moving off in various directions, through the meadow or around it, presumably to circle around the elk. Asgeir waved at Miska to follow him, so he did. Naturally, this was the most difficult of the directions that the others went off in. They were travelling in more-or-less a straight line, keeping low to the ground and darting between and behind hills as quietly and quickly as they could manage.

Asgeir moved like a nature spirit. His feet seemed to brush over the ground like wind, as opposed to stepping. He carried his bow easily, ready to shoot in an instant. Miska, on the other hand, was certain he stepped on dead twigs as often as he stepped on grass. He was glad he could not hear the racket he was making. But Asgeir made no motion of reproach, just kept creeping forwards like it was the most natural thing in the world.

Miska's leg muscles were beginning to cramp from the unnatural crouching by the time Asgeir signalled them to stop. The northman crawled up a steep but short hill. Miska followed, doing his best to be mindful of where he put his hands and his feet. He almost missed, as such, the sight that met him when he reached the top of the hill.

Standing on the other side of the hill, casually grazing in the meadow and looking as if nothing in the world could bother them, stood the most massive wild creatures Miska had ever seen. They were like horses, but bigger. Their legs were skinny and their shoulders muscular. Their fur was short and a muted brown. But most magnificent were the few that grazed among the others, bearing horns on their head that branched off in many directions, looking just as easily like they could kill as not. These were elk. And as to being dangerous, Miska imagined they very much were.

Asgeir touched Miska's arm, causing him to jolt slightly. Asgeir frowned at the motion and Miska tried to smile apologetically. He did not want to startle the elk, not when he was finally being trained. "Get ready to take a shot," Asgeir mouthed, gesturing to Miska's bow. "A buck is best, but a calf-less female will work, too."

Miska's frowned deepened. "Buck?" he breathed. Asgeir gestured to the top of his head. Ah, the ones with the massive horns.

Miska nodded, then followed Asgeir's motions to get the bow into position. He nocked an arrow and drew back the string, arms wobbling with the effort it took to do such a thing. Asgeir rose slowly from a laying position to a crouch, sitting high enough that he could take a shot. Miska did the same, trying to move slowly enough that he would not startle the elk. The buck he aimed for lifted its head and seemed to look right at Miska. He froze, his arms straining with the effort of holding the string taut. The elk lowered its head again. Asgeir nodded.

Miska took a breath and released the arrow. He could not follow it very well, only knew that it flew above the elk he sought and went into the trees a short ways beyond. He was pleased with the effort, thinking that it was not a bad distance to go, even if he did not manage to hit the elk. Then, Asgeir grabbed Miska's arm in a stranglehold.

Miska turned to see what the other man said, but Asgeir's gaze was fixed on the trees where Miska's arrow had gone. There were several birds flying rapidly from the cover of the trees. The elk were bolting, moving in any direction but the forest. And something—large, brown, with hulking shoulders and claws that churned the earth—was running out of the forest, coming straight for Miska and Asgeir, Miska's arrow lodged in the thick fur along its flank.

Miska turned to Asgeir, eyes wide. Asgeir was still for a moment, then said, "Bear. Run."

The two wasted no more time. They heaved themselves to their feet, bows in hand, and started running. The bear was not far behind. Miska could feel the pounding of the creature's feet on the ground. He ran faster.

The ground that they had used to hide from the herd of elk was now doing more harm than good. The dips and divots, the hills and high ground, were slowing them down. Asgeir, used to travelling this sort of terrain, moved faster over the ground, but even he was not able to outrun the bear. Miska saw the trees on the far side of the meadow coming quickly into view. He pushed his legs harder. The ground still shook behind him, signifying that the bear was growing closer.

They were almost at the trees when things went very, very wrong. Miska had leaped over a boulder, but the ground behind it was not where he expected. He fell through the thick grass to the ground a good six inches below where it should have been. His ankle twisted and cracked. His other leg tangled on the ground and sent stabs of pain ricocheting through the broken ankle. Miska's hands scraped the ground in a futile attempt to keep his head protected. He slammed his temple on the ground, the impact reverberating through him. The ground still pounded beneath him. The beating of his heart pulsed through his head like drums he had never before heard. He twisted, ignoring the pain, and saw the bear running towards him.

The creature's maw slavered, its fangs already dripping. It opened its jaws in a roar and surged forwards, legs eating up the ground easily. It stopped before Miska, rising to its back legs so that it loomed over him. Its claws were as large as his fist, its eyes wild with pain and rage. The drumming in Miska's head pounded louder, becoming almost a real sound.

The bear lunged. Miska threw his hands up over his head. The drumming peaked.

Then, silence and stillness.

Miska cracked an eye open, peering between his arms. He half-expected Sisu to be standing there, wielding his battle axe to protect him from the bear. He would never have been able to live down that gratitude, but it would have been more welcome than death. Perhaps Asgeir had stepped in. What lay before him, though, was something entirely different and entirely impossible.

The bear hung suspended in its lunge, unmoving. It was completely still except for the twitching of its jaws and the rage in its eyes. What held it in place was like a multitude of threads, invisible except when they pulsed in a myriad of colours in time with Miska's heartbeat. He sucked in great, heaving breaths and scurried out from beneath the bear, ignoring the fact that his right ankle was assuredly broken and throbbing. Adrenaline assured he did not notice the pain. He limped to his feet and moved a short distance away. The bear remained suspended and still.

Miska shook his head. He wanted the bear far, far away. He wanted this to have never happened. He did not understand what was happening. Most of all, he wanted Ravenna to wrap him in her wings and make him feel safe, the way she had when killing the desert lion that had attacked them.

The air pulsed, the pressure changing so rapidly that Miska's ears popped. He let out a cry and pressed his hands to his ears. The pain in his ankle made it impossible to stand, so he sank to his knees, hoping for relief. The air pressure changed again, a deep beating, throbbing, which ended with the earth shaking. Miska looked up, expecting to see the bear released from its mysterious bindings and rushing for him again. No, the bear was still held immobile, though its eyes were rolling with fear, now, not rage.

Behind the bear, so large he blotted out the sun, was a dragon. It was, without a doubt, Cavaris. His neck curved elegantly as his triangular head wove through the air. His scales shone white, his wings massive, their membranes a slight blue where they were thin enough to have the veins showing through. His red eyes glistened and his obsidian horns rose like deadly spires. The dragon was the largest being Miska had ever seen and despite the fact that he had made his peace with the existence of dragons, seeing Cavaris churn the ground with his talons, his stomach fell from beneath him. Miska knew it. He was about to die.

Who has done this?! Cavaris demanded, his mind-speak echoing in Miska's head louder than ever before. He knew the sound was only in his thoughts, but it *hurt*. He scrabbled at his ears, screaming in pain. Asgeir stumbled close to Miska, his eyes rolling up in his head. Sisu appeared not two moments later, running across the field with his axe swinging, his teeth bared, ready for battle. But even Sisu stopped, shaking, when the dragon whipped his head around to look at him.

Cavaris raised a claw, the point longer than Miska's forearm. He gestured to the bear, still suspended in air. *Who has done this?!* Cavaris repeated. Miska trembled, wrapping his arms around himself. The pulsing of the odd threads around the bear increased in tempo, light shining from them almost bright enough to blind him. Cavaris took in a deep breath, nostrils flaring, eye widening. He opened his mouth to reveal a dangerous line of fangs, and his tongue tasted the air.

Cavaris' head snaked lower to fix Miska in his stare. His eye alone was as large as Miska's head. He had spent two moons in the dragon's presence. He had learned language from the dragon, had discussed the state of affairs in the Red Desert with him. But that was when Cavaris was in a human guise. This… this monstrous being that belonged in myth and dreams, was enough to send a spike of fear straight through Miska. His heartbeat sounded again in his ears, like drums.

Enough! Cavaris said with a jerk of his head. Immediately, the drums stopped. The threads suspending the bear vanished and Miska collapsed to the ground, his body suddenly exhausted and all trace of adrenaline gone. He felt like a great weight suddenly pressed down on him. His ankle screamed in pain. His head swam. He looked up at Cavaris, at his death, with tears in his eyes. Cavaris lowered his head again, resting it on the ground. *Enough*, he said again, this time filling his voice with gentleness. The mind-speak still hurt.

Miska whimpered.

Be not afraid, little human, Cavaris murmured. His tongue snaked out again, the forked ends touching Miska's face briefly. Miska shuddered. *I will not harm you.*

"You're going to kill me," Miska breathed, his muscles too tired to move. Cavaris' eyes widened, then the lids lowered until he was certain that the dragon was smiling at him. His heart nearly stopped.

No, little human. Do you know what you have done? Cavaris asked. Miska shook his head, mouth dry. He hadn't meant to shoot the bear. He hadn't meant to hurt it. He just wanted to bring down an elk, as Asgeir and Sisu had asked. *You have performed magic. You have used the song. You are a sorcerer.*

The threads pulsing around the bear. The drums that were not quite a sound, which seemed to be his heartbeat. The things that Cavaris had sent away with a toss of his head. Magic? No. It was not possible.

Yet, what else could it be?

Miska whimpered again, then gratefully succumbed to the exhaustion plaguing his muscles and the pain radiating from his ankle. The darkness beckoned like an old, comforting friend. Miska closed his eyes, swallowed up by the black.

* * *

THIS WAS the second time that Miska had awoken from the darkness to find himself in Cavaris' tent. This time, he knew precisely where he was when he opened his eyes and saw the walls of the tent rising around him, the fire crackling in the centre of the tent, its smoke rising to the hole in the top. He groaned and sat up, his head pounding. Almost immediately, he was faced with Ib and Asgeir, looking at him with wide eyes. At least Asgeir was smiling.

"Miska!" Asgeir said, standing from where he had been sitting before the tent fire. He put the dagger and sharpening stone away before coming over to crouch beside Miska, looking at him with concern in his eyes. "You're awake! Sisu did not think you would wake so early."

"Why are we here?" Miska asked, pressing a hand to his head in the hopes that the pounding would end. Ib tossed his head, his dark hair escaping its binds.

"Cavaris insisted," Ib said. He said something else, but his face was turned and Miska did not catch the full movement of his mouth.

"What?" Miska asked, looking at Asgeir. Asgeir sighed.

"Cavaris would not let Sisu take you back to Rygirfel, though it was closer. Sisu wanted to put you on a litter and carry you back, so that your ankle could be seen to by a healer. Cavaris refused. He said that there were more important things to attend to than a broken limb."

Miska growled, the sound low enough that he could feel it in his chest, even if he could not hear it. "He had no right," he snapped. He shoved back the furs and swung his legs over the edge. It occurred to him only after he had done so that he should have been in agonising pain, unable to move his right ankle at all. He'd broken bones before, mostly after Qilas and the others beat him. But once a horse had stepped on his foot and Miska hadn't been able to walk for nearly a week until Warra fashioned a crutch for him. Now, though, there was no pain. The ankle was not even bound, though his shoes had been removed. Miska wiggled his toes experimentally, expecting to hiss in pain.

Nothing.

He looked up at Asgeir and Ib, who flinched away. "I don't...I broke my ankle," Miska said, brows drawn together. Ib nodded. Asgeir turned and said something to the other man who wasted no time in darting out of the tent. Asgeir settled back on his haunches and appraised Miska, his light eyes concealing something. Miska clutched the edge of the cot, his knuckles turning white as he did so. He swallowed.

"Cavaris fixed it," Asgeir said. His eyes darted to the entrance of the tent. Miska looked also, but saw nothing there. Asgeir shifted, pulling out his dagger and sharpening stone again. He fiddled with the objects for a moment before putting them back, the dagger to its sheath on his belt, the stone to a pouch. "It was like nothing I've seen before. He just... breathed on your ankle and the bone mended itself. Next moment, it was like nothing had happened. And the bear, he did something to it, too. Healed it, talked to it, I do not know. Now the blasted thing won't go farther than a few hundred metres from the old snake."

Miska's mouth turned dry. He ignored the words about the bear; what could he do about that? But his ankle. He lifted his right foot and stared at it. He knew, without a doubt, that he had broken it. Yet, just as Asgeir said, there was not a scratch marring the skin. This, more than the fact that Cavaris possessed wings and horns and claws, made Miska unsettled. Ravenna had wings—she belonged to religion and myth—but she could do nothing like this.

You are awake.

Miska bolted upright. He reached instinctively for the hunting knife at his belt and wrapped his hands around the hilt. Asgeir stood also, backing away from the dragon subtly, his head lowered and his eyes fixed firmly on the ground. Cavaris watched them both with amusement, his human-esque face showing the emotion clearly. Sisu stood beside him, the big man scowling over the shoulder of the dragon. He glanced at Miska and nodded, his mouth tightening at the corners.

"Sisu, why did you let him bring me here?" Miska asked, the accusation directed at Cavaris rather than Sisu. He might not have been terribly fond of Sisu, but at the moment, his dislike of the great man was less than that of Cavaris. The dragon blinked.

"Why would I not bring you here?" Cavaris asked, his hands spreading so that his robes moved through the air. He gestured to the tent. "This is where you belong."

Miska ground his teeth together but said nothing. He shifted his gaze to Sisu, hoping that he would say something. Miska was not disappointed. "You gave him into my care. You gave him to *me* to train."

Cavaris rolled his red eyes and shrugged. He inspected his claw-tipped fingers, as though he had not a more pressing care in the world. "That was before I knew what Miska was. Now it is more important to have him train with me."

"What I am?" Miska asked. He tightened his grip on the hunting knife, though he did not yet draw it from his belt. Cavaris raised his eyebrows, eyes widening.

A sorcerer, the dragon said. Miska knew that he was the only one who could hear the words. He forced himself to speak rather than answer the sound that plagued his head.

"I am not a sorcerer."

Cavaris inclined his head. His white hair gleamed orange in the firelight. His obsidian horns seemed darker. "What else would you call it? You saw what you did to the bear. You—"

"No!" Miska said. Cavaris and Sisu exchanged a surprised glance. Sisu pushed his way around Cavaris and stopped before Miska. His eyes softened slightly.

"Look, son," Sisu started. Miska shook his head fiercely. Sisu grabbed Miska's shoulder in his hand, resting the stump the other arm, the weight alone keeping it, too, still. "Listen. I… I saw what you did with the bear. You stopped it from killing you and Asgeir. You saved it from its madness at being pinned with an arrow. It was still, in mid-air, with nothing keeping it there. What else could it be?"

Miska shook his head, water blurring his vision. He blinked the angry tears away. "No! It was *not* magic. Magic is evil!"

Cavaris stepped back as if struck. He twined his fingers together and licked his lips as though nervous. Miska knew better. He pointed at Cavaris, not realising that he held the knife in his hand. "You healed me with magic, didn't you?" Miska demanded to know.

Cavaris nodded.

"It's your fault," Miska whimpered. He wanted to blame Cavaris for tainting him. He wanted to blame Cavaris for bringing the magic out in him. Oh, he would deny it as much as he could, but the truth was staring him straight in the eye. He had performed magic. The exhaustion that had followed the act was undeniable, as was the result. But he did not want it.

I do not understand, Cavaris whispered to Miska's thoughts. *Is magic—true weaving of the song—such a burden? It is a gift not seen for some generations! I had thought humans to have lost the ability long ago. I had thought it dead.*

"It's not dead," Miska sneered. He looked at the knife in his hand and the reddish-orange light that glistened on the blade from the fire. Just like that day in the Red Palace. "It is far from dead. In fact, I've seen it before," Miska said.

"Impossible," Cavaris said.

Miska scoffed. "Oh, yes, *dragon*. I've seen the magic before. I saw it the day I had to leave the Red Desert. I saw it kill a whole room full of people. Davorin used it to control the dragon-spirit that infested his captain. It's only evil! Meant only for death!"

Cavaris hissed, his fangs elongating and his white skin taking on the shimmer of scales. *That was an abomination. Far from the song. What you did and what that pretender did are two very different things.*

Miska shook his head. "It doesn't seem that way to me."

"Then you will have to learn," Cavaris said. He stepped forwards, pausing when Miska raised his knife again. It was a useless weapon against a dragon, but it was all he had unless he could figure out a way to use that thing deep inside him, like he had with the bear. He never wanted to do such a thing again.

Sisu stepped forwards, one hand stretched out to stop Miska and Cavaris. "I think you'd better leave him be."

Miska looked away from the human and dragon alike. He did not wish to see any more of this conversation. He wished, not for the first time and not for the last, that he could go back to the way things were before, with Lenore ruling the Red Desert as a proud and strong queen and Ravenna finding her way. He did not even know if his queen was still living.

You hold great power, Cavaris said. *Would you rather your people did not experience the same power? Did not experience the good that can come from such a thing? You cannot understand how different, how unlike the other, the two things are. What you have done and what he has done are not the same. He has a corruption of the song. He does not manipulate the song naturally as a sorcerer should. What he did was accept the blood magic of a long-dead being that should have remained dead.*

Miska frowned. He did not know how Nadezhda had changed, how that thing had come into being. All he knew was that Davorin and that monster had taken his queen as hostage now his people were in desperate need of help. He had gone to the Iron Mountains to do just that. Miska was their hope—he and Ravenna—as much as he would like to deny that fact. But magic? He was not sure he could do it.

"There are things out of stories," Sisu said, "that should be left there. But there are some things that won't stay where they belong. Don't be foolish Miska. This is a gift. This is exactly what you were looking for. Are you going to throw it away because you don't like the means of delivery?"

Miska looked at the knife in his hand. He wanted to use it. He wanted to plunge it into Cavaris' chest and leave it there. To insinuate that he was anything like Davorin…it was hard. Miska flicked his green eyes upwards searching between the two people. "This…can help my people?" Miska asked.

Cavaris inclined his head. "Would you not rather have a defence against someone who uses the song, no matter how corrupted?"

Miska nodded. He sheathed his knife. Then, he lifted his chin determined and resolved. "I will learn," he said. "For the sake of my people, I will learn. That does not mean I have to like it."

Sisu's mouth tightened into a thin line. But he did not say anything against Miska. He just reached up to stroke one of the braids in his hair, then nodded. "And what of your other training?"

Miska looked between the two men. Cavaris blinked languidly. He folded his arms into the long sleeves of his robes and looked at Miska as if he were the one who held the answers. "Well?"

"I...wish to keep training. Real training. With knife and bow and...Please, Sisu."

"And you expect me to track all the way up here?" Sisu asked. "I have other duties, you know."

"Do I have to stay here? Am I...dangerous?" Miska asked. He looked around the tent; it had become a familiar place to him during internment there. He knew precisely where the pots were kept. He knew where to find extra furs to keep warm, and it was the closest thing he had to a familiar place since he had left the Red Desert. Miska did not know what training in magic would entail, but he had a good idea of what was involved in Sisu's form of training. And he wanted to be close to Hullgard for when he had to consult the elders for help. It would do no one any good for him to show up trained in magic without an army at his side. He imagined he would be dead in the first five minutes of battle, no matter whether or not he could match Davorin in the song.

"You may stay where you wish," Cavaris said. "My interests now align with yours. If that requires me to go to Rygirfel, then I shall. Though it has been many cycles since I have interacted with humans on a more than cursory basis."

Sisu's shoulders sagged in relief. He took in a breath and nodded. "Very well," he said. "I will continue to train you. Though after today, I think we may need to start you on something a little bit more remedial than hunting an elk. We wouldn't want any more bears to run after you, now would we?"

Miska felt his skin heat slightly. He swallowed and looked at Cavaris. "Asgeir said that the bear was still here."

Indeed, it still is. Cavaris smiled, the act one of pure amusement at the folly of humans. Miska's flush deepened, though this time it was with anger as opposed to embarrassment.

"How was I to know what would happen?" Miska said. "The bear came rushing after me. I did not mean to shoot it." He shuffled his feet a little bit, so that he would not have to look at the response right away. "The magic did not hurt the bear…did it?"

Cavaris chuckled, the sight a bit startling coming from the dragon; his red eyes crinkled around the edges and his horns waved through the air. *Magic is an unusual substance. Even when one is well-versed in the song, it may not do exactly as you expect. That is why many sorcerers did not live as long as us dragons. We have the song in our blood. You have it in your minds and your heart. But no, the bear is not injured. Though you will find it difficult to send it away.*

Miska looked at Sisu for understanding. The big man shook his head, beard swinging slightly. The extra hair made it difficult for Miska to see whether or not Sisu was laughing, but the wrinkles around his eyes suggested so. "Aye," Sisu said. "The bear won't go away. It's been scaring Ib and Cai something fierce."

Miska clenched his fists. He liked neither Sisu nor Cavaris. Sisu seemed to be making a fool of him, and Cavaris was condescending. Yet both were his only options if he wanted to actually do something for Lenore. He could not find Ravenna. Cavaris knew where she was and yet he would not take Miska there. Instead, he was left to learn how to fight and how to use a magic he never wanted.

"I want to make things very clear," he said. He lifted his eyes to look at both Sisu and Cavaris. Cavaris raised his brows. Sisu said nothing. "I am not your plaything. I will not be manipulated into running from the fish wives so that I might join you on the hunt. I will not be given misinformation that will prevent me from doing what is necessary. You have offered to help; do so. You will answer my questions and I will learn. If you cannot do that then I will find somewhere else to go."

"I think you're finally learning," Sisu said.

Cavaris nodded. "I would agree."

Miska nodded firmly. Then stretching his formerly broken

foot, he loped over to the place where Cavaris had stored his shoes. Miska yanked his sock on, then his boot, then he strode outside to where the others were waiting. They jerked slightly as he approached, as if they were a little afraid of him. Asgeir was the first to recover, smiling brightly and clapping him on the back.

"You told them off something fierce, right?" Asgeir laughed. "Old Sisu really needed the lesson. He's been getting quite insufferable, telling us all what to do."

"Oh and you're one to talk, Asgeir," Ib said. "When Sisu isn't around, you are the one who tells us what to do. Not like we have the same status as hunters or anything."

Miska stopped watching their conversation. He looked around for the bear, wondering if they had just been pulling his leg. But no, there it was. Its shoulders were massive hulking things draped in fur that was probably thicker than anything Cavaris or Sisu wore. Its eyes fixed on Miska, a deep brown that seemed soulful, filled with questions. Sad. Miska walked over to the bear and held out his hand. Without being told, the bear pressed its muzzle into his hand. Its nose was cold, its touch tentative.

"I will not hurt you," Miska said. "And I'm sorry for what I did."

The bear blinked once. It shook its massive head, the ruff of fur following the movements. It dug its claws into the earth, tearing up the loam as it did so. It seemed to be looking at him for answers, or at least some explanation of what was going on. Miska reached out a hand again, this time resting his fingers in the thick fur on the bear's shoulders. "I would change this if I could," Miska said. "But I cannot. Can you live with that?"

The bear ducked its head.

"Good enough," Miska said. "Come on, we have a ways to go before it gets dark. And I have a feeling that Cavaris and Sisu are going to be arguing the whole way."

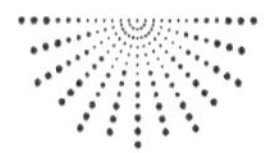

CHAPTER ELEVEN

Miska walked at the back of the group. Cavaris walked a few steps in front of him and the bear, for all that Miska tried to get rid of him, followed a few steps behind. His breath was hot on the back of his neck. Sisu, Asgeir, and the others walked in their own group, chatting amongst themselves as though nothing unusual had happened that day. Miska supposed it was not all that surprising. They had returned to Rygirfel a few times without any meat or prey to show for their efforts for the day. He supposed that fishing was perhaps the more productive means of gathering food. However, the hunting was meant to be good training for him so he mourned the loss. The fact that he had discovered his magic in the process only made things worse, though all seemed to ignore it. Miska could not.

"You once said," Miska said, "that you would not get involved in the affairs of humans unless there were human sorcerers once again walking the land. Now that I'm here, does that mean that you will fight on our side? That you will help me liberate the Red Desert?"

Cavaris dropped back so that he walked beside Miska. He

carried no bag, having left all of his belongings behind in the tent isolated in the forest. Miska wondered if such silly things as possessions actually mattered to the dragon. Somehow, thinking about a dragon requiring possessions like a bedroll or furs or even pots in which to cook food seemed like making a legend far too real for his taste. And yet, he was the one who had fallen in love with a sylph. How strange it seemed to have legends and stories told to children to get them to fall asleep walking amongst them.

Magic was meant to be something that no longer existed. Dragons were meant to be a made up stories. None of this was supposed to be real. And yet Miska himself was part of this legend. He wanted no part of it. But he would do what he must.

"You wish me to fight for you?" Cavaris asked. Miska inclined his head. The dragon switched to mind speak. *Do you know the devastation that you ask?*

Miska shook his head. "I am only repeating what you said. I asked if he would fight for me before, if you help me free my people from this *magic* that Davorin used to enslave them. You refused. Were you lying when you said you would help only when the sorcerers returned?"

It is far more complicated than you understand. My kind... What few of us there are left scattered to the four corners of this land many generations ago. None of us want to get involved in human affairs. We remember what it was like to have to fight wars, to have to use our magic for blood and for death. None of us wish that again. Cavaris sighed, looking up at the trees that stretched far overhead, their boughs still green despite the oncoming winter. Miska wondered if the trees would ever change like they did in the desert gardens. He supposed not. These trees were unlike anything he had ever seen, so why should they obey what he knew of nature?

"So you plucked the impossible out of the air in the hopes that it would never come to pass. Is that it?" Miska's voice must've betrayed his agitation, because the bear drew closer. He nudged him in the shoulder, forcing Miska to turn to look at him. He saw the confusion and concern in his eyes, an unusually human expression for a wild beast that had tried to kill him not too long ago. Miska patted the bear's head and kept walking.

Cavaris shook his head, horns glistening in the dying light of day. Miska noticed that they had already come farther than he had that first trek back with Sisu. It was only a short while ago and yet he was already stronger. Maybe the magic had something to do with it. A song that he could not even hear. How was he supposed to do magic when he couldn't hear this "song" Cavaris talked about?

How ironic. A deaf sorcerer meant to wield a song-based magic. If anything was impossible, it was that.

You have never seen war. You do not understand the sort of destruction that something like me can cause. Cavaris' claws were curled tightly into fists, though the dragon's expression remained impassive.

"Something like me, now, too?" Miska shook his head. He wrapped his hand around the hilt of his knife, trying to draw some comfort from the solid truth of the weapon. All he could feel was the ground falling out from beneath him. He wondered if this is what Ravenna had felt like when she first arrived in the lands of the humans.

Cavaris sneered, drawing up the lip to reveal a slightly pointed fang. Just another example of his lack of humanity. *We are hardly the same, boy. I am as ancient as the earth we walk upon. You are but a drop in the ocean, set to expire before too many cycles gone. You may hold power, but you are nothing more than a child compared to me.*

"Why do you bother living among us at all?" Miska asked, fighting not to return the sneer. "You seem to disdain us completely."

The dragon heaved a sigh and shook his head, like an adult

amused at the antics of child. *We were put on this earth as teachers and guides for the very young. Perhaps once, when the world was new, we were able to do exactly as we wished, when we wished, and however we wished. But our responsibilities have changed. This place was meant for the likes of you. Humans.* Cavaris looked up at the trees once more; his red eyes, which normally looked angry or bitter in the depth of the redness, now just looked sad. *I was there when your people began. We thought that they were nothing more than a nuisance, rodents scurrying around our claws. How wrong we were.*

"Will you help us?" Miska barely breathed words, but they were all he had. The only hope to save his people. If he had to work without Cavaris' help, then he would. He would fight until the very end if it meant he could free his people. He would much rather have Cavaris on his side, though.

Is teaching you not enough? Cavaris looked at Miska, with the bear walking behind him and the warriors in front. *You have more ability than you know. If I did not fight in your war, I would still imagine you to win. You do not need me.*

"Perhaps you are the one who needs me," Miska said. He thought of Ravenna, cold and strong as lonely as the north wind. She hadn't thought she needed his help either, but she had. Cavaris reminded him of Ravenna. They were both legends, trying to forget that truth. "You were friends with Sisu long before I ever arrived. You know the people of Rygirfel well, and yet you claim to disdain us all, to see us as nothing more than a drop in the ocean. Make up your mind."

Miska did not look for Cavaris' answer. He slowed his steps so that he walked beside the wild bear behind him rather than beside the dragon. Cavaris could speak to Miska's mind and had been doing so, but he did not want to hear anymore. He was tired of excuses.

Miska wove his fingers into the bear's fur, marvelling at its density and the fact that the creature existed at all. This being was so much larger than the desert lions that graced the Red Desert. His shoulders alone stood half a head higher than the lion. His claws were thicker, perhaps not as sharp but certainly as dangerous. The bear's muzzle was longer, more square, and likely carried fangs just as dangerous. Certainly, when they had been slavering over him, Miska had been certain he would die. What marvellous or horrible thing was it that had this bear following Miska like a trained dog? Was it cruelty? Or some strange bond that now existed between the two because of his clumsy use of magic?

"I'm sorry for this," Miska said. "All I wanted to do was to find Ravenna and save my queen."

Asgeir tapped Miska on the shoulder. "Who is Ravenna? Who is this Queen?"

"Sisu did not tell you?" Miska shook his head in shock, his braided hair falling into his eyes as the tiny strands unraveled themselves. He noticed that Asgeir did not seem to be nervous about walking beside the bear. He had thought that Ib, Cai and Asgeir feared the beast. All, excepting Sisu and Cavaris, seemed to not like the bear. Cavaris appeared unbothered by any of it, as usual. Sisu just walked on, laughing, and talking with Ib and Cai. Miska doubted very much that anything much at all bothered Sisu.

"No," Asgeir said, enunciating the word. This was probably done so that Miska could understand, but he seemed uncertain. "Sisu said you would tell us when you are ready, or when you went to speak to the Elders. But, I've never met anyone like you. You have skin the colour of sunset. Or soil. You walk and act like someone who has never seen the forest nor lived here. You consort with dragons, and now you are a sorcerer." Asgeir laughed, shaking his head. A slight breeze ruffled his light hair, moving some of the braids away from his face. "I find my curiosity to be overwhelming my patience."

The corner of Miska's mouth lifted, the closest thing he had come to true smile for too long. "I will tell you at the fire tonight, if you will teach me how to shoot properly."

"Sisu is our best archer. Well he was, until he lost his arm." Asgeir waved his left hand, eyes glistening with laughter. Miska would not have thought that the loss of a limb would've been anything to laugh at, but he did not know these northern people.

"How did he do that?" Miska asked. He was so focused on looking for Asgeir's answer that he nearly missed the hole in the ground. The bear nudged his arm, pushing Miska with enough force so that he tripped over the hole, as opposed to into it. Miska looked at the bear and surprise and turned back to Asgeir wondering if he had seen what Miska had.

"Next thing you know, you'll be giving it a name, and riding it like a horse. Or having it fetch like a dog."

Miska sighed. "I don't know what this is. Cavaris hasn't explained what bond lies between he and I."

"I hope he does, and soon. I can just imagine what will happen if you walk into Rygirfel with a tame bear behind you. Especially when you didn't have one before. All of the young ladies will be clambering to get to know you, the Bear Tamer." Asgeir tossed back his head and laughed, drawing the attention of the others in the party. Sisu fell back to walk beside Miska and Asgeir. Cavaris walked on ahead, taking the place of the lead of the party.

"You better not be telling stories about me," Sisu said. "I have enough rumours flying about how I lost this hand. It weren't anything more than an accident with my axe."

"I doubt that," Miska said drily. "I have a feeling there is a lot more to that, and to you, than you would like us to know."

"Is that why you don't trust us?" Sisu asked. Miska took in a deep breath and held it for a beat. He studied his feet for a moment, to save himself from answering and seeing a response. Ravenna had once mentioned that talking with him required more effort on her part because she could not just look away and listen for his response. She had to actually look at him so that he could see what it was that she was saying. She said she both liked that and hated it. Miska, on the other hand, used it to save himself from having to see that which he did not want to see, or from having to answer right away.

Miska looked up at Sisu. "I don't trust *you*," Miska said. "I'm still not sure about Cavaris. At least Asgeir speaks his mind."

"I was just telling Miska that he would be proclaimed Tamer of the Bear by all of the young women in Rygirfel and Hullgard if he cannot figure out how to to keep his bear out of town," Asgeir said, trying to dispel the hostility in the air. He shifted the bow across his shoulder and looked between Miska and Sisu, a forced smile on his lips.

Sisu laughed at that, and clapped Miska on the shoulder. He seemed completely unconcerned by Miska's mistrust. "Indeed, we'll have to be beating them off with a stick, I think. You, a sorcerer, with the bear at your side? Why, you'll be married before the sun sets."

Miska scowled, glaring at both warriors. "I am pledged to Ravenna. No other."

Asgeir pursed his lips as though he had whistled, and looked at Miska, brows raised under knowing smirk on his mouth. "She must be some woman, this Ravenna. I should like to meet her."

Miska smiled ferociously, baring his teeth in a sharp sneer like he had seen Vareis do when training young soldiers. She was just about the scariest person he knew, excepting Ravenna, and she had never been anything so crass as to sneer like that. "I should like to see that, too. She would beat you with her wings before she stabbed you with her sword. Or she would defeat you with her bare hands, like she did with the lion."

"Wings? Lion? I begin to wonder if this woman is real," Asgeir said, the laugh apparent on his face. Miska clenched his fist and tightened his grip on the hilt of his knife, though he left the blade in its sheath. They believed he was a sorcerer and that he had bound himself to a bear. They had acknowledged that Cavaris was a dragon, a creature that should not have existed by all means. Yet Ravenna was the lie?

Sisu tilted his head. "I once knew a winged woman," he said thoughtfully. "It was the loneliest winter I had ever spent, trapped in a pass between vales during a blizzard, mayhap half-a-generation ago it was. I think I hallucinated it all. Some wolf had just eaten my hand. I was starved, dying, and then the most beautiful woman in the world appeared. Come to think of it, I don't think she had wings. I think she was part star, the way she shone. I came back to Rygirfel half-starved, raving about sunshine."

"Ravenna is no hallucination," Miska growled. "She's a sylph. Cavaris has seen her."

"Cavaris has seen many legends," Sisu said. "I doubt most of them exist anymore."

"Believe or not, it doesn't matter. You will meet her on the battlefield soon enough, I imagine," Miska said. Ravenna would come for Davorin just as much was he would. She would not wait for Davorin to come to her, to have the possibility of destroying her people. She would meet him on his own ground, and destroy him there.

Asgeir had been right when he said that arriving back in Rygirfel would be something of a chaotic event for Miska. The bear—Miska really needed to give him a name—was following along as placidly as any trained dog, seemingly unaware of the stares that it was garnering. One of the fish wives dropped her basket of salted fish as it was being carried over to the storage container. The bear raised his nose and sniffed eagerly taking a step in that direction. Miska put a hand on his shoulder, shaking his head.

"Not now," Miska whispered to the bear. "I promise I will get you some food soon."

The bear did not respond, not that Miska expected him to, but there was a sort of understanding that gleamed in his eyes. One of these days, he wouldn't be surprised if the bear started talking mind to mind like Cavaris did.

"What is this, Sisu?" An old, stooped woman, had marched before Sisu and glared at him with all the force of a desert monsoon. Miska only caught the words by virtue of the fact that he was standing directly beside Sisu, trying to figure out how to explain the truth of Ravenna to the old warrior. He gaped at the woman in confusion. Sisu, on the other hand, seem to have no qualms and just tossed his head back, laughing as usual.

"What? You mean the bear? You act as though you've never seen one before, Mother Freya." Sisu reached his hand up towards the bear, walking at Miska's side. The bear looked at the limb, curled one lip to reveal a pointed fang tainted yellow, and growled. Sisu flinched back, looking at Miska in surprise. Miska shrugged.

"The bear is not tame," Cavaris said, walking over to stand beside Miska and Sisu. His words echoed in Miska's head so that he would be sure to understand. "He is a sorcerer's familiar. He is bound to Miska, and will do as Miska asks, but do not make the mistake of assuming that this bear is tame."

We will discuss how the bear is bound to you later, Cavaris said, only for Miska to understand. He sensed disapproval in the dragon's voice. As if Miska had known what it was that he had done and could yet undo it. He had no more idea of what was going on with this magic than he had understood Ravenna's talk of fighting.

"It – it's not *dangerous is* it?" Mother Freya asked, looking nervous. She tugged her shawl, her eyes fixed on the bear's claws. Miska shook his head, resting his hand on the bear's pelt.

"He will not hurt you," Miska said, imbuing his words with a certain command that he was almost sure that the bear would follow. He could sense the bear rumbling beneath his hand; he did not know if that was a sound or if it was a feeling. Either way, he sensed that the bear would obey his order not to hurt the people of Rygirfel.

Mother Freya snorted. "Since when were you a sorcerer? And why is the dragon here? He never shows up unless something strange is going on."

Cavaris inclined his head, slipping his hands into the folds of his robes and looking for all the world like one of the temple priests from the Red Desert. Excepting the horns, the hair, and the blood red eyes. "It is a recent development," Cavaris said. Mother Freya narrowed her eyes, the lines around them making it seem all the more ominous. Having worked with her before, slicing off fish heads and preparing the fish for salting, Miska knew just how dangerous the woman could be. She wielded a knife like she was bred to it.

Cavaris said nothing more. He turned instead to look at Sisu, and raised his brows pointedly.

Sisu blinked, but nodded. He scratched his beard absently, looking around at all of the structures in the village square. Rygirfel boasted more than its fair share of tents, and a few more permanent structures made of wood. Miska had a feeling that he was looking for somewhere to keep him, the bear, and Cavaris. It made sense. Who would want to live with a man who walked around with a bear at his side? Let alone the fact that he would be learning magic from Cavaris, as well as his "usual" training. Sisu turned back to Cavaris, shrugging his massive shoulders. Cavaris shook his head, mouth twisting and something that looked like amusement as opposed to distaste. For a dragon who supposedly seemed to dislike being involved in human affairs, he sure appeared to be keen on them. Why else would he laugh?

"Mother Freya," Sisu said, bowing to the old woman, "I will explain everything in due time. For the moment, I must find a place for sorcerer Miska and his familiar to stay, where they will not alarm people. Cavaris will be staying with them."

Mother Freya twisted her gnarled hands together. She looked around, just as Sisu had. Again, nothing suitable seemed to be found. She looked at Miska, a deep frown marring the normally cheerful wrinkles on her face. "If I didn't know better, I would think that you had been sent here to cause trouble on purpose." Her frown softened, just a touch. "But you are a good lad."

Miska smiled, trying to placate the woman. She had been kind to him, taking the time to articulate her words very well so that Miska might understand. Even now, she was unhappy with him, her words were measured and shaped clearly. "I'm sorry for the bother," Miska said, his words barely more than a whisper.

Mother Freya flapped her wrist and shook her head. "I think there might be a tent on the edge of the settlement." She did not wait for a reply, but turned and marched away. Miska looked at Sisu, unsure as to whether Mother Freya was leading the party to this new tent, or simply going back to gutting fish. Sisu followed her, Cavaris following behind him. Miska fell in step and the bear trudged behind him, nudging Miska occasionally as they passed this fish station. He promised silently that he would try to feed the bear soon, and well. People would be far less nervous about a bear if it were not hungry.

Most of the people they passed looked away quickly as they caught sight of Miska and the bear. Some stared openly. A few children let out quiet shrieks and ran for their parents. One or two warriors even drew their swords, eyes suspicious. Sisu ignored them all, walking with purpose and pride as he usually did. Perhaps it was that which made the march through Rygirfel uneventful. Miska rather thought it was something to do with the fact that Cavaris was also there, and nobody wanted to start a battle they would not win. Asgeir and the others had slipped off after they entered Rygirfel, so it was only Miska, Sisu, Cavaris, and the bear that followed Mother Freya in some bizarre parade to the edge of the village, everyone staring in their wake.

The tent that awaited them was as large as the others: big enough to hold three people comfortably. It would be a little tight with the bear instead of a man, but Miska imagined that it would work just fine. However, the tent itself was in need of repair. The canvas had been worn away, only to be poorly patched with tanned hides that had seen far better days. The entrance of the tent was littered with pine needles and debris from the forest floor. There was a puddle of water sitting just outside the right side of the tent, so it was probably leaking inside as well. On the bright side though, it was far enough from Rygirfel itself but no one would notice Miska and magic. The bear would be out of sight. Cavaris would have privacy. And the questions could, perhaps, be avoided.

Part of Miska winced at the need for such privacy. He would have much preferred a normal life amongst these people. But to save his people, he had to accept how very abnormal he was. The bear nudged him in his shoulder, the movement somehow comforting.

"Here," Mother Freya said. She nodded firmly at Miska, and turned away, striding back to the centre of Rygirfel. Sisu shook his head. He turned to face Miska full on, so there would be no question of understanding.

"You're going to have to be careful," Sisu said. "These are uncertain times. You already came here under the winds of war. Everyone knows that you wish to petition the Elders. Now, you have brought a creature that they all fear into the centre of our home. And you have brought a bear, which is a symbol of strength, power. Killing one is often the first test that many warriors still choose to face. It is not often encouraged now, but it still happens. People will fear you more than ever."

There is nothing to fear, Cavaris said mind to mind with both Sisu and Miska. *Not from me, not from the bear.*

"And is there anything to fear from you, Miska?" Sisu asked. Miska straightened his shoulders, a fire burning in his belly. How dare Sisu ask that question! Sisu had been there when Miska discovered what he was. Sisu new him, knew exactly what Miska was hoping for. He knew of Miska's history in the Red Desert, and he knew what Miska wanted from him. And now he doubted?

"No," Miska hissed. "There is nothing to fear from me."

Sisu jerked his chin in a nod, braids swinging from his hair. "We shall see. I will fight you tomorrow for your training." Sisu turned around and left the clearing with the ragged tent. Miska was alone with Cavaris and his new familiar, whatever that was.

Cavaris heaved a sigh, the movement of his shoulders large enough to tell Miska that the dragon was not terribly pleased with this turn of events. *It used to be that humans respected us. Now I am left with the dregs of settlements, and training sorcerers who have no idea what magic truly is.*

"It's not my fault," Miska said petulantly. He stalked over to the tent and started cleaning out the debris from inside. The interior was as filthy as the exterior, with sunlight showing through the holes where the tent had been poorly patched. There was rotted wood on the floor, pine needles everywhere, and no clear fire pit. Miska started sweeping his foot along the ground, hoping to get as much of the debris out as he could. He hoped that someone would bring by some furs or bedroll, or it was going to be a very cold night.

He rounded on Cavaris, suddenly angrier than he had been since his home was taken by Davorin. "You were the one who swore that you would help me learn this magic! Since you won't help me fight my war, you don't want to be here, what use are you?"

Cavaris waved his hand, as though he expected the motion to do something. The debris that Miska had been beating out with his foot began to move, almost of its own volition. After a few moments—and a pulsing in Miska's temple that was too close to real sound for his liking—the debris shuffled itself outside the tent, leaving the floor clear but for hard-packed dirt. There was even a fire pit, ringed by stones, that hadn't been there a moment before.

Magic is a tool, Cavaris said. *It can be used to do good, it can be used to do bad, but it is simply a tool.*

"Why am I bound to this bear?" Miska asked. The creature had shuffled inside the tent after Miska, watching the movements of the dirt with interest, though not fear. The bear did not seem to be disturbed at all by Cavaris or the magic that the dragon wielded. In fact, except for his size, the bear seemed to be doing his best to not exist at all. Miska wished he understood what it was that the bear was thinking. He did feel a little badly that he had taken this magnificent creature, terrifying as he was, away from his home far in the forest. The bear belonged here no more than he did.

When he attacked you, you drew out what defensive magic you could. But not being trained at all, you did the thing that was most natural. You were an unbound sorcerer, meaning that you could connect your life source to another. Normally, the process of finding a familiar is a dangerous and complicated one. Most creatures to whom you try to bind your life source are not compatible, or cannot withstand the song running through them. The fact that you managed to create a familial bond with this bear is, frankly, astonishing. Instead, you should have just thrown the creature aside, or killed him. But now, the bear is bound directly to your life source. If you die, he dies. If he dies, you will live, but it will feel as though there is something missing. This bond is not to be taken lightly. You have, inadvertently or not, manipulated a living creature into doing your will. The bear will obey you, yes. He will even grow to be stronger than a normal bear, likely even become able to be used as a magical tool. In time, you and he will understand each other's thoughts and desires. You have given this bear a great gift: humanity, or as much as magic can give. But you have also destroyed what he was.

"I don't understand how I could use this magic like you say I did," Miska said. "There was no song. There was only... My heartbeat. And a pressure on my ears when you came and did whatever it was that you did."

Cavaris tilted his head. "How interesting," he said. Miska probably was not meant to see that, but he was looking intently at Cavaris, hoping that some answers lay within his head. Cavaris was busy studying the exit to the tent, the slits in his eyes narrow and his gaze far away.

How to teach someone who cannot hear the song to manipulate the song?

"Why won't you fight for me?" Miska breathed. "You could end this war before it begins, instead of teaching a deaf man music."

Cavaris swiped his hand through the air, as if fighting an unseen enemy. Pressure built up again, this time strong enough to send Miska to his knees. Behind him, he could feel the bear slamming his paws into the ground in displeasure. A sort of twinge in the back of Miska's head spoke of fear and pain. Was this the bond between the bear that Cavaris spoke of?

Just as Miska's head felt as though it was split apart, the pressure stopped. Miska opened his eyes and straightened. Where the tent had been empty before, now it was filled with what looked to be the belongings from Cavaris' tent, all that distance away. The dragon looked unhappy, but not exhausted like Miska had been after his use of magic. Cavaris settled himself on the furs next to the fire circle, and held his hands out over the crackling flames that had definitely not been there before.

I had forgotten how determined you humans can be, Cavaris said. Miska had a feeling that the dragon was going to be speaking to his mind from now on. At least, the furious turn of Cavaris' mouth said so. It was good that Miska had grown accustomed to that means of communication with Cavaris over the moons they had known each other. Elsewise, he had a feeling that his hands would be pressed over his ears and he would be screaming out loud from the pain. There was anger in those words. More than he had ever heard before. But there was also something else. Something indefinably sad.

Cavaris looked up at the hole in the tent, watching the smoke curl its way out into the open sky. The sun was setting, and Miska imagined that many of the people from Rygirfel would be sitting down to their evening meal. Some would be eating venison that more successful hunter groups had brought back. Some would be eating trapped rabbits and some would be eating fresh fish from the lake. Salted fish and much of the meat that was brought back would be left to dry or store for the winter, which was most definitely coming. There was a definitive chill in the air, which even the furs from Cavaris' tent and the fire in the centre did not dispel.

Do you know of the Fire Wars?

Miska shrugged. He crawled over to sit on the furs opposite Cavaris so that they could look each other in the eye. To his surprise, the bear came and sat behind him, his noble bulk providing a comforting warmth that Miska did not even know he had been missing. "Everyone knows the Fire Wars," Miska said. "They are the only thing where magic and dragons and elves and legends exist that is considered history by most people. It is thought to be the time of the gods. I don't know how much of it is real, but even Ravenna acknowledges that it happened."

I was there when the Fire Wars began. No one thought it would be as devastating as it was. Cavaris looked at Miska, his eyes brimmed with emotion. The claws that tipped Cavaris' fingers seemed to lengthen in the dying light in the crackling fire. Cavaris let out a dry chuckle. *Imagine the most powerful things in your nightmares. Then imagine three of them. A whole race of them. Two races. No one really remembers what started it all, just the one day the dragons were at war with the elves. The humans were divided, though most fought on the side of the dragons. Every day, more blood than you can possibly imagine was shed so that it saturated the ground with deaths and magic. Though the dragons were few, each one of us was able to devastate a whole company, even a whole army.*

Cavaris curled his fingers, staring at the claws that appeared there. *I, personally, tore apart thousands of people with my bare claws. It was a bloodied time and a terrible blight upon this land. The aftermath was what set most of modern times on its course. If the Fire Wars hadn't happened, I have a feeling that the world would be far more advanced and enlightened than it currently is.*

"But... I do not understand. Why will you not get involved now? You could stop further bloodshed." Miska was looking directly at Cavaris, and he nearly missed the way the light seemed to dim just a touch around his face. It was gone a second later, but Miska had noticed. And he was afraid.

Do you know what happened to the dragons? Cavaris asked. He waved a hand and the fire seemed to leap higher into the air, the flames taking on shapes that they should not have done. There were dragons, far more dangerous looking than Cavaris had been in the field that day. Some were large, with wings that stretched as wide as the tent. Others were serpentine, weaving their lengths through the air with ease. Cavaris waved his hand again and the dragons vanished, leaving just flames—boring, safe, warm—in their place.

"Surely they didn't die in the wars," Miska said. The bear

rumbled behind him in agreement, it seemed. Dragons were far too powerful for that.

They...slept. They were so tired by the expenditure of magic fighting and battles that should never have happened. Our leader decided that perhaps we were too much for the world as it was. Or that the world was too much for us. So, they slept. Not all; myself and two others remained awake in the thousand cycles that have lapsed since then. I do not know what happened to them. History has not been kind to the names of dragons, and finding out information is as elusive as the legends that they became. The rest, I assume are still asleep, waiting for the world to be a kinder place. Myself? I endured through the history of humankind. I saw wars. I saw revolutions. I saw uprisings. I saw brother killing brother, sister murdering sister, more blood than even I could have thought possible after the destruction of the Fire Wars. No matter what guidance I gave, the blood still spilled on the ground. That, young human, is my legacy. I am tired of war. I am tired of death. So I swore I would not get involved anymore in human affairs, unless a true sorcerer walked the earth again. I thought it impossible. I thought myself safe. Just goes to show that even the old can be fools.

Cavaris spoke no more that evening. Miska could see that he had retreated too far into himself and that it would take rest to return from the history that he was living over and over inside his mind. A thousand cycles. It was impossible, but then everything that Miska had thought impossible seemed to be coming true. And Cavaris just sat there, living legend, history incarnate, lost.

Miska was no longer hungry. He no longer thought about getting up and going to fetch food from the village of Rygirfel so that he and Cavaris and the bear could eat. His mind was on the past, something that had only been told to him in whispered stories of warning regarding where the world could go wrong. He wanted to just wrap the furs around him and sink into the darkness. He couldn't, though. He had to prepare to fight a war.

He had to save his people. Cavaris may not have wished to do so, but Miska knew that he, himself, had no other option. Lenore was counting on him. Ravenna's people would be destroyed if he did not lend his hand. Miska had lingered too long already, waiting for the world to happen to him. Maybe that was why the magic came just as it did. A sign that he needed to act.

The bear rumbled behind him again, this time the meaning very clear. The bear, at least, was hungry, no matter what Miska's own feelings were on the matter. He sighed, then nodded. He rose from the furs and pointed at the bear. "You stay here," he said. "We don't want to scare anybody. When I come back, I'll have food. And maybe a name for you."

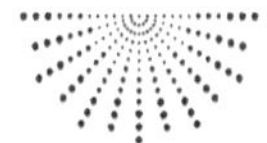

CHAPTER TWELVE

*R*avenna remembered climbing these cliffs three moons before. Tacitus had just died, and it was her duty as his legacy to carry his body to lay beneath the sky. It was ritual amongst the sylphs for the body of the dead to look up at the sky until its bones had been picked clean by the birds and other wildlife. It was a holdover from some long lost time and belief that the sylphs soul could not be freed if this was not done. Ravenna had still been weak from her journey back from the mainland. The scars across her chest had stretched painfully, and her shoulders did not well bear the weight of Tacitus' body. But she had carried him.

And now she was returned. Kratos walked beside her, saying nothing. There was nothing to say. Tacitus had started wasting away the moment that Ravenna had been taken from Shinalea. Kratos had tried to rationalise the disease, called it some wasting sickness. He had said that Tacitus' body was destroying itself from the inside out. She had been gone for a season, and when she returned, her heart-father was dying. He had not known her when she returned, though she may have looked the same. There was too much between them for the easy understanding that had so far graced their relationship.

Tacitus had died, wasted away, without Ravenna at his side. She had been too busy trying to convince the High Council that her war with Davorin was necessary. Well, they had believed her. And Tacitus had died.

Now, the mourning period was over and it was time to take Tacitus' bones from aeries in which they lay and place them in the vaults beneath the Stone Tower. It was time for Ravenna to accept that part of her life was over. She'd known it for some time now. But it was somehow harder to acknowledge it in person.

"What do you think Tacitus would have thought of war?" Ravenna asked as she slowed her pace so that Kratos could easily keep up. The older sylph panted a little, his impressive girth not helping the climb. He could have easily flown up there and waited for her, but it was a kindness to her for him to walk.

"Tacitus…would have understood, eventually. He was a rational sylph through and through. He was devoted to our way of life, to the reading of the histories and the analysis of the natural world. I think that coming to terms with the realities of humans and the necessity of war would have been difficult for him. He would have understood, if you had explained to him." Kratos' wings stretched a little bit as he hopped from rock to rock. It was not far now.

"You know it's all my fault," Ravenna said. "This whole situation, everything that we have done to prepare for war, the sacrifices of our society, it's all my fault."

"I would not say that," Kratos said. He smiled gently at Ravenna. She looked back at him, her face impassive stone. "You are leading our people through a necessary time of change. We know nothing of war. You do."

Ravenna shook her head. Her black hair was unbound, as was tradition when dealing with the dead. It flew about her face in an unfamiliar touch. She brushed it back in annoyance. Just over this ridge now, lay Tacitus' body. Or what was left of it. "No, I mean we would not even be in this situation if it were not for me."

Kratos stared at her blankly, obviously confused by this confession. "I do not understand. How could you be responsible for the actions of humans?"

"The day I went missing, there were humans on the island. I should have warned Tacitus, or anybody. But I was too caught up in my own curiosity. I was wanting to understand, to see if they were anything like the histories or the legends that were whispered to us as children. I soon discovered I was right. No, you say, that cannot possibly be the cause of all of our current woes. Of course you were taken. But you returned." Ravenna shook her head, twisting her lips into a wry, dangerous smile. "I was the one who told Davorin what I was. They kept calling me angel. I did not know what that meant, so I corrected them. And then Davorin discovered that there were more of us. There were journals of the sylph that had left Shinalea generations ago. I should have destroyed them rather than let them fall into his hands. But by the time I learned my error, it was too late. And so you see, Kratos, this whole situation is my fault."

The pair crested the ridge and saw the collection of bones strewn across the open rock. It was a high point on the island, devoid of all vegetation except for a few strong scrub grasses that managed to grow between the cracks in the rocks. No one came here except the birds. For the sylphs, it was only for the dead. Tacitus' bones had been thrown across the expanse of the rock as the birds and tried to tear his meat away from the bones. There was no neat pile to collect. Instead, Ravenna and Kratos did the ghastly job of picking up every single bone and scrap that was left of Tacitus, including the few feathers that remained. They placed them in a small, ceremonial box. There were no words said, no ritual to bring peace to Tacitus and whatever lay beyond. They just cleaned up the bones, closed the lid of the box, turned around and left.

Kratos was the first to break the silence. "Is that why you are so determined to do everything you can fight this war well?"

"People are going to die, Kratos," Ravenna said. "*My people* are going to die. If I stood by in exile, as is our law, and did nothing? I would be worse than Davorin. So yes, I came back for the express purpose of teaching everyone here how to fight, how to protect themselves, how to understand what threats lay beyond our waters. If that means sacrificing myself, working until I am wing-weary and my hands bleed from the effort, then so be it. It is my penance."

"Ravenna," Kratos sighed, the sound somehow amused and yet weary. Wisdom trying to teach youth how not to be foolish. "These things have a way of happening whether we like them to or not. If you were not taken, someone else would have been. And perhaps the consequences would be worse. I think out of all of us, you were the only one who could have been thrust into that depraved situation and come out on the other side stronger than you went in." Kratos turned to look at her, a gleam in his eyes. "Could you imagine Desarra doing what you did? Crispinus? Oh, I grant you, he would have fought. But he would not have won."

Ravenna tried to make Kratos' words sink in. She knew that he was trying to comfort her. She also knew that he was speaking what truth he had. But the fact still remained that she had brought war to the people of Shinalea. She wished she were very far away, laying in Miska's arms with her wings stretched out and peace in her mind. She wished none of this had ever happened. She wished she had not had to return here.

The walk to the Stone Tower was as quiet as the collection of the bones. They were met by others of the Intellecti, who took the ceremonial box and carried it away to the vaults beneath the tower. Kratos clapped his hand on Ravenna's shoulder, smiling. "Tacitus would have said the exact same thing. He would also have said that it is too late to go back and change things now. Do what you must, but it is *not* your fault."

Kratos turned and flapped his wings twice, leaping clumsily into the air. He was gone a moment later.

Ravenna shook her head as she looked after Kratos. He had not been there. He did not understand. Perhaps she did not understand. She did not know why she was thinking about all of this right now. The fault had been hers since the beginning. She had lived with this burden for moons. Perhaps it was to do with the final rights for Tacitus. Ravenna wondered idly how it was that humans went about grieving. They had their gods to comfort them, their Watcher. Did it give them comfort to think of these beings in regards to the dead? What sort of rituals did they have? Did they feel the grief as acutely as she did, in the depths of the darkness where she hid her emotions?

"Ravenna," Crispinus said, alighting beside her in a graceful gesture that was entirely different from what Kratos displayed a moment ago. "Desarra gave me the jewels."

"I imagine she was not terribly happy about that," Ravenna said. She stretched her wings, as though she could taste the breeze that slipped through the trees. Like Crispin. Instead, all she felt was her feathers move slightly.

Crispin shook his head. "I had to...explain the situation to her. She was not pleased. There was nothing else to be done."

Ravenna nodded. Those jewels were a legacy in a place that did not value tradition much. They were a symbol of status, one of the few things that the Chosen Queen had full rights over and could do with as she wished. Desarra would know their value and would not give them up lightly. "What did she demand in return?"

Crispin started, looking at Ravenna with wide eyes that flashed with amber in a rare show of fear. "How did you...?"

"Desarra and I may not have spent all that much time

together during our formative cycles," Ravenna said with a quiet, if regretful, smile, "but we knew enough of each other to understand. She knew I had no interest in this sort of a life. I knew she had every interest in it. She would not give those jewels up for nothing. So what did she want?"

Crispin shuffled his feet on the stone beneath the moss. His leather shoes were wearing thin from all the training that they had been doing. That would have to be another thing to remedy. The weather had started to change, enough so that Crispin covered his dark arms with a long woven shirt, still very much in the billowing styles of Shinalea, but warmer. It was made more for practicality than fashion, which did surprise Ravenna. She had always assumed he was more like Desarra in that regard. After all, they were mates. Though, Ravenna was beginning to understand that her general was something rather different from her sister. She did not yet fully comprehend the difference, but it was there.

"She wishes to be on the battlefield when we go to war." Crispin spoke the words in a breath, barely loud enough for Ravenna to hear. She took in a lungful of air through her nose, held it, and released it slowly. She noted the songbirds winging their way through the air, preparing for their migration for the winter. How interesting that life seemed to keep moving even as the world was falling out from beneath her feet, and her unable to fly.

"Ah," Ravenna said simply. "Is that all?"

"Surely you cannot be thinking of allowing this," Crispin snapped. His wings flared wide, an overt display of his anger. Ravenna had thought she had instilled more control in her trainees, but very few of them were mated. Or perhaps this was all for show, a means of hiding the obvious fear that Crispin so desperately despised. "Desarra should go nowhere near the battlefield."

"Are you going to stop her?" Ravenna shook her head. She

reached back and started braiding her hair into its long tail, preparing for the flight that would come as soon as she had dealt with this conversation. She hoped Itonus and Brianna would be ready. They would have to leave before nightfall. Ravenna turned Crispin who was staring at her like she had sprouted another head, or perhaps a pair of wings that would actually carry her in flight. "You are her mate. You should understand better than anyone. If that's not enough of an explanation, then I ask you this: would you give orders to your Chosen Queen? Of course Desarra wants to be on the battlefield. What sort of queen does not lead her people to battle? If you do not accept that, then at least you should understand that she knows where the power in our society will fall these next few moons. My sister is not stupid."

Crispin recoiled as though Ravenna had struck him. He straightened his shoulders, puffing out his chest like some imposing owl. The snarl on his lips and the bite in his tongue only made Ravenna raise a single eyebrow. She had lost the ability to be intimidated a long time ago.

"You insult me. Do you think I know nothing of my mate? I know precisely what it is that most sylphs see when they look at Desarra. They see a beautiful, vain female who has all of the social graces that one could possibly want, who could be at home in any sort of situation, but who has no real place or power or strength. All that changed when she became the Chosen Queen. She has real power now, and people look up to her, admire her. But they still see that same visage. Desarra is much, much more than that. If only people would stop underestimating her."

"Then why is it that you do not want her there?" Ravenna pretended to dust away debris from her tunic. She lifted only her eyes to look at Crispin, the ice there a little amused.

Crispin staggered, his balance overcome. With a roar, he lunged at Ravenna, his hands outstretched into curled claws, his wings ready with the Dalketh. He might have been a threat to her if she had not trained in the Dalketh for cycles longer than him, and if she had not been taught to fight for her life in the Slave Pits. She let him get close, close enough to see right into her eyes. Then, with a move that she had been taught by humans, treacherous as they were, Ravenna lashed out with her hand and struck Crispin centre-chest. Crispin gasped, the sort of sound that you heard when a body was desperate to get their breath. He fell to the side, wings wrapping close around him for protection as well as privacy. A moment later, he looked up, hands braced on his knees as he tried to catch his breath.

"Gather Itonus and Brianna. As soon as they are gathered, we will leave. Be prepared. It will be a long flight."

"Perhaps Desarra was right," Crispin said after he had caught his breath. He straightened and looked at Ravenna with some sort of pity. But that could not be right. Why in the world would Crispin pity her? "You are perfect to lead our armies."

Crispin leapt into the air as though he had never been struck at all. Ravenna waited exactly where she was, a line drawn in the skin between her brows the only indication that she had heard what Crispin said. She swallowed and looked up at the sky, noting that the rays of sun had turned it deep blood red.

This was the last day of Tacitus' burial. Ravenna should be meditating on her lost heart-father. She should be in her room, weeping as though her loss was the greatest one she had ever endured. Before she had been taken by the humans, she would have done. Tacitus had been her whole world. Now he was just a symbol of the pain she carried with her always. Instead, she would be returning to the place that had put her in chains, hoping to barter weapons from them. Ravenna would hate herself, too, if she had the capacity for the depth of emotion that required. These days though, she teetered on the edge of the wing-weariness, hiding it just enough so that people thought her cold rather than empty.

Crispin returned barely ten minutes later, Itonus and Brianna close behind him. Itonus carried a parcel in his arms that looked nothing like the jewels that Ravenna knew were in the sack slung across Crispin's chest. Itonus held them up to her, a smirk crossing his features. "Our revered general said that you would not be prepared for flying. So I brought these."

Ravenna stepped past Crispin, who would not meet her gaze. Brianna yawned, a quiet smile in the motion. Ravenna picked up the parcel and unwound the string. She held up a jacket, lined with what looked to be rabbit fur. There were tight breeches as well, lined with the same material. Ravenna looked at Itonus in question.

"You would never have had to learn this," Itonus said, not unkindly, "but it gets rather cold when you're flying. Especially when you fly above the clouds, as we will need to do when we cross the human lands. It's the fastest way to travel. And, we wouldn't want to get spotted by some overeager sentry."

"Thank you," Ravenna said. Brianna helped lace the jacket over her wings. The garment felt thick and constricting. Ravenna's swords in their sheaths were almost too tight to fit, but she was loath to give them up. She shifted her shoulders and flapped her wings a few times, trying to better the fit. Itonus made a face.

"Flying leathers do not suit you," he said with a smirk. Ravenna wanted to cuff him over the head. It would be a playful move, perhaps, but she had a feeling that it would be too out of character and he would not understand. Instead, she took off her thin leather boots and pulled on the breeches over her own thin pair. These fit better, but were still awkward.

"They will do," Crispin said sharply. He did not wait for a response. He just beat his wings and surged into the air. Itonus and Brianna looked at Ravenna, unspoken questions in their eyes. She did not answer. A moment later, Brianna followed Crispin, leaving Itonus to scoop Ravenna up into his arms. It was not the most comfortable thing, and Ravenna imagined that after an hour or so of this, Itonus would get more than a little tired. She hoped he did not drop her in the ocean between Shinalea and the desert.

* * *

As expected, Itonus' arms began to tighten just ever so slightly around Ravenna's as they crossed the ocean and into the desert. He was growing tired. They still had a good distance to go and Ravenna needed someone to be able to carry her back. Otherwise, she would have had Crispin or Brianna take her. No, Itonus needed to last a little bit longer. To distract him, Ravenna talked.

"Thank you for the flying leathers," she said. Itonus nodded, but said nothing. Ravenna took a breath. "I…do not know enough about the training of sylphs in flight. How much was involved when you were young?"

"After we learned the Dalketh? Very little. Oh, sure, we were given lessons almost daily in flight, just as we were in other subjects. But flight is something that is so natural to most sylphs that extensive lessons were not often required." Itonus smirked. "Of course, there were some like Crispinus who took flying far too seriously. Is it any wonder he ended up with the Lords of the Wind?"

"He does seem to have a natural affinity for flying," Ravenna said, surprisingly without any longing or bitterness. It had been a time when she would have given anything to be able to fly like that. Or to fly at all, for that matter. She shook her head, tightening her grip on the straps attached to the front of Itonus' leathers. He shifted her also in his arms, the muscles holding, but strained. "No, my curiosity was perhaps more practical. I wished to know how difficult it would be to train you in the art of flying with objects in your arms, or with armour, or with weapons."

Itonus let out a laugh that was more bark than humour. "I see," he said. "You just wanted to be sure I won't drop you."

"If you did, I'm sure Brianna would catch me." Ravenna watched the general in question, her wings wide enough to black out some of the early stars that had appeared in the sky.

"Not Crispin?" Itonus' question was obviously pointed. Ravenna stifled the urge to roll her eyes. She should not encourage him. But, truth was, he was one of the few things that made the emptiness less these days. She would never love him, nor seek that sort of relationship from lust; her heart belonged to Miska, who she could not even acknowledge existed. But it was nice not to be invisible.

"Crispin's loyalties lie closer to Desarra's than they do mine. So when I question the way of things in a manner that our Chosen Queen would not approve of, then I am often the focus of his anger as opposed to his superior. Not to mention, he was the bane of my childhood, and I think I might have been the bane of his."

The desert was passing swiftly beneath them. Ravenna kept an eye out for such things that she recognised, but it was difficult from this height and at this time of night. They were cutting through the thin air far up into the sky, the ground little more than indistinct blurs below. The rocks cast shadows that were far larger than they should have been. The blurs of plant life slowly disappeared, until there was nothing left. Somewhere to their right, almost too close for comfort, would be the Red Palace. How could a place be so much a part of a person that they longed for it, and yet hated the very thought of it? Ravenna checked the stars, the only constant when it came to navigation. They were nearly halfway there.

"Why is it that I never saw you as a child? Or even afterwards. Surely you were present as more than a figment of the imaginations of the Intellecti?" Itonus' voice was beginning to rasp. Ravenna waved her hand and signalled to the others, a sign for them to stop. Crispin banked. Brianna just dove.

"I was there, for those who wished to see me and acknowledge that I existed," Ravenna said. She felt Itonus flinch, but he said nothing. He too angled towards the ground, his wings beating to stop his flight. He let Ravenna down and she did not quite hear the relieved breath of air that he took as her weight left him. She had a feeling that it was perhaps more than just physical weight.

"Why are we stopping?" Crispin asked, anger still a little present in his voice. "There's nothing around here. Certainly not like you described."

"No," Ravenna agreed. "But I have learned something interesting. Why did you not tell me that no one trained you in the more difficult aspects of flight?"

"What are you talking about?" Brianna asked. Her feathers rustled as though they took personal offence at Ravenna's implication.

"How do you expect our army to fly with armour and weapons weighing them down? Let alone supplies? Itonus is, by all accounts, one of the strongest amongst us. And he cannot even carry me the distance to the Pits. If we cannot trust the army to carry itself to the battlefield, how can we trust them to fight for who knows how long it will take to win?"

The three other sylphs shuffled nervously. This was obviously something they had *not* considered. Perhaps once they knew how to fight, they assumed that everything else would fall into place. Ravenna wished beyond hope that would be the case. She knew better.

"We'll deal with it tomorrow," Ravenna said quietly. Brianna nodded and stepped forward, her arms open to take Ravenna's weight. Ravenna nodded also and stepped into her general's arms. With three sharp beats of her wings, Brianna took to the skies, Crispin and Itonus following swiftly behind. They went up where the air was thin, almost difficult to breathe. Ravenna was glad once again for the fur-lined leathers that she wore to keep her warm.

"It is difficult sometimes..." Brianna trailed off, as though she had not the words to explain what it was that she was thinking.

Ravenna took a deep breath and folded her wings tighter against her back. It felt unnatural to have them pinned where she could not move them. Itonus had let her wings dangle as he carried her. They had almost moved instinctively with the movements of the wind.

"I know most people hate me. I am not a pleasant taskmaster. I will not make the shadows go away. Perhaps it comes from my cycles as an Intellecti; we have an impossible need for the unvarnished facts. Or perhaps it is because I was taken by humans." Ravenna looked up at Brianna's face. She was not beautiful, but she was strong she did not hide behind herself the way Ravenna did. "Would it be better if I tried to relate to them more?"

Brianna tilted her wings, catching the air and moving forwards as if without effort or thought. "I don't think so. You do not hide behind artifice. You are precisely what it is that you are, and everyone knows that they can expect that of you. You are perhaps a little cruel. But they expect that of you, too. After all that you have been through, at our own hands and at the hands of humans, I think we would be more shocked if you did not bite."

Ravenna let silence fall between them. Instead, she studied the stars. She felt the way that the currents of the air moved around her. She watched as Brianna's feathers twisted and shifted to catch the air that was impossibly intangible and yet held them aloft. The older dreams of her childhood reared their ugly head. She had thought she had given up on these base, primal longings when she tore the feathers out of her own wings as a child.

"There." Ravenna pointed, seeing the pinpricks of light in an otherwise dark desert. It was not the Red Palace, though there was enough moisture in the air to be either of the two oases. With this place, though, there was an extra tang in the air. Something fetid and wrong. They had reached the Slave Markets. Brianna waggled her wings and the three dropped from the air as though the ground fell away beneath them. It was exhilarating.

They landed dramatically in the centre of town, right where Ravenna had been dragged into Jazer's den and sold for the first time. Being that it was night, there were fewer people about. They were all huddled up in the pleasure dens, or in the slave barracks. But there were some guards about. Enough that when the three sylphs landed, and Brianna let Ravenna down from her arms, the alarm was raised. Ravenna had known this would happen. It would be impossible for any of them to expect secrecy in their dealings with Jazer and the others at the slave pits. So, Ravenna decided to forgo it altogether. Best to control the situation, and the impression is that people would have of them. If she showed up leading three fully fledged sylphs, twin blades strapped to her back, and no sign of her former "master" Davorin, she would be a formidable force. Few would mess with her.

The guards ran, scrambling to find some sort of authority, or weapon, to use against these legends come to life. It had not been so long ago that Ravenna was here herself, and yet everyone seemed to have forgotten. Three of the guards remained standing before them, their swords drawn and pointed at them, as if they could do damage. Their eyes were wide, the whites flashing bright against the night. Ravenna could feel the tenseness in her companions' shoulders and wings. Surprisingly, it was Brianna who was the one to express her distaste.

"Are you certain about this?" She whispered in Ravenna's ear. Ravenna said nothing for a moment, waiting. Her eyes were fixed on the large, stone house that was Jazer's home. She was not disappointed. Her own night black wings flared at the site of the rotund woman who came close out of the shadows. Brianna took a step backwards. Crispin took a step forwards. Ravenna did not move.

Jazer was a grotesque figure, one made from the indulgences that came with power and few morals. She was wrapped in some ridiculous robe that had embroidered feathers on it. Jazer had apparently not forgotten Ravenna's time there. Even as she approached, a grin broke out, stretching her features like some fish long since out of water.

"My Angel!" Jazer said, stretching her arms wide. The rings on her fingers glinted in the torchlight. If she took another step forwards, she would be within wing-reach. Jazer wisely stayed where she was. "I knew you would return. Everyone told me that you were gone, lost by that fool who presumed to purchase you. But I knew. You were mine."

Ravenna tilted her head, expression impassive. "You presume just as much as Davorin did. If I am truly the angel that you say, then you could not have possibly expected me to remain in your captivity."

"And yet, here you are," Jazer said.

Crispin's wings rustled beside Ravenna. She knew that the other sylphs did not understand the humans. Their language was different enough that it would sound completely foreign to any but an Intellecti, and even Ravenna had had trouble at first. She knew if she did not acknowledge the other sylphs soon then she would lose control over the situation. It was enough that she had to return to this wretched place. This was a place of her nightmares, except they existed outside of her dreams. "I am here to trade."

Jazer's eyes widened and her smile seemed to grow inexorably. "So you brought these to take your place?"

Ravenna blinked slowly, looking at Jazer, then flicking her eyes to each of the guards that stood swords at the ready. "No," she said, voice languid as though she had no care in the world. She knew it would drive Jazer to fury. It would also make her companions tense. "I brought them to keep me from killing you."

"You would not kill me," Jazer said, as always, too full of her own importance. Perhaps here, amongst the slaves that she had so carefully cultivated, she had power. But in the rest of the world, she was nothing more than a parasite, easily quashed. "I saved you."

Ravenna did not think this next part through. She did not even hesitate or question. She just drew a blade from her back in her right hand, and thrust it forwards, right into Jazer's heart. Anger surged behind her eyes, turning them to flints of ice in the torchlight. The guards flinched and stepped back, already lost without their master, even though Jazer's body had not yet fallen to the ground. For once in her life amongst the humans, Ravenna was fulfilling her image as the Angel of Death. She pulled her blade out of Jazer and raised it into the air.

"I am going to war!" Ravenna cried. Her voice carried through the desert town without any protest. The humans there stared at her in horror, fear, and admiration. "You can either assist me, or stand in my way. Which will it be?"

One of the guards trembled hard enough that he dropped his sword. Ravenna took three steps forward so that she was a feather's length away from him. She leaned down and picked up the weapon in her left hand, then turned and handed it to Crispin. Ravenna turned back to the guard, raising her eyebrows in question. He swallowed, eyes wide. "W-we will do anything we can, Angel."

Ravenna smiled and nodded. She turned back to where her generals stood, Itonus between them. "You won't even have to use the jewels. Desarra will be pleased."

To her surprise, Crispin laughed. "I told her. I said that we were taking them with us only as a precaution, but that you would manage to make it so that we didn't need to use them at all. I was right."

Ravenna turned around and vomited into a patch of desert scrub-grass.

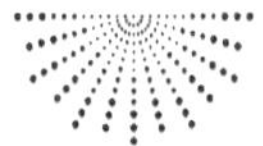

CHAPTER THIRTEEN

*R*avenna sat at the stool at the bar of the pleasure hall, Crispinus on the stool beside her. The hall had been cleared of humans except for the barkeep, who stayed well away from Ravenna and Crispin. Itonus and Brianna had been set to guard the outside, to wait for the humans to come and seek Ravenna. They would come, asking what it was precisely that she wanted. For now, she nursed the horrid sour wine that had been served, and hoped Crispin would not ask the question that she knew was coming.

"What was that?" Crispin asked, without art or artifice. Ravenna hunched her shoulders, her wings lifting to rise above her head so that they almost blocked her from view of Crispin. She had hoped that the question would be delayed by conversation. Her hopes had been, as always, dashed.

"They don't understand us," Ravenna said, delaying the inevitable. "Their language is a derivative of ours, a daughter language. It is very similar, but different enough that they will not be able to understand us when we speak. It took me a while to be able to understand them myself."

"That's good," Crispin said, taking a mouthful of the wine. He winced and set the flagon back onto the bar, his eyes flicking up to the barkeep who flinched back. Ravenna knew that Crispin's charcoal-ash skin and amber fire eyes would be more frightening to him than her own looks, which were almost human. Except for the wings. She had been the one to kill Jazer, though. She was the more dangerous. "But I should like to know the answer to my question."

Ravenna let out a slow breath through teeth, the sound loud in the otherwise silent place. "Would you believe me if I told you that I had never killed before?" She asked, the question barely a breath on her tongue. She did not look at Crispin, afraid to see the reaction. He sucked in a harsh breath, and that was reaction enough.

"What?" Crispin reached over and lifted Ravenna's chin, so that she was looking right at him. He stared at her, eyes searching desperately for some sign that this was a joke, a game. Ravenna kept her expression calm and cool and collected, as ever. There must have been something in her eyes though, because Crispin dropped his hand away as though he been struck.

Ravenna let out a harsh sound that could have been laughter, if you looked hard enough. "Everyone back home thinks that I am…a monster. Their monster, yes, but a monster nonetheless. Why else would I be better at fighting, better at strategising war, better at pointing at harsh truths that no one else wants to listen to? Don't deny it Crispin. I am not an idiot."

"You just seem so…I don't know what to say." Crispin ran a hand through his hair, shaking his head in disbelief. His wings fluttered a little, mirroring his dismay. "I just assumed that you had fought your way out to escape. I assume that you had killed."

Ravenna took another sip of the wine. It reminded her of the watered-down drink that she had taken back when she was a slave. At the end of her days of training, she would eat with the other slaves and drink their watered-down wine and hold conversations that almost felt like real companionship. Being back in this place was difficult enough. The wine was a comfort. "I was trained to fight by these slaves. Do you know when I first got here, I did not fight at all? I did not fight my capture, I did not fight my becoming a slave, nor did I even fight when I fell into the arena."

"Why? How did you get from *that* to *this*?"

Ravenna's wings flattened to her back. She curled a lip. "I fell. And I saw someone fighting a desert lion, a hopeless battle. I did something about it. And then I was trained and sold and then I found—" Ravenna swallowed down the words that she longed to say.

She could not tell anyone about Miska and Lenore, no matter how much she wanted to. She had painted a perfect picture of the demon people that needed to be stopped before they destroyed Shinalea. If she explained that she had felt comfortable among the humans, loved one of them even, she would be ostracised, a traitor and all would be lost. Then, Crispin lay a hand on her shoulder. It was warm, more contact than she had had for what felt like ages. It was not fighting or training or restraint. It was just a touch.

"Why did you come back?" Crispin asked, his words soft in case anyone listening could understand. "What is it that you're not telling me?"

Ravenna closed her eyes and tightened her grip on the wine in front of her. She could feel the wood creaking, but she did not loosen her grip. "As soon as I was taken, I knew exactly what would happen to me. I would never be allowed back on Shinalea. As one of our most ancient laws, I would have to be banished for leaving. Then, I found a place that was comfortable, that had people I could respect and who respected me."

"I know you don't like me, but believe this. I will not betray you." Crispin looked at her, brows drawn together so the lines showed around his eyes. For once in her life, Ravenna believed him. She decided that she would trust him, the enemy of her childhood.

"Not all humans are monsters." Ravenna waited, breath stuck in the back of her throat. Crispin nodded. He traced his fingers over some marking carved into the bar. He did not understand it, but Ravenna did, and the thought made her smile just a touch.

"Is that it?" The question was casual, almost as though the information were obvious.

Ravenna shook her head. One feather in, she might as well give the whole wing.

"When I was in the Red Desert, I made friends. Perhaps the first friends I have ever had in my entire life. I'm not blaming you, not anymore. I just want you to understand. Queen Lenore was the most generous person I've ever met. She gave freely and willingly of everything she had, so that her people might be happy and well. And I became one of her people. And then there was Miska..."

Crispin smiled. He snagged the flagon of wine from Ravenna's hands and finished it off in a single gulp. It was a childish thing to do, like something a brother would have done if you were teasing her. Ravenna did not understand, but she thought she was beginning to. "Miska?" Crispin asked, flashing a smirk in her direction.

Ravenna whacked him in the arm with her wing. "No need to be rude," she said. Crispin laughed.

"I'm happy for you," he said after a moment. "I understand what it must've cost you to finally admit that, to me as well as to yourself. I know you cannot tell the others. I'm fairly certain of what would happen to you if you did. But I'm happy for you all the same."

The smile faded from his face after a few seconds and he turned to her. The barkeep coughed nervously and took another step back. Ravenna said nothing to reassure him. Fear was her trade at this point, she might as well milk it for all it was worth. "If you have never killed before—and I now understand why—why did you kill her?"

Now, Ravenna did smile, though it was something dark and dangerous. "I had hoped to never see her again. She was the one who took me into this life, even if she was not the one who captured me. I have never seen anyone so reviled and so pleased with that opinion. She would have happily lorded herself over me, like some bird of prey lords over a pigeon. I could not kill her before, as I did not have the means. I could kill her now. Part of me says it was the right thing to do. The rest of me knows that I will never be the same. But now, I can at least be the monster that the sylphs expect."

"You may be a monster to them, but I know better."

Ravenna resisted the urge to roll her eyes.

The commotion at the entrance to the pleasure hall had both Ravenna and Crispin leaping off of the stools and into a fighting stance, ready for just about anything. Ravenna did not doubt that there would be consequences to her having killed Jazer. She just thought that it would perhaps take a little longer. Instead, Itonus and Brianna marched into the bar, wings flared. Itonus wore a scowl to match his surly bad mood, and Brianna is simply looked a little confused.

"These two…humans would not stop trying to push their way in. They kept saying your name, as if it was some magical key." Brianna jerked home at two humans who walked in behind her. One was tall and broad, enough so that he could rival Itonus. The other room was smaller, but moved on the balls of his feet as though he could jump into battle at any moment. Ravenna recognised the two immediately.

She surged forward, wings wide. Itonus and Brianna flinched, ready to leap to her aid at any moment. Instead, Ravenna did something that seemed exclusively human. She launched herself into the wide arms of the taller human. He laughed and wrapped his arms around her, careful of her wings. "You came back."

"Tekko," Ravenna said. She extracted herself from the humans arms. She had forgotten how much comfort there was in a hug. Ravenna wanted to stay there for as long as she could manage. Instead, she pulled back so she was standing between Itonus and Brianna. They looked at her, confused and slightly aghast. Crispin strode up behind Ravenna and clapped her on the shoulder.

"Your human allies. The ones who trained you to fight. They hardly look a threat." Crispin's words covered for Ravenna's lapse. Itonus and Brianna still bristled, but they would accept Ravenna's word now. Well, Brianna would. Itonus looked especially put out.

"I never believed that there would be more of you," Radim said. He took a tentative step forward, almost as if expecting Ravenna to hug him as well. Instead, she graced him with a pleasant smile, one reserved for her friends.

"What is he saying?" Itonus said. Ravenna sighed.

She gestured to one of the tables, indication enough to all parties involved they should sit and talk. "Crispin, Itonus, Brianna, I should like to introduce you to Radim and Tekko. These were the two slaves that taught me to fight. They will be the ones to help us get what we need. I will translate as best I can." Ravenna then turned to Tekko and Radim, who were looking at her with wide eyes. Tekko had his hand wrapped around the bronzed leaf shaped blade that he had often carried in the Pits. Ravenna raised her eyebrows. "I'm surprised they let you walk around armed."

"You killed Jazer," Tekko said. "Things change quickly once the head of the snake is gone."

"We never expected to see you again. And as much as I would like to think that you came around and saved us just for us, because you care, somehow I don't think it is true." Radim waved over the barkeep, who supplied them all with more wine before retreating to the other end of the room so that he could not hear. "Wherever you were, Ravenna, you should have stayed there. Times have become dangerous. Jazer was the least of our problems. Though, I think perhaps you knew that."

"I was there just before Davorin launched his campaign. I returned to my people and heard nothing of what happened afterwards." Ravenna took a desperate swallow of wine. She had no reason to believe that these two would know the answer to what she wanted, but what else could she do? She'd had no news of the human world since returning to Shinalea. She had to know if her fears were correct, even though the High Council had said that they had sent a scout to confirm her story. "Tell me."

Tekko exchanged a glance with Radim, who nodded. "Lord Davorin is now the King Consort to the Red Queen. There are rumours that there was a violent coup, and that Queen Lenore agreed to marry Lord Davorin to save her people. But nothing has been confirmed. All we know is that the Salusian Empire stands on both sides of No Man's Land. It is a dangerous position to be in."

Ravenna nodded. Itonus elbowed her in the side, obviously desperate for information. "They are giving me information on the current state of the human world. I will tell you everything later." Ravenna shrugged an apology to the humans. "Do you know why we are here?" She asked quietly.

"I think so," Tekko said. "Rumours of angels and Storm-bringers are not easy things to quell these uncertain times. Lord Davorin has promised that he will bring an army of angels to bear on any who stand in the way of the blessed Salusian Empire. Southron is perhaps the only that stands apart, and they are...not official enemies. Some of these smaller kingdoms have chosen to stand with Southron, but there is very little in the way of resistance. A few fled to the Iron Mountains. And even fewer made it."

"We stand against them," Ravenna said, "whatever his rumours tell you. But we are of limited resources. And we haven't much time. We need weapons. Enough to outfit two thousand winged beings."

Tekko's brow furrowed deeply. Radim gaped, then swallowed, a mixture of fear and awe crossing his face. "It seems so many. When you appeared, I never would have imagined that any of this was real at all. And now there are two thousand of you preparing to fight. And yet, it is a small number in comparison to what Davorin will throw at you. I know it is what you have, what hope you bring, but I weep for us all."

* * *

RAVENNA DID a quick translation of the information that was most relevant—she left out all of her history with Radim and Tekko as well as the news regarding Queen Lenore. Crispin raised his brows a bit, not really believing that she was telling them everything. Itonus and Brianna still shifted uncomfortably.

"These humans can help us?" Brianna asked. She swallowed nervously, glancing between Radim and Tekko and their leaf shaped blades. Ravenna could have told her that the bronze blades were hardly a match for her own steel, or that the sylph means of Dalketh could protect her well enough, but she did not. Radim and Tekko were both dangerous enough to cause serious damage to her sylphs' ego. They did not trust the humans to help them. Understandable, considering that the humans were also their enemies. But some trust needed to be extended. Ravenna was glad the sylphs did not understand the humans and vice versa. That was one advantage she had in manipulating the situation to best suit them all.

"They can," Ravenna said. She looked at Tekko. "I don't know who to talk with to get weapons and armour that we need, now that Jazer is dead."

"You didn't quite think that through, did you?" Tekko asked. He was not accusing her, considering the light smile. Ravenna felt the accusation all the same. Her stomach roiled, sour wine being the only thing left in it after her display earlier. She swallowed and wished for water. "With Jazer's death, this place will become unstable very quickly. Someone needs to be in control, even if that is a former slave. Otherwise, we will fall to the Empire."

"Do you suggest yourself?" Ravenna asked. Tekko shrugged. Radim, surprisingly, nodded vigorously.

"Tekko is the best leader we would have. He is the only one amongst the slaves that actually knows what it means. The others are brutes, bred for fighting and nothing else, or terrified house slaves. After you left, Jazer went through rather a few of the best. Tekko and I only managed to stay alive because we kept our heads very far down. Will you support him?"

"Radim," Tekko said, warning.

Ravenna held up her hand for silence.

"What do you mean?" She asked. Tekko winced. Ravenna's wings flared ever so slightly, causing the other three sylphs to react in kind. Crispin reached for the small hunting knife that he wore at his belt. It was the only weapon he had, but it would be dangerous enough.

"Enough, Crispin. I know what I'm doing. I know it is difficult that you do not understand, but you have to trust me." Ravenna looked at all of her companions, locking gazes with them until each lowered their eyes. She turned her attention back to Radim.

"You are still legends here. Even you alone would have been enough to change the world. But you leading three others? Your support will make sure that there are no questions about who takes over after Jazer's death. The fact that you killed her is going to be considered a symbol, a message from the gods that she was unfit or needed punishment."

Ravenna sighed, twisting her fingers into the braid of hair that hung over her shoulder. She shook her head. "I had forgotten the ridiculous superstitions that you have regarding us. Or at least, had forgotten the intensity with which you people believe them."

Radim shrugged. "We humans are a superstitious bunch. You might as well use that to your advantage. Support Tekko. Stand by his side as he declares his leadership. You don't even have to say anything. Please?"

"If I do this—if *we* do this, you will get us the weapons and armour and supplies that we need?" Ravenna asked. She no longer had any patience for this foray into the human world. As much as she had affection for these two, she had to get back to Shinalea. She was not meant for false messages from gods that she was not even sure existed. She had a war to prepare for. "And one other thing. We cannot spy in the human world. We are too conspicuous."

"Don't worry," Tekko said with a smile. "We will help you. And when the time comes, we will stand against Davorin. You are not as alone as you think."

Ravenna inclined her head. "Then we will support you. Make it quick. we have to be back by mid-afternoon.

Tekko nodded. Radim laughed.

Ravenna explained the situation to the three sylphs, ignoring their indignant looks and protests. At least Crispin appreciated the sense of humour. Itonus and Brianna did not like standing beside Tekko as he declared his intent to lead the people of that desolate place. Crispin remained completely silent and completely still, the most intimidating of them all. Well, excepting perhaps Ravenna, who stood by Tekko's right hand, the hilts of her blades visible above her head, her black wings blending into the night. The angel of death had killed Jazer and now stood by Tekko. As expected, there were no questions and no resistance. The sylphs were in the air an hour later.

"I am not sure that Itonus appreciated the situation," Crispin said as he held Ravenna in his arms. She snorted, shaking her head.

"I think you have missed your calling as a master of understatement," she said. Ravenna clicked her tongue against the roof of her mouth and sighed. "I am going to have to take some time to explain things to him. He is not one for subtlety."

"Noticed that, did you?" Crispin chuckled, then sighed. His wing beats were steady, slow. He was using the cool air over the desert to fuel his speed, though they were flying lower than Ravenna would have thought advisable, given their need for speed. The thinner air up higher was easier to pass through. "Itonus is a good sylph. He cares deeply, if not loudly. And he does not understand why we are allying ourselves with these humans, even if it is just for weapons. I did not understand, not until you explained your particular relationship with these humans to me. This war has set us up as something other than these humans. They believe us to be, what was it you said, messengers of the gods? It is a dangerous power, that influence. I know that this Lord Davorin knows the truth and wishes to seek us out for his own purposes. It is why we are preparing to fight after all. But I cannot help but wonder what will happen afterwards, when the sylphs understand precisely what it is that the humans think of us. How many will act benevolently, as you have done?"

"I wouldn't call my actions benevolent," Ravenna said. "I put Tekko into power because I know him. I can trust him far enough for him to be useful. But it was not benevolent thought that had me supporting him."

Crispin was silent. He flew for perhaps another ten minutes, watching the desert landscape beneath them. Brianna and

Itonus flew beside them, slightly above or slightly below so that they would not interfere in each other's flight patterns. There was a lone human far below, leading some herd animal to a tiny spring of water. Ravenna willed the human not to look up and was successful. The three sylphs passed unnoticed. She had not considered the idea that someone might take advantage of the humans' preoccupation with the legendary aspects of sylphs. It was a dangerous thought, but not one that she could address now. There were too many other things to be doing, not the least of which was training the sylphs in gathering reliable intelligence about the movements of Lord Davorin.

"When we get back," Ravenna said, her words barely audible above the wind. She could tell that Crispin was tiring and that he would have to exchange her weight with someone else before too very long. "When we get back, please don't treat me like the monster that everyone sees. Don't look at me with dismay or fear. I do what I must for the sake of our people. But I think I have been too much alone."

"Everything has changed, Ravenna. If it matters to you that much, I will be sure to look at you the way I look at the others." Crispin looked at her, and Ravenna saw none of the fear or disgust in his eyes that she would have seen earlier. She nodded, thankful. "You know, Itonus would be happy to be your lover."

Ravenna spluttered. "Where did this come from? Especially after what I told you earlier?"

Crispin looked at her in slight astonishment. "Taking a lover does not mean that you love Miska any less. Many sylphs—"

"I'm fully aware of our society's practices involving lovers. As are you, I would imagine, considering that you chose to take Desarra as a mate instead of just lover as many do. Miska, no matter that he is human and the traditions are different, is my mate. I would not dishonour him by taking a lover. Besides, what makes you think Itonus would be happy with such an arrangement?"

"Itonus has no need for false pretences. I am certain that he has already sired one or two children. He has no desire to take a mate, and he admires you. Is that not enough?"

Ravenna shook her head. "Not for me." And that was the end of it. Her heart longed for Miska, longed for the news that had not come from Tekko's report. What would they know of a servant? He was insignificant and unimportant to most people. No one would care where he was when Davorin invaded. Ravenna closed her eyes and prayed to the human gods with all her might that Miska was still alive and had survived the coup. Even if his fate was as dismal as Lenore's.

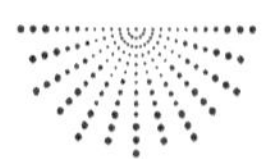

CHAPTER FOURTEEN

Winter was solidly upon the desert now. Lenore knew that the Iron Mountains would be covered in snow. The desert itself was bitingly cold, the moisture from the oasis only making everything that much worse. She hadn't remembered a winter this cold for a long time. Not that she got out much to experience it, but occasionally she would open the large windows in her chambers that led out to the garden so that she might feel the cold just as much as her people.

Davorin had been as undecipherable and insufferable as ever. He had managed his new domain with the practiced hand of one who was used to such fine detailed work. Lenore tried to sneak into the library as often as she could, so that she might see what it was that was happening to her kingdom, but rarely did Davorin leave the papers about. Actually, she rarely saw her husband at all. He was too busy dealing with affairs of state, or dealing with that monster Dagan. She knew from whispers amongst the palace staff that he was training, participating in some strange magic with the demon. All Lenore knew was that when he emerged from the training quarters, his eyes were feverish and red and he rarely spoke sense.

Blodwen, at least, had been more pleasant to Lenore after witnessing Davorin's disdainful cruelty. The lady Seraphina and her husband had left back to Southron nearly a moon before. Lenore was left much alone, a useless ornament in a place that she had once ruled.

"You must drink something," Blodwen said, handing Lenore a steaming cup of bitter tea. Lenore wrinkled her nose and turned away.

"I will happily drink something, but not that." Lenore rose and walked over to the windows. The plants in the garden were dead, few of them strong enough to withstand a freezing desert winter. They would grow again in the spring, she hoped. She tightened the long jacket around her and turned back to her servant. Blodwen looked at her with concern in her eyes. She had still not changed from her Salusian clothes to the styles of the desert, but now at least it made sense. Even some of the other people in the palace had started adopting the warmer style come all the way from the Salusian Empire. Davorin had been pleased when Lenore wore Salusian dresses, and his attentions had been visibly less angry for days following. Now, Lenore was left quite alone.

"My mama gave me this tea special when I came here. She had a feeling I'd be using it for you. It's a special blend, made for women who—"

Lenore rounded on Blodwen, a wry smile making her regal beauty that much more apparent. "I cannot tell you how many times I have heard of a 'special blend'. Warra knows well enough what is necessary for me." Blodwen stepped forward, the tea left behind, thank goodness. She placed a hand on Lenore's stomach, just barely starting to show signs of her condition. The girl smiled.

"I know that this isn't what you wanted. I know that you wouldn't have married Lord Davorin if you'd had proper choice about the matter. I see now that the truth of him is not what I had thought—"

"Blodwen you don't have to—" Lenore started, but Blodwen shook her head.

"Yes, I do. You have taught me what it means to be a true ruler. To care for people who were always less in the Empire. You taught me that there is more than status and perception and conquering. And I just wanted to say thank you. I know that you have been pushed out, that you are only kept around as long as this child is…As long as this child needs you. I will help you, whatever you need." Blodwen lifted her hands and took a step back, perhaps finally realising what liberty she had taken in getting so close to Lenore.

Lenore chuckled, the sound a far cry from a true laugh, but as close as she could manage these days. "This is the fate meted out to me by The One Who Watches. There is not much I can do but learn what lessons must be learned."

"You seem so much calmer than I would have expected," Blodwen said. She turned and straightened a small piece of jewellery on Lenore's side table. Lenore frowned.

"You think I'm not angry? This was *my* kingdom. Now it is only mine in name. Every day, I am angry enough that I could throttle Davorin. But it would do no good. And now I carry his child. I wish to be angry about that, too. I want my blood to boil. I want to set fire in my belly and I want to tear him down, piece by piece. But I cannot. This child is mine, also, and I will do whatever it takes to make sure that it has a good life. It is the only hope I have left." Lenore sat on her bed, fingers running through the fibres of the blanket that she had been weaving for her unborn child. It was pretty much all she had to occupy her time these days, so she wove. Ironic that she was doing so now, when she had hated learning how to do so as a child.

Blodwen looked as though she wished to answer, but the

noise stopped both of them from saying things that should be left unsaid. The window, closed against the bitter cold, was opening. Blodwen reached for the hot tea, ready to pour it on whatever intruder was coming in. It was not Lord Davorin, as he only came in the door when he wanted something. It would not be one of his soldiers, who ignored Lenore as though she hardly existed. Lenore rose to her feet, ready to defend herself if necessary, but desperately hopeful that it was not necessary. Her hands clenched into fists at her side. With her life not difficult enough?

The person that fell into the room was so swathed in thick woven clothing and a hooded cloak that it was almost impossible to identify whether they were male or female. Blodwen let out a little shriek and raised the tea. The figure lifted its head and Lenore nearly fell over in shock.

"No! Blodwen, it's okay," Lenore said, rushing to the figure's side. What looked back at her was like a memory of the lifetime that it happened to someone else. Her face was rough, dried out and red with the cold. Her hair was short, cropped, and her smile infectious.

"You're still alive," she said, reaching a hand out to cup Lenore's face. "Some said you weren't. Some said you succumbed to that monster. But I knew better. I knew my Red Queen would not give in so easily."

"Vareis," Lenore said in a whisper. The old training master for her army. She had vanished when Davorin had taken over, and many had assumed her dead, burned on the pyre of unidentified bodies after the coup. "By the Watcher," Lenore said, her hands running over Vareis' shoulder, her hair, just to make sure that she was real. "I thought you were dead."

Vareis grinned and shuffled into an upright position. She leaned against the wall, breathing a bit raggedly. She watched as Blodwen closed the window. Lenore watched as well, wondering if she should state that Blodwen could be trusted. Here was proof of one thing that Davorin had not yet taken away; she did not want his spies in her household to do the job for him.

"I will say nothing," Blodwen said, kneeling beside Vareis. "I swear it."

Vareis glanced at Lenore. "Do you want to trust her?"

"We have little choice. She has already seen you. But I think she won't speak. If she does, then at least we will know who the traitor is." Lenore spoke without guile, staring straight at Blodwen as she spoke. The Salusian girl blanched and shook her head, ready to protest her innocence. Vareis raised a hand covered in dust and dirt.

"Fine. Trust her for now. She does not cooperate, I'll kill her myself." Vareis grinned wider, the expression almost feral. Lenore looked closer at her once trusted training master. She was wearing clothing that was warm, yes, but also ragged and obviously in need of a wash. Her hair was still cropped, but it looked as though it had been shorn with a knife as opposed to the clean style that was usual. And she wore at least three blades on her person. In short, Vareis was dirty, worn, and probably hungry. She looked more as though she had been through war than Lenore had.

"What happened to you?" Lenore asked, squeezing Vareis' hand.

"Too many things. When I knew what had happened, I wanted to run here as quickly as I could. Maybe I could have done something against the upstart whelp from that stupid Empire. Who did he think he was, taking that which did not belong to him and which did not need his assistance? But I was one person. If he and his mercenaries could take on the Red Palace and win? I knew that I alone could not help."

"He won because the armies of the Red Desert were scattered, as they usually are. No one would be stupid enough to attack the centre without first taking on the perimeter. And yet that is exactly what he did. I let the enemy walk straight into the centre of my kingdom and I'm still paying the price. I now have the demon and his monster living here, as my husband." Lenore took a shaking breath, the fire of her anger rising up. She counted to three to try and calm herself. It would do no help to her or her child.

Vareis nodded, knowingly. From anyone else, Lenore would have happily bitten their head off for the assumption and the arrogance. But with Vareis, she knew that the former training master understood. "I have not been idle these last six moons. You cannot think I vanished for nothing. Your people miss you. They do not wish to be part of this Empire. They wish for you."

"It is done," Lenore said. "I can do nothing to help them."

Vareis nodded, shrugged. "Perhaps. I think you can do more than you think. Surely you know that not all people the Empire conquers accept their new overlords quietly."

Blodwen gasped, the sound breaking through Lenore's anger like a splash of cold water. She sank onto her knees next to Vareis and put her hands inside her robes, ostensibly to keep warm. She tried her hardest to keep her hand away from her belly. She did not want to see the look of pity on Vareis' face when that secret came to light. "You're talking about resistance, rebellion," Blodwen said her words a whisper. She swallowed nervously, eyes darting around as though she expected people to be standing all around the room, listening.

"Yes," Vareis said. "Is it that difficult to believe for someone raised to believe that the Empire is all-powerful?"

Blodwen's hands trembled. She quickly hid them in the folds of her skirts. "There have been whispers of rebellions. But the Salusian Empire quells them before anyone can do more than whisper. The Emperor and Lord Davorin are good leaders. They worked to care for all of their people, to make sure that everyone lives with order and peace and that we do not starve. Rebellions are just people discontent, too hungry for bloodshed and too eager for death."

"Excitable, aren't you?" Vareis said. She coughed, the sound dry. Blodwen's manners won out, and she grabbed the tea that was meant for Lenore, handing it to the woman. Vareis drank it all before grimacing at the bitter taste. "Sheesh, even your tea is oppressive. Pah, you are young, you still believe in your Empire. Is it believed that it is better to be blindly obedient or to stand up for your principles, your morals, or your freedom? Does it matter if you starve if you have your freedom? Or would you rather go to bed with a full belly, knowing that everything that you stood for, everything that you believed, just vanished because you were now part of a different land?"

Lenore clicked her tongue at Vareis. "You are too weak for such eloquence. Blodwen, it is enough to know that the resistance is alive. Even before we became part of the Salusian Empire, the Red Desert was not deaf to the knowledge of the rebellions of the resistance in the Salusian Empire. There were just few enough of them to actually stand a chance. Right now though, Vareis needs food and water and a bath and rest. Please call for a tray."

Blodwen nodded and rose. She darted out of the room, calling for one of the other servants to bring the Queen a tray. Vareis turned to Lenore, squeezing her hand. "I am glad that you are not dead. Hope still remains. If we can but get you away, then we stand a chance."

Lenore closed her eyes and splayed her hand over her belly, fully aware of what Vareis would see. "I am afraid it is too late for me. If I left now, Davorin would come after me. Right now, the tensions are focused on building his army and finding the sylphs. Perhaps it is selfish of me to want to keep that attention away from my people, from myself, but it is all I have. I can trust that Ravenna knows how to take care of herself and her own people. So, I cannot leave."

Vareis closed her eyes, swallowing down a grimace. "No." She knocked her fist against the floor, hardly hard enough to do any damage to her. Vareis opened her eyes, fury and desperation plain. Lenore recognised the emotions as mirroring her own. "No. I come all this way, and... I won't fail now."

"Find a different way, Vareis," Lenore said. "I may hate its father, but I will not jeopardise this child."

Vareis bowed her head. "As you say, my Queen."

CHAPTER FIFTEEN

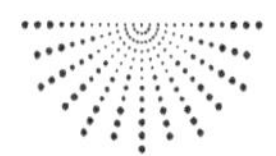

*R*avenna climbed the stairs, stretching her calves as she did so. It was not nearly as difficult to climb the stairs now as it used to be. Moons of training would do that. She had been running around Shinalea with the others under her command, teaching them Dalketh, practicing archery—that was something that Ravenna was not terribly good at, but Brianna and the entire Marauder company were becoming quite talented. Crispinus and Itonus were her best at flying and fighting; they had taken to guiding the others in the aerial techniques while Ravenna focused on groundwork. The first instalment of their weapons was due to be in within the next week. Hence, Ravenna's current trip up the Stone Stairs while her people were training. Someone needed to talk to Desarra and get permission to leave the island.

The guards outside Desarra's chambers seemed more tense than usual. They were cohorts of Ravenna's, assigned to guard duty while they were not training. After all, it would do no one any good if the soldiers were better trained than the guards. Ravenna recognised one of them as having been part of the former Chosen Queen's retinue.

"Thank goodness you are here, Wingsword. The Queen has been out of sorts. She has refused many summons by the High Council to discuss the current war plans." The guard shivered, as though the High Council's wrath would be directed at him. Ravenna tried not to laugh at the mental image of Strygis doing his best to terrify the guard.

"In future," Ravenna said with a gentle smile that she was surprised she felt, "should the Council wish to discuss the war plans, you would do well to direct them to me. As for Desarra, leave her to me. I will see what is wrong. You will not be punished."

The guards nodded eagerly. Ravenna knocked on Desarra's chamber door, though it was more a courtesy than a question. She pushed the door open, just in time to hear Desarra's snarled protest. "The Council can wait! I'm busy."

"I am not the Council," Ravenna said. She looked around the room, surprised at its state of disarray. The wide windows were shuttered, as though there had been a great storm. What little light there was came from a single candelabra on the wall. The neat cushions and table and chairs were all strewn about, as though someone had been performing Dalketh with little regard for order. Desarra lay on the floor, her wings stretched behind her, feathers in disarray. Her burnished gold hair was tangled. Her skin was blotchy with tears. And her eyes looked as though they had seen into the veil beyond and not yet returned.

Immediately, Ravenna was by Desarra's side. She did not care that they did not love one another as much as perhaps they should. She did not even care that they did not like each other. All she saw was that Desarra was in distress, and no one else was helping her. Ravenna lifted Desarra into a sitting position, leaning her sister against her shoulder and wrapping her night black wings around her. "What happened?" Ravenna asked.

Desarra winced. She did not answer. Ravenna nodded, then started running her fingers through Desarra's hair. She worked out the tangles slowly, carefully. It was not the same thing as brushing the hair, but it was comforting even to Ravenna. Once Desarra's hair was slightly more smooth, Ravenna started preening Desarra's feathers. One by one, she tucked the pinions back where they should be. She smoothed the barbs back into place, until every feather was laying neatly between the ones beside it. Ravenna plucked up and errant feather that had fallen out and handed it to Desarra. Desarra's fingers grasped the tiny piece of down. A moment later, she was crying.

"I never wanted power," Desarra said between the sobs. Ravenna said nothing. "Acceptance, maybe. But I never wanted power. All I wanted was to be acknowledged for who I was. I wanted to be with Crispin and I just wanted to live my life, free of the burden of—"

Ravenna nodded. This was not new. "I think we have both been burdens to each other for long enough. Perhaps we should try being friends instead."

Desarra turned her head so that she was hidden from the world in Ravenna's shoulder. Her wings tucked close to her, the feathers shivering as though fluffing up against the cold. It was winter, but Shinalea rarely got too cold. A smattering of snow, the occasional wild ice storm. But in Desarra's quarters it was toasty warm. Ravenna wrapped her wings tighter around her sister.

"I lost it." Desarra's fingers clutched tighter around the downy feather.

"Lost what?"

Desarra looked towards the door leading off to the bedchamber in the bathing room. Her golden skin grew ashy and her fingers trembled. "My child. It was a male."

Instinctively, Ravenna's wings tightened closer. She felt an uncomfortable sensation in her belly. Unbidden, her eyes filled with tears. Ravenna swallowed back the lump in her throat. For one horrible moment, the emptiness that she had been relying on to keep her sane when she was so far away from what she wanted, doing a job that focused on her ability to kill, slipped away. Her emotions screamed at her. Anger. Fear. Revulsion. And for Desarra, grief.

"I did not know you were trying..." Ravenna managed. Desarra shook her head wildly, her hair tangling once again.

"I wasn't. We weren't. Crispin wanted to wait until after this war was over. We decided that it would be too dangerous to bring a child into an uncertain world where death was prevalent and war our new reality. But it happened. And I wanted it. Now it's gone. *He's* gone." Desarra's sobs turned into quiet trembles. Ravenna started stroking her hair again, smoothing it out, offering what little support she could.

"You know how difficult it is for sylphs to bear children. The fact that our mother bore two was unusual. Even if I was not quite as one would expect," Ravenna said. There were enough children born into each generation to sustain the population, but never enough to exceed what Shinalea would support. The Intellecti had been working for cycles with their healers to see if there would be a better way, and easier way, for females to conceive. Desarra's miscarriage was not uncommon. It did not lessen the pain.

"I wouldn't have cared if he were unusual. He would have been mine," Desarra said, her voice soft and twisted. She looked up at Ravenna. "I'm sorry that our mother decided to turn away from you. I was barely three cycles old, but I remember that she was distraught. She would pace for hours, never flying. She would scold me for no reason, until Mariala would take me away. But she was still my mother. I did not understand why she went away when you were born. All I knew was that I suddenly had a sister raised by Intellecti and my mother was gone. I don't understand how she could been so cruel."

"If she were still around, I would ask her. Though, I imagine I was not what she expected." Ravenna carefully started braiding

Desarra's hair, one of the few things that she could do to make herself look more feminine. Tacitus had painfully taught Ravenna how to braid her hair. She didn't know anything about fashion. She knew nothing of face paints or jewellery. But she could braid hair. Desarra seemed to relax under her touch, until her eyes were lidded and her tears had stopped.

"How am I going to tell Crispin?" Desarra breathed. Her fingers clenched reflexively. Ravenna grabbed her sister's hand and smoothed out the fingers. She marvelled at the contrast in their skins, how it did not look unnatural as she had once supposed. It merely was.

"Crispin loves you. He would not have become your mate if he did not. He will understand."

Desarra shook her head. "What if he thinks it's my fault? What if he thinks I took on too much now that I am Chosen Queen and it was that which…This war is going to kill so much more than we imagined. The Council keeps saying that our culture is going to die, that after this is over we will have to do something to return to what we were. But it's not possible, is it?"

"Firstly," Ravenna said sternly, "Crispin will never blame you for what happened. It was an accident, nothing more. You did nothing wrong. Secondly, I have come to believe that change is inevitable. We tried to avoid change for generations, and yet we still managed to be changed. How else could we have forgotten about the Dalketh's purpose? Perhaps this change is more dramatic than others, but it is still part of the inevitable cycle. Either we embrace it, or we run from it. Whatever we choose, we will still change. Yes, we will not be what we once were. More than lives of our people is at stake. You must have faith that we will survive."

"Faith in what?" Desarra asked. When she looked at Ravenna this time, her amber fire eyes were dull with pain. She was no longer crying, true. She was relaxed. She was not even pushing Ravenna away. But the pain was still there.

"When I was with the humans," Ravenna said, "I learned that they worshiped beings greater than themselves. They called them gods. Sylphs were seen as angels, or beings meant to be messengers of the gods, meting out divine will. That is why we are being sought by Davorin. But not all of their gods were as humans, violent cruel and seeking power. Some of them were loving, forgiving, wise. Perhaps that is another thing that we have forgotten in the generations since our interactions with the humans. Perhaps the gods are not their creation, but something that belonged to all the races and were simply forgotten. The elves supposedly worshiped one or more gods. I have heard that even dragons were supposed to have acknowledged them."

Ravenna fixed her gaze on some point far in the distance, something she could not even see if she tried. She shook her head, bringing herself back to the present and the sylph in her arms. Desarra was looking curious, some of the pain lessened. "I don't know. There are many things I don't know these days. Yet here I am, leading an army likes of which has not been seen for more generations than we can count. Maybe it is good I am asking these questions. Mostly, though, it just gives me a headache."

Desarra chuckled. She winced, as though the sound of her own laughter was wrong. Ravenna allowed herself to chuckle as well. Soon, the two were laughing. It was more real than Ravenna had felt since Desarra's crowning. She was not some empty vessel meant only to train in bloodshed. She was alive. And Desarra was too.

Ravenna smoothed the braid back from Desarra's head. "It will be okay," Ravenna said.

"It still hurts." Desarra pressed a hand to her stomach. Her wings seemed to wilt beneath Ravenna's own.

"It will hurt for a while. I don't know how long. But one day, you will rise and suddenly it will be okay. Never forgotten, but okay." Ravenna took a good, deep breath, thinking of the bones that now lay beneath the Intellecti's tower. She had not yet reached the state where living without Tacitus was okay. But she knew it would happen. "If you would like, I can take his body to the ritual place, perform the death rights."

Desarra sat up straight, eyes wide. "He was not even born. Can you do that for a sylph who is not even born?"

"I don't see why not," Ravenna said. "I've seen no rules in the Intellecti's tomes that say otherwise."

"Thank you," Desarra said. "And… I'm sorry for all of the cycles between us."

"They are as feathers on the wind," Ravenna said. This time, when she smiled, she felt it would fill the void where the emptiness had been. Desarra gave a dry chuckle. Ravenna meant it. It would not be quite so easy for them to forget everything that lay between them, but the start had been made. Eventually, Desarra wiped away what remained of her tears and sat up. She stretched her wings and ruffled the feathers, straightening them from her agitation. Ravenna climbed to her feet, stretching her own wings. Desarra rose and walked over to a small pounded metal mirror hanging by the windows.

"I look terrible," Desarra said. "I have to fix this before Crispin gets back."

"I'm sure he'll understand," Ravenna said, righting a cushion and straightening the table. Desarra whirled on Ravenna, eyes wide. She shook her head.

"You won't tell him." This was the first time that Ravenna had heard Desarra give an order with all of her authority. "I know what you said, and I believe you, but we won't tell him."

"As you like," Ravenna said, inclining her head in the closest to a bow she had come in a very long time. "It is not my place to get involved in your relationship."

Desarra closed her fist around a comb and turned back to the mirror. She attacked her hair with vigour, glaring into the mirror. "I can't tell if you're being facetious or if you actually believe that." Desarra turned, straightening her shoulders and flaring her wings slightly. "You're my sister. You're supposed to get involved."

"Am I?" Ravenna tilted her head. "This is all new to me. It will take some time to understand the requirements. If you want me to get involved, then I will. I think you're making a mistake."

Desarra threw up her hands and turned back to the mess that was her hair. She spoke to the mirror, but her anger was visibly directed at Ravenna. "How can you not understand this? Don't you know anything about people? You're supposed to support me. You're supposed to get involved in my life. We're supposed to be friends. You are my blood. You're the only blood I have left. So start acting like it."

Ravenna frowned. She said nothing for a moment, instead walking to each of the windows and pulling back the shutters, opening them once again to the sky. Crisp cold air filtered into the room, held back by the small braziers with burning embers and wood inside. "Is family...always this complicated? For cycles, we have wanted nothing to do with one another. Yet here we are, thrust together through the wings of fate, and we are trying to act as though we have always been friends. You're going to have to give me some time to adjust, Desarra. In the meantime, I will do what I can for your child. But there are things we must discuss first."

Finished combing her hair, Desarra sank into one of the stools by the table. Her wings drooped. "I should have known. No one ever comes by just to say hello. No just checking up on you, Desarra. No how are you handling things, Desarra? Not even a let's have a chat, Desarra. Always I want something. We need to talk. I have something I need from you. The Council demands. You are Chosen Queen. Every now and again, it would be nice to have someone wish to speak with me about something other than duty or work or responsibility."

Ravenna raised an eyebrow. "Until today, we were in the

stages of tolerating one another. You honestly expect that I came here just to talk? I'm glad I did; no one should ever have to go through what you did without someone to talk with. But—"

Desarra waved a hand in dismissal. "You've made your point. Hurry up and get this over with, then you and…You both can be gone before Crispin gets back."

"I've received word, by carrier bird, that the first shipment of our weapons is prepared. I wish to take a company to go fetch them." Ravenna waited, silent. After all that Desarra had been through that day, it was perhaps not the best time to be springing this on her. The weapons had been a serious source of contention between Ravenna and the High Council. Desarra, unfortunately, had been caught in the middle. Eventually, Ravenna had all but challenged Strygis to fight her war without weapons. It had not ended well.

"A company?! Are you mad? You cannot take that many sylphs away from Shinalea." Desarra gaped. That was not a good sign. Ravenna winced and rubbed the back of her neck, watching the feathers on Desarra's wings rustle together. Oh yes, this was definitely not a good sign.

"I would just take who I took the last time, but I cannot. Weapons would be too much for them to carry, let alone getting me involved. They are stronger, yes. Itonus could perhaps carry me there and back—provided he had a rest in between. But we are talking hundreds of weapons and armour. If we do it at night, and meet Tekko outside of the settlement, we should be all right. No one noticed us the last time."

"And what has changed since then? We have scouts doing flyovers, but we do not know the situation on the ground. I can't let you take a whole company. If you are seen, the war could begin in earnest long before we had planned."

"Your tactics are improving," Ravenna said. Desarra straightened at the complement, making the parry that much more difficult. "But I am the leader of the army for a reason. I have been studying tactics from the tomes for moons now. I have been preparing battle plans. I have been gathering rumours and listening to the scouts' reports. I believe this is our only option if we want to get the weapons. And we need those weapons."

Desarra rose and started pacing about the room. She straightened things that had been overturned during her earlier grief. Her wings flared and closed, the feathers rustling as they moved. Desarra was more agitated than even before and this was not a good time to be agitated. Ravenna needed Desarra clearheaded and thinking properly. Today that was obviously not going to happen. "Does no one think I can do anything?"

"You wouldn't be Chosen Queen if that were the case," Ravenna said. She had her doubts at first, but things were different now.

"I'm not stupid. I know the rumours. I am here stuck up in this room, trying my best to learn things that I have never bothered studying before, just so that I might have a grasp on what is going on with this war. The High Council looks down on me like some puppet that they can manipulate into doing what they wish. The army looks to you for guidance. Wings, the rest of the *sylphs* look to you for guidance. I am nothing but a figurehead, can do nothing. I am so tired of it."

"Then do something about it," Ravenna said. She rose and walked over to where her sister was still pacing. She put her hands on Desarra's shoulders, stilling her so that the two could look each other in the eye. Amber met ice and Desarra visibly wilted under Ravenna's gaze. "I know things have been difficult for you. I am not a stranger to difficulty, but yours is different than mine. All I know is that when I was doing nothing, things were worse than when I was doing something. If you are tired of feeling useless, do something useful."

Desarra wrapped her arms around her middle, her wings folding in close. She took a deep breath, paused, nodded. "Very well. You may take your company, if you think it is best. Just be sure that the humans do not see you."

Ravenna nodded her gratitude. "We will be careful. I will leave Crispin behind, just in case things go...So you are not alone."

Desarra's eyes hardened into shards. "Thank you," she said sharply. "But this permission does not come without price. You may lead the army, but I am Chosen Queen. And I say that you will teach me how to fight."

Ravenna stilled. She swallowed, her mouth suddenly dry. "I thought Crispin was—"

"Crispin says I do not need to know. He would rather have one thing that was not tainted by this war, even though I see what purpose it is giving him. He is so much stronger, more sure of himself. He knows his role in the world. And, for some reason, he does not want to share that with me. So you are going to teach me. Every day, you will come, and we will do the Dalketh or whatever it takes. Okay?"

Ravenna let out a long breath. "Ah, I am fairly busy as it is, without adding individual training to my schedule. Perhaps once a week?"

Desarra's lips twitched, the beginnings of a smile at the corner of her mouth. "Daily, Ravenna. You have the generals, do you not?"

Ravenna winced, but nodded. This was important to Desarra. She did not understand why Crispin would not teach his mate, but nor did she understand why Desarra would not tell Crispin about the miscarriage. Something else was going on between the two, and Ravenna did not want to get in the middle. It seemed a little late for that, though. "Very well. I will be here every day at dawn. We will train for an hour, but I can give you no more than that."

Desarra nodded and clasped Ravenna's hands in her own. She stretched her wings forward so that her feathers brushed

Ravenna's. Ravenna sucked in a breath, unused to the intimate gesture of the sylphs. She stepped forward and wrapped her arms around Desarra in a hug. It was a human gesture, but it was the closest she could get to her sister. She pulled away after a moment. "I must go, if I am to be gone before Crispin returns. I promise I shall do the death rites as if he were my own. Did you...Did you want to give him a name?"

"No," Desarra whispered. She closed her eyes, her golden skin once more palid and pain-ridden. "I think my heart would break twice over if I gave him a name."

Ravenna ducked her head. Then, she went into the bathing chamber and gathered the tiny corpse in a scrap of cloth. He was so small. She wrapped the bundle and cradled him close to her chest. Desarra turned away as she left, not another word said between the two. Ravenna left the chambers and started down the stairs. She heard wing beats entering Desarra's chambers and knew the Crispinus had returned.

The trek to the plateau where they left the dead seemed shorter this time. Kratos was not with her, but the sensation was that Ravenna was not alone. Perhaps Tacitus' spirit was here to guide the small child to wherever it was that the dead went. Ravenna added the question to the list that she was compiling for when she next saw Lenore or Miska. So many questions, but she would be just as happy to simply be there in their presence. Especially Miska.

Ravenna lay the tiny corpse on the rock. Birds were already circling overhead, even though the hour was late in the day. "May your wings fly high, and your heart to be free. I release you unto death, dear Silvius."

She turned and walked away, moisture in her eyes. It was time to go and prepare to fetch the weapons.

CHAPTER SIXTEEN

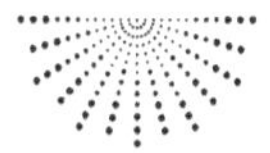

In the moons since Miska had started training with
Cavaris, he learned two things: one, the world was a
far more complicated place than he had first anticipated and
adding magic to it was testing every ability he had; two, he *hated*
snow. Winter had come early and fast to Hullgard, and now that
they were right in the middle of it, the snow seemed never-
ending. If it melted it all, it turned to slush, which froze
overnight. The next day, it was either icy or snowing again. The
fur-lined clothing that Miska had been given seemed to always
be not quite warm enough. He stuffed his boots with extra furs
and only took off his gloves when he had to. He was thankful
for the warmth of Beringer, his familiar, whose pelt had grown
in quite thick for the winter.

Beringer seemed to be growing almost continuously those
days, and sleeping next to a large warm bear was definitely a
perk in the freezing lands of Hullgard. Beringer also seem to be
growing more and more capable the more Miska trained.
Cavaris had Miska practicing communicating with Beringer
mind to mind. He practiced weaving spells around Beringer,
such as wind or snow or warmth. If the spells did not wear him

out quite so much, he would be performing a constant spell of warmth around himself. As it was, he was barely able to control the magic. Cavaris said it had something to do with the fact that Miska could not actually hear the song and therefore conduct it, but Miska was not quite so sure. The only thing that seemed to have come out of his ability was Beringer, and that was pure accident.

During the days, Miska trained with Cavaris. By the time he was angry and snappish—exhausted from trying to conduct a song that he could not hear except through the drumbeats of his heart—Sisu would appear as if by his own magic, ready to take Miska out and beat his body into submission. Miska spent hours on hunts that sometimes brought back a rabbit or two and sometimes brought back nothing at all. Asgeir helped him train in the art of the bow, until he was actually quite capable with it. Still, they never attempted to go after elk again, as that required days away from Rygirfel now that the herds had moved on, and Cavaris would not spare him. In the evenings, Sisu would teach him how to fight. Sometimes the two used battle axes—Miska found the enormous weapon to be almost impossible—sometimes they used hunting knives.

Beringer followed Miska on the hunts, sometimes participated in the training, but mostly, he hung around the people preparing food for the winter. As the snows began, the food became more and more scarce and they had to draw on their stores. Beringer was as it turned out, a very accomplished forager. He was also almost always hungry. The children of Rygirfel had discovered this fact and took great delight in clambering all over the bear in payment for berries, dried meat, fish, even some honeycomb from a wintering beehive. Beringer was a favourite amongst all of the people of Rygirfel. Despite Cavaris' warnings, the bear was friendly with everybody, especially children.

Miska trudged back to the tent he shared with Cavaris,

grumbling profusely. He had a black eye from Sisu and his over-enthusiastic training. Miska was improving, but Sisu was enormous and fast and extremely capable. Miska broke the thin sheet of ice on the water barrel outside of the tent. He sucked in a breath, held it, and dunked his head in. The cold was so intense that the black eye was immediately numb and he was certain he would freeze right then and there. He pulled his head out and shook his hair from the water.

"There are better ways of doing that," Cavaris said, standing just before Miska. The dragon reached out with his hand towards Miska's eye. "There are also better ways of fighting. You could use the magic to defend yourself. Perhaps you wouldn't get quite so hurt if you did."

Miska waved Cavaris' hand away. He scrubbed his beard dry and did his best with his hair. It had grown rather long in his time in the Iron Mountains, and no one seemed inclined to help him cut it. The great-grandmothers simply laughed and re-braided his hair. Excepting his reddish skin, which the harsh winter sun only darkened, Miska was starting to look exactly like the other people of Rygirfel and Hullgard. Well, except they did not often have bears following around behind them.

"How can I fight with magic if I can barely control the simplest of things that you asked me to do? I can't even hear this song that you want me to hear. I don't think I'm going to get any better than I am now."

"It was only a few moons ago that you thought you could not do magic at all. And yet just this morning, you managed to blow up a pinecone." Cavaris smiled slightly, revealing his fangs. It was a little disconcerting when Cavaris smiled. "It is true that I had hoped your progress would be faster, but I think that we can work something out. After all, you adapted to your inability to hear after you were attacked. We just need to find a similar adaptation for the use of magic."

Miska laughed harshly and strode into the tent. He reached

for a cloth lying on a stand beside the fire and dried his face and hair as best he could. His black eye would only stay numb for a few more minutes, but it was better to have some relief from pain than none. In a couple of days, he hoped that it would be gone. Unless Sisu decided to hit him again.

Cavaris stood just inside the entrance to the tent, the flaps open and letting cold air in. Miska stalked over to where the dragon waited and closed the flaps. He turned to Cavaris, folding his arms.

"You're insane. It took me *cycles* to learn how to read people's lips. And it's still an imperfect process. I have to guess more than I am sure about what people are saying. Your signed language is more efficient, but it is still not perfect. And now you want me to adapt something that is intricately more complex than a spoken language. I don't have cycles. I need to be prepared to ride out to war when Ravenna needs me. Or sooner, if my queen is in danger."

"As far as I know, the song magic has never been adapted for someone who cannot hear it. Those who wield the song are always those able to hear it. That is probably why you were never able to wield it before your near-death experience with Beringer. Your body would have never been able to find it if you hadn't been so panicked. And you have made progress. But not enough." Cavaris walked into the tent and sat before the fire. He reached his hands out as if to warm them, but Miska knew from experience that the dragon was never cold. Cavaris walked around in his robes just as he would any other time of the cycle. He never seem to be bothered by snow or ice storms or the bitter cold.

Miska sat on the other side of the fire, scowling into the flames. "I know," Miska snapped. "Stop prevaricating. If I am going to be suited to war, then I need to be able to use magic as well as possible. And I am not doing that right now. If you have some sort of solution where I could see this magic instead of trying to hear for something that isn't there please enlighten me." Miska rubbed his hands together before the flames, though his fingers were nearly always cold these days, no matter how close he drew to the flames. He did not stop trying though. He would never stop trying.

Cavaris sat up straight, eyes growing large as he stared at Miska. Miska scowled deeper. "To see the song. You wish to see song. Instead of listening for notes played together, you would see the tapestry of threads. It is…a novel idea. No, that is not quite right." Cavaris pressed a hand to his head, right where the horn on his left temple grew out of the skull. Was Cavaris getting a headache? Served him right.

"If you have a point to make," Miska said. "Do it. I have been training all day. I am exhausted, sore, in desperate need of food and sleep, and growing towards cranky."

Cavaris' mouth twitched. "You forgot weary. No my point was that I vaguely recall a story from the Darkening, maybe before, about weavers of magic. They were not sorcerers, nor witches. And my memory is vague on the matter. I will meditate later to see if I cannot sift through the numerous pieces that have piled up in my head. It is one of the downsides of being semi-immortal."

Miska shrugged and threw up his hands. "Fine. Do whatever you need. I have to learn this magic if I want to help my people. But I am fed up for today. All I want is a nice meal and a very nice, long, sle—"

The commotion, movement against the fabric outside the tent interrupted Cavaris' thoughts and Miska's longing for sleep. Beringer. Miska groaned, but rose to his feet as though eager to meet his familiar after the day's separation. If there is anything that could make him feel a little less grumpy, it was spending time with Beringer. Over the few moons that they had been together, it was a little bit surprising how fond of one another they had become. Especially considering that Beringer had once upon a time tried to kill Miska. Aside from Ravenna, Miska loved only Beringer. He respected Lenore and was loyal to her, but he did not love her. Not like this.

Normally after a day's training, Beringer simply lumbered his way into the tent, bringing whatever snow and debris happened to come along with him. Today, though, the bear let out small whuffs and made a general commotion about the clearing. Miska pushed out of the tent, sucking in a sharp breath the bitter cold. He saw Beringer's bulk lumbering around the clearing, his shoulders almost as high as Miska's own these days. Apparently that was part of the magic; Beringer would keep growing until his bulk matched Miska's magical strength.

Something was on Beringer's shoulder. It was small and looked to be another animal, given the fur that was covering it. Something was attacking Beringer! Miska rushed forward, only to be stopped by Beringer's snuffling nose to his shoulder. Miska got the sense of patience through his bond with Beringer, and a feeling of unusually strong affection. Miska looked closer at the "animal" upon Beringer's shoulders. A head popped up and bright green eyes—lighter than Miska's own—met him. They were surrounded by a round face with pale skin and wisps of white blonde hair. It was a human. More than that, it was a girl child.

"Beringer?" Miska said, but his eyes never left the girl. "What is this?"

Beringer chuffed. Images flowed through Miska's mind: children running around him as they played during the day; being fed with some precious fresh meat that had been brought back from an elk hunt; a hungry child trying to snatch the meat away from Beringer.

The girl spoke, her eyes bright and yet somehow containing a maturity greater than her cycles. "I am Allora. Beringer is my protector."

"Is he?" Miska asked with a slight smile. "You know he is my familiar do you not?"

The girl looked at him solemnly. She tightened the fur closer around her, eyes suspicious. "He is my protector?" She looked uncertain. As though Miska was about to take this away from her, like other things had been taken from her. He noted that beneath the fur which she wore like a cloak, she was thinly dressed for the weather. She did not have any gloves, nor were the boots on her feet thick enough to stand the snow.

Beringer sent more images, of Allora wandering around the village, being yelled at by adults and shooed away from fires and meals. Beringer then sent an image of Allora running around their clearing, climbing over Beringer. She would sleep next to Beringer, eating her meals with Miska, Cavaris and Beringer, well fed, well clothed, and happier than Beringer had ever seen her. Beringer wanted to *adopt* her.

"Do you have a home?" Miska asked. He did not have time to deal with the child running underfoot. Perhaps Sisu or Asgeir could help him find a suitable place for her to stay that would not be with him as he prepared to march for war. Allora shook her head, then nodded. "Well, which is it?"

"Papa lived in Hullgard, but he's gone. Mama sent me away," Allora said. No home then. Miska sighed.

He looked around and saw Cavaris standing by the entrance to the tent, hands folded casually in his robes. Allora did not seem perturbed by the presence of the dragon, which was a good thing considering that most people were still unsettled by him. "Can we find Asgeir or Sisu or anybody do you think?" Miska asked, flustered enough that his words were barely coherent. He did not know what to do with a child.

"You could do that," Cavaris said. "But your familiar would not thank you for sending her away. Like it or not, Beringer has become fond of the child. I would say that is significant, given the fact that he is a magical being such as yourself, now. Such as myself."

"I cannot take care of a child," Miska said. He looked between Allora and Cavaris. Allora was frowning, her fingers tightening in the thick fur on Beringer's neck. She looked so small up there. Cavaris, helpful as ever, said nothing. Miska turned back to Allora, considering her. "If I let you stay with us, you must promise to stay out of the way, keep out of trouble. I cannot have my training interrupted to take care of you."

Allora straightened, suddenly looking regal and imperious. "I can take care of myself." She sniffed. Beringer huffed his particular style of laughter and nudged Miska's shoulder, a playful look in his eye. Miska blew out a breath and scratched Beringer behind his ear. The bear leaned into his touch, eyes fluttering closed in pleasure. Allora looked a little alarmed at Beringer's obvious affection, as though it was something terrible to see the bear give affection to someone other than herself.

"As you like," Miska said. He reached up, arms outstretched so that Allora could climb into them. "You may stay with us. Understand that we are not your typical collection of people. But we will do what we can for you."

Allora's eyes widened in surprise. Her mouth grew into a smile, and Miska saw that the two front teeth were missing. But that immediate joy was so complete that Miska knew he would never do anything to harm this child. It was like that moment when Ravenna had finally opened up to him. Allora jumped into Miska's arms, her thin limbs wrapping around him like a tree. He hugged her back, carrying her inside the tent where it was warm and safe. This added a whole new set of complications to his plans, but he would adapt. Beringer followed Cavaris into the tent and settled behind Miska, watching Allora with affection.

Miska looked up at Cavaris, smiling—it was genuine this time. "What was that you were saying about threads?"

* * *

THE NEXT MORNING, Miska wondered what exactly had been running through his head when he had decided to adopt a child. Oh, yes, he was doing it out of the goodness of his heart, because he hated to see anyone or anything's suffering. He had done it because Cavaris seemed astonished that Beringer had created a connection with the child. And he had done it because, for one desperate moment, he had felt that emptiness that filled him when Ravenna was near to him fill a little bit. In the light of day, though, a child was more trouble than Miska was certain he could handle.

She had woken Miska long before dawn, complaining that her stomach was hurting. Alarmed, Miska had tried to figure out precisely what she could have eaten to have caused illness, when Cavaris—woken by the frantic rushing about of the tent— pointed out through mind speak that it was likely the child was just hungry. Beringer had seconded the motion to go get food, which meant Miska was trudging through Rygirfel far too early in the morning to get food for a hungry bear and child. He was not sure which one could eat more.

Then, there was the matter of clothing and bathing Allora. She had declared fervently that she was grown up and capable of bathing herself. Miska had happily let her prance away towards the nearest cold stream, only to have to rush after her a few moments later when he felt Beringer's alarm at her screaming at the temperature of the water. He had thought she had broken a limb or cut her hand open on a shard of ice. No, the water was just cold. He had clothed her in her rags again, promising that he would bring her new clothes that evening after his training session with Sisu.

Now, Miska was sitting on the ground with his legs crossed, trying very hard to meditate.

The fire crackled in front of him; Cavaris said it was a

concession to the warmth that humans required. Miska was also meant to use it to visualise glowing threads that stood in the place of the song that he had been struggling to use for the last few moons. Cavaris had told him to pretend that the music of the song that he could sometimes grasp was floating in the air before him, as easy to see as threads that glowed like fire. He was concentrating, glad for once that he was deaf to Allora's incessant chattering. In the back of his mind, he could feel Beringer's interest in the girl's voice and hyperactive movements. But in front of him, he was concentrating solely on the song. The threads.

Something flickered in his vision. It was a blue strand, hardly bigger than a human hair. It was there for a moment as Miska attempted to pull the magic through him in time with his heartbeat. Pulling the magic was one thing that he had been able to do. He concentrated harder.

The blue strand appeared again, flickering once before solidifying. It floated through the air, twisting and turning like some sky dancing creature. Miska pulled on the magic harder, his heartbeat becoming almost a true sound in his ears. Something in his mind cracked and it was like the world was suddenly filled with strands of magic, threads of colours so rich and deep that he had never before seen them. Awed, Miska reached out for thread, afraid to blink. The tip of the index finger on his left hand touched the original blue thread that he had seen snaking through the sky. It thrummed at him, asking what it was that he wanted.

Miska was unsure. He tried to tie the thread into the shape of a butterfly that often flew around the gardens at the oasis in the Red Palace. The thread twisted away from him. Miska tried again, focusing his thoughts on that butterfly. Finally, after a moment of pushing his will towards the thread, it complied. Bright as a blazing sun, barely the size of his palm, a glorious glowing butterfly in the brilliant shade of blue of the thread, took form. It fluttered around the clearing. Miska directed it towards Cavaris who was watching with a quietly satisfied smile. Then, a tiny hand reached out and grasped at the butterfly. A sound like shrill laughter burst through Miska's head. He let out a cry and clasped his hands over his ears. The threads vanished; the butterfly vanished.

The next thing that Miska knew, Beringer was prodding him with his wet nose. Miska looked up, blinking his eyes against the sudden brightness of the sun on the snow. The bear huffed, mentally asking why Miska had ruined Allora's cheerful curiosity at the butterfly. Miska furrowed his brow. He looked over at the dragon, who was surprisingly standing with a hand on Allora's shoulder. The little girl was dangerously close to tears.

The child laughed, just as you were screaming. She thought you were screaming at her. I assume it was the magic? Cavaris tilted his head. It looked like a curious gesture, but Miska knew that it was something far more serious. Cavaris was concerned.

"I'm sorry Allora," Miska said. He reached up and touched a hand to his ear. "Just as you touched the butterfly, I...I *heard* something. I think I heard you laugh."

"So?" Allora snapped, her cheerful good mood obviously ruined. Though, she seemed more upset than angry.

"I do not hear anything, ever." Miska watched her wall the news settled in. Allora's mouth opened in a tiny circle, matching her wide eyes. She reached up with both hands to touch her ears.

"You're deaf? But you can talk to me. You understand me, I'm not using the signed language." Allora seemed just as concerned as Cavaris, though for perhaps different reasons.

"I read your mouth and expressions." Miska looked at Cavaris, swallowing moisture into a suddenly dry mouth. "I saw the threads. And when she touched it..."

"It is an interesting phenomenon. If you are going to hear

something every time your magic interacts with the world, then you are going to have a difficult time fighting your war." Cavaris was saying nothing that Miska did not comprehend, but the realisation was startling. If this was how his magic reacted when someone touched something that he had created, then he would be able to hear again. Perhaps he could hear *everything*. But he had also gone most of his life without hearing a single thing. It would take far longer for him to adapt to sound than otherwise. Miska would have to figure out how to do the magic without that little side effect, or he would be completely useless.

"What war?" Allora asked.

Miska stared at her in complete shock, his jaw dropped. He looked at Cavaris to see if maybe the dragon had put her up to this. Cavaris had some strange notions about learning lessons. But no, Cavaris looked just as he always did. Beringer seemed to pick up on Miska's shock and chuffed disconcertedly. Beringer ran his massive claws through the snow on the ground, revealing the packed dirt beneath. Absently, Miska held out a hand to rest on Beringer's leg. Allora furrowed her brow and looked between Cavaris and Miska.

"What war?" Allora asked again. She was looking a little distressed, as though the lack of answer was somehow her fault, or the adults were angry at her.

"The war in the south," Miska said. "With the Salusian Empire taking over the Red Desert and other places. My queen has been captured by Lord Davorin. That war?"

"No one up here talks about that war. I thought you were just doing this magic thing because Cavaris told you to. And the big man trains all of the people who can't hunt or fight, if they want him to," Allora said. She tugged the small fur blanket closer around her diminutive frame. She still looked a little uncertain, but Cavaris put another hand on her shoulder and squeezed gently. "Can I fight in the war? I've never fought in a war."

"War is not for children," Miska said carefully. He smiled as best he could, but he rather feared that it looked more a grimace than a true smile. Allora wrinkled her nose.

"Grown-ups always say that. When you're older, you'll understand. You have to be older for that. It's not for children. When am I going to be grown-up? I want to have fun too," Allora complained. Beringer lumbered over to where she stood and flopped down on the ground. Allora climbed onto his shoulders and leaned into his fur.

"War is not fun, child," Cavaris said. His expression was little changed from its usual form, but Miska saw enough shift in Cavaris' eyes to surmise that his voice was sharper than before. Then, there was the way that Allora flinched. "War is death. But it is not a peaceful death, nor is it one that you should actively seek out. It is the loss of culture, and of peace of mind, and of safety, and of everything good that you might have known. Perhaps some useful things might come out of war, such as the freeing of a people or the toppling of a government that no longer serves its purpose, but these are rare exceptions. The only thing that is certain in war is that death will come. You should learn this lesson now, Allora, rather than later."

Miska shivered, a thread of energy appearing at the corner of his eye just at the moment that his hackles rose at Cavaris' words. He knew that he had to free Lenore, protect Ravenna and whoever else from Davorin's desperate grasp, but rarely had he stopped to consider the cost. All he knew what was the image of the dead soldiers in the throne room just before Lenore sent him away. It was the most death that Miska had ever seen, and he did his very best to forget the nightmares about it. War was death according to Cavaris. If that was the price for doing what needed to be done though, then he would pay it.

"But he's going to the war," Allora said, pointing at Miska. Beringer shuffled his shoulders enough that Allora was forced to put down the accusing finger and hold on. She smiled and laughed, saying something that Miska could not catch with her head turned at such an angle.

"You are mistaken," Cavaris said. He turned to look Miska full in the eye, the vertically slitted red shining with some dangerous power. "Miska is not going to the war, he is starting it. That is an entirely different matter altogether."

Miska surged to his feet, anger making his emotions flare. The threads appeared again at the corners of his vision, pulsing in time with the heartbeat he could not hear. The colours of Beringer's fur and the trees became crisp. The snow was almost blinding. And Cavaris was outlined in sharp relief. "Is that why you will not help me? Why you will not come with me into battle so that I might save my people? Because you think I am starting a war rather than fighting in one?"

"No matter who started this war, I will not participate as you would have me participate. Who am I to say which side is just? Should one be discounted because I happened to run into the other first? Who is to say that the conquering of people is not a benevolent act? Or is the search for freedom, at any cost perhaps the better cause? I have chosen to help you. Not because I think you are right, nor because I think you are wrong. I am helping you because you have magic and an untamed magic is very dangerous. I have seen the destruction war creates and have no desire to get involved again, no matter the side." Cavaris slipped his hands into the folds of his robes and waited for Miska's reaction, as calm as ever.

For the first time in Miska's life, he struck out in pure anger. He touched the threads that now filled his vision and with a surge in will sent them pulsing towards Cavaris, hoping to bind the dragon or cause him the same pain that Miska was now experiencing. Cavaris simply lifted his hand free of the fabric of his robes. He twitched a finger, then two, and the attack that

Miska had started vanished out of existence. He sucked in a sharp breath and fell to his knees. "I'm sorry," he breathed.

"So were the ones who had started wars in generations past. If you wish to be of any use to your cause, then you must learn to control your emotions. Once you have done that, very little will be outside your grasp. What you choose to do with it then will be your choice. I can only hope that I will have taught you well enough to make an enlightened decision."

Cavaris slipped his hands back inside his robes and strode off into the forest, away from Rygirfel and all of the humans that lived there. He would be back, Miska hoped. He had much yet to learn. If he did not learn, then his people would be doomed. Miska watched Allora sitting on Beringer's back. She was looking at him with a solemn expression, but one that did not bespeak understanding. She knew that something was wrong, but she did not grasp what. Miska rose and walked over to Beringer. He ruffled Allora's hair and sat with his back against Beringer's sturdy side. He could not see Allora, see if she was talking to him. He did not want to talk.

"Don't worry Allora, it will be okay," Miska said. If he said it often enough, perhaps he might start believing in himself.

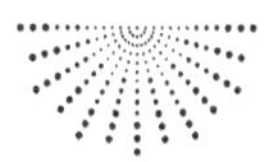

CHAPTER SEVENTEEN

"Miska," Sisu said, "did you know that you have a hanger on?"

Miska looked at the small child that was following behind him, carrying a bow nearly as large as she was. Allora returned Miska's gaze with her own solemn expression and said nothing. Miska turned back to Sisu, shrugging. "This is Allora. Beringer found her running around Rygirfel, no one looking after her. So she has become one of our ragtag little group."

"Beringer found someone to give me a bow," Allora said, holding it out for Sisu to examine. "Miska said I could not come train with him unless I had my own."

Sisu crouched down, so large that even that did not bring him close to Allora's level. He took the bow just as solemnly as the girl offered it, examining it thoroughly. He ran a hand over the smooth wood, looking at the string wrapped around it. Sisu nodded, then handed the bow back to Allora. "It will do. And Miska was right. But, now that you have your own, I see no harm in letting you come with us."

Allora smiled, revealing the toothless gap. She clutched the bow tightly and sidled a little bit closer to Miska. Asgeir approached, frowning at Allora. He looked at Sisu, who shrugged. Miska made another round of introductions and Asgeir bowed his head to the young girl. Then, as like every other day, the three started off into the woods to further Miska's training. He could already feel his eye throbbing in anticipation of Sisu hitting it again. Well, at least Miska had made progress in one area of his training, even if Cavaris was still not speaking with him. And Allora seemed to have forgiven him for his earlier outburst after the butterfly incident.

The odd thing was, though, that Miska kept seeing threads at the corner of his vision. It made him jumpy, constantly looking around for the source of them, even though he knew precisely where they came from. Asgeir raised his eyebrow scornfully as Miska jumped a third time during the first five minutes of their trek, scaring a scrawny rabbit from its hiding place.

"Is there something wrong?" Asgeir finally asked. Miska shook his head.

"It's nothing. Just some side effects of the magical training. I should adjust soon enough. I hope," Miska said. Asgeir nodded, then looked up to where Sisu was walking with Allora on his shoulders. Every now and again, the girl would toss her head back and laugh or tug on one of Sisu's braids. Miska wondered what it was that they were saying.

"Why did you take her in?" Asgeir looked at Miska as though he were almost accusing him. Miska frowned.

"Would you rather I had left her to continue in her abandoned state? She was hungry and had nowhere else to go." An image flashed in Miska's head, of a similarly pale skinned woman with night black hair and wings that wrapped around her, hiding her despair from the world. Ravenna had been hungry and had nowhere else to go when she first arrived at the Red Palace. She had become one of the most important things his life. He wondered where she was, whether or not she was all right. He frowned. Davorin could not be allowed to get to her before Miska could get to Davorin.

"We barely have enough food to spare for keeping you here. You are lucky that Beringer finds his own food most of the time, or the children would not be allowed to give him the offerings for fear that he would demand more. You are learning to hunt, at least, but winter will be difficult. This cycle has not been good for game. And you expect us to prepare to march to war as well, which requires gathering even more resources. I just don't think it was wise to take in a child who is perhaps more trouble than worth. She is probably a thief."

Miska sighed, running his fingers through his hair and feeling the unfamiliar braids that lay there. It was still something to get used to, this northern style. They wished him to look like they did, to fit in. But he was never very good at that. "She is only a child. There is no reason to punish her for things beyond her control. Besides, Beringer likes her."

"Be careful you do not stretch yourself too thin, desert man," Asgeir said before turning away from Miska and walking up to where Sisu was. Miska remained at the back of the group, content to have only his own thoughts to contend with. Allora twisted on Sisu's shoulders to look at Miska, frowning. Miska smiled and waved at her. Her frown deepened and she turned to face front again.

After a while, they stopped. This clearing was relatively sheltered from the weather by trees that crossed their boughs overhead. New snow had fallen over the places where it had become scuffed due to previous training sessions. Still, the ground was uneven and covered alternately in snow or ice. It was an extremely difficult place to walk in the midst of winter, which made Sisu declare it perfect for training Miska. Sisu lifted Allora off his shoulders, telling her something and gesturing to the clearing. He then handed his weapons to Asgeir, hefting the battle ax against a tree. Miska put down his own bow and quiver, though he kept the hunting knives on his belt and in his boot. Sisu did the same.

"Now you just watch this part, all right?" Miska said to Allora, tucking a strand of her white blonde hair behind her ear. She nodded, clutching her bow closer. Miska undid his cloak of fur and wrapped it around the child. In a moment or two, he would not feel the cold as he would be too busy running around trying to keep Sisu from beating him into small pieces.

Training with Sisu was nothing like what Miska had witnessed during his time in the Red Palace. To be fair, he had not paid all that much attention to soldiers and weapons and whatnot while he was serving inside the palace. He much preferred learning how to read or dance or draw. That all changed when Ravenna arrived, obviously needing something to hit. He had watched her training a couple of times, though he was not sure she knew. The motions had been ferocious and graceful and something out of a story from another time. Sisu, on the other hand, was fast, brutal, and brooked no error.

Sisu did not wait for Miska to gather his bearings. He simply lunged forward as Miska was walking to the centre of the clearing, and struck. Thankfully, Miska had been training with Sisu for the last three moons and was fully aware that his mentor was likely to do something of the sort. Miska ducked, then surged upwards and wrapped his arms around Sisu's middle. His arms were not long enough, nor was he strong enough to take Sisu to the ground. However, Miska could use the opportunity to strike with his knee in the soft spot on the inside of Sisu's thigh, where his thick furs and whatever armour he wore did not do much to protect him. Sisu flinched at the strike and did something with his fingers that had Miska squealing in pain and writhing to the ground.

Miska waited for the spots in his vision to clear before he could concentrate on Sisu enough to figure out what the man was saying. He was laughing. "Pressure points, lad," Sisu said, wiggling the fingers of his singular hand. "Don't often get to use those, but if you're going to present me with such a golden opportunity, I might as well practice."

Miska rolled to his feet and swept a leg out to catch Sisu behind the knee. Sisu staggered, catching his balance, but he did not fall. It was enough to allow Miska to duck around Sisu's guard and strike him squarely in the jaw with a closed fist. Sisu's head snapped back, but Miska was not fast enough to get away from the counter strike that followed. Sisu's fist hit him squarely in his already black eye, and Miska was down.

Miska clutched his hand to his eye, wanting to touch it and make the pain go away, but knowing that if he did the pain would only get worse. Colourful threads flared in his spotty vision. Miska instinctively reached out and touched one of the orange ones. It surged in brightness, then vanished. A moment later, and the pain surrounding Miska's eye was gone. In fact, he could see out of it better than he had all day. Miska looked up at Sisu in alarm.

"Well, now, there's something I haven't seen before. Your eye looks good as new. Was that some of the magic that Cavaris has been trying to teach you?" Sisu crouched close to Miska, examining his eye. Allora ran forwards and latched onto Miska's arm from the side. He turned and looked at her, surprised at the shock in her expression.

"Don't hurt him," Allora said. "Cavaris said he can't control magic yet. Cavaris said that they are making progress, but it'll take time. Don't hurt him for it."

Sisu reached out and ruffled Allora's hair. "I won't hurt him, Little Dragon. I was just surprised is all."

"Perhaps we should move on to weapons training for now," Miska said carefully. "That might be better than hand-to-hand combat."

Sisu considered, shrugged, then stood. Miska smiled Allora and shooed her back to where Asgeir waited. "Very well. You definitely need more practice with weapons than you do with hand-to-hand. I never would have thought you would grow so capable."

"Capable? I've never beaten you yet." Miska smiled wryly and rose to his feet, feeling the stiffness of his muscles start to wane away as he finally grew warm from his activities. Sisu clapped him on the shoulder with his metal capped hand, making Miska wince.

"And I very much doubt you ever will. I haven't been beaten in strict hand-to-hand combat since I was probably your age. Weapons fighting, yes, but not hand-to-hand. In case you haven't noticed, I am rather larger than all of my opponents." Sisu walked over to Asgeir, reaching for the battle ax. Allora looked up at the big warrior, her hand entwined with Asgeir's. Miska smiled a little at that; it was difficult to resist that child's smile.

"You're bigger than everybody. Except Beringer," Allora said to Sisu. She puffed out her cheeks a little. "Nobody is bigger than Beringer."

The three men exchanged glances with each other. Sisu was the first to crack, tossing his head back and laughing. Asgeir subsided into quiet chuckles. And Miska laughed clearly, nodding at Allora in pride. "Absolutely, Little Dragon. Beringer has us all beat."

* * *

THAT EVENING, Miska sat next to the fire with Allora, eating stew as quickly as his sore muscles would allow. After training with Sisu on the battle axe, Miska had gone head-to-head with Asgeir in the art of sword fighting. Where Sisu was undefeated in hand-to-hand combat, so was Asgeir with the sword. Miska was lucky that he had Beringer to walk back with him, or he would have been shuffle-stepping his way back to the tent. As it was, Allora had to do most of the cooking, which would have been fine except she had been living for several cycles on her own and had no idea about the amount of spice to put in. She ate her soup happily, smiling at Miska between bites. He tried to smile back, but it was difficult when one was grimacing around mouthfuls of slightly overcooked meat covered in a bit too much salt and pepper. Thank goodness, Beringer would eat just about anything, because the leftovers would be inedible.

"Will Cavaris come back soon?" Allora asked. It took Miska a moment to understand what it was that she was saying, because she was talking around her food. He swallowed his mouth full and set his bowl on the ground near the fire, ostensibly to keep it warm. "It's just, I think you made him mad. I don't know why, he was just talking about war as a bad thing. I don't understand why you want to go to war."

"I think Cavaris will return. We both just needed some time apart in order to think about things. And as for war, I do not want to go to war. But my people have been captured by a cruel and vindictive lord, and I must do what I can to help them. If I do not, then perhaps more than my people will be at stake." Miska was hungry enough that he picked up his bowl and ate more of the over-spiced stew. He chased it down with a large gulp of water that had been melted over the fire, and hoped that his mouth would stop smarting from the pepper sometime soon.

"Couldn't you just tell this lord to go away?" Allora asked, with all the innocence of a child. Miska shook his head, trying to figure out how exactly to explain to her that one did not just ask Lord Davorin to please go away, because they weren't interested in the Salusian Empire as their overlords. Davorin was not as bad as Dagan, who had been more interested in conquering for the sake of glory then for the sake of furthering the Empire, but it was still wrong to think of Lenore and all of the people of the Red Desert suffering under the rule of a people that were not their own.

"I cannot. Some people just want to own things for the sake of owning them. They are power seekers, hungry for things they believe will give their life meaning. Lord Davorin does not have a right to my lands, or my people. We are a free people, who will live only under our own initiative. And we must protect those which Lord Davorin seeks. The sylphs." Beringer lifted his head Miska's words and let out a rumble in agreement. Allora shovelled more stew into her mouth, eyes wide.

"Sylph?" Allora asked. Miska recognised that expression. It was one that he had worn often after first coming to the Red Palace, in the company of Warra. The old healer had steered him directly in the eye, making sure that he paid attention to her words as well as her facial expressions, teaching him as much as she was telling him stories. He had worn the same wide-eyed, eager expression that Allora wore now.

"Sylphs are winged beings, who have lived apart from humans for generations untold. They have been gone so long from our lands, that people have forgotten them, and only know them as angels. Messengers to the gods. Their truth has been lost to the mists of time, just as magic was lost and the innovations that furthered our society were eaten by desperation, hunger, and faulty memory." Miska waved his hands as he spoke, the threads at the corners of his eyes dancing and demanding that he pluck them like strings on an instrument. As he did, images floated around the fire, much like that bright butterfly he had made that morning. Allora watched, absolutely fascinated. The two spent the rest of the evening in the company of stories, the desperation of the upcoming war forgotten for a very short time.

* * *

MISKA WOKE in the middle of the night, pain radiating down his spine. It was so sharp that he was unable to scream, let alone breathe. His hands scrabbled at his back where the pain seemed to be concentrating. He could feel the skin bubbling and morphing, ridges forming in some unknown pattern beneath his very fingers. Beside him, Beringer let out a low roar, rising to his feet and digging his claws into the fur covered ground of the tent. The threads at the corner of his vision were gone, leaving only traces of light in their place. Allora sat up as well, pressing her hands to her ears as she cried out in horror. Miska tried to reach out and comfort her, but he was so twisted in pain that he could do nothing but stare at her, silently pleading that she do something. Anything.

A claw tipped hand rested on Miska's back, the claws pushing into his skin. Suddenly, he could move. He could breathe. He sucked in a desperate breath, the air crisp and cold with an oncoming snowstorm. Beringer was suddenly there, pressing his muzzle into Miska's chest. Miska wrapped his arms around the bear's head as he tried to catch his breath. The pain was still there, but it was less. After a few minutes, it subsided and Miska looked up. Allora was sitting upright in her bedroll, trembling visibly. Cavaris stood over Miska, his eyes glowing slightly.

"There is a price to pay for magic." Cavaris sat on the ground beside the fire, waving his hands so that the flames danced a little bit higher and the light in the tent was brighter. Miska reached back to feel the ridges on his spine. They felt like scars, carved there by some horrible knife. Cavaris waved his hand again, and a mirror appeared in the air, reflecting off of another one pointed at Miska's back. There, across his upper shoulders and the first few inches of his spine, were black lines. They looked like furrows plowed into the ground in some strange, intentional pattern. Between each row were dots of deep black, some smaller some larger. All told, the whole thing only took up a very small portion of his back, though the pain had been blinding.

"How is this a price?!" Miska asked, running his fingers over the ridges. Cavaris lowered his hand and the mirrors vanished.

"In times past, sorcerers would draw their magical energy from the land around them. They would draw it from their familiars. That was why many magical dwellings were surrounded by lifeless lands. Battlefields where sorcerers had fought would be barren for cycles afterwards. If you do not draw the energy to perform magic from the land or the people around you, then the magic will come from yourself. You would not have felt this price had you not healed yourself. That takes a good deal more energy than you would think. The ridges will fade as your energy returns. But be forewarned, Miska. The larger magics that you use will take their toll faster than the smaller. If you do something more than the energy you have available, you will die. If you do something great without drawing energy from somewhere else, then it is possible you will be permanently crippled. Magic is not free."

Miska lowered his hands to his lap, clenching them into fists to hide the trembling. Allora crawled over to him and wrapped her arms around his neck, crying a little. He wrapped her into a hug, wondering how he could ever fight this war if he was so limited. "I never see you paying a price like this."

Cavaris inclined his head, his eyes gleaming a little brighter. "I am not human. Humans were not born of magic. You were gifted magic. And, unfortunately, as the magic passed through your generations, it became diluted. And it required a price."

Miska tightened his arms around Allora, taking as much comfort from her as he was getting. Beringer shuffled his head into the girl's back and the three sat there for a moment. Miska looked at Cavaris, knowing full well that his fear was fully displayed. "Help me, please. I don't want to die and I don't want to kill everyone else around me. Is there another way?"

Cavaris considered. He dipped his hand into the fire, watching the flames dance over his fingers. Tiny white scales formed on the appendage, protecting him from the flames. Cavaris pulled his hand out and the scales disappeared. He looked up at Miska. "Someone will have to pay the price. But I can teach you to strengthen your magic, so that the energy you expel can be extended, so that you will be able to do more with less. Nothing in this world is free, Miska. You said you were willing to help your people, no matter the cost."

Miska nodded. He stared into the fire. The threads were appearing once again at the corner of his eyes. They started swimming, blurring in the pool of water that filled his eyes. Miska blinked away the tears as best he could. "Nothing is ever going to be the same, is it? Not me, not my people, not Ravenna."

"That is the price of living. Once you can consider whether or not that price is worth paying, only then can you do something with your life. Choose carefully, for this price is not yours alone to pay." Cavaris dimmed the fire with the twitch of his fingers. Allora shuffled in Miska's arms, and he leaned back onto Beringer. The girl and the bear were quickly asleep. That left only Miska and the dragon, keeping vigil until the dawn.

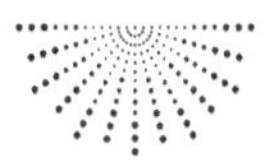

CHAPTER EIGHTEEN

Ravenna waited at the plateau with Itonus, Brianna, and most of the Harrower company. She was strapping the flying furs into place, under the watchful gaze of Itonus, when desperate wingbeats filled the air. Crispinus dropped to the ground in front of her, his wings spread wide in the most threatening gesture he could possibly manage. His hands were curled into talons and his eyes flashed with more fire than usual.

"Would someone care to tell me why it is exactly as I am being left here while you go and fetch the weapons?" Crispin asked, pacing before her and drawing ever so slightly closer. Ravenna watched him cautiously, not unaware of the fact that Itonus was bristling a little bit on her behalf. This was the last thing she needed right now. "Or perhaps you would like to tell me why it is that my mate refuses to talk with me except to say that she is going to be training with you from now on every morning. I don't need her to know how to fight. At least one of us should be untainted from this…this nonsense!"

"Have you asked Desarra precisely how she feels being left out of the deliberations that most of her society is taking part in? Do you think that she is a nothing more than a pretty picture, a sculpture to be polished and admired as she sits on the throne? She is not a human queen. She is the embodiment of our society. She is the Chosen Queen, the best of us." Ravenna took two steps forward so that she was uncomfortably close to Crispin. She fisted her hands on her hips and looked up at him; he was several inches taller than she but Ravenna had stood down more dangerous creatures.

"Do you mean to suggest that I think my mate is incapable?!" Crispin snarled, glaring down at Ravenna with his wings spread wide. She did not bother matching his stance. She just casually stretched her wings open then closed, feigning boredom.

"Have you actually told Desarra this?" Ravenna asked. Crispin hissed wordlessly and strode away, flapping his wings in distress. He paced a few moments more.

"Why am I ordered to remain here? I have dealt with the humans before with you. I know what it is that you need of me. They know me." Crispin folded his arms and glared. Itonus stepped forward, slurring his own wings slightly.

"Are you going to disobey a direct order?" Itonus asked. Ravenna sighed; this was really not the time for male sylph posturing. They had to get into the air soon.

"Itonus, enough. This is between Crispin and I, and apparently his mate. Have you actually spoken with Desarra today?" Ravenna wanted to know what it was that her sister had told Crispin. She had a feeling that if Desarra had told Crispin the truth about what was going on, that he would not be anywhere near the plateau, demanding to be taken along to fetch the weapons. The question was whether or not Ravenna was going to say anything. Desarra would have her wings if she did. The alternative could be much, much worse.

"Of course I have spoken with Desarra," Crispin huffed. He wrinkled his nose and glared at the ground. "She was...in a mood. Which is probably why she demanded to be taught how to fight. She wouldn't even let me touch her after I disagreed."

Ravenna sighed, lifting her eyes to look at the state of the sky. It was a fairly cloudless evening, and the sun would be setting before too very long. She knew that sylphs had decent night vision, but they had to be in the air soon. It would take time for them to collect the weapons, make sure that they would work and that the armour could be fitted properly. She did not want them to be flying during the day more than they had to. Ravenna looked at Brianna, who was watching all of this with a solemn expression. Ravenna gestured to Itonus with her eyes, and Brianna got the message.

"Itonus, come," Brianna said. The two walked away a little bit, though Itonus remained close enough so that he could to see Ravenna, if not hear her.

"What have you done to my mate? Filled her head with ideas that you learned from your precious humans?" Crispin demanded. Ravenna looked at him, expression as icy as ever. She took a deep breath and let it out slowly, shaking her head. This had to be dealt with now, or things would only get much worse.

"I went to find Desarra today as you were training the others in flight manoeuvres. I found her in the dark, shuttered in, weeping. Would you like to know why?" Ravenna asked. Her voice was sharp, shadowed. Crispin backed up a step, his eyes growing wide.

He swallowed nervously. "Weeping?" He breathed.

"I performed the death rights for your unborn son today." Ravenna jerked her head to the peaks off in the distance, where the body of Silvius was probably already picked clean. "Desarra did not even wish to name him, for fear that…She did not wish her heart to break any further."

Crispin staggered backwards. He fell to his knees,, his wings laying limply by his side. His mouth opened and closed, but no words came out. His amber fire eyes filled, and the charcoal black skin became streaked with tears. "My son? My son. I did not even know she was—and you're just standing there, as if nothing has happened?! They're right, all of them. Whatever happened to you in the human lands broke you. How could you do this to me?"

Perhaps it was because of the strained day that Ravenna had endured. Perhaps it was because she had finally given up on trying to succumb to the emptiness. Perhaps it was because the things she felt could no longer be swallowed up. Whatever it was, something in her snapped. With a single beat of her wings, she surged forward to where Crispin knelt on the ground. She wrapped her hand into his tunic and lifted him to his feet, ignoring his resistance.

"I buried my kin today. You think I feel nothing, after that? I know you see me as a monster. I am nothing more than a weapon, meant to train you all to fight in this war. I don't exist outside of that purpose. I am nothing more than the swords on my back, the Dalketh, the blood, the death. I am the humans' avenging angel. I am anger. I am wrath. I am righteousness. But to you, I am nothing more. I am not even a sylph." Ravenna turned to face all of the sylphs who were watching and listening with bated breath. She let out a laugh that was more darkness than anything. "When this war is over, you will all go back to your lives, and I will be left as remnant. I am only your Warlord. You expect me to be ice. You expect me to kill. And I will do all of those things. But never forget that I, too, have blood pumping through my body. I am not empty. I am not stone. For your sake, I will be all the more dangerous because of it. But after this is done, leave me be."

Ravenna released Crispin. She walked over to Itonus, her eyes hard and her jaw set. He said nothing, just spread his arms and gladly lifted her into the air. The company of sylphs that were to accompany them to go fetch the weapons followed

Itonus. And they flew off into the oncoming evening, leaving Crispin and Ravenna's words behind.

"I will never see you as stone, or ice," Itonus said. Ravenna barely caught his words above the wind whispering in her ears. She replied with a thin smile, and leaned her head against his shoulder. For a brief moment, she allowed herself to take comfort in another. As soon as they landed, that moment of weakness would have to be forgotten and she would have to return to her normal state of fearless ice. There was no place for emotion in war, not for her.

Ravenna had made a mistake. She tried not to think of it that way as she was held in Itonus' arms on their way to go fetch the weapons. She tried to think of it as caring for a friend, rather than betraying a confidence. But the fact of the matter still stood. She had told Crispinus precisely what it was that Desarra did not wish her to say. Worse, Ravenna had said it loud enough for more than Crispin to hear. She would have to have a word with the company before they flew back to Shinalea, or Desarra would have her head.

"Don't tell anyone what happened," Ravenna said into Itonus' ear as he flew. He looked at her in surprise.

"Don't tell anyone that you are as they are? That you feel just as much as they do and that you are more than your swords? You may think that you need to be empty to be strong, but you can be just as strong without giving into the emptiness," Itonus said. Ravenna tilted her head back so that she was looking at the quickly darkening sky above her. That was not quite what she had meant. Nor did she think that Itonus knew what it was that he was speaking of. The cold façade that she showed was not a feigning of emptiness, but precisely what she was.

"I meant about Desarra. Our relationship has been difficult to say the least. I should hate to have caused her pain for a lapse in judgment on my part. Crispin needed to know; that much I do not deny. But no one else did." Ravenna spoke loud enough to be heard over the wind as the currents changed. The weather was cold and it made flying a bit more difficult. At least there was no headwind.

"No one will say anything," Itonus said. "You are their Warlord. Desarra may be Chosen Queen, but they do not see her in their lives on a day-to-day basis. They see you. You are the one who commands them, not she. She is intermediary between you and the High Council. They do not care about her as much as they do about you. As much as I do."

Ravenna did not have a response for that. Her words earlier on the plateau should have made everything quite clear. After this war was over, she would no more be part of their lives. The position of Warlord would be irrelevant. The sylphs should care about their monarch, the best of them. Desarra's fears were apparently not unfounded.

Thankfully, Ravenna did not have to engage in conversation with Itonus, to either defend Desarra or answer to his increasingly obvious declarations regarding her. The wind was picking up, coming in off of the sea and over the desert. They were swept along much swifter than they would have been otherwise, which was good as they needed as much time as possible to get the weapons and then fly back. Ravenna kept an eye out on the ground below, though she could not see as much as she had hoped. She had hoped that they would perhaps fly closer to the Red Palace than they had before, but there was no such luck. The fastest way to go out was far enough off that they were not even close. Still, she felt her heart being pulled in that direction. Did that mean Miska was still alive? That he was there and waiting for her, as was her friend Queen Lenore?

The former slave markets appeared before too very long. Ravenna was impressed; she had not been required to change flyers. Itonus, and the others, had grown in strength and ability, even considering the fact that they have been flying all their lives. Ravenna saw a fire on a small hill some distance away from the slave markets. That was where Tekko and Radim would be waiting. Ravenna signalled, her light skin easy enough for the other to spot in the dark that there would be no chance of confusion. She heard the shifting of feathers as the company banked towards that fire in the dark.

Itonus was the first to land, Ravenna slipping out of his arms as soon as they touched ground. She saw Tekko standing with a sword at his hip, a pleasant smile waiting for her. Then, the rest of the sylphs landed and the smile faded. She imagined how they looked to the human; in the firelight, the charcoal ash skin and the gold skin, coupled with gold feathers of all different shades was a terrifying site. Ravenna looked mostly human, except for the fact that her wings existed. The others did not appear human. To be faced with hundred sylphs was something that would make many tremble. Tekko certainly did.

"When you came with those others, I knew that you were not alone. But it is one thing to think it, the other to see it. You have a formidable army," Tekko said, bowing slightly to Ravenna. Beside her, Itonus shuffled uncomfortably. Ravenna knew that the others did not understand the humans, but she really hoped that things would not end badly.

"This is but one company. Tekko, it is good to see you," Ravenna said, stepping forward so she could clasp hands with the human she called friend. Time away from being a slave obviously agreed with Tekko. He was looking healthier and stronger than he had when he was fighting in the arena. Radim stepped into her line of sight, and Ravenna was shocked by the change. He looked even more capable than Tekko.

"Twenty companies of flying warriors," Radim said, clasping Ravenna by the hand. He whistled in admiration. "It will be an impressive site. I only hope it is enough. Rumours are that Lord Davorin is gathering his forces. Now that he has access to resources from the Salusian Empire, there is not much that can stand in his way. No one quite knows what his ambitions are, but he has made no secret that he will be searching you out."

"Have you heard of anything regarding the Red Desert? Of its people?" Ravenna asked, before she could stop herself. No matter the fate of Miska and Lenore, Ravenna had to fight this war. Her very people were at stake. If she could liberate with her friends at the same time, then she would. But knowing would not help her.

"It is difficult to say," Tekko said. He turned towards the fire and reached his hands out as though to warm them. The desert air was crisp, but Ravenna was still warm in her flying leathers. "Under the current Emperor, some many cycles ago when he actually took an active part in the ruling of the Empire, the Salusian Empire was a relatively benign force. It was no great economic powerhouse, nor was it overly oppressive to its people. Under the guidance of Dagan, the borders expanded rapidly, often at the expense of its economy and its people. I have heard rumours of many cultures that were lost due to Dagan's interference. I had thought that Davorin was more rational than his brother. But recent events have not proven that to be the case. At first, he seemed to only be solidifying economic bonds and ensuring the rebuilding of places decimated by Dagan's attacks. Now, resources have been moved to places that do not need them, from places that will not survive without them. The economy moves only in one direction: up. People who struggled before are now starving. There seems to be no logic behind his rule, but the current Emperor does not interfere. No one seems capable of interfering."

That had not answered Ravenna's question. She wanted to demand a proper answer from Tekko, but she had a feeling that this was the best she would ever get. It was strange, though, that Davorin should be so imprecise and illogical in his movements. During the time that she had been enslaved under him, he was angry and cruel, but intelligent and with purpose. So Ravenna asked a different question. "Does this mean that there is a chance that the Stormbringers will not be the only ones fighting?"

Tekko exchanged a glance with Radim. Tekko grimaced and said nothing. Radim hesitated a moment before speaking. "I don't know. Those who would wish to do so are not always in a position to help. There have been whispers of possible resistance workers throughout the desert. But nothing concrete. And there's always Southron ready to snap at the heels of anything the Salusian Empire leaves behind. Frankly, Southron frightens me more than Davorin. But our information is not complete. After Jazer and her empire were dismantled, our resources have not been what they were. Much of what we have has been put towards arming you."

"And we thank you for that," Ravenna said. "Without you, we would be fighting with nothing more than staffs and our fists. We will repay you as we can."

Tekko smiled benevolently and clapped Ravenna on her shoulders. Itonus bristled further at that, but Ravenna ignored him. She knew her people were getting restless, that they did not want to be standing around while Ravenna and these humans spoke in a language that was familiar but not intelligible. They would see it as a waste of time. But this was the first time in a long time that Ravenna had not felt quite so alone. She revelled in it.

"There is no need for that. You gave us our freedom, and you supported me as leader of this place. That alone has brought new and interesting opportunities to our door. Unfortunately, though, the rumours of your involvement here have spread. You cannot be shrouded in secrecy anymore. Still, that is trouble for another time. For now, let's get you your weapons." Tekko waved his arm broadly and a few young people started unloading wagons that had been just outside of the firelight's reach. Ravenna heard the clanking of metal and the rasp of leather. Itonus straightened.

The young people moved into the light of the fire, their arms full of weapons and armour. There were swords, made much in the style of the ones she wore at her back. There were also long, curved knives that seemed as though they could perhaps take off a head—or a wing—with a single strike. Ravenna nodded to Itonus, who stepped forward and picked up a weapon suitably large enough for him. It was a double-headed axe with a shaft long enough to be wielded in both hands. Itonus swung it experimentally, using motions that she recognised from some of the more advanced pieces of Dalketh.

"It is easier to manoeuvre than I thought," Itonus said with a slight frown.

Tekko nodded at the axe. "We only have a few of those. Most of what you probably needed are swords, so that is what we made. There are three hundred swords, fifty scimitars, and three axes. We made enough armour for two hundred."

Ravenna picked up one of the pieces of armour. It was made of boiled leather with metal plates, adjustable to multiple sizes, with removable panels that looked as though they could be replaced easily enough if needed. The backs were made specifically for those with wings. Tekko had something very similar made for her when she first stepped into the arena. It was very effective.

"The armour is reinforced with pieces of metal where we could manage it. It won't stop a heavy sword, but it will do fairly well protecting you against strikes that are not perfectly precise. Still, you're going to have to be careful. Davorin will be wearing heavier pieces, and I have heard that he is outfitting his armies in the latest technology. I think your wings are going to be extremely vulnerable." Radim reached a hand out as if to stroke Ravenna's feathers. Itonus stepped in front of her, flaring his wings. Ravenna put a hand on his wing and he stepped aside, eyes wide.

"He was going to touch you in a way that he did not deserve," Itonus snapped. Ravenna narrowed her eyes slightly.

"You know no such thing. He was discussing armour for our wings," she said to Itonus. She turned back to Radim and spoke to him in his own tongue. "I apologise. Itonus is rather antagonistic these days. I agree with you about the wings. But we cannot armour them. It would be too heavy to fly. I can manage it, but I still need to be flown to battle. No, we shall have to make do with what you've done. How long will it take for the rest?"

"We've gotten new supplies. Working flat out, it should take another three moons. I know that is not as quickly as you might need, but we have brought on all who can manage and we are doing our best." Tekko sighed and looked a little weary, despite the fact that he was healthier now than he had been. Ravenna lay a hand on his arm.

"It will be enough," she said. "We are doing our best to make bows and arrows as well. If you have other news of Davorin, send a bird. I will try to have someone keep an eye out at all times. I do not know how long it will take before he makes his move. I can only hope that we are ready."

Tekko and Radim eyed the company of sylphs standing behind Ravenna and Itonus. They were eyeing the weapons and armour with interest. "If you have more of these at your disposal," Radim said nodding to the sylphs. "Then you will be ready. Hope instead that it will be enough."

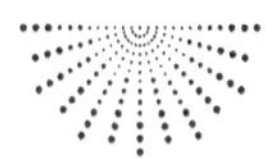

It had been three days since Vareis had returned. Lenore and Blodwen had managed to get Vareis cleaned up, fed, and were seeing to the few injuries that the former training master had managed to pick up. Vareis told them of the time spent in the various rocky places of the Red Desert, trying to meet up with rebel forces discreetly. They were few in number and disorganised and had nearly been captured by the army more than once. As a result, Vareis was sleep deprived and had a few injuries that had not been seen to. Lenore and Blodwen did the best they could, but it was difficult. They could not fetch Warra for fear that the news would get back to Davorin.

Lenore had not seen her husband in all of the time that Vareis had been there. This was becoming more and more common; she would often not see Davorin for days at a time. She was not even sure he knew about the fact that she was pregnant. She only begun showing very recently and Blodwen was the only one who knew about the symptoms.

Lenore rested her hand on her stomach as she wove the shuttle through her loom. Vareis was standing by the window, ducking away as soon as any patrol passed by. Lenore wondered how soon it would be before her friend left, returning Lenore to that state of being where she did not quite exist. Blodwen opened the door and slipped inside, carrying a tray of food. Lenore's stomach growled as the smell of the food simultaneously brought about her nausea.

"Can you force anything down?" Blodwen asked, walking over to her queen. Vareis turned to the tray and took one of the bowls of soup. Lenore swallowed down her nausea and tried to focus on the weaving.

"I think that would perhaps be a bad idea," she said. "It wasn't too bad a week ago, but things have escalated."

Blodwen rested a comforting hand on Lenore's shoulder. "My sister was the same way. Just fine at first, but couldn't keep a morsel down until she was in her fifth moon. We all thought she was going to waste away, but she birthed a fine, healthy son. I asked the kitchens to see if they had something simple and plain, but the flatbread was the best they could manage. It might be too spiced for your tastes at the moment."

Vareis practically tossed the half-empty bowl of soup down onto the tray again. "We have to do something. We can't just stand around and talk about the pregnancy and babies and forget that the rest of the world exists. I was meant to come here and bring you away."

Lenore sighed and folded her hands in her lap. "I have already explained to you why that is problematic. I told you to find another way."

"What we can't very well have you leading the rebellion from here," Vareis said, throwing up her hands. Lenore understood all too well that feeling of restlessness that her former training master was experiencing. She had gone herself from being an active monarch that took an interest in the daily lives of her people, to a solitary queen in name only, who spent her days weaving and playing with her hair. She did not even know if

Davorin was doing a good job, as he refused to let her see any of the paperwork and none of these soldiers were willing to report on things for her. Blodwen did not have the access, and Vareis was out of touch.

"You do not need me to fight your rebellion. Why do you not talk to some of the other protectorates of the Empire, get recruits from outside the Red Desert? Surely there are others who would be willing to join our cause to liberate all who wish it, rather than just us. Should we not be working with our allies, no matter where they be?" Lenore asked. Vareis let out a rumble in her throat and turned back to the tray of food. She picked at it, tearing apart a piece of flatbread.

"All we need is for the Empire to get out of the Red Desert," Vareis said around a mouthful of bread. "That will demoralise the Empire enough for the others to rise up on their own time."

"If we go at this piecemeal, then nothing will get done. You are talking about taking down an overwhelming force with nothing but a few annoying bee stings. Enough stings, and you will die. Anything less and it is just an annoyance," Lenore said. It was a struggle for her to keep her voice even. The fire that burned inside her wanted to promise to help Vareis with anything, take back control of her lands. She had never been so disconnected from her people in her entire life. But she had something else to consider, now. It was time to think smarter.

"Surely they don't need Queen Lenore to run the rebellion?" Blodwen asked, keeping her voice quiet. She had grown slightly more use to talking about these things in the last few days, but she was born into the Salusian Empire and it was difficult for her to betray what she had known.

"Having Lenore lends us an air of truth and respectability. If she is not there, officially sanctioning us, then we are nothing more than a group of ragtag troublemakers. No one will take us seriously."

"What about those angels that Lord Davorin keeps talking

about?" Blodwen asked. Lenore closed her eyes. She hoped that Ravenna had made it back to her people. Otherwise, hope would be lost for them. She had to believe that Ravenna was all right, and preparing for Davorin. But she could not expect the freedom of her people to lie on the wings of Ravenna's.

"Even if Ravenna manages to create a fighting force with her people," Lenore said, pulling the shuttlecock through and turning it the other direction. "We don't know what their strengths will be. Surely they cannot possibly stand up to the entire army of the Salusian Empire. Davorin does have to keep his forces a little more scattered, as they are required to manage the Empire, but even the standing army he has at his disposal is great. We would need help from multiple quarters to face it and have a hope of surviving."

Vareis turned around to reply and was stopped by a knock on the door. The three women froze, eyes wide. A moment later and Vareis was dashing into Lenore's bathing chamber. Blodwen quickly opened one of the windows and dumped out the third bowl of soup, putting the empty bowl on the ground just outside Lenore's window. She closed the window in a hurry and then turned around and faced the door with her hands folded demurely in her skirts.

Lenore nodded and ran a self-conscious hand over her stomach before rising and walking to the door. Whoever it was knocked again, this time more fervently. Lenore opened the door with her chin tilted upwards and saw her unfortunate husband standing there. He had obviously been training with Dagan, because his eyes were rimmed with dark circles and red. He looked at her with teeth bared, not quite seeing her.

"And what it is that my wife does all day while I am busy with the affairs of state?" Davorin asked. He started to push past Lenore into her chambers, but she stopped him with a frigid look. "It seems I married a worthless trophy as opposed to a useful person."

Lenore sniffed. "I am only as useless as you choose me to be. I ran my country well before you came along. You were the one who took away my means of administration."

Davorin paced the hallway, his heavy boots echoing on the stone. He rounded on Lenore, pointing a trembling finger in her direction. "I wouldn't be in this situation if it weren't for you. I wouldn't be in the situation if it weren't for Dagan. Ah, yes, Dagan. Where would I be without Dagan. You know that it is helping me to understand."

"Understand what?" Lenore asked. She drew her brow together, not entirely sure what it was that Davorin wanted with her. Normally, he came to her in the middle of the day, she would have suppose he wanted to gloat or demand more information about her people. But this was something else entirely. He did not act as though he wished to bed her or to gloat. That and the fact that he had not pushed past her to get into her chambers was equally confusing. Davorin hated being forced to stand in the hallway, where anyone could see him appealing to his wife.

"Everything," Davorin said with a chuckle. He held his hands up to his temple and paced in a circle. "I am understanding everything. What futile efforts I have been making all my life. Wandering the royal palace as a child, thinking that great things were laid out for me. Now I know that I am the one doing the laying out. And all who stand in my way are nothing more than tiny beetles to be crushed beneath my boots."

Lenore wanted to draw back, but she stood her ground. She did bite her lip to keep silent though. Davorin was not acting like himself. He had always acted with purpose. Now he seemed to be ranting for no reason.

He turned and pointed another finger at her, this one accompanied by a wide smile the likes of which Lenore had never seen before. "I killed Dagan," Davorin said. He leaned against the wall and folded his arms as though expecting Lenore to act astonished or surprised. She knew that it was more than likely Davorin had killed his brother, but such rumours had never been whispered widely throughout the Salusian Empire. Seraphina, though, had intimated as such.

"Why? Was he a threat to you?" Lenore asked. Maybe if she played along, then Davorin would reveal a weakness to be used against him.

Davorin snorted. "I think it was more that I was threat to him. After all, he was Heir Apparent. He was the Firstborn Son. His line to the throne was clear. Mine was not. No, I spent considerable more time perfecting the role of ruler to the Empire. I learned economics and I learned all the names of the people we had conquered. I learned of the history of our Empire and I learned what it meant to make it great again. Dagan cared only for his glory. He wanted his legacy to be immortalised amongst the stars. He wanted to be immortal." Davorin turned to Lenore, exaggerated question on his face. "Do you know what it means to be immortal?"

"Immortality no longer exists. It is lost to the past, as is magic and all of the things that went with it." Even as soon as she said it, Lenore knew that it was a mistake. Davorin's eyes darkened and the corners of his mouth dropped. Some sort of undefinable energy crackled around him and he reached out to drag his fingers through Lenore's hair. She did her best not to flinch away.

"History is not as dead as you would think, my dear. Ravenna taught us that, did she not? The fabled messenger to the gods, walking amongst us as though it were nothing astonishing that she existed at all. Can you imagine what it would have been like if she stayed where she was? If I had never found her at those Slave Pits? Why, then I wouldn't be searching for people to stand beside my army and make me immortal. I wouldn't have found Dagan again. Then, I wouldn't understand everything. But it *has* happened. And I am so close to completing my understanding. The only thing after that is to go and find Ravenna again; convince her of a truth that I think she's forgotten. Do you know what that truth is?"

Davorin was looming over Lenore, his eyes wide, pupils mere pinpricks against the dark brown. Lenore swallowed and splayed her fingers over her belly as if trying to protect it. Davorin did not even notice. "No," Lenore said simply.

Davorin pulled away, frowning. Some semblance of his usual self seem to be returning. But when he spoke, it was with the same madness. "Neither do I."

Without saying another word, Davorin walked back down the hallway. He seemed to have forgotten that Lenore was there, or why he came to see her in the first place. He just walked down the hallway, twiddling his fingers through the air as if playing with that impossible energy.

The words fell out of Lenore's mouth before she could stop them, and she had never regretted anything more. "I'm pregnant."

Davorin took a few more steps, so perhaps he hadn't heard her. Lenore clapped a hand over her mouth to prevent the words from being said again. Davorin paused. He turned his head to look at her, that familiar scowl present. The earlier spark of insanity was now completely gone. The dark circles under his eyes had vanished and he spoke with a clarity that frightened Lenore more than his seeming madness moments before.

"I see. Good. I will set extra guards on you, so that my future child will never be put into danger." Davorin paused another moment, then turned to face Lenore fully. She saw that the twin blades at his hips were missing, the sheaths empty. Why did that feel more like a threat than a comfort? "Actually, no. I have a different plan for you in mind. I think it is time that we allow the people to build up confidence in our new life with the Empire. You will be by my side for every moment. Once the pregnancy is notable, then we shall go on Progress. I will gather my army and we shall make ourselves known to the people at the same time. Once the Progress is done, then I will go and find the Stormbringers. I will conquer them, and then we shall see about my immortality."

Lenore kept her hand pressed over her mouth so she could not scream. Water filled her eyes, but she was afraid to blink away lest something changed in Davorin between that moment and the next. Davorin said nothing more, merely turned and continued his way down the hallway. She thought she heard him humming. A heartbeat later and he was gone.

Lenore stumbled back into her rooms. Blodwen closed the door behind her and stared at Lenore, eyes wide and terrified. She had heard everything. "He killed Dagan?" She asked, barely more than a breath. "No. I don't understand. It doesn't make any sense."

Lenore reached out and clasped her hand and Blodwen's. "The Davorin that came to the Red Desert nearly a cycle ago was a man not of great intelligence and cunning and strength. He was cruel, but he had sense. Do I think he killed his brother? Yes. But the Davorin that I just saw…he was mad."

Vareis emerged from Lenore's bathing chambers, her face grim. She perhaps had not heard everything, but then Davorin had made no efforts to be quiet. Judging by the shards of determination and anger in equal measure that Vareis was showing clearly in her eyes, Lenore imagined that the former training master had heard all. And was far from encouraged by it.

"I had not thought that things could get worse. But they have. One does not conspire against a madman. One endures. We cannot predict what Davorin will do. He claims to want to be immortal, but what does that mean?" Vareis waved her hands through the air before drawing them through her shorn hair. She sucked in a breath through her teeth and then hissed it out.

Vareis shook her head. "I don't know how to help. I don't know how to fight against this."

Blodwen straightened. "You fight against him just as you always did."

"You think it's so simple to—" Vareis started, stopping as Blodwen dropped Lenore's hand and stepped forwards.

"You keep fighting. You stop trying to predict what he'll do and you keep fighting. Fight against his army, fight against his trade, fight against *him*. Who cares if you cannot predict what he'll do? You have a duty to your people and to your *queen* to keep fighting. You want to run your rebellion, you do it. Find your information. Find your weapons, your allies. You talk to others and you get their support. You gather your forces and you *fight!*" Blodwen's chest was heaving for air after her unexpected speech. Her words rang through the room and Lenore was suddenly eternally grateful to Davorin for bringing Blodwen with him. She had turned out to be the most surprising ally.

"He's mad," Varies argued. "Our strategy will be worthless."

"No it won't. Lord Davorin may not be what he was, but the rest of the world does not know that. He still shows a whole front to the rest of the Salusian Empire. You don't slow the machine of state down quite so easily. So focus on that. And the madman will topple as his kingdom crumbles," Lenore said. She stood, her legs shaking beneath her. She pressed her hands against her stomach, wanting to feel her unborn child. "I am now in a position where I can see what's going on. I won't do anything to put my child in danger, but I will do everything I can to free my people. Use that. Use *me*. Please do not give up on us, Vareis."

Vareis considered, silent. She watched Lenore for a moment, then flicked her eyes to Blodwen. Finally, she nodded. "Alright. If you can get us that information, this might work out after all. I'll…talk to the others. Gather what allies we can. Rumours talk about people gathering at the Slave Pits. They say that Jazer is dead, killed by a legion or a legend or something. And they say that there are things stirring that haven't been dreamed of in a thousand cycles. It's little more than whispers after dark, but it's not nothing."

Lenore walked forwards and took Vareis' hands in her own. She smiled, the smile of a Queen to her loyal and beloved subject. "No. It is assuredly not nothing."

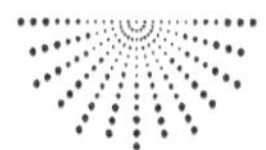

CHAPTER TWENTY

*S*pring was well and truly in the air by the time Ravenna decided that her army was as prepared as she could make it. She had gone through every tome to find out information about how wars were fought. She had let her people practice with what weapons they had, picking up more as they were finished by Tekko's people. On ground, they were masters of Dalketh, using blades and staffs as well as any depictions of the Stormbringers that Ravenna had ever read. The archers were competent and had mastered the art of shooting whilst flying. Her generals were well-versed in battle tactics and they had practiced drills over and over and over again until all of the sylphs could do them in their sleep.

Even Desarra had improved in her dedication to Dalketh to the point where Ravenna almost wanted her fighting at her side. Every morning, the two practiced with wooden sticks in place of blades so that they would not hurt each other. Desarra was particularly vicious with her wings, buffeting Ravenna thoroughly each time that the dark winged sylph got close enough. Desarra had grown in confidence and strength and no longer did anyone question her ability to lead them. The High Council was growing quite frustrated with their inability to cow Desarra into submission.

Crispinus was still not terribly happy with Ravenna. Desarra had nearly snapped Ravenna's wings off when she learned what Ravenna had done, but she and her mate were still talking. Crispin preferred only to talk to Ravenna, however, when it was to do with the army and the upcoming battles. He had insisted on coming with her the last two times she had gone to see Tekko. He spent the whole time sneering at the humans and admonishing her for her fondness for them when the two were alone. He was the only one who knew how fond she was of certain humans. As far as anyone else knew, they were all enemies.

Ravenna had taken to sending scouts to the Red Desert to watch and see what it was that Davorin was doing. They were to stay high in the sky and be sure not to be seen. It was bad enough that rumours of their involvement with the former Slave Pits were spreading throughout the land. She had heard of a grand Progress being made through the majority of the desert. Apparently, Davorin was gathering his army while he went from village to village, parading about. The scouts had reported that the human army seemed vast and well-prepared. But no one had fought a flying force for generations on hold, so there was an advantage.

A slight one.

Still, Ravenna had hoped that some of the remaining forces of the Red Desert would be fighting at her side. Her people would have to be overwhelmingly capable if they wanted to destroy Davorin's army. As for facing Davorin? Ravenna reserved that right for herself.

She sat on the edge of the cliffs where the Aerial City had been built. The plateau behind her had been pounded into empty dirt and mud from all of the training. Ravenna sat with the sun rising directly into her eyes, warming her wings.

Desarra had left her only a few minutes before, gliding back down to the city so that she could oversee the gathering of supplies for when the army flew into battle. That time was not long off, now, and there seemed to be a countless number of things to do. Those who were not fighting would still be coming, carrying supplies and seeing to wounded sylphs as best they could. Only a few would remain on Shinalea, mostly the old and the young. Ravenna had a special wooden platform made that her people could carry, so she would not have to depend on one sylph for that. Though, Itonus and volunteered for the "honour" more than once.

"Crispin told me I'd find you here," Itonus said, sitting at the edge of the cliff besides Ravenna. "I thought you would be back at the Tower, preparing more strategy discussions."

"I have no more strategy to prepare," Ravenna said with a wing shrug. She spread her hands, looking at the calluses that were now permanent additions there. She thought about the scars running across her chest and the one between her wings. There was the brand on her hip and the scratches on her wrists from the desert lion. "The volumes in the Stone Tower are not infinite. There is a reason why the Stormbringers are legend even among us why our culture fell to philosophy and curiosity more than remembrance of war. There are not that many tomes discussing such matters. The ones that do exist are old and decaying and must be treated with care. Even so, I have gone through everything we had. We have done everything to prepare except engage in battle itself. I fear that once we actually get that far, everything I've taught will be for nothing."

Itonus spread his wings behind her and stretched one out so that the tips of his feathers brushed her shoulder. It was the closest thing to a true embrace that the sylphs could manage. Still, Ravenna longed for Miska's human embrace, his human touch. His human love. War was impending. It was anything but sudden. It had been the sole focus of her life for nearly a cycle.

Now, it felt like her purpose was almost at an end. Ravenna did not know what she would do afterwards. So she sat in stead, her face calm and betraying nothing of the roiling emotions beneath the surface. She sunned her wings and thought about the weight of the blades at her back.

"Is...Is fighting really that much different than what you've taught us?" Itonus asked in a quiet voice. Ravenna turned to look at him and saw a surprising amount of uncertainty in his eyes. His ruddy golden skin was healthy with the glow of strength. The single braid on his left temple was tucked behind his ear. But his amber fire eyes betrayed uncertainty.

"You challenged me nine moons ago. You wanted to see what it was that I could offer. What did that feel like?" Ravenna asked. Itonus frowned and looked at her as though she were a little bit crazy. Perhaps she was. Ravenna kept silent, waiting.

"It was like nothing I've ever experienced. Even our fighting practice, the learning of the Dalketh, the sparring, the drills, nothing was quite like that." Itonus looked down at his hands folded in his lap. He flexed his arms, stretching the fighting leathers a little bit. Everyone was wearing them as often as possible to break them in. Truth was, sometimes Ravenna felt like she had never taken hers off.

"My first experience with fighting was a literal fight to the death. I fell off a balcony and into the slave pits where a battle was going on between a human—Radim—and a starved desert lion."

"Lion?" Itonus asked. Ravenna silently cursed herself. She had been trying to teach some of the others about the human language differences between the generations that stood between them. Only the Intellecti were interested. Kratos was fairly fluent in the human tongue. Brianna had suffered through language lessons as a matter of course, but she was far more interested in other things. Crispin had not even tried.

"It's like the cougars we have here, but bigger by about two.

This one was half starved so it would be meaner to fight. Radim had a gash in his leg that made it difficult for him to walk properly. If I hadn't fallen between him and the lion, then it is more than likely he would be dead. But I fell and I distracted the lion. And if I hadn't fought, I would be dead. When you fight with everything on the line, the world falls away. The pain is there, yes. But you have no choice but to do something or die. The thinking I've had you do all these moons, the consideration of your next move, the endless drills to get Dalketh into your muscle memory, none of that matters in the end. All that matters is your will to live and the desire to protect something worth fighting for."

They were silent for a moment. Ravenna was remembering past pains and hoping that she could do better this time. She hoped she would never be again in a position where humans were holding her wings out to her side so that Davorin could draw a blade up her spine. She remembered stepping in front of the second lion she had faced, protecting Miska from certain death.

"Ravenna," Itonus said, drawing her name out so that it hung in the air like a conversation. Ravenna wanted to close her eyes pretend that none of this is happening, but she knew that she couldn't reasonably put this off for any longer. So she listened. "When we go into battle—it's coming soon, isn't it?"

Ravenna nodded. "Yes."

Itonus swallowed and started again. "Well, when we do go into battle, I would like to fight for you. Shinalea, our people, they matter. Of course they do. But, you matter more."

Ravenna tried her best not to wince. Giving into her feelings for Miska had been difficult enough, not to mention awkward at times. But that felt natural and real. This felt like she was trying her hardest to make someone see what wasn't there. And Itonus was determined to see something entirely different.

"Itonus—"

He shook his head, turning so that he faced her. He pressed his wings against hers and she made no move. To pull back now would be problematic. She had to see this through and explain the situation. "Now, listen. I know that you think you should be nothing more than our Warlord. You need to be something strong for our people to rally around. You need to be careful what emotion you show so that they are not afraid. But, you are so much more than that. You let yourself be vulnerable with me. And that means a great deal."

Ravenna inclined her head in a slight nod. She had let herself be vulnerable around Itonus, but more as a sign of friendship than anything else. She was not very good at friendship apparently. Cycles of being alone but for the Intellecti had not prepared her for dealing with the social niceties of her current predicament. Itonus reached out as though he wished to grab her hands. Ravenna kept them squarely where they were.

Itonus twined his fingers together and looked at Ravenna with a slight smile. "I'm sure you're well aware of the fact that I have taken many lovers amongst the sylphs."

"It is not uncommon," Ravenna said. "That is our way after all, more often than not."

Itonus straightened. "That's what I mean," he said, starting to smile. *Oh dear*, Ravenna thought. *Shouldn't have said that.* "You are uncommon. You are unique and intelligent and more capable than I would have ever imagined. You may not be able to fly, but you haven't let that stop you and it's amazing what sort of a female you've become. I know we never have gone anywhere near the idea of being lovers, but please consider what I'm asking. I want to be your mate. I want you to be mine. I want to fight at your side and fly with you in my arms from now until the end of everything. We'll face this war together; with you fighting beside me, I know we can come through this."

This time, Itonus did not hesitate. He grabbed Ravenna's hands and wrapped them in his own. She also did not hesitate;

she pulled back. Ravenna pushed herself to her feet and walked a few steps away from the edge of the cliff. She looked at the dead patch of ground that now replaced what used to be a lush and fertile plateau. Everything she touched seemed to move in that direction these days. Her relationship with Crispinus, the fact that her friends in the Red Desert were lost to her. Ravenna did not even know if Miska was alive to hope and wait for, but she wasn't going to risk it.

"I can't," Ravenna said, facing away from Itonus. She pulled her wings in tight around her and thought about what sort of a conversation this would be if Miska were there. She would have been forced to look at him, so that he could read her mouth and understand her words. With Itonus, Ravenna could feel the safety of having distance between them. There were walls that she was not willing to overcome.

Itonus flew over to stand in front of her, his wings spread wide. He did not look angry, but his eyes were dark and stormy. "Why not? Is it that you're not interested?"

Ravenna sighed and shook her head. She fisted her hands on her hips and felt her blades shift between her wings on her back. Her feathers rustled. "It's not that, Itonus. It's...Before I was taken from here, I never even thought that I would grow close enough to anyone to want to have that sort of a bond. I always assumed that I would follow the path of my heart-father, Tacitus, and become a full Intellecti. I assumed that I would be separated from society and that I wouldn't have to deal with the emotions or the disappointments that were sure to be mine. Things changed."

Itonus spoke up before Ravenna could continue and explain about Miska. He grabbed her hands again, this time holding them close to his chest. "That's exactly it, Ravenna. Things *have* changed. There is no need for you to try and be invisible anymore. You have become what you were meant to be, and it is glorious. You are strong and proud and confident and beautiful."

Ravenna pulled away again, this time flaring her wings so that Itonus was forced to take a step back. She shook her head again. Ravenna fixed Itonus in her gaze and tried to make him understand. If she had to explain her whole history with Miska, then she would. "You're not understanding me."

Itonus ran his fingers over his scalp and whirled around. He turned back to Ravenna, frowning. "It's because of him, isn't it? The human."

Ravenna did not even have to consider how he knew. Her fractured relationship with Crispinus was causing problems. They had never had a loving relationship, but things had been getting better. She was even starting to like him. And then he had to go and do something like this. Ravenna did not bother answering, she just nodded. Itonus snarled in frustration and whirled round again. He paced for a few moments, his wings flaring wide and then closing as he muttered to himself. Then, he turned back to Ravenna with a grim expression on his face. "I understand. So I will go and prove my admiration for you. I will take care of this."

With a few mighty beats of his wings, Itonus surged into the air and was gone. The direction he had gone was directly towards the mainland. Panic gripped Ravenna in a way that she hadn't felt since she was first taken by the humans. Her heart turned to ice and fear. She screamed after Itonus, hoping that he could hear her. But there was only the wind, mocking her.

Ravenna fell to her knees. She had to fix this. She had to save Miska. If she had to face Davorin without Miska by her side, or at least in her thoughts as waiting for her, then why bother? Ravenna curled up, her head between her knees. She took three deep breaths, trying to calm her racing heart and swallow her panic. When that did not work, she rose to her feet and ran off the plateau swifter than she had ever run before.

It seemed to take an age to reach Desarra's chambers. Ravenna did not even acknowledge the guards outside the doors, she just burst in and hoped beyond all hope that Crispin was there. Desarra greeted her, rising from a late breakfast, looking as though she had just bathed. Thank the stars, Crispin was there also. He looked coolly at Ravenna and inclined his head in a semblance of a greeting.

"How dare you?!" Ravenna hissed. She stalked towards Crispin, her hands itching to reach for her blades. She wanted to draw the swords and slice through his wings. She wanted to make him understand what it was that he had taken away from her.

"Ravenna? What's going on?" Desarra asked. Ravenna ignored her sister and stared down Crispinus. He rose from the table, his hands held up to defend himself and his wings held neutral. He must have seen something in her eyes because he widened his own in a rare show of alarm.

"I just had a conversation with Itonus," Ravenna said, her voice low. "He wants to be my mate."

"Congratulations!" Desarra said. She stepped around the table to be kept in Ravenna's eye line at all times, but Ravenna was still focused on Crispinus. He said nothing at all.

Ravenna pointed at him accusingly. Her wings rose over her head in the most threatening gesture she could make. Her feathers spread wide and her shadow fell over Crispin. "Only, you know exactly why I can't take him as mate. And Itonus took that information about as well as you would expect. He's gone. And now, he's going to kill Miska."

Crispin choked. "He *what?!*"

"Don't pretend that you don't know what I'm talking about," Ravenna snapped. "You told him. You told him about Miska, about what stood in his way. Only, because Miska is human, Itonus thinks that he should kill him. Undo this!"

Crispin stepped out from behind the table and walked up to Ravenna. His wings were pressed flat against his back and his hands were still up. He was shaking his head as he spoke. "I know things have been strained between us for the last few moons, but I would never say anything that you told me in confidence. I did not tell Itonus *anything*. I knew he was interested in you, but I didn't know that he wanted to take you as mate. And I would never have told him about Miska."

"Who is Miska?" Desarra breathed. She stepped into Crispin's side and flattened her hand against his chest, relaxing when he wrapped his wing around her. Neither Crispin nor Ravenna bothered to answer; that would have to be explained later.

"Then if you did not tell him, what was Itonus talking about when he said the human stood between us?" Ravenna asked. She had told no one else about Miska, had not even spoken his name in moons. She stiffened. There was one human whose name she had spoken frequently. It was the human that stood between them and the war. It was the one she had hoped to kill herself.

Crispin must have realised it about the same time that she did. He dropped his hands to his side and tried to get words out. None were forthcoming.

"You have to go after him," Ravenna said. Her own wings fell to her side like stones. She would have flown after Itonus in a heartbeat if she could manage. Crispin nodded, and a moment later he was running for the window. He stopped to grab his sword on the way and then he, too, was gone. Desarra and Ravenna stared at the place where he had been.

"What's going on?" Desarra asked, voice hard. Ravenna's legs were trembling and she collapsed into the stool at the table. In slow, halting words, Ravenna told her story—all of it—to her sister. About Miska. About Lenore. And about the fact that Itonus was now going to try and kill Davorin on his own.

CHAPTER TWENTY-ONE

Miska lifted Allora above his head and raced with her towards one of the remaining snow piles under a clump of pine trees. Most of the snow had melted, but there were several large piles that would remain for a while yet. At least, that was what Cavaris had told him. Providing that there was no other snowstorm, as it was only spring. Allora wiggled in Miska's grasp and he could feel her laughter through his hands.

"Oh no!" Miska said. The snow pile grew closer, close enough for Miska to toss Allora into it. "The snow monster ate you!"

Allora pawed her way out of the snow pile, turning to face Miska with a wide grin. Her white blonde hair was wrapped in a long braid and she still wore furs to keep out the cold, but she looked much more like a normal child of Rygirfel than a starving waif. She folded her arms imperiously, though she was unable to keep the grin from her face. "What you fail to understand, bear man, is that I am mistress of the snows. Those I command will give you your comeuppance."

Miska frowned. Something cold and wet hit him in the back

of the neck, dribbling down his furs. He spun around in wide-eyed astonishment to see Sisu, Asgeir, and Cavaris all standing there with packed balls of snow in their hands. Asgeir was, suspiciously, missing one. Sisu raised his singular hand and the massive ball of snow contained therein. "Now!" He cried.

As one, the three hurled their snow towards Miska. He did not even have to think; he just touched one of the threads that now continuously outlined his world and the snow halted mid air. He directed it back toward his attackers, conveniently forgetting to hit Cavaris with the snow. The dragon was devious and better at getting back at pranks than anyone had anticipated. Allora had learned that well when she put pine cones in Cavaris' bedroll. Asgeir yelped as the snow hit him full in the face. Sisu caught a mouth full of it and was too busy coughing to help.

Miska smiled and turned back to Allora. "I have vanquished your followers. What do you say now, mistress of the snows?"

Allora returned with an impish smile. A shadow fell over Miska, massive and tipped with claws. Again, Miska turned to find his opponent waiting for him. This one was not bearing snow. Beringer towered over Miska, standing on his hind legs, his forepaws spread wide in the air. Beringer showed his teeth in a bear grin and let out a playful roar. The snow remaining on the tree branches fell to the ground at the sound, covering Allora with snow. Miska could not help himself; he burst out laughing at Allora's dismayed expression. Even Beringer looked as though he was laughing.

Beringer fell to his feet and shuffled over to Allora. He grabbed her by the scruff of her furs had lifted her out of the snow, setting her at Miska's feet. She grinned up at the bear, even more massive than he had been before. He nosed her hair in return.

Moments like these seemed to be fewer and farther between than before, Miska thought. So much of his life seem to be devoted to training, preparing for a war that was beginning to feel farther and farther away. It was not that he no longer cared about freeing his people, about finding Ravenna and helping Lenore, but he had also found a home here in the Iron Mountains.

Beringer had grown larger off of Miska's magic, until it was impossible that he could become any bigger. He rivalled many of the sturdy, massive horses that the people here favoured. Miska had taken to riding Beringer just as he would a horse. Allora had grown confident and strong, though she still seemed to be a little bit afraid that Miska and Cavaris would vanish at any moment. Miska had even stopped hating Sisu, though he still felt the results of Sisu's fighting abilities more often than not. Asgeir had become uncommonly fond of Allora and had taken to teaching her how to read. And Cavaris seemed to have given up on scolding him into wisdom, instead teaching him how to better utilise his magic and, on occasion, smiling.

Miska now used his magic almost instinctually. He was able to do, as Cavaris had shown, more with less. The payments still came, in the middle of the night more often than not. But none were as extreme as the one before. In fact, at the moment, Miska had only two dots on either side of his neck to demonstrate his payment. Good food and good company would soon set those two rights and they would vanish as his life force was replenished.

A small part of Miska's mind had started wondering if it would perhaps be better if he did not go to war at all. It was the most selfish thought he had ever endured and he tried not to bring it out except in the darkest parts of the night, when there was no one else around to judge him. He still longed for Ravenna. And he knew that every day he stayed here, Lenore was suffering more at the hands of Davorin. So Miska still trained, hoping that he would do the right thing in the end. As

Allora looked up at him in that moment, her eyes loving and bright, he was not sure he would.

Miska looked up from Allora and met Cavaris' gaze. Cavaris blinked slowly, his vertical pupils dilating slightly. Cavaris took a deep breath through his nose, then nodded. He started walking away from the group, tilting his head for Miska to follow. Miska left Beringer and Asgeir and Sisu behind, but Allora would be the one to run after him. She slipped her hand into his hand. He did not have the heart to tell her to go back.

They followed Cavaris off into the forest for a few feet before Cavaris turned and stopped. His hands were folded into his robes as usual, and his horns seemed to brush the lowest branches of the trees. If Miska looked closely, he could see tiny white scales forming at the corner of Cavaris' eyes. Cavaris said nothing for a moment, still taking those deep breaths.

"Under traditional study, a sorcerer would take many cycles to learn his craft. Your study has been anything but traditional, and as such I have taught you only that which I considered absolutely necessary for your chosen task. What do you think is now the result?" Cavaris asked. Judging by the way he moved his mouth slowly and carefully, Miska imagined that his words were being well measured, perhaps quietly said. He took a moment to consider—even that was more than he would have done two moons ago.

"You think it's time I go and see the Elders," Miska said after a moment. Allora tugged his hand and he turned to her, seeing that brightness turned into uncertainty.

"I thought that if you were going to see the Elders, you wouldn't...You won't come back." Allora rubbed her eyes with her free hand, hiding her tears as best she could. But she was still young and not well versed at controlling her emotions. Miska knelt before her and grabbed her hands in his.

"I love you, Allora," Miska murmured. He smiled at her, trying to impress the truth upon her. "Ravenna told me that she had been adopted by a heart-father. You are my heart-daughter. I will never leave you behind, no matter where that takes me. You matter more than anything."

"You promise?" Allora asked flatly. Miska nodded. He knew that if he left her behind, she would simply follow him. He knew that war was no place for a child, but also that being abandoned would damage her irreparably. He would make sure she was safe when the time came, but until then, he could at least show her the world.

Miska stood again and faced Cavaris once more. "How do you know I'm ready?" He asked before the words could be stopped. This is what he had been working for all these moons. Why was he questioning it now?

Cavaris inclined his head. "Because you wish to ask at all. That is how I know."

Miska nodded, though he did not really understand. That much had not changed in all his time here. "I'll go tell Sisu and Asgeir and we can head to Hullgard before nightfall."

"No. If you wish to approach the Elders, you must do it under your own power. No horses or supplies will be provided to you, nor directions. You shall have to rely on your own training to make it to where the Elders are. No one in Rygirfel or Hullgard will direct you to the place of meetings. You have until midday tomorrow. I will place a binding upon your magic and then you must make your way."

Cavaris reached out a hand and touched Miska's forehead. Miska could feel the magic, this in the form of the song that Cavaris was so keen on. It pulsed through his veins like drums that he could not hear. Miska let out a silent cry and fell to his knees. When he opened his eyes again, the crisp detail and the outline of threads that he had grown so accustomed to seeing was gone. The pounding of his heart that signified the song, gone. Cavaris, too, was gone. Allora remained at his side, and Beringer loomed over them.

Miska pushed himself to his feet, trying to hide the fact that he was already breathing heavily. The forest around them looked unfamiliar and he knew that they were nowhere near Rygirfel or Hullgard. Beringer leaned his shoulders down. Miska helped Allora onto the bear's back and then climbed up himself. He looked up at the sky, the position of the sun, the trees around him, and pointed in a direction he hoped was correct. Beringer started forwards. And, just to make everything a little bit worse, the air chilled and a few flakes of snow started to fall.

* * *

IN TRUE IRON MOUNTAIN FASHION, those few flakes turned into a proper snowstorm within a matter of hours. By the time the sun was setting, Allora was huddled close to Miska, her hands tangled in Beringer's fur. The trees and landscape were becoming more familiar to Miska, but that was even more disconcerting. Judging by his—admittedly poor—navigation skills, they were at least a day's journey from Hullgard. This would mean that they had to travel through the night. There would be little time for stopping to warm up by fire, let alone hunting for food. That was Miska's biggest worry; a young child of Allora's size needed food to keep her heat up in this weather.

"Miska," Allora said, turning to look up at him. It was difficult to see her speak through the snowstorm. If he'd had access to his magic, Miska would have done what he initially did with the butterfly and given a means for them to communicate verbally. He had tried it a few times in the past three moons, each time flinching away at the sounds. But he would have happily done it now for Allora sake. She rubbed her stomach and Miska understood without the words.

"I know," Miska said. He hated doing this to her. In truth, he hated the fact that Cavaris had sent Allora along with Miska even though she could have stayed behind with Sisu and been at the Elders' meeting place by the time Miska arrived. Beringer easily withstood the snowstorm, his bulk making more progress than Miska would have thought. The fact still remained, though, that Cavaris had sent them on this ridiculous trek without supplies or guidance. It was supposed to be some sort of symbolic journey, Miska figured. Would he be able to protect his family whilst under difficult circumstances. What did Cavaris want? To prove a point that Miska was incapable? That he should leave Allora behind when he went off to war? No matter that he knew only bloodshed could await him, he had made a promise to Allora and he was not going to break it now.

Beringer huffed. Miska's annoyance must have rubbed off on him because the bear sent a thought of Cavaris being buried under a pile of snow through their familial bond. Miska laughed a little. He patted Beringer on the shoulder and replied with an image of the snow freezing over Cavaris' form. Then his own stomach rumbled from hunger and the humour vanished. If Miska was that hungry, Allora would be famished. And her trembling had slowed, which was not a good sign. They needed to stop, but if they did then there was little chance that Miska would make it to the meeting place of the Elders in time.

The sun dropped below the horizon and with those last few rays gone, it felt like the temperature dropped even more. Allora moved as close to Miska as she could, her shoulders hunched against the snow. His anger rose up to him, sharper than he had felt for a long time. If this was the game that Cavaris wanted to play, then fine. It was clear that the dragon had no intention of helping Miska at all with his war against Davorin. Cavaris had made it plain that he was "tired of the bloodshed" and that he thought humans were destructive monsters. It was clear that Cavaris was sabotaging Miska's attempt to find the elders. If he arrived there and Allora was the worse off for it, then it would be clear he was incapable. If he did not arrive in time, then it would be clear he was incapable. But he was not going to risk Allora simply for the chance to have other people sneer at him and his desire to free his people. If he had to ride into battle alone except for Beringer and Allora, then he would.

Miska silently gave the command for Beringer to stop. The bear found a slightly sheltered copse of trees and lowered himself a little bit so that Miska could slide off and take Allora with him. With a few sweeps of his massive paws, Beringer cleared the ground of snow as best he could. Miska quickly gathered what bits of wood he could while Allora huddled against the trunk of a massive pine tree. Miska formed a fire ring and did his best to provide dry kindling. He reached for a flint at his belt and paused. He did not have it. He had not taken his flint with him when he was going out training with Sisu, and the training session had turned into a snow fight. Miska had only his hunting knife.

Instinctively, he reached for magic. A sharp pain flared through his skull and Miska doubled over, clutching his temple. The pain subsided and Miska straightened. He saw Allora huddling against the tree, her eyes glazed over and dull. Cursing, he found a rock and scraped his knife against it, hoping that the sparks would be enough to kindle a flame. He spent probably ten minutes trying to light the fire, his knife edge growing increasingly dull and the storm raging about them. After a while, a tiny ember caught in some dried leaves. Miska held his breath for a moment until the ember spread. Then, he blew on it carefully and watched as a few flames flickered to life. Ten minutes later, there was a roaring fire—enough to keep them all warm.

Now it was just a matter of food. Beringer lumbered off into the storm and returned a short time later with a squirrel in his jaws. It would be barely enough for Allora and Miska, but it was better than nothing. Miska thanked Beringer and set to cooking the squirrel. They ate, then huddled around the fire in silence until Allora managed to drop off to sleep. Miska stayed awake until the dawn.

Despite the snow that had fallen the day before, everything was bright and clear. The air was warm enough that it would be fairly certain the snow would melt soon. Even as Miska put Allora onto Beringer's back, just after sunrise, he could already feel the accumulated snow softening. Soon, he realised, that he would be back in the desert where no snow fell. Whether or not he had an army by his side would be a different matter, but it was unlikely that Miska would ever return to the Iron Mountains.

Miska swung up onto Beringer's back beside Allora and the three set off. Having already wasted so much time, Miska did not feel the need to press on at the expense of his companions. So when he felt Beringer's immense hunger through the bond, and saw the pleading in Allora's eyes, they stopped to find food. They did not have time to hunt, but there was some bark to chew on that had a flavour not unlike cinnamon. Miska promised that they would find real food once they reached Hullgard.

As expected, midday came and went before reaching Hullgard. By the time they strode into the settlement outskirts, the sun was well on its way down to the horizon. The few people out and about looking at Miska and Allora riding astride the most massive bear they had ever seen and quickly ran off. He soon had a trail of people following him, pointing and whispering. He did not look too closely to see what it was they were saying.

He did notice that the binding Cavaris head laid upon his magic was slowly fading away. The sharpness of vision was returning, and Miska could see minuscule threads outlining everything again. He felt that now-familiar hum of power pulsing through his blood. Little good it would do him now.

Beringer seemed to know the way to the Elders. Miska did

not even have to direct the bear; he just walked through the increasing busyness of Hullgard, his claws gouging slashes into the hard-packed dirt. Miska had a feeling the bear was doing it on purpose. Even Allora seemed to be out of sorts. Her hands were fisted tightly in Beringer's fur and she sat ramrod straight. Too late, Miska remembers that she had been born in Hullgard had been sent away. He lay a comforting hand on her shoulder, but she did not relax.

Miska had never been to Hullgard. After so many moons, the open forests and wide walkways of Rygirfel felt like a ballroom compared to this place of tight quarters and buildings made out of wood and stone. This place felt more permanent and more overwhelming. It did not help that the people following him were now many. Miska did his best to ignore them, but he could not help straightening his back just as Allora did.

After what seemed to be an endless march through winding streets, Beringer drew to a halt. They had stopped outside of a low, long building. It looked to be half set into the earth. But what set it apart from the others around it was that there were two people standing outside, holding long shafted battle axes and wearing some sort of ceremonial garb. They were guards, the most organised thing that Miska had seen in a society that appeared to value independence and individuality just as much as it did the ability to fight and hunt. This was the place of the Elders.

Miska slid off of Beringer's back. He allowed Allora to stay up there, knowing that she would be comforted by the bear's presence and that if any harm were to come their direction from Miska's inability to make it on time, Beringer would see Allora safe. Miska straightened his furs as best he could and strode into the building, Beringer falling into step beside him. The guards did not stop Miska, but they did look at him disapprovingly. He opened the door with a perhaps too-showy display of magic. Inside, the building was dark, illuminated only by a couple of torches. The ground was hard-packed dirt covered in a layer of dried pine needles, lending the air a forest sent where there should have been none. The building was also one long room, completely empty except for a stone table, behind which sat three people all nearing the end of their lives. On either side of the table stood Sisu and Cavaris. Their faces were expressionless.

The elders were two females and one male. The women were as different as could be, one short and squat with long silver hair flowing over her white furs and without many braids as adornment, the other tall and rail thin her hair done up in a multitude of tiny braids that reminded Miska of his queen. The man seemed to be a warrior who was bitter about his inability to fight anymore; he wore a permanent scowl and his silver hair was tied back in the same style that Sisu and Asgeir wore.

The squat woman raised her bushy eyebrows at Miska's entrance. "You are late," she said. "We were just about to go home."

"Due to the snowstorm, I had to rest for the sake of myself as well as my traveling companions." Miska stood there with his hands calmly at his side, fully conscious of the fact that he wore only a hunting knife as opposed to the myriad of weapons that were displayed in this room.

The man banged his fist on the stone table, making it echo. "You offer us excuses?!" He demanded, already halfway out of his chair as the ready for a fight.

"Simply an explanation," Miska said. The man snorted and sneered, but sat back down.

The thin woman, perhaps the most levelheaded of the three, spread her hands in a slightly placating gesture towards Miska. "We were prepared to hear your argument for why we should support you in your efforts to fight a war that has not come near our borders or interests. But that was at midday. Now, we are deciding whether or not we want to hear your arguments at all. You have not shown much to be confident about. You have failed the task set to you, to reach us at an appointed time."

Even though Miska had known this was coming, it was still difficult to face. He clenched his hands into fists to keep from doing anything stupid, like striking them down with the threads at his disposal. He looked between Cavaris and Sisu, wondering if either one of them would perhaps come to his defence. Cavaris simply watched, his hands folded into his robes as usual. He seemed no more interested in this affair then he would be in the affairs of squirrels. Sisu, on the other hand, would not even look Miska in the eye. He just stood there with his hand resting on his battle axe, the other stump resting on his hip. Anger flared through Miska like a wildfire.

"The fact that you are willing to judge my cause on my ability to walk through the woods is absurd," Miska snapped. This time the old man did stand fully upright, his outrage plain. He twisted his mouth to say something and yell back at Miska, but Miska simply turned his attention to the others. He could not hear the yelling, and so ignored it. He was not ready to start with counter arguments before he had even gotten his anger out.

"I came here more than a season ago, having just lost my queen and my people at the hands of a tyrant who is obsessed with proving to the world that he is great. I saw a twisted magic come into the world again. I saw death and an insatiable appetite. I came looking for help. Instead, I received training in the ways of bow and the blade and of magic—true magic. It was a valuable lesson, one I will never forget. But that does not change the fact that I still am one person. I thought that coming here would be a chance for me to present my case to you, telling you all about how dangerous Lord Davorin is, how his desire for conquering will be greater than his dead brother's. How Lord Davorin has already declared war on legends and how nowhere in this world will be safe from him if he is allowed to do as he wishes. I came here to tell you that we should stand up to him, joined with the sylphs of Shinalea, the rebels in the Red Desert, the fallen people that the Salusian Empire has crushed beneath its boot. Instead, I was greeted by people who were not even sure that they wished to to hear my case, because I could not manage the day's walk through a snowstorm with a young companion in a half-day. You wish to know why you should risk your people and your isolation for a cause that is not your own? I say it is your cause. If you do not wish to help me, very well. I thank you for the training I have received, as well as the companionship that has seen me through this winter. I am going to go fight my war. And for your sake, pray we meet again. Because if we do not, then assume all is lost."

Miska did not wait for a response. He turned away, making it impossible for anyone to call him back except Cavaris, who would not interfere. Then, opening the doors with magic as before, Miska strode out with Beringer and Allora. He did not look back once. After a few hundred feet, Miska paused long enough to climb back onto Beringer's back and be borne the rest of the way out of Hullgard. Once they were in the forest, Miska stopped and tapped Allora on the shoulder. She turned around to face him, so they could talk.

"I think you spoke really good," she said. She was looking up at Miska with a sad smile, as though he would be angry at her.

"Thank you, Little Dragon." Miska ruffled her hair, which Allora immediately smoothed down with a playful scowl. "Before, when I said that you could come with me, I thought that we would be going to the Red Desert with lots of supplies and lots of people with us. It's going to be very different now."

Allora shrank back. "Are you saying that you don't want me to come? You going to leave me behind?"

Miska reached forward to grab Allora's hands. He shook his head firmly. "I meant what I said. You are my heart-daughter and if you want to come with me, then I would be more than glad of your company. I only wanted to offer you the opportunity to remain behind. Asgeir and Sisu would look after you. You would be safe here."

Allora shook her head fervently. She wrapped her arms around Miska's waist and looked up at him. "I'm going with you."

Miska smiled. "Okay. Let's get back to the tent and pack our supplies. We'll leave tomorrow."

The question of whether or not they would be marching to their deaths would have to be one addressed another day. For now, Miska knew only that he was finally going home. Yes, it had been severely disappointing dealing with the reception the Elders had offered, but he was at least some help. And he would soon see Ravenna again. He wondered what Allora would think of her, and what Ravenna would think of Allora. That thought had him smiling all the way back to Rygirfel.

CHAPTER TWENTY-TWO

After three moons dealing with the Grand Progress, Lenore was both disheartened by the current state of her lands and extremely tired of her husband. Every day, it was the same routine. Lenore would be woken by Davorin, informing her that it was time to get ready and presentable for the day, according to whatever wishes he chose. He would then leave the tent to go off and practice his magic with that monster Dagan while Blodwen helped Lenore prepare for the day.

At six moons pregnant, this involved rather a lot more work than Lenore had anticipated. Yes, the nausea was gone, but there was pain in her back and her ankles, she often felt as though she could not control her bladder, and every move she made felt ungainly and absurd. Not to mention the child she carried was extremely active and often hit organs that should have remained untouched.

On this particular spring morning, Davorin had decided that he wanted to bedeck Lenore in a dress that looked as though it had been made of flowers. It was in no desert style that she knew of and it itched. Lenore sighed as Blodwen did up the fastening's on the back of the dress. "Where are we going today?" Lenore asked.

"It's a tiny place near some cliffs. I'm not sure why Lord Davorin is bothering, but there are rather a lot of people gathering here. Do you have any...news you would like to spread?" It was Blodwen's polite way of asking whether or not Lenore wished to sprinkle useful information to people known to be in the rebellion. She had passed a missive off to a message runner not two days before. And if they were where she thought they were, near the border with the Iron Mountains, then this place was small enough to barely be on the map. It was a tiny village known only for the oil that it pressed from olive trees that grew sparsely around here.

"I have no new news," Lenore said. She winced as Blodwen dragged a comb through her hair, placing bejewelled flowers in the copper strands. "I do know that this is ridiculous. I know that Davorin wants to gather his forces, and parade me about, but do I have to look like a garden to do so? This dress is uncomfortable and surely we both have better things to be doing than walking through this place."

Blodwen clicked her tongue in a sympathetic sound. Lenore grumbled; she hated being this petty and concerned with such matters, but there was little else that she could do. Every day she had been wandering through her lands watching her people being made to give their tithe to the Empire and being told things that made no sense. Why would Davorin care if a primarily pastoral people should have unexcavated ground? Why was he making them dig? Why was he making people concerned before with making earthenware and weaving fabric instead start crafting from stone. Lenore did not understand, Vareis did not understand, and the people did not understand. The Red Desert was not in danger of collapse yet, but if Davorin continued this way then it would soon be over. Her people would not be able to fight back because they were starving and beaten.

"Well, at least the Progress can't continue much longer," Blodwen said. She smoothed out a strand of Lenore's hair and pinned it into place. "At this point, surely you've been through the entire Red Desert. Unless Lord Davorin intends on going back to the main arm of the Empire, then there are only some outlying lands left. Unless there are settlements closer to the coast?"

Lenore shook her head. "The land that way is too arid for life, and the few that choose to live that way are reclusive and solitary. There are no settlements. No, what worries me is that Davorin doesn't seem intent on stopping. He has made no mention of any plans to me. But then, I'm only carrying his child."

Blodwen shrugged, a wince on her face. She placed a last flower in Lenore's hair and then tried to smile encouragingly. It did not work particularly well. Blodwen let out a shaky breath and threw her arms around Lenore's shoulders. "I have this horrible feeling that something is going to happen today. Please be careful."

"I am allowed to go nowhere without three guards and at least one spy to watch my movements," Lenore said. "Whatever happens today will happen. If something does happen to me, then you must be sure that all our plans are not for nothing. Promise me."

Blodwen nodded silently. Lenore squeezed Blodwen's hands and then turned to walk slowly out of the tent, one hand pressed to her back the other to her belly. She was greeted by the bright morning sun and an overeager Davorin pacing before the tent. He turned to her with bloodshot eyes rimmed in that familiar red that showed he had been training with Dagan.

"Don't you look a mess," Davorin said with a grin. Lenore resisted the urge to roll her eyes. It seemed as though her husband chose her outfits simply for the effect they would cause. Or to humiliate her, she was unsure which.

"It is said that my lord married a great beauty," Lenore said with a slight bow of her head. "It is for you to judge whether or not you believe them."

Davorin waggled a finger at Lenore as he slipped his arm through hers. "You've been practicing. Your tongue is sharper than it was before," Davorin chuckled. He ran his free hand through his hair, making it even more mussed than it was before. He no longer looked the precise and proper warrior of the Salusian Empire, a prince among his people. He looked like he had been to battle and to a pleasure house in the same day.

There was some missing piece of the puzzle that Lenore did not grasp, but she pushed that thought aside for speculation on a later day. For now, there were people gathering outside the village with flowers and tithes at the ready, looking a little bit uncertain as to the size of the army that was bearing down on them. Davorin travelled with his entire force close at hand. Yes, some were left behind to guard important places, and others were gathering supplies, but the majority of Davorin's army was always with him.

Davorin walked right up to the people at the edge of the village. He looked at them with some strange smirk, his eyes wide and eager. Lenore did her best to look a little more dignified, despite the ridiculous clothing she was wearing. After a few, awkward beats, Davorin started to speak. "People of the Red Desert, I am Lord Davorin, Firstborn Son of the Salusian Empire, Heir Apparent to the throne, King Consort to your beloved Red Queen. I have come before you today to show your queen and the child that she carries, to you, so that you may see her and adore. I have come to collect your tithes so that my army may flourish in our coming battle. What battle you may ask? The one against the legends that make up our very history. I shall reach forth my hand and wrap it around the world, so that the dangers that face us may be quelled. I shall become great so that you may know the truth about our world. As I gain understanding, so shall I give it. But first, we have to fight for this understanding, facing dangers that you have forgotten existed. So bring forth your tithes and be safe and secure in the knowledge that I am working for your greater good."

His speech did not even make sense, Lenore thought. Every visit was something along the same lines, but recently Davorin's thoughts had become more and more unusual and illogical. If Lenore hadn't seen those moments of fierce clarity, she would have thought that he had gone mad.

One sorry looking man, about the same age as Miska had been—Lenore's heart tightened for a moment—shuffled forward. His brown hair was scraggly and he looked as though his belly hadn't been full for quite some time. "I am Qilas, headman of this village. To honour you, we offer—"

The air shifted, something making it move. A shadow blocked out the sun and everybody turned to look up at it. It was large, larger than any bird Lenore had ever seen. And it was moving to the ground dangerously fast. The creature landed with an earth shaking thud. It straightened and unfurled massive golden wings. Lenore's breath caught in the world shifted beneath her feet. A guard caught her and kept her steady.

Standing before them, facing Davorin with a sword that looked suspiciously like the ones preferred by desert people, was what could only be a sylph. He had skin the colour of burnished gold, a single braid of golden brown hair hanging off his left temple. His shoulders were broad and powerful, his eyes burning with amber fire. Lenore hadn't believed Ravenna when the sylph woman had said that her wings were small, that she was not representative of their kind. Ravenna was something out of a legend. This man was something entirely different.

"Davorin," the sylph said, his accent twisting the name so

that it sounded like a curse. Davorin giggled and stepped forward.

"I am Lord Davorin," he said, bowing. The sylph tightened his grip on the sword and pointed it at Davorin. He spoke something that didn't make any sense, though it sounded almost like real words. All Lenore could catch was the name Ravenna. But surely that couldn't be...

"So you were sent by the Angel of Death herself," Davorin said, clapping his hands in glee. Lenore took a step back from Davorin; whatever sanity her husband had laid claim to a few short days ago, it was gone now. The sylph did not hesitate, he surged forward with a beat of his massive wings, sword raised in a motion to kill. Davorin did not even blink, let alone draw his own swords. He just raised a hand and the sylph halted. His feet were suspended inches off the ground, his wings wide and trembling with rage. Davorin squeezed his hand, sweat beading down his brow. But that smile did not dissipate at all.

The sylph dropped his sword, eyes widening in dismay as he fought against whatever magical bond Davorin had keeping him in place. He managed to move far enough to grasp at his throat, trying to suck air into a place that could not hold it. His eyes flicked to Lenore, perhaps some instinct telling him that she no more wanted his death than he did. If Ravenna had really sent him, then surely she should have sent someone better prepared for what Davorin was capable of these days. Ravenna had left before Davorin gained the ability to use magic, though. She did not know. And now one of her own was dying for it.

Water fell from Lenore's eyes as she watched the sylph struggle for breath, his wings moving uselessly through the air. "I'm sorry," she breathed. The sylph blinked and reached for her, then collapsed. Davorin released whatever hold he had on the sylph, his smile now formed in a grimace and his face perspiring. The sylph fell to the ground in a puff of desert dust. He did not move.

"Pluck his wings. And then I want them sewn into a cloak for me," Davorin said. The glee was gone from his voice, instead replaced by a burning fierceness. "I will wear them when I go into battle against his compatriots. The Stormbringers are coming. And we will meet them with open arms."

Lenore's hands trembled. The guard that was holding her steady tightened his grip. Lenore looked up at him and saw that his eyes were wide, his mouth hanging open, his skin two shades paler than usual. She looked at the dead sylph on the ground, his life ended in a few short heartbeats. Why was he here? Did it matter? If Ravenna was going to come and help Lenore's people, then this did not bode well.

Lenore should have killed Davorin the first time she laid eyes on him. Now, it was too late. She was carrying his child. And she was watching him march her people to war.

CHAPTER TWENTY-THREE

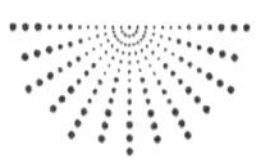

It was almost a full day before Crispin returned. Ravenna did her best to go about her normal routine, training Desarra and the other soldiers, preparing supplies, oiling her leather armour and sharpening her swords—two tasks learned from ancient tomes and taught to her people—but her nerves were wound tight. Desarra, after learning the truth about Ravenna's time amongst the humans, would not leave her sister's side. She had not yet made any official declaration to Ravenna about her thoughts on the matter, but the silent show of support was quite welcome. Unfortunately, with Ravenna's distraction, it was also quite plain that something was wrong.

Near the end of that second day, Brianna flew to Desarra's chambers where Ravenna was staying and found the two sisters struggling to talk over an evening meal. Desarra did not want to speak about her relationship with Crispin—whether or not it was doing better than before, things were still strained—and Ravenna did not want to talk about her fears of what Crispin would find. Brianna landed with a thump, causing both Desarra and Ravenna to jump. Ravenna reached for her weapons, only relaxing when Brianna folded her arms and her wings in expectant silence.

"Is there something you would like to say?" Desarra asked before Ravenna could order her general away. Brianna ducked her head respectfully to the Chosen Queen then turned to Ravenna.

"I want to know what is going on with you," Brianna said. "Actually, most of the companies want to know what's going on with you. You've been distracted and irritable all day."

Ravenna growled into her drink. "I'm irritable most days," she said. "Why should this day be any different?"

Brianna tilted her head and sat at the table beside Ravenna, not waiting for permission to do so. Ravenna sighed and glared. Desarra leaned back and folded her arms. "Actually, you're not irritable most days. You're cold and sharp. Today, you're irritable. I don't like it. However, I'm not an idiot. Crispinus has been gone all day—he had promised to take the Wing Dancers out for a training flight. I had to take the training flight instead, despite the fact that I have already been on two reconnaissance flights in the last three days. I would have asked Itonus, but he is also missing. Is there something I should know?"

Ravenna snarled and slammed her fist down on the table. "When it comes to matters regarding the army, perhaps you should trust my decisions. I appreciate you taking the training flight, but please don't question—"

"It is no secret that Itonus is half in love with you. He is loyal to the cause, yes, but more loyal to you. The only reason he wouldn't be here is if something had changed that. And, since you cannot go after him, Crispin must have done so. Would you like to explain things to me now?" Brianna asked with that annoying smile said she knew she had won. Ravenna's hand tightened around her cup until it shattered, spilling wine over her fingers, pieces of ceramic littering the table. Desarra flinched and Brianna widened her eyes.

"I will thank you to leave my personal life out of this," Ravenna said flatly. Her eyes had turned to shards of ice and she made it very clear that if Brianna had actively challenged her then Ravenna would have acted.

"I am concerned on behalf of all of our people," Brianna said carefully, enunciating each word as she thought it out. "If you, our Warlord, are distracted and temperamental, then our people are going to be nervous. Nervous flyers make mistakes. And we are feather spans away from flying to war. I think you should perhaps—"

This interruption was a flurry of wing beats, pushing the still chilly spring air through the open windows. Crispin landed, looking haggard. His feathers were mussed and his hair and clothes looked dirty. No, not dirty. Sandy. Ravenna rose from the table faster than the others could move. She rushed towards Crispin and rubbed some of the sand from his hair. It was familiar. Too familiar.

"You have been to the Red Palace," Ravenna said, her wings held stiffly behind her. Crispin nodded, more sand falling to the floor.

"I went there first, since that was where you thought maybe…Davorin was not there. Actually, the place was almost deserted. I had to go search almost the whole of the Red Desert to find out where they were. I found Davorin. He has amassed an army bigger than anything we could have imagined. Apparently they were touring the land, gathering forces." Crispin's left hand opened and closed reflexively, reaching for the sword he wore at his hip. His right hand was still, something clasped within.

Ravenna nodded slowly. She was not surprised about Davorin gathering an army. She had expected that he would be doing so and would also be searching for the sylphs and Shinalea. Ravenna felt more than saw Desarra moving behind her, steps slow and measured. Her sister reached her back and pressed a wing against her in comfort.

Ravenna swallowed and spoke again. "What of Itonus?" she asked.

Crispin let out a strangled laugh. "He always was more foolishness than brains. But I never thought he would fly into the middle of an army and challenge Davorin to a fight. I got there just as it was ending. I could not even land for fear that someone would see me and do the same thing. Davorin…He did not even touch Itonus. He just reached out, and the life was taken." Crispin fixed his eyes on Ravenna and she had to forcibly stop herself from staggering backwards. She forced control onto her emotions and stood there, watching Crispin and waiting for the next words that would start a war that had been in the making for too long.

Crispin opened his right hand and offered the object within to Ravenna. It was a single golden brown feather, the ruddy colour signature to Itonus. She picked it up, marvelling at how empty it felt. The shaft was broken and the barbs had been mussed. "Itonus is dead." Crispin looked at the ground.

Ravenna closed her eyes. She smoothed the barbs of the feather as best she could before tucking it away in her armour.

"This was one lesson that I could not teach. And it is perhaps the most important lesson of all." Ravenna opened her eyes, feeling the wetness there. She blinked it away, took a deep breath, and was as cold and hard as she had ever been. Her voice was steady when she spoke. "Some of us are going to die. And we will know their names. Take me to the plateau and call the others. All of them."

The others did not move for a moment. Crispin stared at Ravenna in shock. Desarra kept her wing pressed against Ravenna's back, but the feathers trembled. And Brianna did not move but to gape. Ravenna waited a wing beat, then was snatched up by the haggard looking Crispin. The others followed. Ravenna was dropped at the edge of the plateau, a few wing spans away from where she had refused Itonus and inadvertently set this all into motion. Desarra stood by her side. Crispin and Brianna went to gather some of the others.

"We are at war," Desarra said. Ravenna nodded.

"Blood has been spilled. And we are going to answer for it, one way or another," Ravenna said quietly. Desarra flinched. Then, she twined her feathers with Ravenna's. Ravenna reached out and took Desarra's hand, weaving their fingers together. They waited for the others to arrive. And arrive they did.

Two thousand sylphs filled the sky, their wings beating in formation, the sound drowning out anything that might have been happening. It seemed the very wind was shaped to their desires. It sounded like the oncoming storm. They landed before Ravenna in precise form, standing firmly, weapons at the ready, expressions hard. Ravenna waited until they were all still, wings folded. Then, she reached into her armour and pulled out the feather that Crispin had brought back.

Ravenna held the feather aloft.

"Itonus has fallen," she called. After the flurry of wing beats, her voice was surprisingly quiet. But there was no doubt that they all heard her. "He flew off to confront the enemy we have been preparing to fight, hoping that he could make a difference in this war before it even began. He thought that if we could end this before we all flew off to an end the likes of which none of us have ever seen, then maybe there was hope for the future. But Itonus was wrong! Not wrong to hope, not wrong to want to do something to protect us. But to think that this war was preventable, there he was wrong. The human killed Itonus. And we are his next target. What do you say, will we stand up to this plague, this monster that seeks to control every living being, to use legends long forgotten for his own purpose, to glorify himself at the expense of others? Will we protect our future and the generations that follow by taking flight now? Or are we going to stand here, isolated, and let Itonus have died in vain? I have been teaching you all to fight. I have gone through everything I know, I have gone through all of the oldest tomes, and I can teach you no more. You are as prepared as you will ever be under my watch. Now, you have only one choice before you: decide that it is not worth it, that facing possible death under bloodied and terrible circumstances could never be worth the sacrifice, or that it is time to raise our wings and do what our ancestors did."

Ravenna kept the feather aloft. She held it, and herself, perfectly still, staring down her people before her. Silence descended over the plateau. One beat. Two beats. Then, Desarra raised the hand entwined with Ravenna's.

"I stand with Ravenna Wingsword, Warlord of the Stormbringers. We fly to war!" Desarra cried. Her words were echoed, a whisper at first, then louder. Finally, the whole plateau was ringing with the words that Ravenna had hoped she would never hear.

"We fly to war!"

Wings beat the air. Feet stomped the ground. The sylphs drew their blades and their bows and held them in the air as Ravenna did Itonus' feather. Slowly, she lowered it, tucking it back into her armour and wishing she could just throw it off a cliff. On the morrow then, they would fly. The reckoning was coming no more. It was already here.

* * *

CAVARIS WALKED into the tent and closed the flap behind him, sealing it with magic so that no one could intrude. He considered for a brief moment returning to his isolation in the forests about half-a-day's walk from Hullgard. But, it seemed more prudent to remain close to humans. They were a hasty species, and when things changed within their communities, they changed rapidly. Given young Miska's inflammatory words and swiftness to depart the day before, Cavaris had a feeling that change was upon them.

He let out a slow breath and waved a hand. The fire rose to an appropriate height and warmed the tent almost immediately. The empty space left behind when Miska and Allora took their belongings became filled with more supplies transported from Cavaris' tent. Cavaris sat on a padded fur and folded his hands on his knees. He would be the last to admit that the tent felt empty now that the two humans and the bear had gone. Miska was perhaps a bit too idealistic, hoping to shape the world into something that had not existed since before the Fire Wars. And young Allora was possessed of far too much energy; Cavaris had forgotten how much trouble younglings could be, and how enjoyable.

Still, it was better that they were gone. And that they were gone without the armies of Hullgard behind them. Sisu had been furious after Miska stormed out of the meeting with the Elders. The Elders had been so offended by Miska's blatantly disrespectful tone that accompanied his challenging words that they had simply sniffed and turned their backs on him. They left without another word. Which left Sisu to deal with Cavaris.

"This is your doing," Sisu said, jabbing his amputated hand into Cavaris' chest. The dragon could have responded, could have easily turned Sisu into particles of dust. But there was no point. The human was correct. "You sent Miska too far away. You knew that it would take too long to get here."

"He could have gotten here within the allotted time if he had chosen to push himself," Cavaris had said. That had caused Sisu's face to turn a strange shade of red.

"He was traveling with Allora. They had no supplies, no weapons, nothing. You expected Miska to endanger Allora for the sake of this meeting?"

Cavaris shrugged. He would not defend himself. He had

known that he did the right thing, and that was all that mattered. These humans were insignificant before him and he had already tried his best to prevent nightmares. It was not his doing if they chose not to listen. "It was a test merely to see where Miska's priorities lay. That has been determined, and the consequences were there for his own doing. It is too late to change it now."

Sisu's response had been to curl his lip and back away from Cavaris. The large human shook his head, braids rattling an echo into the open room. "I thought you were here to help us. Your kind are the guardians of us, as you have said multiple times. Perhaps you are too far removed from your original purpose. I trusted you. Miska *trusted* you. And you betrayed him, and me. Well, fine. We will fight our wars without you, dragon. Go languish before your fire. Alone."

Sisu had stormed from the room, leaving Cavaris in solitude.

Now, Cavaris sat before his fire and tried to face down his rare moment of doubt. Memories of blood-strewn battlefields filled his head. He could feel flesh rendering before his claws, could see the destruction that was caused when his kind chose to go to war. And the cost? The cost was that people were now stuck, fighting one another and eking out some sort of survival. Their world had been grand and beautiful. Magic had been free-flowing and used for amazing purposes. Now the humans were stuck in an endless cycle. Their history was forgotten and they were the lesser for it. Yet, Miska was a sorcerer. He was a weaver of magic that had not been seen in this world for generations. Perhaps it was a sign that things were returning to the way they should be.

No. Cavaris shook his head and stoked the fire. He had done his duty. He had taught Miska, shown the human that there were choices to be made and consequences to face. He had explained things as best he could and there was nothing more that he could offer. Miska had made his choice. Sisu would follow him. And Cavaris would remain behind, tending a fire in vigil as promised. The time of the dragons was over. It was time for the humans to stand on their own and forget the dragons completely.

A gust of wind blew through the opening at the top of the tent. Cavaris looked up and something flew in. No, not flew. Floated. Cavaris reached up and plucked it out of the air, his claws lengthening so he would not drop it. As soon as he touched it, he felt the world rend in two. Magic the likes of which should have been forgotten and had not had touched this...this feather. This was magic that ended worlds. It had ended the world of the dragons. Cavaris had thought it forgotten. He had hoped it forgotten.

Miska had warned him about this. About that evil human and the death he had caused. Cavaris had not realised the truth until now. It was impossible to deny, with the feather of a sylph —a species even more lost and forgotten than the dragons—in his hand. Cavaris himself had confirmed their existence, flying over their isolated island. He had seen them preparing for battle. And here was the result. One was dead at the hands of forgotten monsters.

Cavaris thrust his hand into the fire and released the feather. The ruddy golden barbs burst into flames as though made of tinder. The fire sparked, flared, and the feather was gone. The magical taint seemed to linger. Cavaris tried to resume his vigil, tried to resume his meditations on the past and the decisions that he was making. He was an immortal, or as near enough as made little difference. He was slow changing and set in his ways. And he was not wrong in them. So why did he feel doubt?

Cavaris increased his flow of magic to the fire. He bowed his head and dug his claws into his legs. Another war was beginning.

EPILOGUE

The Lady Seraphina, Queen of Southron, paced before the screaming woman. The room was hot and close and there seemed to be too many people about, bustling and murmuring orders to one another. The midwives looked at Seraphina askance, silently questioning whether or not she should be there. But no one dared voice those questions aloud. They were not fool enough for that.

Seraphina would wait until Nadira gave birth to the child. Davorin's child, incidentally. Seraphina's brother had been a fool when he came to her encampment. He had stolen her prize from her—that dragon claw was irreplaceable, and no amount of excavations had unearthed anything even close to it. But, her scheme with Nadira had gone well. Oh, Nadira thought that she was doing Davorin's will. But after the moons went by and her pregnancy became obvious, and Davorin's lack of contact or interest became even more obvious, Nadira had once again sworn her loyalty to Seraphina. As if there had been any doubt.

Davorin was a fool. More foolish than Dagan. Dagan was a brute, interested in little more than his own glory and the bloodshed of others. It was a boon that he was dead, even more so one that Davorin had killed him. Seraphina admitted that she had underestimated her brother. She had not thought Davorin's ambitions ran so strong. She had thought him interested only in the competent running of the Empire, perhaps as a vizier to his brother's Emperor. Davorin had shown her otherwise. And now, he was prancing around his newly acquired desert kingdom, showing off his new wife in the most ridiculous fashion. She was pregnant. But little did she know that Davorin's heir was in Seraphina's hand.

"Push, woman!" one of midwives snapped at Nadira. Nadira wept openly, taking a few deep breaths before she pushed and screamed. The child crowned, and one more push had it slipping into the midwife's hand. The old woman bent over the child for a moment, clearing its airways. A baby's scream rent the air; Seraphina's lips split into a smile.

"A girl," the midwife said flatly. She delivered the wrapped baby into Seraphina's waiting arms. It was an ugly creature, still bloody. Its tiny fists beat the air as it screamed. As she screamed. Seraphina smiled. Davorin's heir, a healthy daughter, in her hands. Seraphina handed the child over to another waiting woman, to take away and clean and check for any problems.

"How many nursing mothers do we have here?" Seraphina asked casually. Nadira was still panting and exhausted from her labours. Tears still streamed down her face, but she seemed slightly calmer. Perhaps it would be beneficial to keep the mother around as witness that Davorin was in fact the father. But, no. Seraphina wanted no ridiculous sentiment to get in her way. Then, she would also require things that the mother would perhaps not allow.

"Two," the midwife said, washing her hands in a basin of water and drying them on her skirts. "One is about to be weaned. The other just born."

Seraphina nodded. She walked over to Nadira and rubbed the woman's sweaty hair from her for head. "Did I...do well?"

"Very well," Seraphina said. "All of Southron thanks you for your service."

Seraphina drew a sharp, bejewelled dagger from her gilded skirts. She pulled it across Nadira's throat in a swift motion, not hesitating an iota. Nadira choked on her own blood. Seraphina looked down at her skirts and sighed in annoyance. She would have to get these cleaned. And swiftly. Blood was so difficult to get out.

"Deliver the girl to one of the mothers. I do not care which." Seraphina started to walk away, leaving the room.

"And what are you going to do, my lady? Davorin is a good distance away, preparing for his little war," the midwife asked. Seraphina graced her with a smile and silently contrived to kill her in the morning. Or perhaps not, as she was witness to the birth and would be useful in her machinations against Davorin.

Seraphina turned and walked from the room, tossing words over her shoulder as she went. "I am going to prepare for a war of my own."

END, Book Two

ACKNOWLEDGMENTS

Despite the rumours, the number of people that actually go into the making of a book is impressively more than just the writer. I should like to thank all of them.

These include my editor, Michael Evan, who dealt with all the strangeness that comes with dictation (because my software really doesn't understand "the" and "a" and "and") to make this book as good it could be. Then there is Fay Lane, who took the cover from the first book, made it green and added a dragon. Basically, I think it's the most beautiful thing ever and it's perfect for this book.

Then there are the actual readers. People who got through the first book and are waiting for the second. People who have been the most wonderful to talk with and whose opinions I value a lot. A lot. Basically, they tell me things and I try to make things better.

To the people whose support has helped make this book reality, thank you.

ABOUT THE AUTHOR

E.G. Stone is an independent author who has been writing, quite literally, since the age of six. Since then, E.G. has improved rather a lot and has written (so far) twenty-two full-length novels, various short stories, a screenplay, snippets of poetry, and various blog entries that may or may not make sense.

E.G. enjoys writing in many different genres. The favourites are science fiction, mystery (preferably of the murder variety), adventure, fantasy — basically anything where the world isn't quite what you would expect. When not writing, she is off musing about the workings of languages, both real and created, or wandering around and experiencing new people, places and things. E.G. reads voraciously, perhaps to the point of slight-insanity. She also is enjoying making a go of this writer thing full-time. Weird, nerdy, perhaps a little crazy, she is having a grand old time writing, reading, reviewing, interviewing, and causing trouble.